a Whisper of Death

DARCY BURKE

USA TODAY BESTSELLING AUTHOR

OLIVERHEBERBOOKS

Cover Design by Wicked Smart Designs

Published by Oliver-Heber Books

0 9 8 7 6 5 4 3 2 1

For Loki
My sweet, snuggly rescue Maine Coon

A WHISPER OF DEATH

After being viciously stabbed and left for dead, Hadrian Becket, Earl of Ravenhurst struggles back to health only to discover he is cursed with a vexing ability to see visions he can't explain. Terrified he may be going mad, he must keep the disturbing skill secret. But when it proves helpful in tracking his would-be killer, he has no choice but to embrace the newfound power. The retrocognition leads him to the house of a man recently deceased, where he encounters the clever and intriguing Miss Matilda Wren—who may be able to help him solve the many questions raised by the attack.

The death of Tilda's cousin has left her and her beloved grandmother in a precarious financial position when she discovers their investments have gone missing. Between the lost money and the mysterious Lord Ravenhurst's incessant queries, Tilda begins to wonder if her cousin may have been murdered. Desperate to determine what happened, she'll exhaust every possible line of inquiry to stave off destitution. For a price, Tilda agrees to work with the earl to uncover the truth, though she suspects he's hiding a dark secret.

As their investigation grows, so does the body count, but can they trust each other enough to expose the puppet master pulling the strings? Or will the villain's malevolent machinations end with more than a whisper of death?

Do you want to hear all the latest about me and my books? Sign up at Reader Club newsletter for members-only bonus content, advance notice of pre-orders, insider scoop, as well as contests and giveaways!

Care to share your love for my books with like-minded readers? Want to hang with me and see pictures of my cats (who doesn't!)? Join me in my Facebook group, Darcy's Duchesses.

PROLOGUE

London, January 1868

rost had formed on the lampposts as Hadrian Becket, Earl of Ravenhurst, strode away from Westminster toward Whitehall. He had a meeting with an inspector at Scotland Yard about the Clerkenwell explosion and the Fenians. The air was chilled but thick with the ever-present fog that clung to the streets at this time of year.

Hadrian pulled his hat down closer to his ears, regretting that he hadn't taken the scarf his valet had pressed upon him earlier that afternoon. But Hadrian had been in a hurry to get to Westminster.

There weren't many people about at this late hour—nearly midnight—but the streets weren't empty either. Hadrian kept his attention rapt as he surveyed the area while he walked. It wouldn't do to be surprised by a footpad.

A boy came toward him, dirty-faced, his dark eyes round and hollow. "Ha'penny for me younger siblings, guvna?"

That slight distraction was all it took.

A hand gripped Hadrian's right shoulder from behind tightly, viciously. Turning his head, Hadrian saw a man, his hat pulled low over his brow and a scarf covering most of his face. He pulled at Hadrian's outer garments just enough to expose his side. Hadrian caught the flash of a knife as it flicked toward him, slicing just beneath his ribcage.

The blade was long and sharp, neatly piercing Hadrian's clothing and his flesh. Pain flashed, but he didn't think of it. He clasped the man's wrist while the knife was still embedded in his side.

Hadrian pivoted. The man was a few inches shorter than Hadrian's six feet, two inches and thick and muscular. A gray scarf covered his neck and the lower half of his face, leaving just his dark, narrowed eyes exposed. The ruffian had been smarter than him, it seemed. In more ways than just guarding against the cold.

The man's gaze swept over Hadrian's face then lifted to meet his eyes. Surprise registered briefly. Did the brigand know him? Hadrian had never seen him before. But his eyes were now emblazoned in his mind.

Angry and desperate to free himself, Hadrian tightened his grip on the man's wrist. The ruffian twisted the blade. Hadrian sucked in air as a pain he couldn't ignore shot through him. He had the sense to cry for help, his panicked voice thundering in the night. Someone would hear him. He wasn't that far from Westminster.

The man withdrew the knife from Hadrian's flesh, but Hadrian wouldn't release him. He would know why this man wanted to kill him.

The villain tried to pull away. "Leggo!" Growling, his eyes now furious, he kicked his leg against Hadrian's calves and pushed him forward.

Hadrian had nowhere to go but down. He fought to keep

hold of the man's hand, but it was futile. In the end, he fell to the cobblestones. Unable to get his hands in front of him to break the fall, his head hit the rough stone.

Agony exploded in his head, forcing Hadrian's eyes closed. A terrible weakness spread through him along with a helplessness.

As darkness descended, he realized he had something in his hand, something that didn't belong to him. He managed to shove it into his pocket as he gasped for breath. Then he moved his hand to the wound in his side where thick, sticky blood flowed freely.

Anger coursed through Hadrian as he fought to remain conscious. This was not the way things were supposed to end. Murder would not be his fate.

However, he couldn't keep the shadow from claiming him. He drifted softly and infuriatingly easily into the abyss.

CHAPTER 1

One week later

"*S*harp!"

Hadrian's valet, a solidly-built man in his middle thirties with gray eyes that assessed every aspect of a person—in an effort to see how he could be of service—hastened toward the bed where Hadrian was struggling to sit up.

"Yes, my lord?"

"I'm bloody tired of lying abed. I'm going to the sitting room." It was a short walk as it adjoined his bedchamber, but it would be the longest distance he'd traversed since he was stabbed.

"The doctor did say to take things very slowly," Sharp cautioned, his thin mouth turning down. "What if you just sat in that chair there?" He gestured toward the chair beside the bed where Sharp, his mother, the butler, and a few other people, including the inspector from Scotland Yard who'd visited yesterday, had perched whilst gazing worriedly at

Hadrian. Except the inspector. He hadn't appeared concerned or even that interested in being there, truth be told.

"No...thank you." Hadrian added the last through gritted teeth. He hadn't been a very good patient, but lying about and sleeping for hours upon hours grated him horribly, even if he did need it. Honestly, his head had hurt so badly following the attack that sleeping was the only relief. "To the sitting room, if you please." He swung his legs to the floor.

Sharp hurried to help him, grabbing his arm, but Hadrian waved him away. "Just fetch my banyan, please."

"Of course." Sharp went to the other side of the bed where Hadrian's dark-blue silk banyan lay. Fetching the garment, the valet returned to help Hadrian into it.

Standing, Hadrian felt a rush of satisfaction, along with a pull in his side—where a neat row of stitches kept his knife wound closed—and a sharp throb in his head. Blast, but the head injury was worse than the wound in his side. Though, donning the banyan made his side hurt more than his head for a brief moment.

Sharp brought a pair of slippers, which Hadrian pushed his feet into. Taking a deep breath, Hadrian shuffled toward the sitting room, feeling with every step that he aged a year. Or that he'd aged years as a result of the attack and was somehow forty instead of thirty. Dammit, but that made him angry. The entire event was infuriating. Why on earth would a footpad, which was what the inspector had concluded Hadrian's assailant to be, stab him and not steal anything before running off? It made no sense.

The moment Hadrian stepped into the sitting room he felt better. For whatever reason, just the change of room was comforting. No, not comforting, invigorating. And that was what he needed.

He forced himself to walk the perimeter of the room. He grew tired before he finished but pushed himself to reach the table near the windows. Frustratingly exhausted, he sat and slumped back against the chair. Lifting his hand to his brow, he tried to massage the pain away. It helped slightly.

"Would you like to break your fast here?" Sharp asked. There was a tentativeness to his question.

"That would be agreeable. My apologies, Sharp." Hadrian wiped his hand over his face and straightened—slowly. "I know I have not been the best patient."

"There is no need to apologize," Sharp said crisply. "You have suffered a terrible attack. You nearly *died*."

Unfortunately, Sharp was not being overdramatic. Hadrian *had* nearly died. His assailant had barely missed his liver, and Hadrian would likely not have survived that. "But I did not die, thankfully, and I am eager to return to my former activities." Riding in the park, working at Westminster, meeting friends and colleagues at one of his clubs.

Why did that all sound boring suddenly? Perhaps because nearly dying made one examine one's life. Was this where Hadrian imagined he'd be at the age of thirty?

No, he'd expected to be married with an heir and perhaps a spare. Or with a bright-eyed daughter he could teach to fish at Ravenswood, his estate in Hampshire.

Alas, he was not married and didn't know when he would be. That would require him to actually court someone, and though it had been four years since he'd last tried, he wasn't ready to do so. Catching one's betrothed in the arms of another man didn't instill trust or confidence. Or any desire to put oneself in the position of cuckold ever again.

"The doctor said you may not ride for a month or longer," Sharp said, his brow creasing.

Hadrian gave him a weak smile. "Never fear. I will listen to him on that score. But a walk in the park would not come amiss." A pain streaked through his temple. "I fear I'm a way's off from that yet. I shall endeavor to enjoy this foray into

another room. Perhaps in a few days, I'll try going downstairs."
The thought nearly made him giddy. Well, it would have if he
were not entirely spent.

"I know you're frustrated," Sharp said quietly. "But may I
repeat myself and say how glad I am to have you here. I'd much
rather you disagreeable than...gone."

This made Hadrian chuckle. "Have you ever known me to
be disagreeable?"

"Not until now." Sharp grinned. "Apparently, it takes nearly
being murdered to provoke you." His smile faded, and he
paled.

"No," Hadrian said with a shake of his head he immediately
regretted. "Let us make light of it, for wallowing in the sense-
lessness and frustration of what happened serves nothing."
Perhaps if he said that enough, he'd believe it. Or at least stop
thinking about what had happened and why.

He'd been attacked after being distracted by a boy. Were he
and Hadrian's assailant working in concert to fleece gentlemen
from Westminster? That was the conclusion Inspector Padgett,
who'd called yesterday, had arrived at. The inspector had actually come a few other times, but Hadrian hadn't felt well
enough to see him.

Padgett's theory made no sense to Hadrian. Why would a
footpad stab him without asking for Hadrian's valuables—
which he had not?

Despite Hadrian raising that question, Padgett had insisted
the attack was the work of a footpad. He said that they occasionally panicked and did something foolish.

Such as stabbing people? Hadrian had asked. Padgett had
nodded, then informed Hadrian that he would be closing the
case. And that was *after* Hadrian had noted that his assailant
had seemed surprised when Hadrian had turned to face him as
he'd fought back, almost as if he'd expected someone else.
Padgett had shrugged that away, too, saying anyone would be

surprised if a fancy gentleman such as Hadrian would fight. The inspector had even had the gall to laugh about it.

"I need to speak with Inspector Padgett again," Hadrian said to Sharp. The inspector may have closed the case, but Hadrian was not satisfied that the investigation was complete. "Please bring me writing supplies so I may draft a note."

"Or you could have Elton write it," Sharp suggested, referring to Hadrian's secretary, whom Hadrian hadn't spoken to since before the attack.

"Yes, that would be fine. I should speak with him anyway. Tomorrow." Hadrian suspected this excursion to the sitting room would be the most complicated thing he did today. *Blast.*

"It's good that you speak with the inspector again," Sharp said. "There's the matter of the ring I found in your pocket when I went through the clothes you were wearing that night."

Hadrian had forgotten about that entirely. But now he remembered it distinctly. He'd pulled the ring from his attacker's finger. "Where is it?"

"I'll fetch it." Sharp disappeared into the bedchamber, and it sounded as if he'd gone through to the dressing room. A moment later, he returned with the gold ring and set it on the table. "You should eat. I'll be back directly with your tray."

"Thank you," Hadrian murmured, his attention completely focused on the ring. It was not something a ruffian such as his attacker would wear. The man's clothes had been rough and cheap. This ring was expensive—and old. Hadrian could see it wasn't quite round as it had molded its shape to the wearer's finger.

Hadrian picked it up between his thumb and forefinger. It was a signet ring with an M engraved into the gold. No, this was not a common footpad's ring, which raised even more questions in Hadrian's mind. Perhaps when he presented this ring to the inspector, the man would change his theory about Hadrian's attack being a simple theft gone awry.

An image passed quickly through Hadrian's mind. He saw himself on a dark street, his eyes round with shock. Surprise and then anger flowed through him along with a terrible pain at the front of his head.

What the devil?

Inhaling sharply, Hadrian sought to clear the strange vision and sensations from his brain. Then it happened again, only it wasn't his face he saw but a tall monument. This was followed by the flash of a pretty, red-haired woman with plump scarlet lips drawn back in a sultry smile. He didn't recognize her. Another image emerged, that of a battered face of a young man. His lip was cracked, and he said something that Hadrian couldn't hear. A fist—as if it were Hadrian's—smashed into the man's cheek. He felt an overwhelming rage and need to commit violence, but those feelings didn't come from him. Hadrian sensed them like one would catch a breeze or a scent.

Gasping, Hadrian dropped the ring as agony ripped through his head. The visions ceased as did the sensations and emotions that didn't belong to him. None of it belonged to him.

Putting his hands to either side of his head, Hadrian closed his eyes and tried to breathe calmly as the intense pain continued. It took a few minutes for it to finally decrease, but it did not completely subside.

Opening his eyes, he looked at the ring on the table. Curiosity won out over caution as he picked it up again. Nothing happened.

Exhaling with relief, Hadrian turned the ring over between his fingers, then he slipped it onto his pinkie. He was immediately assaulted with pain and anger and visions of people and things he didn't understand. Swearing, he pulled the ring off and set it away from him on the table.

What cursed object was this? What was he seeing and feeling?

He daren't pick it up again. At least not today. He was too spent, and his head was on fire with pain.

But he couldn't let the ring go either, definitely not to Inspector Padgett whose interest in what had happened to Hadrian seemed passing at best. Apparently, the stabbing of a man as he walked along the street did not warrant significant investigation.

Hadrian disagreed entirely. This attack had been more than a footpad behaving foolishly. The assailant had been wearing a ring that likely hadn't belonged to him and that carried an inexplicable power to produce visions and emotions—and pain. Hadrian didn't like any of that, but if it would help him sort out what happened and lead him to his would-be killer, he'd use the tool as best he could. Even if he felt like a madman doing so.

Sharp returned with the breakfast tray and came toward the table. The ring was sitting in the middle, so Hadrian quickly moved it to the side. He barely touched it, but there was still an accompanying flash of a bell in his mind. Rather, a sign with a bell on it.

"Would you mind putting the ring in the dresser next to my bed?" Hadrian asked. "Top drawer."

"Certainly." Sharp picked it up, and Hadrian watched closely for any sign that he felt or saw the same things that Hadrian did. There was no reaction from the valet as he slipped it into his pocket then set about arranging Hadrian's breakfast.

"Where have you been keeping that?" Hadrian asked.

"The ring?" Sharp poured out Hadrian's coffee. "In the box with your other jewelry."

"And you haven't done anything with it since the attack?"

Sharp blinked. "No. Should I have?"

"Not at all. It's just...it's an odd object."

Sharp's light brown brows gathered together. "Is it?"

It seemed as though the valet thought it was simply a regular ring. That was extremely perplexing. And made Hadrian feel as though the blow to his head had triggered some sort of mental defect.

Or, perhaps this had just been a random occurrence caused by his head injury. Yes, that was it. He'd probably pick the ring up tomorrow and nothing at all would happen.

Except that was not remotely the case.

CHAPTER 2

Late February

The door swung open before Miss Matilda Wren could reach for the handle. Mrs. Acorn, the housekeeper, greeted her. Tall and slender with dove-gray hair tucked beneath a white cap; she was in her early sixties and possessed a keen aptitude for keeping an exceptionally tidy house, baking the best tarts in London, and caring for Tilda as if she were her daughter. Which was most welcome, since Tilda's own mother had remarried nine years earlier and relocated to Birmingham.

"How did things go with Mr. Forrest?" Mrs. Acorn asked as Tilda walked into the small entrance hall of her grandmother's compact terrace house in Marylebone.

Mr. Forrest was the barrister for whom Tilda did occasional investigative work. "He was most pleased with the evidence I provided regarding Mrs. Paine's case."

Mrs. Paine was seeking to divorce her husband on the

grounds of abuse and adultery. Tilda had collected a statement from the owner of the brothel where Mr. Paine had spent every Thursday evening for the past four years. They already had proof of abuse from Scotland Yard where Mrs. Paine had filed a report last month. Mr. Paine was a truly horrid man, and Tilda was delighted to help Mrs. Paine be free of him.

Indeed, Tilda would have done the work for free, but she could not afford to be charitable. The money left by Tilda's grandfather only stretched so far, and there had been no money from Tilda's father—not for Tilda anyway. Her mother had inherited a small sum and taken it with her when she'd remarried. She'd told Tilda that her grandmother would care for her, particularly since Tilda had decided to stay with her rather than join her mother and her new husband in Birmingham, where he resided.

Whilst Tilda could probably ask for money from her stepfather, Sir Bardolph, she would not. He'd been delighted that Tilda, at the age of seventeen, had chosen to remain in London with her grandmother. Since then, Tilda's relationship with her mother had diminished to monthly letters and one visit each year when her mother traveled to London with her husband so he could see one of his own adult children. They never came to just see Tilda.

Mrs. Acorn smiled as she nodded at Tilda with encouragement. "I hope that earned you a fair price."

"Fair enough." Investigating for Mr. Forrest wasn't lucrative work, but every little bit helped. "Unfortunately, he doesn't have anything else for me at the moment." Tilda chose not to work on cases for husbands, preferring to focus her investigative attention on helping women, for they had little enough assistance.

"Ah, well, things will work themselves out," Mrs. Acorn said, brushing her hands on her apron. "I'd best get back to the kitchen so I can bring tea up shortly."

Leaving her hat and gloves in the small entry hall, Tilda made her way past the staircase into the sitting room where she was sure to find her grandmother. As expected, Grandmama was settled in her favorite chair near the fireplace, her feet propped on a small stool and a blanket covering her legs. Half-moon glasses perched on her nose as she read a newspaper. A lantern on the table beside her chair gave her the additional light she needed to adequately see the print.

"I've returned, Grandmama. Mrs. Acorn will bring tea soon."

Grandmama looked up at Tilda over the rim of her glasses. "Splendid. How was your meeting, my dear?"

"Very pleasant, thank you." Tilda sat in the other chair situated before the hearth. It once matched the one her grandmother occupied, but its cushion was fuller and the dark gold and brown fabric more vibrant since it was not used as regularly as Grandmama's.

"Your grandfather would be so proud of you, even as he would be troubled by the idea of you being employed in such a manner." Grandmama set the newspaper in her lap and removed her glasses, setting them on the small, square table beside her chair.

"I'm sure if Grandpapa were still with us, he would have accepted how things have changed—and continue to change— for women."

"I'm sorry you feel the need to work at all." Grandmama frowned, the curved lines that bracketed her mouth from her nose to her chin deepening.

They'd had this conversation many times. It wasn't at all that Tilda *felt* the need. There was, quite simply, a need. Even so, she knew why her grandmother thought it was more due to Tilda's own desire. Tilda did enjoy her investigative work and even if there wasn't a need, she would want to do it. If she could, she would have taken up a position at Scotland Yard, just as her father had done. He'd taught her so much about what he did—how to gather evidence methodically and thoroughly, how to consider and deduce, how to ask questions and adopt the right demeanor to ensure you obtained answers. She couldn't help but possess a keen appreciation for justice and helping others. How she longed to make a difference to people as her father had done.

Without that, what would she do? Besides be invisible, as all unmarried women became.

Though, in truth, since her father's death, Tilda had felt, if not invisible then...small. When he'd died, the light from their household had gone with him. Things were much brighter here with her grandmother, but Tilda still thought a part of her remained in the shadows and probably always would.

Tilda turned her thoughts to addressing her grandmother. "As it happens, Grandmama, our finances are stretched rather thin. We'll need to speak with Sir Henry about increasing your quarterly stipend." Grandmama received payments on an investment, but there was a second investment that was to be used as Grandmama aged, which Tilda had only learned of a few months ago.

Sir Henry Meacham was Tilda's grandfather's cousin and their closest living male relative after Tilda's father had died. At that time, Sir Henry had taken over management of Grandmama's funds.

"Is that really necessary?" Grandmama asked with a slight purse to her lips.

"Yes. I will call on him." Tilda knew her grandmother disliked asking him for more money. She found it a "ghastly" subject. "I'm sure you remember that the rent increased last year." Tilda wasn't at all certain that was true but would give her grandmother the benefit of the doubt. "And I'm afraid some expenses have simply inflated." It seemed odd to Tilda that the quarterly stipend hadn't changed even once since she'd come to live with her grandmother eight years earlier. When she'd attempted to speak to Sir Henry about that and, more recently, about the secondary investment, he always said it wasn't convenient, but that they would discuss it "soon." She understood he was a busy man, but she was beginning to think she and her grandmother were not important to him. Perhaps she should see about taking over the management of the finances herself—if she could.

"It's my new medicine, isn't it?" Grandmama's worried blue eyes met Tilda's. "If it's too expensive, I'll stop taking it. My hands are much better."

"Owing to Mr. Harvey's cream," Tilda said. "Your medicine is necessary. We can afford it." In truth, it *was* one of the reasons they needed more money. Tilda budgeted to their very last pence. "Grandmama, please do not fret about any of this. I will speak with Sir Henry tomorrow and all will be well." Tilda regretted saying anything to her grandmother. She should have gone to see Sir Henry without mentioning it.

"If you say so, my dear. Only promise me you won't press Sir Henry unduly."

Tilda would if she had to. She would brook no further procrastination.

And she would hope for more work from Mr. Forrest. If she couldn't work for Scotland Yard or become a private investigator in her own right, that was the next best thing. She ought to consider different lines of work, but she didn't really have other skills besides investigation. She couldn't sew or mind children—she had absolutely no experience with anyone younger than herself. Working as a clerk might appeal to her, but the truth was that helping people solve their problems was all she *wanted* to do. Sometimes she wondered if she was just being selfish.

Exhaling, Tilda reasoned the day may come when she would take a position as a clerk or some other passionless job.

Or worse, that she would marry. She wanted that even less than employment that didn't inspire her. For now, she could make do with her occasional work for Mr. Forrest, especially if she could persuade Sir Henry to increase their quarterly stipend.

Mrs. Acorn brought in the tea tray and poured out before departing for the kitchen once more.

Grandmama sipped her tea with a smile then reached for a lemon cake. "I saw Mr. Orchard this morning," she said before taking a bite of cake.

Tilda responded with a vague, "Mmm." She did not want to engage her grandmother on the topic of Mr. Orchard. A widower with two children, he was very nice. He was also clearly interested in Tilda as a potential mother for his offspring. If she wanted to care for children, she would seek a position as a governess.

"You could at least consider him," Grandmama said. "You are not so firmly on the shelf, are you?"

At twenty-five, Tilda regarded herself as a spinster and had no quarrel with that. To marry would be to surrender every-thing, and given that she had so little, she was not willing to do that. Marriage as an institution also held little appeal, but then Tilda had only ever been privy to an unhappy one—her parents'. How she wished she could have known her grandfa-ther and seen her grandparents together. The love her grand-mother had for him was still very present, even if he wasn't.

"I think I am, Grandmama," Tilda said. "What's more, I find the shelf comfortable. The view is most diverting."

"Well, then I shall put Mr. Orchard from my mind." Grand-mama's gaze drifted to her teacup but not before Tilda caught the sheen of sadness in her eyes. She wanted to know that Tilda wouldn't be alone once she departed this earth. Tilda could only console her by saying she didn't mind being alone, that she actually enjoyed independence. To which Grandmama would scoff—with a smile—and say there was nothing wrong with being dependent. That caring for someone and having someone to care for you was indeed lovely.

Such comments never failed to bring Tilda's father to the forefront of her thoughts. How she missed him. He'd cared for her greatly—more than her mother ever had. His loss still hurt, and Tilda knew it always would.

Tilda set her teacup down. "I think it's time for our word puzzles." One of their "luxury" expenses was a book full of word games published monthly. Most afternoons, they did a few pages together.

Beaming, Grandmama leaned forward. "Oh, yes, let's."

Tilda moved the table next to her chair between them and fetched the book. Opening it to their last completed puzzle, she flipped the page to the next one.

Grandmama rubbed her hands together. "This one looks quite complex."

They settled in to decipher the rebus, and Tilda set her financial worries aside. For the moment.

~

*A*fter five weeks of recuperation, Hadrian was more than ready to leave the confines of his home in Mayfair. But the destination of his first foray back into the world would have surprised anyone. There was no way he would reveal his intentions, not even to Sharp. He simply could not.

"You look very well, my lord," the valet declared as he stepped back.

"I feel well, thank you." The lingering ache in Hadrian's right side where he'd been stabbed had finally subsided.

The pain in his head had also diminished, though he still had the occasional headache. He'd taken a hard blow, so the doctor had said. Hadrian had to agree, for things had not been the same since he'd struck his head on the pavement. But did he really blame the injury, or was that confounded ring he'd taken from his assailant at fault?

Hadrian had continued to see visions and feel sensations whenever he handled the ring with his bare hands. Indeed, the more he touched the ring, the longer the visions lasted and the more detail he could discern. Though, it was never quite enough—not until the last few days when he'd finally determined what he was seeing. He was fairly confident the visions were like memories, but they belonged to whomever had owned the ring.

Keeping the ring from Scotland Yard hadn't been a concern. The inspector had not returned to speak with Hadrian despite Hadrian sending two letters requesting his presence. Whilst Hadrian had no intention of surrendering the ring, or even mentioning it just now, he was still eager to have his case reopened.

Perhaps calling on Padgett at Scotland Yard should be Hadrian's first excursion, but Hadrian had something more pressing—finding answers to whatever he was seeing when he touched that bloody ring. If the visions could lead him to his assailant, Hadrian could discover the truth behind the attack, for there was no way the man had been a common footpad. This crime carried a different sort of motivation, and Hadrian intended to solve this mystery. He'd always felt he had a purpose in life, but this was something different. This was a visceral need to determine why he'd almost died.

Releasing the ring, Hadrian took his hat and gloves from Sharp whose vertical creases between his brows had formed deep crevasses. "Erase the worry from your mind. I'm truly fine, and I'm quite looking forward to being outside."

Hadrian set his hat atop his head and departed his dressing chamber. Making his way downstairs, he drew on his gloves.

His butler, Collier, greeted him in the entrance hall. "It's good to see you going out, my lord."

"Thank you. Do see that Sharp has some tea. He seems nervous about my departure. I've assured him all will be well."

"I will do so," Collier replied with a nod. "We are all concerned for your welfare. Do take care."

"Always." Hadrian strode from the house onto Curzon Street. He'd already decided to walk to Piccadilly where he would hail a hack to his dubious destination.

It felt good to be out, even if the air seemed worse. Or perhaps in the weeks since his injury, he'd simply forgotten how bad it was. Every summer he spent weeks at his estate in Hampshire and was somehow shocked by the quality of the air when he returned to London.

Once he reached Piccadilly, he had no trouble hailing a hack. "Fish Street Hill," he told the driver as he handed him payment. Hadrian climbed inside and pulled the door closed in front of him.

"Aye," the driver responded, and they were quickly on their way.

Hadrian felt the energy and bustle of the city as they traveled east. Smartly dressed ladies and gentlemen gave way to people of business rushing along the pavement. The farther east they went, the number of people increased—and they were of a decidedly lower economic class. Children dashed about, and some worked alongside their parents, hawking pies or coffee or any number of goods. Some children worked alone, selling matches or flowers. He only saw one of the latter, as it was still early in the season. The child had clusters of barely blooming daffodils, their bright yellow a glimpse of the coming spring sun.

Blinking, Hadrian wondered at his sense of curiosity and even nostalgia today. He had been too long cooped up, he reasoned.

At last, they arrived at Fish Street Hill. The image he'd seen most in his mind rose before him, tall and unmistakable, though it had taken him more than a week to hold the vision long enough to discern what he was seeing.

Hadrian departed the hack and walked slowly toward the monument. Erected more than two hundred years ago, it commemorated the Great Fire that had destroyed most of the city of London. This obelisk had lived in Hadrian's mind for weeks now, along with a sign featuring a carved and painted bell. Turning in a circle, he looked for that sign.

Of course it wasn't immediately visible. He began to walk, deciding to follow Fish Street Hill toward the river. After a few dozen steps, he saw the sign, precisely as he'd seen it in his vision. It hung over a tavern—the Bell.

Hadrian quickened his pace until he stood outside the pub. Taking a deep breath, he stepped inside. And had no idea what to do next.

The ring had led him this far, and he needed help to continue. He hated relying on the vexing object with its inexplicable power, and it wasn't just because seeing and feeling things from it made his head ache most fiercely. The strange ring made him question his sanity. It was bad enough that he saw and felt things, but to follow them? He'd end up in Bedlam before long.

Which was why he'd told no one about the ring.

Steeling himself, Hadrian removed his glove and reached into his pocket to stroke the ring. Nothing came to him at first, which wasn't unusual.

Come on, Hadrian urged silently. He just knew the ring was trying to lead him somewhere. Why show him the monument and this tavern?

Because they had something to do with the man who'd worn the ring. The footpad who wasn't a footpad, no matter what Scotland Yard had resolved.

The door behind Hadrian creaked as someone pushed inside. Hadrian hurriedly stepped away, his eyes adjusting to the dim, low-ceilinged interior. The pub's common room was long with a rough collection of tables taking up the bulk of the space. Two dingy windows looked out onto Fish Street Hill. A bar stretched along the back of the room, behind which stood a burly barkeep with a beard. He spoke familiarly with the man who'd just entered and gone straight to the bar.

Was the man who'd worn the ring in Hadrian's pocket a patron of this pub? If the visions Hadrian saw in his mind were indeed the man's memories, somehow trapped in the ring he'd worn, then it was likely. Unless his assailant had never actually walked into the pub. Perhaps he saw the sign as he walked past it to his lodgings.

Hadrian could very well be wasting his time and energy. And for what? Was he going to haul the footpad to Whitehall himself? Or inform Scotland Yard that he'd found his attacker...through visions from a magic ring?

Not that last part, but the rest, hell yes. If Scotland Yard wasn't going to properly investigate this crime, then someone needed to. Hadrian had considered hiring a private investigator, but for now he wanted to determine whatever the ring was trying to tell him.

And how would he explain that to the man he hired?

Hadrian shrugged those thoughts away. He needed to concentrate on whyever the ring had driven him here.

He thrust his hand into his pocket once more and pulled out the ring out to slip it onto his little finger. Wearing it generally gave him the best results, as far as seeing visions and perchance grasping them for more than a flickering moment. It was also the best way to ensure his head was pounding, but that was a risk he would take now that he was here.

Running the forefinger of his right hand over the engraved M, Hadrian wondered what the initial stood for. Probably a family name, but whose? Certainly not the man who'd attacked him. He did not seem the sort whose family would have such a treasure.

The ring never failed to make Hadrian feel unsettled, as if he'd just received bad news. It infused him with a sense of anxiety that he didn't care for, but his need for information outweighed that discomfort. For now.

A few of the tables were occupied, but most were not. Likely, that would change as the day aged. Empty tables meant Hadrian could stop at each one and see if something, *anything* would flash in his brain.

After moving about from table to table and feeling nothing save a growing ache behind his temples, Hadrian became aware of the barkeep and the man who'd walked in after him looking in his direction. And why wouldn't they? He was behaving oddly.

Frustrated, Hadrian sat at a table and put his palm on the pocked wood. Something flickered within him, like an energy. Hadrian closed his eyes and pressed his bare hand more firmly against the tabletop.

There! An image rose in his mind. But it was impossibly brief. He tried again, focusing on his mind's eye. "Show me," he whispered.

"Ye need something?"

Hadrian opened his eyes to see the barkeep standing over him. He didn't want to be thrown out for behaving as though he belonged in an insane asylum, which seemed imminent given the barkeep's wary gaze and the hard set of his mouth. "Ale, thank you," Hadrian said pleasantly.

The barkeep returned to the bar. As he did so, Hadrian saw another image. It was definitely a man's face. The only other faces he'd seen were the red-haired woman and the bruised man. Seeing them repeatedly had not increased his recognition. Hadrian didn't know them, and why should he?

But something about this face tickled his brain. A sense of excitement rushed through him. Hadrian took off his other glove, wondering if pressing both hands against the table would help. Hell, he had no idea what he was doing. He just knew he needed to see that face again.

The barkeep deposited a tankard on the table, and Hadrian paid him. "Thank you," he said, eager for the barkeep to go away.

"Ye seem a long way from home," the barkeep said.

"Not that far." Hadrian narrowed his eyes slightly as he looked up at the man. He would prefer to be genial, as that generally smoothed disagreeable situations. However, this man was rough, his demeanor that of distrust and suspicion. "I'm in the neighborhood conducting business and fancied an ale."

The barkeep eyed him another moment then nodded before returning to the bar.

Suppressing a scowl, Hadrian swept up the tankard and took a long drink. The ale was weak, but it was wet and eased the ache in his head a bit.

Hadrian took a second drink then set the tankard down. Summoning all his focus, he pressed his hands against the table once more and closed his eyes. Nothing.

Then he realized he typically saw more when his eyes were, in fact, open. He silently cursed himself for not noticing that sooner. Fixing his gaze ahead, he moved his hands to a new position.

The image of the man came again. He was older, his thinning hair gray, the flesh of his face loose and weathered. His eyes were wide. He seemed frightened.

Hadrian felt he knew this man, but he couldn't see him long enough to know for certain. He drank more ale and, over the course of nearly an hour, kept chasing the image, taking breaks to allow the pain in his head to ease. At last, Hadrian recognized him. Without a doubt, he knew this man. But what, pray tell, did he have to do with the man who'd attacked Hadrian?

Head aching and his body thrumming with excitement, Hadrian removed the ring and slipped it into his pocket. He pulled on his gloves then rose from the chair, intent on following the path the vision had laid. Hopefully the man he'd seen would be able to tell him the identity of Hadrian's assailant.

How Hadrian would ascertain that knowledge was uncertain, but he would not be daunted. He would determine why he'd been stabbed, for he was convinced that theft had nothing to do with it.

Hadrian strode from the pub, aware that he may very well be on a fool's errand.

CHAPTER 3

Tilda stepped from the hackney coach and walked toward Sir Henry Meacham's house in Huntley Street only to stop short. A yew wreath with black ribbons hanging on the door turned her blood cold. Sir Henry must be dead. They would not hang a wreath for one of his retainers, and his wife had died two years ago.

Still, her grandmother hadn't received a notice, and surely Sir Henry's daughters would have sent one. Unless the death had just happened, and they hadn't yet had them printed.

The cool wind pulled at Tilda's bonnet, but she'd tied it securely beneath her chin. Shakily, she made her way forward and summoned the courage to knock on the door. She wasn't intruding. She was family. Sir Henry's second cousin. Or was it third?

Her knock was soon answered by their decrepit butler, Vaughn. He'd been a tall man but was now stooped. Still, he was taller than Tilda and a great many others. His faded blue gaze met Tilda's. "As you can see, miss, death has visited this household."

"I'm sorry Vaughn. What, pray tell, happened to Sir Henry?"

The butler's aged skin pulled taut over his cheekbones as he grimaced. "He collapsed at one of his clubs last evening. He suffered an attack of some kind. Dr. Selwin, his physician, said it was his heart. He examined Sir Henry before he was brought here. Mrs. Forsythe was summoned and has been here since early this morning. However, she is not receiving." Millicent Forsythe was Sir Henry's eldest daughter. Tilda wondered where his other daughter, Belinda, was.

"Of course not," Tilda said softly. "Please convey our deepest sympathies."

"The funeral's to be here on Friday," Vaughn said. "Mrs. Forsythe just ordered the cards a few hours ago. I presume you and your grandmother will be in attendance."

"Most certainly." Tilda briefly touched the butler's forearm. "I know you've been with Sir Henry a very long time."

Vaughn exhaled roughly, his chest sounding as though it were shuddering. "Suppose it's time for retirement." He sounded rather despondent, which was to be expected after such a shocking tragedy.

Tilda bid the butler farewell and turned away from the closing door. Though she hadn't been terribly close to Sir Henry, she felt a wave of sadness.

She walked slowly back toward the street, her mind reeling from this shocking news. Grandmama would be very upset. In many ways, Sir Henry had kept the memory of her husband alive. They often shared stories of time spent together decades earlier. Tilda couldn't do that, for he'd died seven years before her birth. Even so, he'd loomed large in her life because of the way her grandmother and her own father spoke of him. The death of his cousin would likely bring up many emotions for her grandmother.

Reaching the pavement, Tilda stopped short once more as a gentleman stood facing the house. "I beg your pardon," she said just before colliding with him.

She had to tilt her head to look up at him, for he was most certainly over six feet tall. His eyes, beneath a wide forehead, were a deep blue with thick, dark lashes. A strong, square chin supported his full lips. The gentleman was most arresting.

"My apologies," he murmured. "I was distracted by the mourning wreath." His gaze swept over her. "Are you a member of the family?"

"I am, albeit somewhat distantly," she said. "Sir Henry was my grandfather's cousin." She would need to see about a gown of black crepe. Yet another burdensome expense. She wouldn't need to wear it long for such a distant relative. Perhaps she could adapt something of her grandmother's, though it would likely be desperately out of fashion.

The gentleman's brow puckered beneath his top hat. "It is Sir Henry then? I'm sorry for your loss."

"Were you calling on him?" Tilda asked.

"I'd hoped to."

"I'd hoped to do the same." Tilda thought of the reason for her visit. How was she to obtain an increase in her grandmother's stipend now? Indeed, what would happen to her grandmother's investments now that he was gone? He had no sons, only two daughters, one of whom had no children, and the other, Mrs. Forsythe, had just a single daughter. Tilda would need to speak with Sir Henry's solicitor. After the funeral, of course.

She cocked her head to the side and looked more closely at the gentleman. He was not familiar to her. He was, however, expensively garbed. His attire was somewhat formal, and if she'd had to guess, she would put his address squarely in Belgravia or Mayfair. He might even be nobility.

"How do you know Sir Henry?" she asked.

"We worked together somewhat before he retired from the Home Office." The man frowned faintly. "When did he die?"

"Last night. The funeral is Friday." Tilda wondered why she

was sharing so much information with a stranger. She reasoned she'd been jolted by this shocking news. And he wasn't a stranger to Sir Henry.

"Is it here?" the man asked. "I should like to pay my respects."

She blinked at him, clutching her purse more tightly before her. "Forgive me, but who are you?"

He shook his head. "My apologies. I am not usually this poorly mannered. I am Lord Ravenhurst."

She'd been right about his potential nobility, and she was more confident than ever that he was nowhere near his large, certainly fashionable home. "I'm sorry we had to meet under such circumstances."

"I am the one who is sorry, both for my lapse in behavior just now and because you are the one with cause to be grieved since Sir Henry was family. At the risk of breaching etiquette even further, may I ask how he died?"

Though Ravenhurst knew he was verging upon rudeness, he chose to flirt with it anyway. He must be very keen to know what had happened. Why? His curiosity rivaled her own. But then an investigative mind demanded one ask questions.

"He suffered an attack," Tilda said slowly, uncertain of this man's interest or motives for calling on Sir Henry. "Why are you calling?"

"I wished to speak with him about a private matter." He drew a quick breath. His blue eyes sparked with intensity though his features remained passive. He seemed to be well practiced in schooling his expressions, for the most part. "Where did this attack happen? Do you know if anything was stolen from his person?"

Tilda stared at him as she realized what he meant. "He wasn't attacked by someone. He collapsed due to some sort of attack. His heart, apparently." That was all she would say, not that she knew much more. "Your interest in the specifics of Sir Henry's death is most curious, my lord."

His lips turned up in the briefest of smiles. No, it wasn't really a smile, but a resetting of his face into something more pleasant upon realizing he'd displayed too much of... something.

"Again, I must apologize. I'd hoped to speak with Sir Henry about an important matter, and I find myself perplexed as to how to move forward. But that is most selfish of me. Please accept my deepest condolences." He touched his hat, then turned and walked away from her.

Tilda's own curiosity was quite provoked. What private, important matter? She couldn't help noting that he'd been purposely vague whilst asking her a series of questions. If she didn't know better, she would assume he was an investigator.

But he was an earl, if she recalled her Burke's Peerage correctly, and what reason could he have for investigating Sir Henry?

She trailed after him. "Pardon me, my lord?"

He turned to face her. "Yes?"

"Your interest in Sir Henry's death has piqued my curiosity." She narrowed her eyes slightly, seeming to assess him. "Perhaps I could help you with your *private, important matter.*"

Surprise flickered in his gaze before he blinked it away. "I wouldn't want to trouble you today on the heels of such a tragedy."

"Another time then," Tilda said benignly though she wanted to press him. That he'd neatly obtained information from her whilst she'd gleaned nothing from him grated on her.

He smiled and nodded before turning away once again. This time, Tilda watched him go, her mind silently repeating their conversation.

Botheration. She couldn't focus on the perplexing earl right now, not after what had happened to Sir Henry. Turning on her heel, she walked in the opposite direction from the earl to hail a hackney to return home. She was both anxious about informing her grandmother of this tragedy and how it may affect their livelihood. She was eager to speak with Sir Henry's solicitor at the earliest possible moment.

She could only hope the man had clear instructions regarding Grandmama's investments. Waiting to confirm that would be somewhat agitating. Alas, there was nothing else to be done.

~

*T*he rain had lessened as Hadrian had returned to Sir Henry Meacham's house in Huntley Street on Friday for the funeral, but now as he arrived, it came down in buckets. He waited in the coach a few minutes before giving up on the downpour lessening.

Pulling his hat down, he jumped from the coach and hastened to the door, which was promptly opened wide by one of the oldest butlers Hadrian had ever encountered.

Stooped, with rheumy blue eyes, the man barely looked at Hadrian. "The parlor is just through there." He gestured behind him to a doorway on the left side of the entrance hall.

"Thank you," Hadrian said, removing his sodden hat and handing it to the poor man. There was already a collection of damp headwear atop a slender table.

Moving into the parlor, Hadrian felt as though he'd stepped directly into a funeral shroud. Black crepe was draped over mirrors and the windows. The space was dark and close. Gloomy.

As Hadrian scanned the room, he recognized several faces, many of whom were—or had been—with the Home Office. And not just clerks, but the secretary, Lord Cranbrook and even a former secretary, Mr. Spencer Walpole.

There were strong smells, like perfume, wafting about. This was typical at a funeral to mask the scent of death, especially in warmer months. However, the smells here were rather pungent —floral and citrus.

"Afternoon, Ravenhurst," a deep voice said from behind Hadrian.

Turning, Hadrian recognized the man who had to be around seventy but appeared quite hearty. "Ardleigh," he said with a nod.

The viscount, thick-waisted with dark gray hair and patrician features, glanced about the room before focusing his gray eyes on Hadrian once more. "Didn't realize you knew Sir Henry all that well."

"Well enough to receive an invitation," Hadrian said. He'd been surprised when it arrived but reasoned the woman he'd met outside the house the other day had included him on the list of people to receive invitations. And he was not going to pass up the opportunity to come and learn whatever he could about Sir Henry's sudden death. It was too bloody coincidental that Hadrian would see the man in a vision associated with Hadrian's own assailant.

"Nice to see a hearty turnout," Ardleigh said with a fleeting smile. "But then Sir Henry was well liked."

Hadrian recalled that about him. "Sir Henry was always most genial."

"He had a fine laugh." Ardleigh smiled again, this time for longer. "I'd known him a great many years."

"I'm sorry for the loss of your friend."

"He had better friends than I, but I shall be grateful to be considered among them. Please excuse me. I must pay my respects to his daughters." Ardleigh moved past Hadrian toward a pair of women encased in black from their veiled hats to their footwear.

"Lord Ravenhurst, you did come," a feminine tone said from behind him.

Hadrian turned. Though he'd recognized the voice as belonging to the woman he'd met the other day, he jolted to see her in black, thinking he preferred her in the blue walking dress she'd been wearing that day. She was a striking woman with moss green eyes, sharp cheekbones, and a small, cunning cleft in her chin.

"Were you hoping I would?" Hadrian asked, an odd pleasure sweeping through him.

"I made sure you received an invitation since you claimed to know Sir Henry."

Her use of the word 'claimed' made Hadrian wonder if she doubted him. She had seemed somewhat skeptical of him the other day, following him down the street to offer assistance. And curious, which made two of them.

"Thank you, Miss—I'm sorry, I don't how to address you." He smiled politely. She hadn't offered her name the other day when he'd given his.

"Miss Matilda Wren."

He knew that name. "Was Alexander Wren, the magistrate, your grandfather?"

She nodded. "You knew of him?"

"Certainly. He was highly regarded. Such a shame he died at too young an age."

"I never knew him, but I feel as if I do, living with my grandmother." Her gaze moved to an older woman leaning on a cane as she spoke with one of the women Ardleigh had identified as Sir Henry's daughters.

"Is that her?" Hadrian asked.

"Yes." Miss Wren looked at the women with marked concern. "This has been a shock for her. Sir Henry hadn't been ill, as far as anyone knew."

Hadrian noted the sleek column of Miss Wren's neck rising

above the high collar of her ebony gown. She wore a stylish black hat atop her red-gold hair which was gathered at the back with curls cascading to her shoulder blades. Her gown, however, wasn't the least bit fashionable. He was no expert, but he would have guessed it was over a decade out of style. The skirt was too full.

She turned her head toward him, her eyes narrowing slightly. "You were exceptionally curious about Sir Henry's death the other day, particularly when you assumed he'd been attacked."

Though she hadn't asked him a question, Hadrian again sensed her skepticism as well as her own curiosity—about him. "I heard of another attack recently and wondered if he'd suffered the same." Hadrian wasn't going to reveal the attack had been on him or why he would think the two would be connected. For then he'd have to explain the magical, preternatural ring.

Miss Wren's brow furrowed, as if she too wondered why he would think an attack on her distant cousin would be related to an attack on someone else. She opened her mouth, and Hadrian was certain she was about to ask that very question.

Only they were interrupted by the arrival of her grandmother.

Miss Wren's demeanor changed, her features softening. "Lord Ravenhurst, this is my grandmother, Mrs. Wren. Grandmama, this is Lord Ravenhurst. He was an associate of Sir Henry's."

"Please accept my condolences on the loss of your cousin-in-law," Hadrian said solemnly.

Mrs. Wren was petite, and like her granddaughter, wore a black gown that was somewhat outmoded. "Thank you. It is still quite shocking to me that he is gone. Such a strange coincidence that my granddaughter had gone to speak with him about financial matters only to discover he had perished."

Hadrian tucked that piece of information away, not that Miss Wren's financial state had aught to do with him and whatever it was he was investigating.

Miss Wren pursed her lips briefly. "It isn't all that strange, Grandmama. It *is* a tragedy, however."

"Well, I suppose he lived a good life," Mrs. Wren said with a light sigh, her blue eyes shuttering as she dipped her head briefly. "To go suddenly and without fuss is rather fortunate, I say." She looked to her granddaughter. "I have always been grateful that your grandfather went in the same manner."

"Do ailments of the heart run in the family then?" Hadrian asked.

Miss Wren's gaze snapped to his. But it was her grandmother who replied. "My husband did not die of a heart attack as his cousin did. He was thrown from his horse and hit his head. He died instantly." Her eyes lost focus for a moment, and her lips turned down, deep creases forming in her soft flesh.

"I'm sorry for your losses—both your husband, and his cousin." Hadrian gave them a solemn nod and a slight bow before moving away.

He was aware of Miss Wren's attention on him as he moved toward the open coffin to view the deceased. But he did not make eye contact with her. He'd already stirred her interest enough with his probing questions. He needed to find and employ subtlety if he meant to continue on this path.

And what path was that? Did he fancy himself an investigator? Perhaps, since it seemed Scotland Yard wasn't interested in doing their job. Hadrian could scarcely believe Inspector Padgett had closed his case. Since when did footpads stab their marks?

Sir Henry looked much the same as Hadrian remembered him. Perhaps his jowls were a little meatier. He was definitely paler, but Hadrian credited death for that.

If Hadrian touched the dead man, would he see another

vision? Quickly removing his left glove, he reached into his pocket and clasped the troublesome ring between his thumb and forefinger for a moment. Again, he saw the sign of the Bell as well as a dingy living space with a small table next to a dirty window, which Hadrian assumed was his assailant's lodgings. Unfortunately, he never saw enough of that to aid him in finding where it might be located.

He released the ring and moved away from the coffin to a table with a handful of photographs, all of them turned face down. Pity, for Hadrian would have liked to view them.

Curious, he brushed his bare hand against the table. He had hoped for a vision, but there was nothing. But of course, there wouldn't be—he wasn't wearing the ring.

Suddenly, he felt a sense of agitation and of something darker and more arresting. Fear, almost. He pulled his hand away with a slight frown. The sensations diminished and faded away. Hadrian put his hand against the table once more, this time gripping the edge. The feelings from a moment ago, which made no sense for him to have in this moment, particularly without touching the ring, returned. They were not his emotions. Though he wasn't touching the ring, he was certain he was sensing someone else's feelings. Sir Henry's perhaps. The darker emotion was more pronounced. It was definitely fear.

Taking his hand from the table, he drew his glove back on. What did this mean? Was the ring not the conduit for whatever Hadrian was seeing and feeling? Did the ability come from... him?

He thought about the visions at the Bell when he'd touched the table. Would he have seen them even if he hadn't been wearing the ring? Now, he wanted to touch everything in the parlor, but the funeral was about to begin.

Frustrated and confused, Hadrian made his way toward a chair. He passed one of Sir Henry's daughters—Mrs. Forsythe, he thought—overhearing her as she was speaking with another woman. "I had to wash and dress him," she said in a low tone. "It was shocking to have to see my father like that."

The other woman patted her arm. "You poor dear. I had to do that for my neighbor a few years ago." She shuddered. "He had a horrible, stitched incision down his front. They said it was from the autopsy."

"My father also had a stitched incision," Mrs. Forsythe said grimly. "But it was on his right side. I suppose that was from an autopsy too."

"The funeral's about to begin. Let me get you to your seat," the other woman said, taking Mrs. Forsythe's arm.

Hadrian thought of Sir Henry having an incision on his right side as he continued to a chair in the back row. It would not have been from an autopsy. Autopsies, as far as Hadrian knew from a physician friend who'd dissected a fair number of bodies during his education, were conducted by cutting the cadaver open along the front of their chest from neck to waist in the way the other woman had described her neighbor.

Why would he have had such a wound? Was there a chance Sir Henry's death hadn't been due to a heart attack?

Glancing about the room, Hadrian wondered what he could hope to accomplish. Well, he'd just learned that Sir Henry may not have died from a heart attack. And that he had a wound on his right side, just as Hadrian had suffered. Was this another connection between Hadrian's attack and Sir Henry?

Hadrian realized in that moment that he absolutely *was* conducting an investigation. The ring he'd taken from his assailant had led him here to Sir Henry, who was dead. And whose death may have been unnatural.

Solving Hadrian's own attempted murder had been reason enough to continue following these infernal visions, but now it seemed he could have stumbled onto something bigger. He needed to confirm Sir Henry's cause of death, and he wanted more information about how it had happened. What had Miss Wren said, that he'd collapsed? What if that wasn't really what had happened?

But why would she lie?

He saw her seated in the front row next to her grandmother. She hadn't struck him as hiding anything from him, but she had seemed wary. He'd attributed that to his being aggressive with his curiosity, but perhaps there was more going on.

A pair of clerks whom Hadrian recognized from the Home Office sat next to him. They exchanged nods and compliments regarding Sir Henry's life and contributions to the Home Office. "He was an excellent undersecretary," one of them, a fellow in his middle fifties called Ernsby who'd served as the supplemental clerk overseeing the criminal department, said.

The funeral progressed with an appropriate shroud of melancholy. When it was finished, the pallbearers, which included the other of the two clerks who'd sat near Hadrian—the man was younger and more spry than Ernsby—walked toward the coffin. Hadrian helped move the furniture so the casket could be carried out.

Hadrian waited to join the procession and was able to approach Miss Wren briefly. She and the other women would not attend the burial.

"I am truly sorry for your loss," he said to her. "I hope you are able to resolve your financial issues."

Miss Wren's nostrils flared slightly, and he deduced this was a sensitive issue. She leaned toward him. "And I would like to know about the *private matter* you intended to discuss with Sir Henry. My offer to help you remains."

"Today is not the time," Hadrian said softy, but perhaps she would allow him to question her about Sir Henry's death.

"No," she said, her green eyes glittering with a heat Hadrian could not define. "Perhaps you'll call on me in Marylebone Lane."

"Perhaps I will." Hadrian had every intention of doing so, but he would give them time to grieve.

He gave her a benign smile before stepping around her into the entrance hall. The butler ambled toward the hats and accurately retrieved Hadrian's, which was more than a little surprising. But perhaps the man's faculties were far nimbler than his body.

Setting his damp hat atop his head, Hadrian stepped out into the drizzle and joined the funeral procession.

CHAPTER 4

$\mathcal{A}$ mere five days after Sir Henry's funeral, Tilda sat in the office of his solicitor, Mr. Charles Whitley. A decade or so older than Tilda, he had a high forehead and a receding hairline. He possessed a round face with a thick, dark-brown mustache. His eyes were small and his smile ready as he'd greeted her.

"I am sorry for the loss of your cousin, Miss Wren," he said from the chair across from hers. A secretary brought a tea tray and set it on the small round table between them. "I do hope your grandmother hasn't suffered from the tragedy."

Though Tilda nor her grandmother had ever met Mr. Whitley, he seemed to know of them at least. Which of course he would since he was overseeing their financial matters.

"I appreciate your condolences, Mr. Whitley. What is most pressing for me and my grandmother at the moment is determining the state of her finances. She has been living on the income from her investment the past thirty-three years, however that income has not changed in eight years now." That was the length of time Tilda had been living with her grandmother and had taken over management of the household.

When she asked her grandmother if it had fluctuated before that, she'd only shrugged.

Mr. Whitley poured their tea then generously sugared his cup. "Not at all? I'm sure it has."

"It has not. I wanted to speak about this matter as our expenses have increased over the years, which is to be expected. However, since Sir Henry has died, I must ask for your help instead."

"I understand," Whitley said solemnly and with just the slightest condescension. "Perhaps you should review the payments Mrs. Wren received. You will likely find they *have* increased, just not as much as you might have liked."

Tilda kept her lip from curling. "I have been managing my grandmother's household for eight years. That is how I *know* the income has not increased. Perhaps you can provide me with a summary of payments for that time period so I can make sure she received all that was due. Furthermore, I would like to see your records for Mrs. Wren's secondary investment."

The solicitor flattened his lips. "I'm afraid I only have records for the past three years, as that was when I took over from the previous solicitor who retired." He frowned. "Furthermore, I am not aware of an additional investment."

Tilda's pulse quickened. "But there most certainly is. You must review your records. Perhaps a mistake was made during the transition from the former solicitor."

Mr. Whitley sipped his tea making a soft but unmistakable slurping sound. He set his cup down and gave her a sympathetic look. "I can have my clerk review the records, but I highly doubt there was a mistake. I will provide a summary of the transactions regarding Mrs. Wren's that have occurred since I have been Sir Henry's solicitor. Will that be acceptable?"

It was better than nothing, even if it didn't ease Tilda's frustration. "Yes, thank you. My grandmother said her husband made that second investment before he died. It was meant to provide for her as she aged and serve as a supplement to the primary investment."

"I see. That is helpful to know," Whitley said.

There had to be another investment. The interest from the one wasn't enough to meet their needs. They'd have to reinvest the money or perchance put it into an annuity. Tilda wasn't sure *what* they would need to do. "If you don't have record of it, I must address the issue with the prior solicitor. Will you provide me with his direction?"

"Yes, though I must tell you he no longer has all of his wits about him," Whitley said with a faint grimace. "I should also inform you that he was forced into retirement after he was caught embezzling money from a client. He paid the money back to avoid imprisonment."

Tilda gasped. That was the probable "mistake" then. "Is it possible he stole my grandmother's investment?"

"I suppose it's possible, though Hardacre claimed he'd taken them from the client by accident, that he was confused, that he'd had no intent to steal anything." Whitley blew out a breath. "Given his mental decline, I don't find that difficult to believe."

Whatever the truth, Tilda would find it.

"I think it's far more likely the investment money was used before you assumed management of Mrs. Wren's household," Whitley continued. "Or that the investment was poor, and the money was lost—and your grandmother simply forgot." He lifted a shoulder as if he were discussing the weather and not the livelihood of Tilda's grandmother and her household.

Tilda's pulse sped once more, as her frustration grew. "My grandmother did not use that money." She had, however, forgotten about it for a time, so Tilda supposed it *was* possible she'd also forgotten the investment had failed. Grandmama had also not tracked the amount of income Sir Henry had given her. This was what could happen when women did not have agency over their financial decisions and weren't even encouraged to do so. Tilda was determined to assume control of these matters.

Tilda would speak with her grandmother and gather every detail she could. Tilda's investigative skills would be most useful, though this was not how she imagined employing them. She reached for her cup and took a drink of tea before realizing she hadn't added any sugar or even a splash of cream. Still, the moisture was welcome.

Setting her cup down, she said, "I will confirm the details of the investments with my grandmother, and I will await your summary. For now, please write down Mr. Hardacre's direction."

Whitley took a small piece of parchment from his desk and scrawled out the retired solicitor's name and address. "I wish you good luck. It will likely take my clerk several days to retrieve all the records, and I want him to look for anything that might have been retained from Mr. Hardacre. I do understand that this is a great deal for you to take in. I will be happy to help with your financial matters however I can. I'm sure we can come up with a strategy to provide additional income."

Whilst Tilda appreciated Whitley's willingness to be thorough and that he genuinely seemed to want to help, she couldn't miss his slightly condescending message reminding her that women were not expected to concern themselves with such matters. "Thank you." Tilda rose, her emotions a knot of irritation, worry, and fear. What if the money was gone? Unfortunately, it seemed that was the case.

"Good day, Miss Wren," he said with a smile. Did he not realize this had been a devastating meeting?

She turned and left his office.

Outside the building, she made her way across Chancery Lane. She was most eager to speak with her grandmother. She would call on Mr. Hardacre as soon as possible. At this point, she had to hope he'd stolen the money, for that was the only chance she had of recovering it.

And if she could not, then Mr. Whitley's strategy had better be a good one.

~

*B*ack in Parliament for the first time since his attack, Hadrian was welcomed robustly by his colleagues. And perhaps somewhat less so by his political adversaries. It was a Tuesday, the same day of the week he was stabbed.

After business concluded and Hadrian was making his way out of the building, he encountered the Viscount Ardleigh who gave him a cheerful smile. "Welcome back, Ravenhurst. When I saw you at Sir Henry Meacham's funeral last week, I suspected you'd return to your chair here soon. I apologize for not mentioning that dastardly business you suffered. Seemed inappropriate at the funeral."

"No need to apologize," Hadrian said. "I am much recovered, thank you."

"And we're glad to see it," an MP called Gilbert said. He came up behind Hadrian and clapped him on the shoulder. "Could have been so much worse," he added soberly. "Like Crawford."

Patrick Crawford was an MP from Kent. Hadrian frowned. "What happened to Crawford?" He was a relatively young man, not even forty years old.

"He was attacked, same as you," another MP who'd joined them said. The man, Dillingsworth, was young and earnest, serving in the Commons for the first time. "But he died."

Hadrian was shocked to hear this news. How had he missed it? "I wasn't aware of any of that."

"How can that be?" Gilbert asked in surprise. "He was stabbed the week after you and in the same location."

Hadrian had to work to keep from gaping at the man. But had it been the same man who'd stabbed Hadrian? That would be awfully coincidental, though Crawford being attacked in the same manner and in the same place as Hadrian a week later was the definition of coincidence. There was no way, in Hadrian's mind, that the assailant was a simple footpad.

Ardleigh's expression was solemn. "It was a shock after you'd also been attacked in a similar fashion, and both of you on a Tuesday evening."

"What sort of footpad stabs the person they are robbing?" Dillingsworth asked.

His question nearly made Hadrian smile. Finally, someone with common sense that was apparently lacking at Scotland Yard. "Crawford was determined to have been killed by a footpad?" Hadrian asked.

"That's what we heard," Gilbert said.

"That seems incredibly reckless—and pointless. Unless the man wasn't really a footpad, but some sort of twisted killer," Hadrian said with more than a touch of anger. He realized he was furious about what had happened to him and that the case had been solved in a most unsatisfying fashion.

Ardleigh looked aghast. "A killer? I can't imagine that. Surely, this footpad became scared or something."

That hadn't been Hadrian's experience. His assailant had stabbed first and then hadn't even stolen from him.

Gilbert nodded. "Same as you, and on the same stretch of Parliament Street. Crawford was on his way to our Tuesday night card game at the White Stag. We're headed there now." The man blinked at Hadrian. "I hadn't realized before, but you and Crawford are about the same height and have a similar build. And your hair's the same color."

A chill raced down Hadrian's spine, and he had to quash a shiver. "Has anyone else been attacked since?"

That would be weeks ago now that Crawford had been

killed. Hadrian was still surprised he hadn't known. Surely, he would have seen the notice in the newspaper. But it was possible he had not. He hadn't kept up on reading it during the first few weeks of his recovery. He'd been too busy sleeping and being distracted by the cursed ring.

"Not that we've heard," Ardleigh said with a shake of his head. "I, for one, have avoided that area. Not that I walk about London much at night."

Dillingsworth nodded in agreement. "I don't think anyone has walked alone down Parliament Street after dark since. A footpad who stabs people is bloody terrifying."

Yes, it was, and Hadrian couldn't believe Scotland Yard wasn't trying to make sense of that. He would go there now, demand to know if they'd perchance reopened his case after Crawford was killed. Though, he doubted it. Wouldn't they have informed him?

"Was Crawford robbed?" Hadrian asked. "If it was the same assailant, he left me on the pavement without claiming a single prize."

"I believe Crawford was relieved of his purse and pocket watch," Gilbert replied. "Terrible shame. Crawford was a good man."

Though Hadrian hadn't known him well and they didn't share the same general political beliefs, Crawford had seemed a dedicated and thoughtful MP. "It is a shame indeed," Hadrian agreed.

"You're welcome to join our game at the White Stag," Gilbert said, turning toward the door.

"Not tonight," Hadrian responded with a faint smile. "I do appreciate the invitation, but I think it's best I don't overdo it."

Gilbert gave him a nod. "Have a good evening then. Glad to have you back." He and Dillingsworth left together.

"Smart to take it easy," Ardleigh said. "Evening, Ravenhurst."

As the viscount departed, Hadrian's mind turned over the

information he'd just learned. Though he had no proof whatsoever, he felt certain the same brigand had stabbed him and Crawford. The coincidence was too great. But why attack Hadrian and then Crawford in the same place on the same day in the same manner, then stop? He supposed it made sense the assailant would move on to another location, but it made even more sense that he would have done so after his failed assault on Hadrian—if thievery was his goal.

The fact that Crawford and Hadrian resembled each other was an important detail, as was the fact that they'd been attacked on the same night of the week, a night that Crawford was known to walk that length of Parliament Street on his way to the White Stag. Hadrian had to deduce that Crawford had been the assailant's target, not Hadrian. It explained the assailant's surprise when he'd seen Hadrian's face.

A moment later, Hadrian departed the same way as the others and set his hat atop his head as he stepped outside. The late winter evening was cool with a stiff breeze. However, he didn't don his gloves as he hastened toward Parliament Street.

Instead, he put the horrid ring on his little finger and urged it to show him something new. Could he perhaps see something to do with Crawford? That would be most helpful.

Walking quickly, he made his way to Parliament Street, a surprising apprehension catching hold of him. Hadrian looked about, and he realized he was looking for young boys who might distract him or men with their faces covered. Shivering, he crossed Bridge Street and worked to push the fear away. He didn't have time for such sensitivity, nor would he fall prey to it. His assailant had already stolen weeks of his life and left him with an abundance of unanswerable questions. Perhaps that was why he was so driven to discover the truth of why he'd been stabbed.

Hadrian began to slow as he drew nearer to the site of his assault. When it was but twenty paces in front of him, he stopped. Trepidation slithered up his spine. Twitching his shoulders as if he could dislodge the fear like a physical thing, he put all his focus on that night and what happened.

He recalled his errand that evening—he was to meet an inspector at Whitehall about the horrible explosion at Clerkenwell in December. The Fenians had allegedly blown a hole in the side of the prison to break out one of their own. However, the prison had learned something was afoot and exercised the prisoners in the morning instead of the afternoon when the explosion occurred. As a result, no one had escaped. Instead, the blast had killed and injured many innocent people who lived on the opposite side of the street.

The inspector, whose claimed an Irish lineage, wanted to make sure the investigation was conducted with the utmost integrity. He'd sought Hadrian out because of his work on police and justice reform. Hadrian was even now lending his attention to a bill that would end public executions, which he found utterly barbaric.

Hell, now he was distracted. Taking a deep breath and mentally scolding himself, he refocused his mind on that night specifically. He'd been on his way to meet Inspector Teague. The night was cold, the street perhaps emptier than usual. But there'd been a boy. He'd asked Hadrian for money. The interaction had been enough to distract Hadrian just as his assailant had accosted him.

Had the boy's presence been a coincidence, or did he work in concert with the brigand who'd stabbed Hadrian?

Moving toward the place he'd been attacked, Hadrian saw the boy's face in his mind. This wasn't a vision from the ring but his own distinct memory.

Suddenly, he became overwhelmed with sensation. Surprise flowed through him then a sliver of fear. He felt a powerful urge to run. From what?

He was not afraid, regardless of what was washing over him. Why should he feel surprised?

A face flashed before him—a vision, and this time from the ring. But it was a face he knew better than any other: his own. There was the surprise and the fear, though not the need to run. No, he hadn't wanted to run that night, nor did he wish to do so now.

What he was seeing and feeling belonged to the man who'd worn the ring. He'd seen Hadrian's face in the lamplight and known surprise then fear. Then he'd wanted to flee. And he had.

Hadrian chased the vision once more, summoning his own face. It took several minutes, and his head began to ache. At last, it appeared along with the sensations. Then everything went instantly and completely black, as if the moment had been wiped away. As if there was nothing more.

That was the moment he'd pulled the ring from the brigand's finger.

Breathing heavily as if he *had* run, Hadrian removed the ring and returned it to his pocket. He didn't really have any new information, save the overwhelming emotions he'd felt. He grew more certain that the brigand had been targeting someone specific, and it hadn't been Hadrian.

But had it been Crawford who had perished the very next week?

It also seemed clear now that the ring gave him the thoughts and impressions of the man who'd worn it right up until the moment it had left his finger. Hadrian thought of the table at the Bell and the table at Sir Henry's. Those objects had also given him visions and impressions, so he had to conclude that the ability came from *him*, not the object. They were merely conduits for this newfound power. He sounded as though he was losing his mind. What other explanation could there be for what was happening to him?

Hadrian massaged his forehead as he continued along Parliament Street until it met Whitehall. A few minutes later, he turned into Whitehall Place. Scotland Yard, the headquarters of the Metropolitan Police, stood ahead.

It occurred to Hadrian as he walked into the main doorway that Inspector Teague may not be present this evening. Nevertheless, Hadrian would inquire. He had too many questions about these attacks and was most eager to find answers. As it happened, he was in luck. Teague was still on the premises.

A clerk showed Hadrian to the inspector's office. The door was slightly ajar, but Hadrian rapped on the wood. "Inspector Teague?"

"Come."

Hadrian pushed the door wider and stepped inside. "Good evening, Inspector. I hope I'm not disturbing you."

In his middle thirties with dark red hair and a pale, angular face, the inspector looked up from his desk at Hadrian. "Lord Ravenhurst, what a surprise. I trust you received my note following your attack."

Teague had conveyed his regards and hope for Hadrian's full recovery in a missive that also included his regret that he hadn't been assigned as the investigator on the case.

"I did, thank you. I appreciate your kindness."

"I'm glad to see you walking about." Teague folded his hands atop the desk. "That was a nasty wound you suffered, and I understand you were also concussed."

"Quite. I had a beast of a headache for weeks," Hadrian replied. His head ached now, in fact, because of the visions he'd had a short while ago.

"Fully recovered now though?" Teague asked.

Unless one counted his deteriorating sanity. "I believe so. Though you weren't assigned to my case, I was hoping you could share what was learned during the investigation. I would ask Inspector Padgett, but I found him rather dour." His interview of

Hadrian had been short and devoid of concern, not to mention the fact that Padgett believed a footpad would stab his quarry and then not steal anything. Hadrian had to question the man's capability.

"Take a seat," Teague said, indicating a chair next to his desk. "I'm happy to help but since I wasn't involved with the investigation, I may not be able to answer your questions. You may need to speak to Padgett after all, though he's not here this evening."

Hadrian removed his hat and sat down. "I understand. Is there a report I could read?"

"Certainly. I can fetch that for you."

"Thank you. I Just learned that Mr. Patrick Crawford was killed the week after I was attacked—in the same location and he was stabbed as I was."

Teague's brow creased. "Yes, that was somewhat of a coincidence."

"Too much of one, don't you think? Surely a footpad wouldn't hunt the same ground where he'd stabbed someone so recently. And why would a footpad stab his mark in the first place? He didn't even steal anything from me." Hadrian chose not to point out that *he'd* done the stealing—he was not prepared to surrender the ring just yet, in case it had more to reveal. "That's a murderer, not a footpad."

"But he stole from Crawford, I believe," Teague pointed out.

"You think it's the same culprit?" Hadrian asked.

"I don't know because I didn't investigate. I'm not sure what Padgett concluded. I only know what I do from the constables who came to your aid and found Crawford." He pressed his lips together in a sour expression. "Padgett is a solitary bloke, and he doesn't work well with others. You should read the coroner's inquest about Crawford's death. I can fetch that for you as well."

"That would be much appreciated, thank you." Hadrian

considered sharing his suspicion that the alleged footpad hadn't meant to attack him at all. But he wasn't ready to reveal that. He wanted to read the report to see if there was any evidence that might lend credibility to his speculation. As it was, he had inexplicable visions and intuition. Those didn't exactly make a compelling case.

Instead, Hadrian said, "I hope you won't mind me asking you about something else. An acquaintance of mine died last week—Sir Henry Meacham. His death was sudden and apparently attributed to a heart attack, however, at his funeral his daughter said he'd suffered a terrible wound to his right side. I wondered if there'd been an inquest into his death." Hadrian was all but certain there hadn't been. Surely, someone at the funeral would have mentioned it.

Teague narrowed his eyes at Hadrian. "Forgive me, my lord, but why are you inquiring about such a thing?"

Hadrian decided a minor fabrication would be beneficial in this instance. "The family found it odd that he would have a wound like that if he'd died of a heart attack. I offered to obtain what information I could for them."

"While that is kind of you to offer your assistance, I shouldn't discuss the matter with you," Teague said. "Though, I am not aware of an inquest."

"The way his daughter described the wound brought my own injury to mind," Hadrian pressed. "I couldn't help wondering if he'd been the victim of a stabbing." Saying this out loud made Hadrian realize how incredibly foolish he sounded.

Teague gave him a patient look tinged with something between pity and sympathy. "I think perhaps your attack has made you...hypervigilant." Was that a polite way of saying Hadrian's sanity was slipping?

Or was he implying that Hadrian had been shaken by his

attack? He bloody well had been, though he hadn't realized how much until he'd walked along Parliament Street tonight.

Whatever the man had meant, he'd made Hadrian feel as though he were a child who required coddling, which he did not. He only needed better judgment, for he never should have mentioned Sir Henry. He was going to have to find another way to learn about the man's death and what his connection had been to Hadrian's assailant.

"I'm sure you're right," Hadrian said benignly. "I fear the threat to my mortality has left me questioning a great many things."

"Wait here whilst I see about those reports and the inquest." Teague stood and departed the office, leaving the door ajar. He was gone at least ten minutes.

Hadrian turned his head as he heard the inspector return. He noticed the man was carrying a thin sheaf of papers.

"Here's Crawford's inquest," Teague said handing the papers to Hadrian. "However, the clerk says both your and Crawford's cases have been closed. The reports are filed away, but I can retrieve them tomorrow."

Disappointment curled through Hadrian as he skimmed the first page of the inquest. It was not a long document.

Teague sat down in his chair. "I shouldn't let you leave with that, but there will be copies. I can get one for you tomorrow, if you like."

"It says Crawford was murdered," Hadrian said. That was no surprise. He read the next page containing testimony. Only the constable and Inspector Padgett had been interviewed. But who else would they have spoken with? Hadrian looked over at the inspector. "Did anyone even try to find, let alone arrest, the assailant?"

"I can't say. Were you able to provide a good description of your assailant?"

Hadrian scowled. "No. His face was mostly covered. I

would recognize his eyes anywhere, though." And he was fairly certain the man lived near the Monument to the Great Fire not Westminster. There was no way he could explain to Teague how he knew that, however.

"These kinds of crimes often go unsolved," Teague said. "It's almost impossible to find people such as this footpad."

"You won't convince me this was a footpad. I would hope that constables are patrolling that area more heavily, in case the man returns." It seemed unlikely, since he'd struck two weeks in a row and not in the several weeks since. And *that* was perplexing too.

"I confess, this is an odd situation," Teague mused. "These two attacks were very similar. I'll find these reports tomorrow and look at them myself."

Hadrian was glad to hear it. "I appreciate that, Inspector." Setting his hat atop his head, Hadrian rose.

"Good evening, Ravenhurst," the inspector said as Hadrian left the man's office.

The headache from earlier persisted, and now Hadrian's frustration seemed to strengthen it. Stepping into the cold night, he hastened toward Whitehall where he would hail a hack to take him home.

It was time to call on Miss Wren. She'd offered, twice, to help him with his private matter. Whilst he had no intention of telling her of his curse, he would hope she could help him solve the mystery of Hadrian's assailant and how he was tied to Sir Henry.

CHAPTER 5

The day after Tilda had met with Mr. Whitley, she sat at the desk in the library, which had been her grandfather's study before his death. She went through every drawer and cranny searching for anything to do with Sir Henry and her grandmother's money. Grandmama sat next to her, alternately fidgeting with her hands and commenting that she still didn't understand what happened with the secondary investment.

Upon returning from her appointment with the solicitor, Tilda had queried her grandmother about the specifics of the secondary investment: the amount, the date, anything she could remember. Unfortunately, Grandmama wasn't able to recall anything with specificity, just that she'd asked Sir Henry to invest a sum of money that wasn't already in an investment that Tilda's father had made while he'd managed the money. Then Tilda had asked her where she might find a record of the investment. Grandmama hadn't known that either.

"It can't be gone," Grandmama said again as Tilda carefully studied a ledger she'd found in the bottom drawer of the desk.

It was old, and she hoped it contained something about the money given to Sir Henry.

"Mr. Whitley has no record of it, Grandmama." *And neither do we.* Tilda hadn't told her that she suspected embezzlement by the former solicitor. She didn't wish to upset her grandmother further when nothing was certain.

Grandmama sucked in a breath. "Did someone steal it? You must tell me the truth, Tilda."

Looking up from the ledger, Tilda turned her head toward her grandmother and offered her a comforting smile. "I am not aware of any theft at this time. But I am worried that we can't find a record of the investment. This ledger is from years after Grandpapa died, and it is the oldest one I've found." It was also not terribly detailed as far as Tilda could tell.

Tilda recalled how devastated her grandmother had been when Tilda's father had died. To think she'd taken the time to accurately record the distribution of funds amidst her grief was too much to hope for. Indeed, Tilda didn't think she could have done it, for that had been the most painful time of her life.

Shaking that dismal thought away for the moment, Tilda finished reviewing the ledger.

"I don't think there are any ledgers stored elsewhere, but I will ask Mrs. Acorn to look in the storeroom on the top floor." Grandmama stood.

"Yes, please." Tilda should have already thought of that and silently chastised herself for not doing so. She reasoned that she was simply overtaxed with the situation and how to resolve it.

"I do wonder if it's worth you calling on Millicent," Grandmama suggested. "There ought to be records in Sir Henry's study."

Millicent was staying at her father's house whilst she cleaned and prepared it for sale. Whilst Tilda hated to bother the woman after her father's death, it appeared to be necessary.

Tilda was running out of places to look for evidence that the investment existed. Tomorrow, she planned to call on Mr. Hardacre. She'd first wanted to thoroughly search her grandmother's house.

"I will call on Millicent and pray it isn't too much of an imposition," Tilda said.

"She will understand." Fine lines tracked across Grandmama's forehead, revealing her concern before she turned and left.

Tilda finished reviewing the ledger, which was—as expected—completely unhelpful. Still, it had needed to be done.

A thought struck her—what if Millicent had already disposed of things? The records could be gone by now. Tilda stood, deciding she would go to see Millicent right now.

Driven by a sudden apprehension, Tilda started toward the door but halted upon seeing Mrs. Acorn. "I need to go see Millicent. Did Grandmama speak with you?"

Mrs. Acorn nodded. "Yes. She is resting now. I will look for ledgers on the third floor shortly. First, however, I came to inform you that Lord Ravenhurst is here to see you."

Tilda could not have been more surprised. She wondered if he'd forgotten her offer to help him—or hadn't wanted to accept.

Botheration, she was incredibly eager to reach Millicent before she disposed of anything. Exhaling, she brushed her hands over her skirts. "I don't suppose I can tell an earl that I don't have time to see him?"

"Of course you can," Mrs. Acorn replied firmly. "I'll inform him."

Before the housekeeper could turn, Tilda stopped her. "No, just show him to the sitting room, and I'll be down directly." Whilst she didn't really want to take the time, she had to admit she'd been wondering when he might call. It seemed he was ready to discuss his *private matter*. The investigator in her thrilled at the idea of solving at least one small mystery.

"If you're sure." Mrs. Acorn didn't sound as though she was.

"Were you looking forward to refusing an earl?" Tilda asked with a small smile.

Mrs. Acorn smiled, her features softening with affection. "I always look forward to supporting you, my dear girl, especially during trying times. I'm not entirely certain what is troubling you, but I can guess, and I'm sorry for it."

The housekeeper knew about the household finances suffering, but Tilda hadn't told her about the investment's disappearance.

"Thank you, Mrs. Acorn. Do not offer the earl tea. If you could put my hat and gloves in the entrance hall, that would be most welcome."

Nodding, Mrs. Acorn left, and Tilda followed her out, going downstairs to the parlor at the front of the house off the entrance hall. Lord Ravenhurst stood near the bowed window facing the street, his hat in his gloved hands. His dark, wavy hair was combed back from his high forehead. He offered her a smile as she entered, and she was reminded that the earl was a rather handsome gentleman. "Good afternoon, Miss Wren. I appreciate you seeing me."

She stepped farther into the room but did not invite him to sit. There wasn't time for such hospitality. "My I presume you've come to discuss the private matter you had with Sir Henry?"

"Yes." He took a deep, almost hesitant breath, as if he were about to reveal something of great import. "I was stabbed several weeks ago, and during the attack, I removed a ring from my assailant's hand. I thought I had seen Sir Henry wearing that ring and wished to ask him about it."

Of all the things Tilda might imagined he would say, this hadn't been anywhere in her mind. "You could have asked about this the day we met."

"I didn't want to trouble you with such a thing when you'd just learned Sir Henry had died."

Tilda supposed that made sense. "I am not aware of any rings that Sir Henry wore, but that doesn't mean he didn't ever wear one. Why would a man who stabbed you—and I am very sorry to hear that happened—have a ring that may have belonged to Sir Henry?"

"That is the question I would like answered. I do realize it seems far-fetched, but it's all I have to go on at the moment." His gaze fixed on her more intently. "When I was at Sir Henry's funeral, I overheard his daughter describing a wound to his side that sounded suspiciously like the one I sustained—both to our right sides. It seems too much of a coincidence."

Tilda's investigative senses came fully alert. The earl certainly sounded as if he were conducting an investigation. "It seems as though you are investigating your attack. Didn't Scotland Yard do that?" If he hadn't reported the incident, her estimation of him would plummet.

A deep frown creased the earl's features. "They did; however, the case was closed but not solved. They did not capture the assailant, nor did they even appear to look for him."

Though she wasn't surprised to hear this had happened, Tilda was as frustrated by it as the earl appeared to be. "My father was a sergeant at Scotland Yard. Unfortunately, a great many cases suffer from a lack of investigation, particularly those that are difficult."

"That is disappointing to hear," Ravenhurst said, still frowning. "The inspector resolved that I was attacked by a footpad, but why would a footpad stab their mark? That doesn't make sense to me, especially because the man didn't even steal anything from me." He took a deep breath, his expression smoothing. "My apologies, Miss Wren. I nearly died, and I am frustrated this matter wasn't investigated more thoroughly, as far as I can tell. I should like to know *why* I was stabbed. This does not seem to me to be the case of a footpad who resorted to violence. In fact, he stabbed me straightaway and did not ask for my valuables at all."

Why would the inspector have concluded this was the act of a footpad? Footpads did not normally nearly kill their marks, as far as Tilda was aware, and she knew far more than the average person about crime. Her curiosity had been piqued when she'd met the earl, and now it was completely engaged. "That does sound very strange. Who was the inspector on your case?"

"Padgett. Do you know him?"

"The name is familiar," she said, thinking of the many people she'd met at Scotland Yard over the years. "I believe he was with the police when my father worked there. He wasn't one of my father's friends, however, so I am not acquainted with him personally." She knew a few sergeants and a handful of inspectors, all of whom had worked with her father. But he'd died eleven years ago, and she hadn't kept in touch with most of them. Though, her investigative work for Mr. Forrest had led her to become reacquainted with a couple of them over the past few years.

Tilda's investigative instincts took over. "What did Scotland Yard say about the ring?"

The earl's gaze darted to the side, and Tilda instantly knew he wasn't being entirely honest with her. "They don't know about the ring. I'm afraid I didn't realize I had it until after the case had been closed. Given Scotland Yard's lack of persistence with the case, I decided I didn't want to surrender the only piece of physical evidence I have."

That was completely understandable to Tilda. It was also very smart. But the earl was keeping something from her, and she would tread carefully. She reviewed in her mind what he'd already told her and made a deduction. "You think this ring may have belonged to Sir Henry and once you heard he had an odd wound, you wondered if he may have been stabbed as you were?"

"I am wondering a great many things. At this point, I'm only trying to ascertain if there was some connection between Sir Henry and my assailant."

Tilda recalled what she knew of Sir Henry's death and shook her head. "Whilst I am also perplexed by a wound in Sir Henry's side, he wasn't stabbed." Tilda would most certainly be asking Millicent about this wound. "He collapsed in a public house or a club of some kind and was taken directly to his physician who determined he'd died of a heart ailment. Then he was taken home." Tilda now wondered why there hadn't been an inquest. Though, if Sir Henry had been determined to have died of natural decay, there would likely not have been one. Still, he'd collapsed in a public place. An inquest would have been best.

When she considered these oddities along with her grandmother's missing investment, she began to think that investigating Sir Henry's death was necessary.

"And there was no inquest despite his sudden death?" the earl asked.

Tilda nearly smiled at how the earl's mind had followed her own. It seemed he possessed some measure of deductive skill. "There was not. You have piqued my interest in this matter, Lord Ravenhurst." She didn't like it when things did not make sense or when there were unanswered questions. Such as why he'd allowed her grandmother's investment to go missing. And how long he'd been suffering from a heart ailment no one knew about, not even his daughters. Furthermore, there was the odd wound and her grandmother's missing investment.

She was compelled to solve any mystery, no matter how small. And this did not sound small. "Let us assume this ring you have belonged to Sir Henry. Why would the man who attacked you have it?"

He inclined his head. "You ask an astute question, Miss Wren. I find it beyond puzzling that Sir Henry's ring—and I may be mistaken about it belonging to him—would be on this alleged footpad's person. I should also mention that a week after I was stabbed, another man was attacked—stabbed in the same manner and in the same location along Parliament Street. Unfortunately, he did not survive." Ravenhurst paused briefly. "What sort of footpad returns to the scene of a crime he wasn't able to complete? As his victim, I would be able to describe him, and one would think the police would patrol that area more frequently and in greater numbers."

"One would think. However, Scotland Yard doesn't always have enough constables for every shift. They don't pay as well for those working at night." Tilda recalled her father taking extra shifts at night, even as a sergeant, because there hadn't been enough constables.

His gaze met hers and held it for a moment. "I will also tell you that I am fairly certain I was not his intended victim."

"Why do you think that?"

He lifted a shoulder. "While his blade was still embedded in my flesh, I gripped his wrist and turned on him. I looked into his eyes, and I saw surprise—he was not expecting me."

"Perhaps he was surprised because you were fighting for your survival. I would guess most victims do not have the wherewithal to grab their attacker." She had to admit she was impressed he'd done so. But Ravenhurst wasn't a doughy-faced nobleman who likely slept all day and drank all night. He appeared athletic and fit. And clever.

"I did consider that, and you may be right. However, I can't shake the sensation that I was not his target—and that was before I learned that someone else had been killed the very next week. On the same night of the week, in fact." He took a breath, his gaze intense. "The victim—Patrick Crawford—went to a card game every Tuesday night, and he and I share the same coloring and build. I think it's possible the assailant was looking for the man he killed the week after my attack but stabbed me by mistake."

Tilda could see where he was going with his logic, but that didn't make it true. "That is a great deal of circumstantial speculation."

The earl narrowed his eyes. "Why visit the precise same location on the same night of the week the following week to commit the same crime and then not once since?"

"Because he'd failed in his endeavor the first time when he stabbed you in error, then returned to make it right," she concluded, latching on to the earl's theory. "If your supposition is true. I can't help pointing out that much of your investigation and deduction relies heavily on your intuition rather than evidence."

He exhaled, sounding frustrated. "That is why I am trying to collect evidence and continue to bother you with my questions. I could be entirely wrong about everything, in which case I will have wasted your time—and my own. However, I can't give up until I am satisfied that I have chased every avenue of possible intelligence. Someone nearly killed me, and I would know why." He said the last with a cold determination that resonated with her more than anything else he'd said today.

She could understand a visceral need to learn the truth about something so primal. "Were you near death?"

"I sustained an injury to my head when I fell. That took weeks to heal, and I still suffer headaches. The wound in my side was serious, and I lost a great deal of blood." His right shoulder twitched, and she assumed he'd been stabbed in the right side. "I was fortunate to be repaired by an excellent surgeon."

"Indeed," she murmured. "Everything you've told me is a great deal to take in." Tilda planned to write down every aspect of this case at the earliest opportunity, for she was now more than intrigued—she was invested. The tale of a footpad stabbing an earl so close to Westminster and not stealing anything from him did not make sense, especially along with all the other things he'd told her. And if Sir Henry was somehow connected to this criminal, she absolutely could not turn away.

There was only one way to find out. "As it happens, I was about to pay a call on Sir Henry's daughter," Tilda said. "She is staying at his house and overseeing the dissemination of its contents. I will ask her about the ring you have and about Sir Henry's odd wound."

"Or I could come with you and ask her myself," he offered benignly, a placid smile doing a poor job of masking his anticipation. She noted the subtle rocking of his heels. It was slight, but she could see he was eager to join her.

Tilda recalled how he'd obtained information from her when they'd met. "Are you an investigator, Lord Ravenhurst?"

"No."

She smiled at him. "As it happens, I am. I consult with a solicitor regarding divorce cases. You could leave this to me, and I'd be happy to report what I learn."

"It seems more expedient if I just go with you," the earl said, his expression eager.

Tilda crossed her arms over her chest. "I can't help noticing you are somewhat aggressive in your search for information. As someone who regularly conducts investigations, might I advise you that this can be off-putting. You want people to help you not be annoyed by you."

This was a lesson her father had taught her when she was

perhaps seven years old. Tilda had lost her favorite hair ribbon at school. Upset, she'd demanded the other children help her to look for it. Some did, but one girl in particular had said she wouldn't help because Tilda hadn't asked nicely. Later, when Tilda had cried about the loss of the ribbon to her father and how one girl refused to help search for it, he'd hugged her and said, *"I know you were upset, my darling, but sometimes we have to set aside our true feelings and employ kindness and even charm. I must do this often in my work with the police, especially when I need information from someone who doesn't want to give it."*

He exhaled. "My apologies. I *do* want your help, most fervently. Seeing as you are an investigator with connections to Scotland Yard, I wonder if I might hire you to assist me with this investigation."

Assist? Tilda didn't know whether to laugh or glower. "As you pointed out, my lord, you are not an investigator whilst I am. I would consider allowing you to engage my services as the investigator of your case. I will not assist you, nor will you assist me."

His expression darkened. "I'm afraid I'm not the sort of person who is content to wait at home for answers. I've been doing that for weeks whilst I recuperated. I nearly died, and I would be involved in the resolution of this crime."

Tilda could understand and appreciate his need to do that. Indeed, she could feel his tension. This matter was of the utmost importance to him, and she wanted to help him. "Let me clarify what you are asking for. You wish to hire me to solve the matter of your attack—who was responsible and why. And you want to accompany me throughout the investigation?"

"Yes, to all that," he said firmly. Enthusiastically. "Do you wish to be paid a flat fee, or will you bill for the time you spend?" He asked blithely, as if the cost were no matter to him. And why would it be? She imagined he didn't have to budget in the way she did.

Mr. Forrest paid Tilda a flat fee. However, she didn't know what this investigation would entail. "I would prefer to bill you for the time I spend." Her breath caught as she waited to see if he would agree. It seemed he would, but at the same time, she was overjoyed that this opportunity had come when she'd needed it most.

"Very good. Let us see what we learn from Sir Henry's daughter regarding the ring."

"If there is no connection to Sir Henry, do you still want my help?" Tilda asked, almost afraid of the answer.

He nodded. "I do."

"We will need to visit Scotland Yard," she said, feeling a joyous relief. "I would like to review the reports that were made on your case as well as that of the man who was stabbed the following week."

"As it happens, I met with an inspector last evening, and he is retrieving those reports today. I planned to stop by later this afternoon."

They could do that after visiting Millicent, Tilda supposed, however Tilda had things to discuss with her that she did not wish her new client to overhear. The earl did not need to be privy to her grandmother's financial concerns.

"I'm afraid I won't be able to do that this afternoon. We can go tomorrow morning," she suggested, though that would delay her visit to Mr. Hardacre. She hated to do that, but she was also keen to earn money. She could, hopefully, conduct both errands.

Ravenhurst's wide brow puckered. She could feel his disappointment. "I suppose that will suffice."

"Excellent. Now, let us go to Sir Henry's house. Do you have a coach?" She realized as soon as she asked the question that it was silly. Of course an earl would have a coach.

"It's right outside."

"Then let us depart." Tilda turned and went into the

entrance hall where Mrs. Acorn had left her hat and gloves. She also donned her cloak, which hung on a rack along with her grandmother's. Her client hurried to assist her, and she murmured her gratitude.

Her *client*. Tilda pressed her lips together to keep from grinning.

CHAPTER 6

*H*adrian looked across the coach at Miss Wren as they began moving. Today had not progressed as he imagined. Indeed, it was exceeding his expectations. It felt good to have an official investigation of his stabbing with someone who seemed to know what she was doing.

Normally, he would have sought a reference, but he wanted Miss Wren. Sir Henry was somehow tied to Hadrian's attacker, and Miss Wren was connected to Sir Henry.

The question that remained, however, was how he would convey the connection between the ring and Sir Henry, for she would soon learn the ring hadn't belonged to him. Then what? Hadrian would reveal his inexplicable visions so she could stare at him in disbelief then suggest he consult with a doctor regarding his clear mental illness?

He noted that she'd taken the rear-facing seat. He would insist she take the forward facing in the future.

He actually had no trouble believing she conducted investigations. He could practically feel her skepticism and curiosity. They were like an aura about her.

Had she inherited those traits from her father who'd

worked for Scotland Yard? Her grandfather had been a magistrate. It seemed law and order must flow through her veins.

"Does your aptitude for investigation come from your father?" he asked idly, not only to pass the time to Huntley Street but to get to know Miss Wren better. He found her most engaging.

Her long, light lashes fluttered as she glanced toward him. "I should hope so. He was an excellent investigator. At the time of his death, he was to be promoted to inspector."

"I'm sorry he passed in what was surely the prime of his life."

"He was just forty-one years," she said softly. "That was eleven years ago. There is not a day that goes by that I don't miss him."

He heard the love in her voice and was doubly sorry for her loss. "How wonderful that you shared such a closeness with him." In an effort to dispel any sadness, he asked, "It's just you and your grandmother now?"

"Here in London. I do not have any siblings. My mother remarried and now lives in Birmingham. I chose to remain with my grandmother."

"I'm sure she was delighted when you did," he said with a smile.

Her gaze turned wary. "As my client, you don't need to befriend me, Lord Ravenhurst."

"Forgive me if I am being intrusive." He didn't wish to make her uncomfortable. "I am making idle chatter as one does, but I also find you fascinating, Miss Wren."

"Why?" she asked bemusedly, the corner of her mouth lifting.

"You are a capable, independent young woman. I don't meet a great many of those. Honestly, I don't meet a great many young women anymore."

"And why is that? I should think an unmarried earl would

be in high demand on the Marriage Mart." She paused. "Or perhaps you are already married."

"I am not," he confirmed. "Nearly, but I was thankfully spared what I now realize would have been a dreadful mistake."

One of her brows arched in an elegantly mischievous manner. "That sounds like an interesting story. Too bad we have arrived at Sir Henry's."

It was indeed too bad, for Hadrian found himself wanting to confide in her. And he rarely ever spoke of his broken betrothal. The coach drew to a stop, and Hadrian reached for the door. "I shall regale you with it on the return trip if you like."

She did not respond, but he was already climbing out of the coach. He helped her down, and they made their way, side-by-side, to the door, which still bore the yew wreath with the black ribbons.

The door was soon opened by the elderly, stooped butler. His faded blue gaze fell on Miss Wren. "Good afternoon, miss."

"How are you, Vaughn?" she asked with deep concern.

"We are forging ahead," he said with a slow nod. "Cook has found a new position and will be gone in a fortnight, and the maid seems close to securing employment." He opened the door wide, and Miss Wren moved inside.

Hadrian followed her into the entrance hall.

"Vaughn, allow me to present Lord Ravenhurst," Miss Wren said as she removed her gloves and tucked them into the pocket of her cloak.

The butler's eyes narrowed to focus as they moved over Hadrian. "You attended the funeral." It wasn't a question.

"I did," Hadrian replied, impressed by the man's memory and attention to detail.

Vaughn took Miss Wren's cloak and hung it on a peg. "If you'd care to wait in the parlor, I'll inform Mrs. Forsythe you are here."

"Thank you, Vaughn." Miss Wren moved into the parlor where the funeral had taken place. The room was still draped in black, and the coffin stand was still present, as were Sir Henry's mementoes.

Hadrian recalled the funeral and specifically what Miss Wren's grandmother had said about her granddaughter wanting to speak with her cousin about financial matters. He may regret what he was about to do, but he apparently couldn't help his curiosity. That shouldn't have come as a surprise as he was always asking questions at Westminster, much to the chagrin of many. Could he help it if he liked to be well informed about everything?

"Have you come to speak with Mrs. Forsythe about whatever financial issues you'd hoped to discuss with Sir Henry?" he asked.

Miss Wren sent him a furtive glance and pursed her lips. "My, but you are inquisitive. I don't see how that's your concern."

"It seems we both had business with Sir Henry that became unfinished by his sudden death. I only meant to point out we have something in common."

"Our *business* with Sir Henry was quite different," she said somewhat tersely.

"I didn't mean to offend," he murmured, but he still wasn't sorry he'd said it. She was clearly troubled by these financial concerns. Her tension was palpable when the subject was mentioned He was glad he'd hired her and hoped it would ease her worry.

Mrs. Forsythe entered then, her black dress rustling as she walked. About fifty with light-blonde hair and a round face supported by a double chin, she smiled upon seeing Miss Wren. "Cousin Tilda."

Miss Wren met her in the middle of the room, and they briefly embraced. "Please forgive our intrusion. Allow me to present Lord Ravenhurst. He attended the funeral, so perhaps you met then."

Mrs. Forsythe's brow puckered as she regarded Hadrian. "I don't recall. How do you know each other?"

"I am conducting an investigation for Lord Ravenhurst," Miss Wren replied. "Though that is not why he attended the funeral. He was an associate of your father's." She glanced over at Hadrian.

He stepped forward. "Please accept my condolences, Mrs. Forsythe. I worked with Sir Henry over the years when he was with the Home Office. I'd planned to introduce myself to you at the funeral, but my timing was poor, and I didn't have the chance."

"Well, I do thank you for remembering my father," Mrs. Forsythe said. "He was never proud of anything as much as his work with the Home Office."

Hadrian detected a faint note of bitterness in her tone. Had he neglected his family in favor of his work? He would not be the first man to do so. Hadrian's own father had been egregiously inattentive to his wife and children when compared to his duty as the earl.

Miss Wren continued, "Lord Ravenhurst has accompanied me today because we wish to speak with you about a matter involving his investigation. The earl was stabbed several weeks ago, and he took a ring from his assailant. He thinks he recognizes it as one that Sir Henry wore."

"It bears an M, which I assumed was for Meacham." Hadrian hadn't removed his gloves, so when he retrieved the ring from his pocket there was no faint sensation or hint of a vision. It was just like any other object. He opened his hand and moved the ring to his palm. "Did it belong to him?"

Mrs. Forsythe squinted at the ring and leaned toward it. She reached for it then paused, meeting his gaze. "May I?"

"Of course." He had no expectation she would be familiar

with it, of course. This was all a farce. Though the M corresponding to Meacham was another striking coincidence.

She picked up the ring and brought it closer to her face. "I don't recognize this, and I've never known my father to wear a ring. But you've seen him wear one?"

"I thought I had, but I could be mistaken."

"I think you must be," Mrs. Forsythe said, placing the ring back onto Hadrian's open palm.

And that was the end of that. He tucked the ring back into his pocket.

"I didn't think Sir Henry wore rings either," Miss Wren said. "However, I thought it was worth asking. If it did belong to him, I would think you'd want it back." She gave Mrs. Forsythe a supportive look. "How are you doing? This all must be terribly taxing."

Mrs. Forsythe seemed to relax, her shoulders flattening. "It is. Things would be far more manageable if Belinda were helping. However, she can't be bothered, particularly since there is no inheritance."

There was no mistaking the bitterness in her tone now. Hadrian presumed Belinda must be her sister.

"There's nothing?" Miss Wren asked, her features creased with alarm. She glanced toward Hadrian and pressed her lips together then looked back to her cousin. "We can discuss it later," she murmured.

"It's most distressing," Mrs. Forsythe said.

Miss Wren nodded in agreement. Hadrian wondered how bad her own financial situation was. He recalled the dated furnishings at her grandmother's house, but that could just be due to Mrs. Wren having a preference for things she'd had for years and didn't wish to replace. Hadrian had also noted Miss Wren's outmoded mourning garb. She was wearing the same gown today that she'd worn at the funeral. And when they'd first met, she'd been wearing a gown that was also out of current fashion.

Had Sir Henry been in control of her grandmother's finances? He was a male relative and perhaps the closest one. Had he mismanaged everything and left them, as well as his own daughters, in poor circumstances? But no, his daughters at least had husbands, as far as he knew. He wasn't sure Miss Wren and her grandmother had anyone. He was even gladder now that he'd retained her services.

Miss Wren waved her hand. "It's all distressing. Your father died so suddenly. It was a shock as we weren't aware he had any problems with his heart."

Mrs. Forsythe clucked her tongue. "He wasn't doing a very good job taking care of himself since Mama died a few years ago. He was likely ignoring the symptoms."

"I do wonder if they may have mistaken the cause of his death," Miss Wren mused. Hadrian suspected where she was going and marveled at her skill. "I don't remember if you said, but was an autopsy was conducted since he died so unexpectedly?"

"I only know that his physician declared his cause of death to be natural decay. He sent a copy of the death certificate along with my father's body." Mrs. Forsythe's gaze turned contemplative, and she ran her fingertips along her jaw. "I would assume he'd had an autopsy. He had a wound on his side, and autopsies leave wounds, don't they?"

Miss Wren frowned, her forehead creasing. "The wound was only on one side? I'm not sure that is how an autopsy is conducted."

"How would you even know that?" Mrs. Forsythe asked. Then she gave her head a shake. "Never mind. Your father worked at Scotland Yard."

"You're sure that was his only wound?" Hadrian asked. "Was it stitched closed?"

Both women turned their heads to look at him. They blinked, their expressions mildly surprised, either by his presence or that he'd dared speak.

"Yes, that was his only wound, and it was stitched." Mrs. Forsythe's shoulders twitched, and she held up her hand. "You must forgive me, but I'm afraid I can't continue this topic of conversation."

"Of course not," Miss Wren said soothingly. "I'm not even sure how we got here." She flashed her cousin a comforting smile. "Why don't I show Lord Ravenhurst out, then I'll stay for a while to help you with some of the sorting."

Mrs. Forsythe relaxed again, as she'd done earlier. "Thank you, Tilda. That would be ever so wonderful."

Hadrian bowed. "Thank you for allowing me to call, Mrs. Forsythe. I am deeply sorry for your loss."

"Thank you, my lord."

Miss Wren led him from the sitting room into the entrance hall where he put his hat back on. The butler was not present. "I'm sorry we are no closer to determining where that ring may have come from, though I must say I can't imagine what sort of connection Sir Henry would have had to the man who stabbed you."

"I assumed the man stole it from Sir Henry," Hadrian said with a shrug.

She looked at him shrewdly. "But I think we're agreed that this man who stabbed you is not a thief."

Damn, she had him there. "True. I'm very glad I hired you, Miss Wren. You are much better at this than I am."

She inclined her head. "I have experience and the benefit of the knowledge my father imparted to me."

"Well, I must congratulate you on your investigative skill with Mrs. Forsythe. That was a deft turn bringing up the wound."

Miss Wren lifted a shoulder. "It is not difficult to steer conversations in certain directions."

"Do not discount your abilities," he said earnestly. "It is a skill some do not possess. I suppose the next step in the investigation will be visiting Scotland Yard tomorrow." He cocked his head. "What of your own investigation?"

"My investigation?"

"Regarding Sir Henry," Hadrian said. "The circumstances of his death seem somewhat suspicious."

"They do, and I will look into it. You needn't concern yourself with the matter."

Except Hadrian was completely concerned with how Sir Henry was connected to his attacker. He would need to find a way to obtain information from Miss Wren, or he'd have to tell her the truth about the connection between himself and Sir Henry. And that simply wasn't happening, not if he wanted to stay clear of an asylum.

"You may fetch me at ten tomorrow," she said.

"How will you return home today?" he asked. "If you like, I can wait in my coach until you are finished."

"Thank you, but I don't know how long I'll be, and I wouldn't wish to trouble you. I will take a hack."

"You must include the expense with your invoice for your services. I shall see you tomorrow." He touched the brim of his hat before departing.

As he settled into his coach, he realized what a fool he'd been not to touch whatever he could in Sir Henry's home today. There could be no doubt that Miss Wren was the superior investigator.

After seeing Ravenhurst out, Tilda returned to the parlor, but it was now empty. She assumed her cousin had gone to Sir Henry's study, which was just through a doorway from the parlor.

Tilda removed her hat as she walked into the study but there wasn't a place to set it down. Every surface was covered with something. Stepping back into the parlor, she set her hat on a chair and returned to the study where Millicent sat at the desk, her faced creased in what was likely a perpetual frown since she'd begun her task of sorting through her father's things.

"This is a great deal to manage," Tilda said lest she jump straight to querying Millicent about the lack of inheritance form her father. The fact that more money had gone missing was of dire concern.

Millicent looked up at her with a weary gaze. "It's over-whelming. I do appreciate your offer of help. I should have thought to ask you."

"What can I do?" Tilda asked, tamping down her eagerness to discuss the financial situation.

Millicent turned her upper body toward Tilda. "I started going through everything in the house to determine if I wanted to keep or dispose of it. I plan to sell most of the furniture and some of the contents, but a great deal will need to be burned, probably. Such as all this." She gestured to stacks of correspon-dence on the desk. "Since the solicitor informed me there is no inheritance, I've started looking for any mention of money. I'm hopeful my father had other investments or accounts."

"Were you relying on inheriting money?" Tilda asked, glad for a way to broach the topic at last. Perhaps Millicent and her family were in similar financial straits to Tilda and her grandmother.

"I was expecting it, but we can manage without." Millicent pursed her lips briefly. "I do wonder if that's the case with Belinda. She has avoided committing to helping me, but she eagerly accompanied me to see Mr. Whitley on Monday regarding Papa's will. That was when we learned the house was mortgaged to the rafters, and Papa had no money. I'll have to sell what I can from the house just to pay for the funeral expenses and a few outstanding debts. I'd no idea my father was in such horrible financial straits."

Tilda didn't like hearing any of that one bit. She hesitated telling Millicent about her grandmother's missing investments. However, if Millicent had been expecting money and there wasn't any, perhaps the potential embezzlement of funds extended to more than just Tilda's grandmother's investment. "I also met with Mr. Whitley. As it happens, an investment your father made on my grandmother's behalf has gone missing—Whitley has no record of it. What's more, he said the prior solicitor, whose business he assumed about three years ago, embezzled money from a client."

Millicent gasped, her fair brows shooting up her forehead. "Do you think that solicitor stole your grandmother's investment?"

"I don't know, but I plan to call on him and ask for his records as Whitley didn't have those."

"Oh, please do," Millicent said earnestly. "Perhaps he'll know what happened to all of Papa's money. Whitley only said that Papa was a spendthrift, which I knew. I just didn't expect he would have spent *everything*. I suppose my mother kept him in check. But if the previous solicitor has more information, I'd be keen to hear it."

"I'll inquire and let you know." Tilda noticed a brooch on the desk. It was a cameo made of coral. "That's a beautiful cameo."

Millicent reached over and ran her finger over it, her lips curving into a warm smile. "Isn't it? I found it yesterday in my father's jewelry box. I'd never seen it before, but I suppose it could have belonged to my mother and she never wore it. She wasn't one to wear much jewelry."

"I'll wager it did belong to your mother. It's a nice memento."

Millicent smiled. "I was so happy to find it. It's been the one spot of brightness in this dreary, overwhelming task."

"You deserve brightness and joy, especially right now."

Millicent lifted her attention from the brooch. "I really do, and I'm glad you're here to help. You could start by going through those ledgers on the table over there."

Nodding, Tilda sat at the table and opened the first one. It was from more than twenty years ago. Pushing it aside, she looked at the dates of the others. They were all from the 1840s. She was really hoping to find some from the time of her father's death or afterward since that was when Sir Henry took over management of her grandmother's money.

"Are there more ledgers besides these?" Tilda asked.

"I suspect so, but I haven't found them yet. I've set everything from this room out where we can see it—that is why there isn't anywhere to put anything in here. I'm sorting the books from the personal documents. There is a great deal of correspondence to my mother. I didn't realize he'd kept all this."

"What will you do with it?" Tilda recalled her mother throwing away most of everything that had belonged to her father. Still, Tilda had managed to keep a few of his things—a letter opener, one of his hats, and his pistol. She also had the club he'd carried when he'd patrolled the streets, though he'd done less of that after becoming sergeant.

She wished he never had, for it was how he'd met his end. Always eager to serve, he'd been filling in one night when they were short of constables. Public safety and justice were his guiding principles. One night, he'd caught a thief breaking into a shop. The man had killed her father, cutting his throat.

Tilda squeezed her eyes shut. She hated thinking of that. Indeed, she mostly avoided doing so. But here in this house where death had so recently been, she was perhaps struggling to keep those thoughts at bay.

"I'm not sure," Millicent answered, drawing Tilda back from her melancholy. "I find myself reading them and then I've lost an hour or more. Some of them are quite engaging—from my mother's sister and her cousin who moved to Scotland. I've started setting them aside and will keep those to read later. Perhaps I'll dump all the boring ones on Belinda's doorstep."

Laughing Tilda said that was a good idea then stood to poke about the room and see if she could find more ledgers. "Would you mind if I took these ledgers home to review?"

"Not at all. If you don't find anything useful, please go ahead and burn them."

Tilda nodded as she picked up books and letters, moving things about in search of ledgers or anything financial. There was nothing. There appeared to be ledgers on the corner of the desk, however. "What about those?" Tilda asked, gesturing toward the small stack. "Should I review them?"

"These are from the past few years, but I already went through them. Please feel free to take them home and do so again. I know you are looking for your grandmother's investment, but I daresay you won't find anything since it sounds as though the previous solicitor embezzled the funds." She clucked her tongue. "He should be in prison."

Tilda didn't disagree. "I understand he returned the money that he stole to the client and went into retirement to avoid being prosecuted."

"But he could have stolen from other people," Millicent said, aghast.

"That is what I intend to find out."

"Bless you, Tilda. You've more heart for such things than I ever could."

It wasn't heart but intelligence and deductive skill. Tilda

was eager to determine the truth. "What else can I do whilst I'm here?"

"You could look through the cabinet in the sitting room," Tilda suggested. "I doubt there is anything of import, but if you want to put the contents out somewhere I can see them, that would be helpful."

Tilda went into the sitting room and felt a chill. She blamed it on the funerary hangings and coffin stand. Moving to the cabinet in the corner, she opened the cupboard and found linens. Rather than take them out, she just left the cupboard open. The drawers held candle stubs, a couple dozen newspapers that looked to be from the last month, and odds and ends. She looked about for a place to put the items, but the hard surfaces in the room were still covered with Sir Henry's mementos.

She went to the nearest table, which bore photographs. They'd been turned down at the funeral but were now sitting upright. There was a rather nice one of Sir Henry with his wife and daughters. Tilda imagined Millicent would be happy to have that.

Her gaze fell on a particularly old image. It was fuzzy and pale with age. She picked it up and squinted to recognize Sir Henry on the left side. There were three other men, but the two on the right weren't identifiable. Their images were too blurred and faded, as were many photographs Tilda had seen from that time.

Setting the photograph back down, she moved them all to one side to make room for the items from the cabinet. When she'd removed everything and organized the table, she turned and went back to the study.

Millicent was massaging her brow. She looked up as Tilda came toward her.

"I've emptied the cabinet drawers," Tilda said. "I put the contents on the table with the photographs, which I moved to one side. I hope you won't mind that I did that."

"No, that's fine. Thank you for your help. You needn't stay any longer."

Tilda was eager to review the ledgers. "I should get home to Grandmama, but I'll let you know if I find anything in the ledger books."

"I doubt you will. And even if you did find something questionable, what would we do?"

"We'd notify Scotland Yard, and there would be an investigation." Tilda would make certain of it.

"I'm not sure I believe they would investigate, but perhaps with your lofty new friend, you might persuade someone." Millicent's mouth tipped into a slight smile.

Tilda wasn't sure who Millicent meant at first but then realized she was referring to Ravenhurst. "The earl isn't my friend; he's a client."

Millicent appeared skeptical, her eyes gleaming with something akin to amusement. "Well, that's a shame. You could do worse than an earl."

"Millicent, you can't imagine I'd be socially connected to Ravenhurst."

"I suppose not, but it would be lovely, wouldn't it? I imagine your grandmother would be delighted."

Tilda wondered what her grandmother would think of him calling today. She assumed Mrs. Acorn will have told her. Later, Tilda would inform them both that the earl had hired her as an investigator. Grandmama may not entirely approve, but Mrs. Acorn would likely be delighted.

Millicent narrowed her eyes. "I just realized what you said, that the earl is a client, and earlier you said you were investigating something for him." She gaped at Tilda. "Are you a private investigator? I've never heard of a woman doing that."

Tilda laughed. "Because we aren't allowed. I've actually worked for a solicitor to help with divorces, but this is my first case." She could still hardly believe it. In hindsight, she should not have put Ravenhurst off until tomorrow. But this time with Millicent had been important.

"That's exciting," Millicent said warmly. "I imagine your father would be proud."

I hope so, Tilda thought.

"Millicent, I am going to use my investigative skills to determine what happened to your father's money and my grandmother's investment. If there is a way to recoup any of it, I will find it."

Tilda was more motivated than ever, and not just because she and her grandmother were in dire need. She'd warmed to the investigation itself. There were so many questions, and she would not rest until she'd answered them all. If only she could be paid to solve this mystery too.

CHAPTER 7

"Here again, my lord?" Mrs. Wren's housekeeper asked somewhat cheekily when he arrived the following morning to fetch Miss Wren to Scotland Yard.

Hadrian acknowledged their household was likely far more relaxed than his own. His butler would never pose such a question to someone outside Hadrian or the other retainers. But then, Mrs. Wren didn't have a butler, and her household was certainly smaller and more informal. Hadrian couldn't find fault with that. In fact, he found himself charmed by the housekeeper's humor.

"Indeed, I am," Hadrian said with a smile. "Miss Wren and I have business to attend."

"So I understand. You have made an excellent choice hiring Miss Wren to conduct an investigation for you."

Hadrian heard the woman's pride and smiled. "I think so too, though I am glad to hear your endorsement."

The housekeeper nodded. "Do come into the parlor. I'll fetch Miss Wren." As he walked toward the doorway, the housekeeper added, "I should tell you Mrs. Wren is there." She flashed him a smile before taking herself off.

Hadrian entered the parlor where Mrs. Wren was seated in a chair by the front window doing needlework. She looked up as he entered.

"Lord Ravenhurst, how charming to see you."

"Good afternoon, Mrs. Wren."

She peered at him over her half-moon spectacles. "You've caught me during prime needlework time. This window has the best light for my poor eyes."

Miss Wren swept into the room wearing the same mourning gown, and he was now certain it was the only one she owned.

"Tilda, your Lord Ravenhurst is here." Mrs. Wren possessed a barely concealed enthusiasm.

"He is not *my* Lord Ravenhurst." Miss Wren's lips pursed ever so slightly.

"He is *your* client, is he not?" her grandmother asked, sounding a trifle annoyed. Hadrian wondered if it bothered her that he'd employed her granddaughter. It was unusual for a woman to do such work. Mrs. Wren looked to Hadrian. "I understand you've hired her to determine who stabbed you. What a horrid event. I'm so sorry, my lord."

"I'm much recovered," Hadrian said.

Miss Wren had remained near the doorway to the entrance hall. "Grandmama, I'll be back later this afternoon."

That long? Hadrian didn't think their errand to Scotland Yard would take hours, but Miss Wren was the expert, and he would follow her lead.

As Miss Wren moved into the small entrance hall, Hadrian bowed to Mrs. Wren. "A pleasure to see you again."

"For me as well." Mrs. Wren smiled, her features crinkling with the ease of a woman who had known joy in her life. "Perhaps next time you'll stay for tea."

"I should like that," Hadrian said before joining Miss Wren in the entrance hall as she was donning her gloves. Her bonnet was already atop her head, and a reticule hung from one wrist. The housekeeper stood nearby. Presumably, she'd fetched the accessories for Miss Wren.

"I'll be out several hours, I expect, Mrs. Acorn," Miss Wren said. "Do not hold tea for me."

The housekeeper nodded then sent a smile toward Hadrian just before he opened the door for Miss Wren. "Good afternoon, Mrs. Acorn," he said, glad to know the woman's name.

Following Miss Wren outside, Hadrian closed the door behind him. His coachman stood at the coach and held the door open for Miss Wren. She did not require Hadrian's assistance as she climbed inside.

She sat on the rear-facing seat again. As Hadrian took the opposite one, he said. "It was your turn to ride facing forward. Indeed, you must always do so."

"Nonsense," she said. "It's your coach. I am merely your employee. How about if we take turns?"

"That seems fair," Hadrian said with a nod.

"Is fairness important to you?" she asked.

"Yes."

"It is to me too, actually. I will take the forward-facing seat next time." She turned her head toward the window as they started moving.

"What does your grandmother make of you working as an investigator?" Hadrian asked.

Miss Wren exhaled. "She was not entirely enthused, but she knows how much it means to me to do this sort of work."

Hadrian was intrigued by her drive toward a career that was not available to women. Or a career at all, really. Women of his class worked for charitable endeavors and managed households. He admired Miss Wren's ambition and persistence.

"Did you prepare an invoice for your work yesterday?" he asked.

"I started one, but I thought to wait to complete and submit it to you until after we concluded today's errand." She looked at him intently. "In truth, my lord, you really needn't accompany me as I work to solve this case for you."

"But that is our arrangement." Hadrian wasn't going to miss anything, especially since he couldn't tell her everything. "I am personally invested in every aspect of this investigation."

"Because you were nearly killed." She nodded. "If at any time you are unable to participate, please don't feel you must. I know you have other responsibilities, and I am quite capable of managing on my own."

"I don't doubt that for a moment," Hadrian said. He had to admit he was also looking forward to watching her work. "I hope you realize that is not at all the reason I insist upon joining you."

She only inclined her head in response. After a few moments, she said, "I am hopeful these reports from your and Crawford's attack will help us today. I confess I am not sure where to begin looking for your assailant, though the ring you have in your possession may help."

Hadrian jolted. Of course she couldn't know how the ring had aided him thus far. Her choice of working had just given him a start.

Miss Wren continued, "It's not as if we can go flashing it about London. We need to narrow our search somehow. I suppose we'll begin in the vicinity of where you were attacked. Though he hasn't stabbed anyone else in that area—that we know of—that doesn't mean he isn't still around."

Hadrian didn't think she would find him near Whitehall or Westminster. He was farther east because he'd been to the Bell tavern on Fish Street Hill. He could lead her there, but how would he explain why he was doing so? If he told her the truth, she'd think him mad. And she may not be wrong. He'd handled the ring again last night, hopeful that he might see something new, but he had not.

"It sounds daunting to try and find him," Hadrian said, though he had the added benefit of knowing his curse may be able to help them. He simply had to find a way to share the information he learned from his visions without telling Miss Wren the truth about how he knew. He nearly laughed at the thought of that being remotely simple.

"We have to start somewhere," she said with a shrug. "Today, we will speak with Inspector Lowther, who worked with my father. I sent a note yesterday asking to see him. He has helped me from time to time with my divorce investigations." She paused before continuing, "I should tell you that I don't plan to inform Lowther that you've hired me to conduct an investigation. I am not sure how he, or anyone at Scotland Yard, would feel about that. I've told Lowther you are a family friend and that I offered to help you gain answers about your attack."

Hadrian hated that they had to misrepresent her role, but he understood why it might be necessary. "I find it frustrating that anyone at Scotland Yard could fault me for hiring an investigator when they have done such a poor job of investigating."

"They may not mind you doing *that*. They will mind, however, that you hired *me*."

"And I mind that they mind," Hadrian said crossly. "I can hire whomever I like."

She smiled but quickly sobered. Hadrian wished she hadn't. He liked her smile and wondered if she didn't have enough opportunity to do so.

A few minutes later, they arrived at Scotland Yard. The coachman opened the door, and Hadrian stepped down. He held up his hand for Miss Wren. She hesitated briefly but took his hand as she climbed out. It was silly, but Hadrian felt a tremor of exhilaration shoot up his arm. Was this his curse? No, he was wearing a glove.

Hadrian informed his coachman to return in a half hour's time then escorted Miss Wren to the main entrance. She entered before him and led him along a corridor to an office, presumably Inspector Lowther's. The door was open, and a man sat behind the desk. He rose when he saw them.

"Miss Wren." The inspector greeted her with a smile as he moved around the desk. He appeared to be in his mid-forties and sported a thick shock of nearly black hair. Bushy brows crested deep-set brown eyes. He was burly and tall, a model physical specimen of the Metropolitan Police. "It's good to see you. How is your grandmother?"

"Well, thank you. And how are Mrs. Lowther and your children?"

"Very well," Lowther replied with a nod. "My youngest just had his eleventh birthday. He makes good marks in school."

"You must be proud," Miss Wren said with a smile. "Please allow me to introduce my associate, Lord Ravenhurst. He is a family friend, and I am helping him with some matters."

Lowther held out his hand, and Hadrian quickly removed his glove to shake it. There was a sudden flash of pride and the face of a boy bloomed and faded in Hadrian's mind.

"Pleased to meet you, my lord," the older man said.

"Likewise," Hadrian managed to say as he tried to under-stand what had just happened. He'd touched that man's hand, and his curse had activated. His hand shook slightly as he pulled his glove back on. He quickly dropped his arm to his side but still felt unsettled.

"I didn't realize your family had such lofty friends," Lowther said to Miss Wren with a smile.

She only inclined her head then removed something from her pocket which she slid into his hand. "I am glad to hear your family is doing well. We have had some upset as my grandfather's cousin, Sir Henry Meacham, recently died suddenly."

Lowther slid the item she'd given him—an envelope—into his pocket. Was that a...bribe? "I'm sorry to hear that." He moved to close the office door.

"It has been a blow," she said. "However, that is not why we've come today."

Hadrian wished it was because he wanted answers about Sir Henry's death. He would try to find a way to steer the conversation in that direction, just as Miss Wren was capable of doing.

"How can I help?" Lowther said amiably.

"Perhaps you are aware that Lord Ravenhurst was stabbed several weeks ago," Miss Wren said.

"I am. All of Scotland Yard hears when an earl is attacked." He looked at Hadrian. "You seem well recovered."

"I spent several weeks recuperating. I am fortunate to be alive."

Miss Wren went on, "It seems Lord Ravenhurst's case has been closed, and yet he has questions about the resolution. He spoke with an inspector recently and requested to review the report of his attack as well as the report for an attack on Mr. Patrick Crawford."

"Wasn't he stabbed the following week?" Lowther asked. "Infuriating that we didn't catch the culprit. We should have been watching that area very closely after his lordship was attacked. Could've prevented Crawford's death." The inspector frowned.

"Does that mean both crimes were committed by the same person?" Miss Wren asked.

"I'm not sure," Lowther said. "Though, that makes the most sense to me."

It made the most sense to Hadrian as well. "It is infuriating that the culprit was resolved to be a footpad. I am not aware of footpads who stab their marks," Hadrian said wryly.

"That is not typically how they operate," Lowther said in agreement.

Hadrian was encouraged that the inspector seemed reasonable. "I spoke with Inspector Teague the other night, and he was going to retrieve the reports yesterday. Given Miss Wren's connections here, I thought it prudent that she accompany me."

"I would say so, though as an earl, I'd wager you could get whatever you asked for," Lowther remarked with a chuckle. "I'll go and fetch the reports from Teague. I'll be back shortly. Please, sit." He gestured toward a pair of chairs opposite his desk.

When he was gone, they moved to sit. Hadrian realized this was his opportunity to press her about the other part of the investigation that she didn't realize was connected. "It occurs to me, Miss Wren, that you should query Inspector Lowther about Sir Henry's death whilst we're here."

Her golden brows pitched into a V. "I couldn't do that when we are here to investigate your attack."

"It seems silly for you to make a separate appointment. You should take advantage of having his attention."

"I suppose I could," she said slowly, as if she were warming to the idea. "I would like to ask why there wasn't an inquest given the circumstances of Sir Henry's death."

Hadrian had another pressing matter to discuss. "What did you give Lowther after we arrived?"

"I gave him a pound note. Bribes are commonplace, though I only give them to a few select people. Doing me a favor can be a risk, so I compensate them. These are men with families who need the money. Lowther in particular has five children, one of whom is sickly."

"Don't *you* need the money?" Hadrian asked, thinking Miss Wren had a kind heart. He was not surprised.

"I'll be including the cost of the bribe in your invoice," she said with the flash of a smile.

"What if I don't agree with bribery?" It did not sit well with him.

"Then we may run into difficulty, because it is sometimes necessary."

"Was it today, though?" It had seemed as though Miss Wren and Lowther were at least friendly acquaintances. She wasn't asking him to break any rules or laws.

She shrugged. "Perhaps not, but Lowther is now incentivized to help us to the best of his ability, and I like knowing that."

"I should like to think he'd help you because it's his job," Hadrian muttered. "I didn't realize the police were this corrupt."

"Corruption is almost ubiquitous, I'm afraid." She almost sounded sad. "My father didn't like it, but he understood why some men sought additional funds for their families."

"I have to say that my faith in the police is shaken." Hadrian wondered if he ought to launch a parliamentary investigation into the Metropolitan Police.

She looked at him with sympathy. "I'm sorry. I would feel the same after what's happened to you."

Lowther returned, but he was empty-handed. He sat down behind his desk, appearing flummoxed. "Teague said those reports have been marked as confidential. I'm afraid we're not able to share them."

Miss Wren glanced at Hadrian, her brow creased. "That is odd. Why have they been classified that way?"

"I don't know, but I'll look into it. I can try to speak with the inspector who worked on those cases." Lowther grimaced. "I say 'try' because Padgett can be a bit sour."

"That was my impression of him," Hadrian said.

Lowther reached into his pocket and withdrew the envelope Miss Wren had given him. "I should return this since I wasn't able to help today."

She waved at him to put it back. "Keep it for now. You're going to see about obtaining those reports for the *earl*."

"I should hate to have to speak with the Home Secretary to obtain them," Hadrian said, thinking it wouldn't hurt to use his rank. Was that any better than bribery? "But as you so aptly pointed out, I am likely to receive whatever I ask for."

"I would tell you to go ahead and do that," Lowther said. "However, the superintendent won't like it. Let me try to obtain them first, then you can go over our heads."

Hadrian nodded. "I may wish to speak with the superintendent at some point. I would like an explanation as to why my attempted murder and Crawford's murder were blamed on a common footpad. It just doesn't make any sense to me."

"Nor to me," Miss Wren put in.

"I can't say I disagree with you," Lowther said, and Hadrian's opinion of him, already improved when he'd offered to return the bribe, climbed. "I'll do my best to help you with this matter." He looked to Miss Wren. "I'll send word as soon as I have something to share."

"Thank you," Miss Wren replied. "I have an additional matter I'd like to ask you about. I mentioned earlier that my grandfather's cousin had died. He collapsed in a club or a tavern, I'm not sure where, and was found to have died from a heart attack. He was taken to his physician who completed a death certificate."

Lowther stroked his chin briefly. "How odd. The burial registry would have been sufficient."

"My thoughts exactly," Miss Wren said. "Sir Henry had a wound on his side that had been stitched. That does not sound as though it was due to an autopsy, so I'm curious what caused it."

"No, that doesn't sound like an autopsy. He would've been

cut down the middle, as you know." Lowther was quiet a moment. "You said his physician completed a death certificate. Can we assume he performed an autopsy?"

"I don't think we can assume anything. I don't understand why there wasn't an inquest. Sir Henry died in a public place and apparently had a wound of some kind."

"That is strange." Lowther tapped his fingers atop the desk. "I'll look into the matter and let you know what I find out."

"Would you be able to obtain the autopsy report if one was completed?" Miss Wren asked.

"Yes. In fact, let me try to find it now. Excuse me again for a few minutes." He stood and left the office once more.

"Lowther seems most helpful," Hadrian noted. Was it because of the bribe? "How well do you know him?"

"Well enough. He was a new constable under my father and had a great deal of respect for him. Lowther was a solid source of support when he died." She did not meet Hadrian's eyes.

"I can tell how much your father meant to you," he said quietly. "How did he die?"

She flicked a glance at him and straightened her spine against the back of the chair. "He happened upon a crime and was killed when he tried to stop it. Lowther was the first constable to arrive. He found my father."

Hadrian was surprised the man would take money from her, but then the whole scheme of bribery was distasteful to him, even if it was necessary.

Lowther returned, closing the door behind him and returning to his chair behind the desk. "I can't find an autopsy report, so I presume one wasn't conducted. That would not be strange if the cause of death could be easily determined, and it sounds as though it was."

"Except it doesn't account for his mysterious wound." Miss Wren stood abruptly. "Thank you for your time today, Inspector."

Lowther rose. "I'm always pleased to see you, Miss Wren. We'll speak soon."

Nodding at the inspector, Hadrian escorted Miss Wren from the office. On their way out of the building, they encountered Inspector Teague.

He nodded once as he saw Hadrian. "Afternoon, Ravenhurst."

Hadrian gestured to Miss Wren. "This is Miss Wren."

Teague inclined his head toward her. "Lowther informed me that Thomas Wren's daughter was in his office with you. I'm Inspector Teague. My father also worked for Scotland Yard, and before him, my grandfather worked for Bow Street. Your father's reputation was well known and admired."

"That's kind of you to say," Miss Wren said with a soft smile.

Hadrian appreciated this moment for her.

Teague arched a brow at Hadrian. "I'm surprised you didn't come to me since I am the one who offered to fetch those reports for you." His tone wasn't exactly accusatory, but he sounded a bit put out.

"My apologies," Hadrian said. "Miss Wren is acquainted with Inspector Lowther, and she offered to help me obtain information." He hoped he was saying the right things.

"I'm not sure you need both of us looking into the same matter, but I'm afraid I'm too curious about this case to leave it to Lowther. He told you the reports have been classified as confidential?"

Hadrian nodded.

"Why classify the report of a crime that's been attributed to a common footpad as confidential?" Teague mused.

"It does make the whole situation seem even more suspicious, does it not?" Hadrian asked.

Miss Wren interjected, "Inspector, since Lowther is looking into this matter, you don't really need to do so."

"I understand, but as I said, I'm rather invested now,"

Teague said with the flash of a smile. "I don't like that the police have let his lordship down. We can do better."

"It can't hurt to have you looking into things." Hadrian thought two inspectors had to be better than one, especially if neither of them were named Padgett.

"I'll send word when I know more." Teague looked to Miss Wren. "It's a distinct pleasure to make your acquaintance, Miss Wren." He nodded at Hadrian. "Ravenhurst."

Hadrian escorted Miss Wren from the building and was pleased to see his coachman was just returning. She settled into the forward-facing seat, much to Hadrian's satisfaction. Hadrian sat opposite her.

"You interfered with my investigation," Miss Wren said, her gaze cool.

"How?"

"Having two inspectors looking into the same matter involving cases that have already been closed and are now classified as confidential will rouse suspicion," she replied evenly. "It may be more difficult for them to learn anything."

"It sounds as though you think someone at the police is concealing information."

"I think the way your case and Crawford's have been handled warrants investigation, but some people, namely Padgett, won't like that. We must proceed carefully."

Damn. He *had* interfered. "I didn't mean to impose myself. I've hired you to manage this, and I must let you do it. My apologies."

"Thank you."

Hadrian wanted to ensure he remained privy to her investigation into Sir Henry. And yet he couldn't tell her why he was certain his death and Hadrian's own attack were connected.

A part of him wanted to confide in her. He found her easy to talk to, and he admired her intellect. But that very intellect likely wouldn't allow her to believe the absurdity he would tell her, that he could see things when he touched objects and, apparently, even people.

God, he hadn't even had time to think about what he'd seen and felt when he'd shaken Lowther's hand. Whilst he hadn't seen anything troubling, the experience had been shocking. He didn't want to consider that he could never touch a person again without seeing something he didn't want to.

"Miss Wren, I can't help wondering if Sir Henry wasn't stabbed in the same manner that I and Crawford were stabbed."

"That seems highly unlikely. What possible connection could there be between you, Crawford, and Sir Henry? I do see how your attack and Crawford's are related, but Sir Henry died weeks later at an alehouse or wherever he was." Her eyes shuttered, and he had the sense she was thinking.

"I don't know," Hadrian said, feeling frustrated. "After our interview with Lowther, it seems clear to me that you must speak with Sir Henry's physician about the night he died."

"I was thinking the same thing. I may call on him after you drop me at home."

"I could take you, if you like." Hadrian tried not to sound overly enthusiastic—or what had she called him, aggressive?—though he was anxious to accompany her. "I'll even compensate you for your time, since I have it in my mind that Sir Henry's death is somehow connected to my assailant."

"Specifically, to your assailant?" she asked sharply, her gaze shrewd.

"Perhaps," Hadrian said, thinking he'd nearly exposed himself. He needed to be careful. Miss Wren would surely discover his secret if he wasn't. "I only mean that it's possible the same man stabbed Sir Henry in the same way he stabbed me and Crawford." He sounded absolutely cracked just saying that. How could he ever tell her he saw visions and felt sensations?

She pondered what he said for a moment. "If you want to pay me to accompany me to Harley Street, I won't object."

Hadrian relaxed against the squab. "Brilliant. I would also offer my assistance should you require it. I understand the matter of Sir Henry's death is concerning to you, particularly in the manner of financial problems it has caused."

She gave him a beleaguered look. "Lord Ravenhurst, you are somehow even more aggressively curious than I am."

Hadrian couldn't help but laugh. "I can't decide if that is a compliment."

"It is merely a statement of fact," she said with a shake of her head. "It does occur to me that having a man at my side whilst I make certain inquiries could be beneficial. I will consider your offer."

That was all he could hope for.

CHAPTER 8

*T*ilda wasn't certain that allowing Lord Ravenhurst to assist with her financial situation was the right choice. She could not deny, however, that she was sorely tempted to have an earl at her side when she called on Mr. Hardacre.

As the coach returned toward Marylebone, Tilda thought back over the interview with Lowther as well as the encounter with Teague. She also kept thinking of Ravenhurst's certainty that Sir Henry's death was somehow connected to the attack he'd suffered. And the death of Crawford.

Tilda couldn't dismiss the feeling that the earl wasn't telling her everything. Perhaps that was why she'd endeavored to keep her own investigation into her grandmother's investments from him. That and the fact that she didn't wish him, or anyone outside of their family, to know of their financial difficulties.

Ravenhurst flicked a miniscule speck from the sleeve of his expertly tailored coat of burgundy superfine. Tilda tried not to look too closely at his clothing. She felt like a pauper next to him. A terribly unfashionable pauper.

"When we speak with Dr. Selwin, we will need specific roles," Tilda said.

When her father had taught her to pretend certain behavior, he'd also said that on occasion he had to adopt an entirely different demeanor, as if he were a character in a play. That had been thrilling to Tilda, and she'd looked for opportunities to pretend to be someone else. She hadn't realized how valuable the skill to assume a role would be until her father had died and she'd had to pretend for her mother that she wasn't completely devastated.

Pushing that maudlin thought away, she went on, "I will be the bereaved family member who desires the truth, and you will be the helpful family friend, who is asking the troubling questions we all have. My hope is that the doctor will respond better to an earl demanding answers." She hated that he would hold more sway, but her pride would not stand in the way of investigative progress.

"Roles?" He sounded surprised. "Your investigative prowess exceeds my expectations, Miss Wren."

She couldn't help feeling flattered. "I'm glad, since that is what you are paying me for."

Tilda was prepared for the doctor to be irritated by their questions. She was already suspicious of what happened the night Sir Henry died, and the doctor would have had to be complicit in whatever had gone on. How else would he have missed a wound? She doubted he had, since it had been sewn. Who had done the stitching?

More and more, she suspected Sir Henry's death had not been due to a heart attack. But if there had been foul play, someone—or multiple someones, including the doctor—was going to a great deal of effort to cover that up. And what did this concealment have to do with her grandmother's missing investments, if anything?

They arrived at Dr. Selwin's in Harley Street, and Hadrian

departed the coach. As he had at Scotland Yard, he helped her down. It was silly, but Tilda wished she looked more the part of someone who would be associated with an earl. Her gown was atrocious, but there was nothing she could do about that. She looked forward to returning to her regular wardrobe next week. Whilst it also wasn't up to noble standards, it had at least been chosen by her and wasn't a horridly uncomfortable reused frock. The neck of the black crepe gown made Tilda want to itch. How she hated donning it every day.

She walked with Ravenhurst to the door of the physician's office. Ravenhurst opened it for her, and she moved inside.

A clerk sat behind a desk and greeted them with a stern look. Middle-aged with gray hair and spectacles, the woman looked as though she could herd sheep with a single glower.

Ravenhurst gave the clerk a smile that should have melted her into a puddle, but she didn't seem affected at all. "Good afternoon, I'm Ravenhurst and this is my associate, Miss Wren. We'd like to see Dr. Selwin, please."

"Do you have an appointment?" the woman asked.

"Do we need one?" Ravenhurst asked in surprise and perhaps a bit of affront.

"My cousin was a patient of Dr. Selwin's," Tilda added with a slightly pleading tone. "He died recently, and I have a few questions that are troubling me." She wrung her hands for added effect. "I was hoping Dr. Selwin could offer some comfort."

The clerk was only slightly more affected by Tilda's performance than she had been by the earl's smile. She pursed her lips in response then stood, much to Tilda's relief. "I will see if he is available."

The woman opened a door and closed it behind her with a firm click.

"I do hope she isn't expected to provide any form of solace to Dr. Selwin's patients," Ravenhurst noted in a quiet tone.

"I can't imagine she possesses that skill," Tilda replied softly, pleased when Ravenhurst smiled.

The fearsome clerk returned a moment later and said Dr. Selwin would see them. She gestured for them to go through the door she'd used.

"Thank you," Ravenhurst said with another charming smile that did nothing to impress the woman.

They entered a small sitting room just as a gentleman, who was likely nearing sixty, came in through another doorway. He smiled warmly, already far more genial, at least in appearance, than his clerk.

"Good afternoon, my lord," he said to Ravenhurst before transferring his gaze to Tilda. "Miss Wren. If memory serves, you are related somehow to Sir Henry Meacham? I am sorry for your loss."

"Yes, he was my grandfather's cousin. His death was very sudden. We are still somewhat in shock, especially my grandmother."

Selwin's jowled face drooped as he met her gaze with sympathy. "I'm sorry to hear that. Sir Henry was a fine man. My clerk says you had some questions?"

"I do, and I appreciate you seeing me." Tilda smiled prettily. "I understand he died of a heart ailment; however, we were not aware that he had any problems of that nature. Neither was his daughter, Mrs. Forsythe."

The doctor exhaled. "It's odd that he didn't tell you, but not surprising. He didn't seem terribly interested in taking the diagnosis seriously. He'd been having pains for a few months, and we discussed the need for him to simplify his diet and not become overexerted. But I fear he must not have followed my advice."

Tilda glanced toward Ravenhurst to signal that he should speak next.

The earl gave the doctor a brief, benign smile. "Are you

certain it was his heart? As there doesn't appear to have been an autopsy, the family wants to be sure. And since he was brought here after collapsing, we knew you could confirm this."

"I can assure you it was his heart," the doctor said firmly, though Tilda noted his right eye was twitching. "And why have you accompanied Miss Wren?" he asked.

"I am a friend of the family and sought to provide support." He gave Tilda a comforting smile, and she thought he was rather good at playing a role. Add that to his incessant curiosity, and he had the makings of a fine investigator.

Ravenhurst's expression turned contemplative. "You must have performed a thorough examination of Sir Henry's body."

The doctor pushed his chest out. "I most certainly did."

"And the wound to his side?" Ravenhurst asked. "Did that not figure into Sir Henry's death at all?"

Dr. Selwin's face lost a shade of color. "Er, I don't recall seeing a wound. I am certain he died of a heart attack. He'd been suffering pains. The men who brought him from the club said he grabbed his chest."

"What men were those?" Ravenhurst asked politely, though his eyes glittered with expectation.

"I'm sure I don't recall." The doctor's eye was twitching again, and he looked away. "They weren't people I knew."

"Not friends of Sir Henry's?" Ravenhurst prodded. Tilda would love to know who those men were so they could question them. As it was, they would need to visit the place where Sir Henry had collapsed.

"What was the name of the club again?" Tilda asked softly. "I've forgotten, and I should like to send a note of gratitude to them for taking care of Sir Henry."

"I'm sure I don't know that either," Dr. Selwin said as he clasped his hands together then immediately pulled them apart.

Tilda sent the doctor a hopeful stare. "And how long ago did you diagnose his heart ailment, Dr. Selwin?"

The doctor frowned more deeply. "I can't recall."

"I'm sure your clerk will have a record of it." Ravenhurst glanced at the door that led to the reception room.

"Yes, yes, I'm sure she does. However, you are disrupting our day." Selwin rubbed his hand over his forehead, which appeared damp. Though he didn't meet either of their eyes, Tilda could see that he was agitated. "I would prefer you set an appointment to return another time."

"We can certainly do that," Ravenhurst said affably. He removed his glove and offered his hand to Selwin. "We're sorry to have troubled you, and thank you for your time."

Selwin shook his hand, and the connection between the two men seemed to go on a trifle longer than would be typical. The earl flexed his hand before he replaced his glove. A single furrow deepened across his brow only to be followed by several more. Lines bracketed his mouth.

"Good afternoon, Dr. Selwin," Tilda said as Ravenhurst turned and went to the door to the reception room.

Once they were with the clerk again, Tilda asked for an appointment to see Dr. Selwin to obtain Sir Henry's medical records. The clerk pursed her lips and said there was no availability until the following week.

"That is fine," Ravenhurst replied, his brow still creased. "We'll take the earliest opportunity, if you please."

"Next Tuesday at one," she said. "Unless there is an urgent matter requiring his attention, you understand."

"Of course," Tilda said. "Thank you." She moved toward the exterior door, and Ravenhurst hurried to open it for her.

They didn't speak until they were settled in the coach once more. It would be a relatively short ride to Tilda's grandmother's.

"I found him completely lacking in credibility," Tilda said as the coach pitched into motion. "Unless Millicent was mistaken about the wound in her father's side."

Ravenhurst massaged his forehead briefly. "Listening to her discuss it, I would say that isn't possible. One remembers things they've seen preparing their father for a funeral," he said wryly. "Not that I would know personally. I also found the doctor's replies and behavior dubious."

Tilda couldn't allow herself to be distracted by talk of fathers and funerals. She had not prepared her father either, and she wished she'd been allowed to. "I would wager he told us to come back to see proof of Sir Henry's diagnosis because it never happened, and he needs time to fix his diary to add it."

Ravenhurst's brows shot up. "You think he would fabricate an appointment in his diary?"

Tilda lifted a shoulder. "I think it's possible. As you noted, he was upset by our questioning. Why not just show it to us now? Then he wouldn't have to see us again since that was clearly stressful for him."

"But why was he agitated? And why was he lying about Sir Henry's cause of death?"

"It seems to me that if Sir Henry had a wound, he was stabbed, and that fact was concealed by Dr. Selwin. But why?" Tilda couldn't deny the rush of anticipation coursing through her at the onslaught of questions their interview with Selwin had prompted. "I can't believe the men who brought Sir Henry to Harley Street were people unknown to him. Was he truly at the tavern alone? How would these unknown men even know to take him to his personal physician? The whole scheme appears to be covering for something else. I would dearly like to know what this has to do with the state of his finances, if anything."

"You pose excellent questions," Ravenhurst said with something akin to admiration. "We must discover the name of the club—Sir Henry used the word club—where he collapsed and interview the employees and patrons about what happened that night."

"Do you think Selwin was lying when he said he didn't know where Sir Henry had collapsed?"

"It seems he could be lying about a great many things."

Tilda nodded. "I will ask Millicent for the name of the club or tavern or whatever it is."

"You mentioned the state of Sir Henry's finances," Ravenhurst said almost cautiously. "I have the sense that you don't wish to discuss the matter, but I hope you know you can trust me. Whatever you share will be kept in the strictest confidence."

Though she still thought he was keeping something from her, she decided she could confide in him. She would have to if she wanted him to accompany her to see Mr. Hardacre, and she was all but certain she did. "Sir Henry died in debt; his house mortgaged. As my grandmother's nearest male relative after my father died, he oversaw her investments. I've been troubled by the fact that the interest payments from her investment have not changed since I began managing her household finances eight years ago. There was also a second investment, and that has simply disappeared."

Ravenhurst leaned forward. "What do you mean it disappeared?"

Tilda explained the timeline of the investment and Mr. Hardacre's embezzlement of a client's funds. The earl's eyes had grown larger as she spoke.

"You think your grandmother's money has been embezzled?" he asked.

"I think it's likely. And Millicent—his daughter—was expecting an inheritance, but you heard her say there was none. I do wonder if the solicitor stole a great deal of money."

He settled back against the squab, his expression determined. "We must speak with Mr. Hardacre."

"Yes. I'd hoped to do so today, but I should get home to my grandmother."

"I imagine she's distressed about the possible embezzlement," Ravenhurst observed.

"I haven't told her that part," Tilda said. "She would be very upset, and she's already unsettled by Sir Henry's death. What's more, she feels badly that she didn't keep better records." Tilda stretched her neck by moving her head from side to side. "I've been combing through all the ledgers I can find—both my grandmother's and Sir Henry's."

"You shoulder a great deal of responsibility," he said softly. "How old were you when you began managing your grandmother's household? You couldn't have been twenty."

"Seventeen," Tilda replied. "It gives me pleasure to care for my grandmother. The loss of my father was difficult for us both. I think when I came to live with her, we both found joy again."

"That's lovely." His mouth curled into a warm smile.

The coach drew to a stop in front of Tilda's house.

"Have you looked through Sir Henry's correspondence?" Ravenhurst asked. "Perhaps there is a letter or letters between Sir Henry and his solicitor, probably the former one—Hardacre—I'd guess."

Why hadn't she thought to look through the correspondence? She'd been too focused on the ledgers and the actual accounting of money. Except if there was no accounting, she ought to look elsewhere. "Millicent had a great deal of correspondence to review. I didn't even think to ask if she'd found anything, though we've discussed this matter, so I do think she'll tell me if she discovers anything helpful."

"Would she know what is helpful? Perhaps you should offer to assist."

He was right. She wanted to call on Millicent now.

"Would you like me to take you there now?" he offered, as if hearing her thoughts. "I don't mind. In fact, I'd like to, if it's convenient."

He really did seem to want to help her.

She was glad for his offer, for she was burning with a sense of urgency. "That would be most kind, thank you."

"I'll just inform the coachman." Ravenhurst departed the coach and returned a moment later.

They were shortly on their way to Huntley Street.

When they arrived, Ravenhurst helped Tilda from the coach once more. "You're becoming rather accomplished at this," she quipped.

"Was I lacking before?" he responded with a smile.

"I couldn't say." They walked to the door, but Tilda's knock was not answered.

They waited a few moments before Ravenhurst tried again, rapping his knuckles against the wood more loudly. Tilda hoped nothing had happened to Vaughn. But perhaps he'd taken his retirement, as was his due. Though, she doubted that would have occurred since yesterday.

At last, the door opened. Millicent stood on the other side, her face pale, and her eyes somewhat glazed. "Thank goodness you're here. Please, come in."

Tilda entered and the earl followed. "Is something amiss?" Tilda asked.

"It's poor Vaughn. He's through here." Millicent led them to the back of the house to a small sitting room.

The butler was stretched out on the settee, his frame too long for it, so his legs dangled off one end. He was paler than Millicent—no, he was gray. The maid was standing near his head, a cloth in her hand. It appeared another cloth was wadded beneath his head.

"What happened?" Tilda asked amidst a wave of concern for the elderly butler.

Vaughn's eyes slowly opened, and he started to speak, but

Millicent went to put her hand on his shoulder. "I'll tell them. You rest. The doctor will be here soon."

"Did you send for Dr. Selwin?" Tilda thought it might be awkward to encounter the doctor again this afternoon.

"I don't know what doctor is coming," Millicent said. "Cook went to the neighbor to ask for help. They sent for a doctor. She returned and is downstairs fetching hot water and a tonic for Vaughn's head since he will likely be quite sore."

"What happened?" Ravenhurst prompted. Tilda sent him a grateful look.

"I left to take a short walk," Millicent said. "My eyes were tired from going through correspondence, and I was weary of being caged in here. But I should not have gone." She looked down at Vaughn with great distress. "Someone stole into the house. Vaughn heard something and caught them in my father's study. The brigand hit Vaughn in the head and fled."

"I'm so sorry this happened," Tilda said, her gaze moving to the poor butler.

"I'm sorry he—or she—surprised me," Vaughn muttered, his eyes closed.

"Why would you think it was a woman?" Tilda asked.

"Smelled like one. Never known a man to wear so much perfume. And it smelled like flowers, perhaps lilies?"

"Were you able to see him at all?" Ravenhurst asked.

"He wore something covering his face," Vaughn said. "His hat was pulled low over his forehead. That's all I can remember. And the powerful scent."

"That is all helpful," Ravenhurst said encouragingly. "Did you lose consciousness?"

"I think so, at least for a moment or two." Vaughn grimaced. "I wondered how I came to be on the floor before I recalled what happened. Then Mrs. Forsythe returned and found me."

"I didn't hear a thing," the maid put in, her eyes damp and her cheeks red from crying. "But I was on the second floor, cleaning out one of the rooms." She wiped the back of her hand over her nose and sniffed.

The cook came in with a tray bearing steaming water, cloths, and a bottle. There was also a pot of tea and a cup. She set it on a table, and Tilda moved to help her, though she wasn't sure what to do.

"Did you bring tea?" Vaughn asked.

"I said I would," the cook replied.

As she prepared his tea, Tilda moved closer to Millicent. "What did the thief steal?"

Millicent turned her head toward Tilda and blinked. "I don't know. Everything is such a mess. I'm not sure I'd notice what was missing."

Vaughn spoke from the settee. "If he stole anything, it would have had to be small because his hands were free. He would have had to tuck it into his coat or pocket."

"Despicable that someone would prey upon a house in mourning," the cook said bitterly as she took the tea to the settee. The maid helped Vaughn to sit up and sip the tea while the cook held the cup.

Ravenhurst looked to Tilda, his gaze skeptical. Was he thinking what she was, that this was not a simple instance of someone taking advantage of a house in mourning?

"We should fetch Scotland Yard," Ravenhurst said. "I'll go at once."

"Thank you, my lord." Millicent looked to Tilda. "Why have you even come?"

"We can discuss it later," Tilda replied before patting her cousin's arm. "I'll just see Lord Ravenhurst out."

The earl inclined his head for Tilda to precede him then followed her into the entrance hall. She turned to face him.

"Something is not right here," she said quietly.

"I agree. There are too many strange happenings. I do think

we can conclude that there was definitely something amiss the night Sir Henry died."

"Yes, though I am still not convinced it has anything to do with your attack." She studied him intently. "I must say it seems you are keeping something from me on that score. I do hope you'll take the time you are fetching someone from Scotland Yard to reconsider whether you would like to trust me completely. I trusted you enough to tell you about our financial problems."

The way his nostrils flared told her she was right. She did not feel victorious about it, but she was glad her instincts had proven accurate.

"I'll be back as soon as I can," was all he said before he departed.

Tilda thought back over everything she knew and observations she'd made about the earl. Something wasn't quite right, but she couldn't identify what. And yet, while she was certain he hadn't been fully honest, she didn't think he was untrustworthy. He had a reason he was withholding information from her.

If he wouldn't tell her when he returned, she would need to tell him that she couldn't properly investigate his case if she didn't have all the facts. If he didn't confide in her after that, she'd have to reconsider whether she could continue working for him.

She hoped it wouldn't come to that. Besides needing the income, she was too invested to walk away.

CHAPTER 9

On the way to Scotland Yard, Hadrian couldn't help but think of what Miss Wren had said to him. She knew he wasn't being completely honest with her. And she was demanding he change that. But how could he when doing so would ensure she severed their association? Or worse, tell people he belonged in Bedlam.

Which was perhaps precisely where he ought to be.

When he'd shaken the doctor's hand, he'd been overwhelmed by feelings of fear, agitation, and guilt. There'd also been a strong sense of deception. Then Hadrian had looked into the man's eyes and seen those emotions mirrored there. It had been the most discomfiting encounter. And it had been accompanied by the usual shock of pain to Hadrian's head.

Setting aside the horrid curse, Hadrian tried to focus on what the encounter revealed. All of it pointed to the doctor lying.

When he arrived at Scotland Yard, he gave a report to the sergeant on duty. The man said they'd dispatch someone to Huntley Street as soon as possible. Frustrated that no one would return with him, Hadrian made his way back to Sir Henry's.

Again, his mind turned to their meeting with Selwin earlier and how many questions they now had as a result. And now with the attack on poor Vaughn, they had even more questions. This investigation was fast exceeding its scope, and Miss Wren wasn't even aware of how this was all related to the investigation he'd hired her for—his own attack.

He was going to need to find a way to tell her the truth. But today was not the time. They needed to deal with what had happened to the butler.

As the coach stopped in front of Sir Henry's house, Hadrian worked to clear his mind. Departing the coach, he breathed deeply of the cold, late winter air and hoped it would provide some ease, for there was still a mild ache in his head.

Miss Wren admitted him just as the doctor—who was not Selwin—was finishing with Vaughn. The butler had suffered a mild concussion, and the doctor prescribed strict bed rest for a week and suggested he may want to consider stepping back from his duties. It seemed Vaughn's retirement had come upon him even more suddenly than he'd originally anticipated.

Hadrian stood in the entrance hall with Miss Wren as the doctor departed. A moment after the door closed, there was a knock.

"Did he forget something?" Miss Wren mused as she opened the door.

However, it wasn't the doctor returning. It was Inspector Teague. His brown eyes fixed on Miss Wren first, then his gaze found Hadrian.

"Afternoon," Teague said.

"Come in, Inspector," Miss Wren invited as she opened the door wider.

"Is it a coincidence that you are the one to come and investigate what's happened?" Hadrian asked.

"Somewhat." Teague removed his gloves and took out a notebook and pencil. "I had just arrived for my shift after you left, Ravenhurst. I did see that you had made a report and would have volunteered to come, but I was the only inspector available, as luck would have it."

"It's certainly convenient for us," Ravenhurst said. "Come back to the parlor where you can speak with the victim and the residents of the house."

Miss Wren arched a brow at him, and Hadrian realized he'd taken charge where he shouldn't have. He was merely a helpful associate of someone who was actually attached to this household by family ties.

"Forgive me, Miss Wren," he murmured.

She pressed her lips together then addressed the inspector. "Do come along to the parlor where you can speak with Vaughn. He is the butler and the one who was attacked." She led him along the corridor past the stairs to the rear of the house. "The others present are my cousin, Mrs. Forsythe, who is Sir Henry's daughter, the cook, and the maid."

Teague nodded just before they entered the parlor. Hadrian trailed them and stood on the periphery.

Vaughn was now sitting up on the settee. Mrs. Forsythe slumped in a chair nearby, still looking somewhat pale. The maid stood near the settee, and the cook fussed with the tea tray, crowding everything she'd brought up earlier onto it.

"Everyone, this is Inspector Teague from Scotland Yard," Miss Wren said. "Inspector, allow me to present my cousin, Mrs. Forsythe."

Mrs. Forsythe looked up at the inspector but didn't say anything. Miss Wren introduced the retainers next.

"I'm sorry for what happened," Teague began. "How are you feeling, Vaughn?"

"Head's as heavy as lead," the butler replied, his eyes nearly closed. "Mildly concussed, the doctor said. I'll recover."

"I'm glad to hear it," Teague said. "I don't wish to trouble you too much as I'm sure you need to rest, but if you could tell me what happened, that would be most helpful."

Vaughn detailed the events, starting with hearing a noise in the study and going to see what it could be. After he shared his surprise at finding someone there, he described what he could of the intruder, including the smell of perfume, and the subsequent attack, as well as the fact that assailant hadn't been holding anything.

"Did he hit you with something?" Teague asked.

Vaughn nodded then winced. "Something in the study, but I don't know what. It all happened very quickly."

"I'll go there shortly and take a look," Teague said. "Have you any idea how he stole into the house?"

"No, but I suppose he could've slipped in the front door," Vaughn said with a frown. "I was in here tidying."

"But you didn't hear him come in that way?" Teague prodded.

"I did not. The first I heard was a shuffling noise, as if furniture was being moved."

Teague had been scratching notes in his book the entire time and continued to do so. "Can you think of anything else I should know?" Teague looked up from his book to query the butler.

"I believe that's everything. I'm sorry I can't better describe the thief," Vaughn said rather bitterly, his brow creasing deeply.

"You call him a thief, and yet you didn't see him carrying anything out of the house," Teague noted. "Are you certain he took something?"

"No, I'm not certain," Vaugh replied with a morose expression. "I just assume he came in to take something, that he saw the wreath on the door and thought to take advantage of a grieving household."

"Yes, that can happen." Teague gave him a reassuring nod.

"You've done very well." He transferred his gaze to the cook and then the maid. "Did either of you hear anything?"

They both explained that they'd been occupied on other floors. The cook seemed most distressed. She quickly left with her overloaded tray.

Teague looked to Miss Wren's cousin in the chair. "Would you join me in the study, please, Mrs. Forsythe? I should like to see where the attack took place."

The woman rose, albeit it somewhat shakily. Miss Wren moved to steady her and murmured something near her ear. Mrs. Forsythe nodded and said something in response. Though Hadrian couldn't be certain, he thought she'd said she would be all right—if he was any good at reading lips.

Miss Wren led the procession to the study. Hadrian trailed behind and hoped it was all right that he was still there. He was entirely invested in what had happened. Indeed, he was invested in anything to do with Sir Henry's death, and that included the attack of his butler in his house. But it was more than that. As he'd come to know Miss Wren, he was invested in *her*, and this affected her.

Teague surveyed the study, walking slowly about and writing notes. "It looks as though he ransacked the room."

"He did not," Mrs. Forsythe said, sounding smaller than she had when Hadrian had spoken with her previously. "I was in the middle of going through my father's things. I must clear the house as soon as possible so it can be sold. I'd gone for a walk to take a break from the work. You can see how cumbersome it all is."

"I can." Teague gave her a sympathetic look. "You were out walking when the attack occurred?"

She nodded. "When I returned, I found Vaughn on the floor here." She gestured to an area just inside the doorway. "He was there."

Teague went to the space and crouched down. "I see a bit of

blood on the carpet. Was Vaughn's head bleeding after the attack?"

"Yes," Mrs. Forsythe replied with a shudder.

"And was this pottery broken before?" Teague asked, gesturing toward what looked to have been a Grecian urn or probably a replica of one. There were three large pieces on the carpet, and there looked to be a smudge of blood on one of them.

"No. That was on the corner of the desk. It belonged to my mother, and I liked having it nearby as I worked." She sniffed and wiped a hand over her eye.

Miss Wren moved closer to her cousin and patted her shoulder.

"Perhaps it can be repaired," Hadrian suggested. "I'd be happy to try."

Mrs. Forsythe looked at him with a bleary eye. "I'm not sure I want to keep something that nearly killed my parents' butler."

Hadrian could understand that.

"Is there anything missing?" Teague asked.

"Not that I can tell, but I haven't looked terribly closely. I was worried about Vaughn."

"Of course, that is understandable," Teague said with a solemn nod. "If you do find that something has gone missing, please send word to Scotland Yard as soon as possible."

"I'm not sure I would even know," Millicent said, glancing around the room with a bleak expression. "This isn't my house. I don't know that I'd recognize if something was gone."

"Also understandable," Teague said.

"There's no chance you'll catch this person, is there?" Mrs. Forsythe looked and sounded defeated.

"It's unlikely," Teague replied quietly. "And I do apologize for that."

"I feel so unsafe here now." She covered her hand with her

mouth and again, Miss Wren comforted her by stroking her shoulder.

"I doubt the assailant will return," Teague said. "If that gives you any comfort."

At last, some fire showed in Mrs. Forsythe's gaze. "It does not, Inspector."

"I understand. I'll take my leave of you now. Please accept my condolences on the loss of your father. I'm sorry this incident happened so soon after, while you are already grieving."

"Thank you." Mrs. Forsythe sniffed and pulled a handkerchief from her pocket as her eyes began to leak.

"I'll see you out, Teague," Hadrian offered. He led the man back through the sitting room to the entrance hall.

At the front door, Teague turned. He'd tucked his notepad and pencil back into his coat and now drew his gloves back on. He wore a frown, and his gaze was apologetic. "I'm afraid there isn't much we can do in a situation like this. I do think it's unlikely the man will return—if it was as the butler surmised, a thief taking advantage of a house in mourning. We see it not infrequently. Someone dashes in and takes something without being noticed because the household is lax."

Hadrian frowned briefly. "I'm not sure I agree with your assessment that the criminal won't return or that this was a random attempt at theft. There is something very wrong about Sir Henry's death, and today's attack on the poor butler only underscores that."

"It is a terrible incident, to be sure, but there is no evidence that it was anything more than an interrupted burglary."

"I think it was definitely an interrupted burglary, but I don't think it was random," Hadrian said. "Someone came here looking for something and apparently left empty-handed. I fear they may try again." Once again, Hadrian had no proof, just his bloody intuition. At least this time it wasn't due to visions and sensations he couldn't explain. There were just too many unanswered questions about Sir Henry's death and now this. It was too coincidental.

"What makes you certain that is what happened?" Teague asked.

Hadrian exhaled in frustration. He could not share his intuition, which was, at least, based on his cursed new abilities since they'd led him to Sir Henry in the first place.

He could, however, update the inspector on what he'd learned earlier that day. "Miss Wren and I called on Sir Henry's physician, Dr. Robert Selwin, in Harley Street. He insists Sir Henry died of a heart ailment but is unable to recall when he made the diagnosis. We are to see him next week after he's had a chance to review his diary."

Teague blinked. "He couldn't just look while you were there?"

"Apparently not," Hadrian said pointedly. "Furthermore, when we queried him about Sir Henry's wound, he said he hadn't seen it. Either he is lying, or Sir Henry's daughter is mistaken."

"She does seem rather upset," Teague said, glancing toward the study.

Hadrian frowned at him. "That would not prompt her to see something that wasn't there, such as a wound that had been stitched closed. There is something off about Sir Henry's death. I am skeptical that Dr. Selwin performed an examination at all."

"You think he was being lazy?" Teague asked.

Hadrian shrugged. "I don't know his motivation for not ensuring an autopsy was performed, but I think one should have been. Sir Henry collapsed in a club, and despite the doctor's insistence that Sir Henry was suffering from a heart ailment, none of his family were aware. I also find it strange that Sir Henry's body was conveyed to Dr. Selwin that night. The doctor says he doesn't know who they were, but how can that be? How did these men know to bring Sir Henry to his personal physician?"

Teague was silent a moment as if he were pondering all that Hadrian had told him. "Sounds as though you may want to speak with someone who witnessed the event. What is the name of this club where Sir Henry collapsed?"

"Selwin couldn't tell us that either, but we'll hopefully find out from Mrs. Forsythe. If Scotland Yard decides to take an interest in our investigation, do let me know," Hadrian added with a bland smile.

"I will," Teague said pressing his lips tighter. "I admit my investigative curiosity is more than piqued."

Hadrian opened the door for the inspector and watched him go. This day had certainly progressed in a shocking fashion.

Closing the door, he walked back into the parlor where he encountered Miss Wren. She motioned for him to join her near the front windows, which was on the other side of the room from the doorway to the study.

"Millicent would like to return home this evening," Miss Wren said in a low voice. "I don't blame her."

"Nor do I." Hadrian glanced toward the study. "Is she still in there?"

"She's putting all the correspondence into crates. I've offered to finish looking through everything for her."

"That was kind of you," Hadrian said.

"I also wanted to do as you suggested and review the correspondence myself." She glanced toward the study. "There is a stack of letters to Millicent's mother that she is taking with her, and I can't argue with that."

"Hopefully there isn't anything pertinent in what she's removing."

"Even if there is, I can't very well say anything." Miss Wren shot another look toward the study, her features etched with concern. "Poor thing is terribly upset."

"I imagine it's a shock to find one's butler has been attacked."

"Yes, and Vaughn has been with them since Millicent was a child." Miss Wren's brow creased further. "I wonder if the retainers will be comfortable staying here. What if the brigand returns?"

"I can have someone watch the house, if you like," Hadrian offered.

"I couldn't trouble you," Miss Wren said with a shake of her head. "The cook already has a new position and was to leave in a fortnight. While you were gone, she told Millicent she wishes to leave tomorrow. And the maid said she could go stay with a cousin temporarily and has already interviewed for a new placement."

"That leaves the wounded butler," Hadrian said.

"It does, but he can come stay with me and my grandmother while he recuperates. Then he will retire."

"Can you manage that?" Hadrian asked. While he didn't know the specifics of her financial situation, he could surmise that an additional person in the household may be taxing.

"I will." Miss Wren exhaled softly. "There is simply no other choice. And we must expedite matters here. The house needs to be emptied with haste so it can be sold."

Hadrian thought ahead to when everyone dispersed, as soon as tomorrow, apparently. "Once there is no one living here, I suspect whoever attacked Vaughn today may return to find whatever they were looking for."

Her green gaze was shadowed with apprehension. "Do you really think he—or she—would be so bold?"

"I think we must be wary of anything that might happen. What can I do to help?"

"All the rooms must be emptied of personal items—we can

leave the furniture for now. Millicent had begun this process, and I will complete it over the next couple of days. I'll work there this evening and return first thing tomorrow. I'll see if the maid can help me through tomorrow at least."

Hadrian frowned. He didn't like the idea of Miss Wren being here tonight. While she wouldn't be alone, the butler hadn't been either. "Will you please allow me to post someone to watch the house overnight while the maid and cook are still here?"

She gave him a small smile. "All right. That is very kind of you."

"It's my pleasure." He felt quite strongly about it and would have insisted if she'd refused him. "I will also help you this evening. And tomorrow, though in the afternoon I need to be at Westminster."

"That would be most appreciated, but really I can't ask that of you."

"You didn't ask," Hadrian said. "I'd like to think that we are becoming friends in addition to professional associates." Except friends didn't keep things from one another, did they? Hadrian knew he had to tell her about his curse, but it could wait until after she sorted through this mess.

Small pleats gathered between her brows. "I don't know that it's wise for us to become friends whilst you are employing me, but I appreciate your assistance."

"I'll help as long as I'm able, and I'll bring a footman who can act as the guard." Hadrian knew exactly who he would assign to the position. He'd send his coachman home shortly to fetch him. "Then I'll have a second footman join him, so there will actually be two of them here overnight."

"Thank you. I'm sure the cook and maid will be grateful." She turned toward the study. "Let us get to work. We've much to accomplish and that's just with packing things up to be moved. We shouldn't take time to look through anything. I can do that at home."

"What will your grandmother say when everything shows up at her doorstep?" he asked with a smile.

Miss Wren chuckled. "She won't like it initially, but she'll understand why it is necessary." She sobered, her features growing worried once more. "She will be distressed to hear of the attack on Vaughn. But I can't keep it from her if he's to come and stay with us."

"Would you rather he stay with me?" Hadrian offered.

Her brows shot up as her eyes rounded for a moment. "I couldn't impose on you even further. You are already helping a great deal. Besides, I think Vaughn will be more comfortable with people he knows."

Hadrian couldn't argue with that.

"I believe there are crates in the storeroom downstairs," Miss Wren said. "Would you mind fetching them?"

"Not at all." As Hadrian found his way to the servants' stairs, he wondered what the intruder had been looking for that afternoon. Since Hadrian would need to remove his gloves to help, perhaps he'd detect a clue somehow.

While he hated to encourage the terrible curse that had befallen him, he realized it was their only hope of discovering the truth. But if he did see or feel something, how would he share it with Miss Wren?

CHAPTER 10

Two days later, Tilda was very pleased with her progress regarding the contents of Sir Henry's house. She'd managed to sort and empty all the rooms of personal items, moving them to the parlor downstairs. Then she'd crated everything she wanted to go through and transferred them to her grandmother's house. There was one crate left that she needed to fetch, but everything else at Sir Henry's was either furniture or items that could be sold or given away.

She would not have been able to accomplish the massive effort in such a short time without the help of Sir Henry's maid, Dora Chapman. In her late twenties, Dora was thin as a rail but somehow also strong as an ox. She'd been indispensable. Indeed, Tilda wished they'd been able to take her on at her grandmother's house for she was a hard worker and in possession of a cheerful disposition—and that was after everything that had gone on at Sir Henry's of late.

Lord Ravenhurst's pair of footmen had also been incredibly helpful, both in their assistance with moving things about and simply being there as protection. Their presence had made her feel safer, and Dora had confessed the same.

Yesterday, Ravenhurst himself had come to help before he needed to be at Westminster, just as he'd said he would. He'd worked with the footmen to move many items from the upper floors to the ground floor and had sorted things in the sitting room. He and the footmen had also taken down the black crepe and the coffin stand so that the room felt less like an undertaker's place of business.

But Ravenhurst had left rather suddenly after packing up the photographs in the sitting room. As Tilda thought back on it, his behavior had reminded her somewhat of how he'd seemed after shaking Dr. Selwin's hand. He'd appeared a shade lighter than usual and had massaged his head, as if it were aching.

Did he have some lingering effects from his attack? He'd had a serious concussion. Perhaps he suffered headaches. She wanted to ask but also didn't want to pry. Though, he probably wouldn't mind. He thought they were becoming friends.

Tilda didn't really have friends. She hadn't ever been interested in the same things as other young ladies. She detested needlework and saw no benefit in marriage or motherhood.

However, she liked the earl, which surprised her. She would have thought they had little in common, but that was not the case. They shared an avid curiosity as well as a drive to accomplish things that mattered to them. She could well understand his need to not only solve the mystery of his attack but be a part of it. And she couldn't deny that he'd been most helpful with everything to do regarding Sir Henry's death.

Did Ravenhurst still think it was connected to his attack? She hadn't been able to focus on his investigation whilst she dealt with Vaughn and clearing Sir Henry's house, but Tilda was eager to get back to it. However, it was difficult when her own investigation into Sir Henry's death seemed to be gathering steam.

Tilda blinked and looked back down at the stack of correspondence she was reviewing. She sat at the desk in the sitting room, alone as her grandmother was in the front of the house using the afternoon light to work on her embroidery.

Mrs. Acorn walked in, a hesitant expression on her face. "Sorry to bother you, Miss Wren."

"Not at all," Tilda said with a smile.

"Aside from wondering if you wanted tea, I came to talk with you about Vaughn." Mrs. Acorn clasped her hands in front of her.

"Is he too much of a burden?" Tilda asked. He'd been abed all day yesterday and, as far as Tilda knew, was today as well, which was what the doctor had instructed.

"Goodness, no." Mrs. Acorn exhaled. "I had to stop him from polishing what little silver there is. He said it was the butler's duty, and he didn't feel right lying abed all day."

Tilda covered her mouth lest she laugh. She'd visited with him for a while last night, and he seemed in good spirits despite being annoyed at having to remain bedridden. She was not surprised he hadn't stayed abed. Lowering her hand to her lap, she murmured, "I see. I assume you explained to him that he is not, actually, our butler?"

"I did try, along with the fact that we don't need the silver at present. He replied most adamantly it was important to always be prepared, saying one never knew when nobility, such as Lord Ravenhurst, would drop by." Mrs. Acorn looked at Tilda expectantly. "Will he be dropping by soon?"

"Not today," Tilda said. "But even if he did, we don't require the silver. We haven't brought it out on the occasions he *has* come." Tilda had the sense Mrs. Acorn was fishing for information, but she wasn't entirely sure why. She could, however, guess, though she wasn't going to indulge the housekeeper's desire for matchmaking. *If* that was what Mrs. Acorn was getting at.

"How are you enjoying working with his lordship?" Mrs. Acorn asked.

"I'm finding it most gratifying," Tilda replied with a smile. "I should be delighted if this leads me to more investigative work. Only think what an earl's recommendation could do."

Mrs. Acorn blinked in surprise. "Would he recommend your services?"

"I believe he would." Tilda hadn't asked, but she would. Once she solved his case.

"Even though you are a woman?"

Tilda thought of Ravenhurst's reactions and things he'd said. He hadn't liked that she thought it best Scotland Yard wasn't aware that he'd hired her. "Yes, even though I am a woman. The earl does not seem bothered by that in the slightest." That alone should ensure that they became friends. He was refreshingly forward thinking, and she'd met so few gentlemen like that. Only her father and Mr. Forrest came to mind.

"Dare I hope something more might bloom between you and the earl?" Mrs. Acorn asked with a smile.

"No, you should not. Ravenhurst and I are becoming friends, and that is all. I believe I've made clear my opinion on marriage." Tilda had set Mrs. Acorn straight a couple of years after she'd come to live with Grandmama. The housekeeper had assumed Tilda wouldn't be living with them much longer as she would certainly wed. Tilda had explained that she had no desire to shackle herself in that manner.

The housekeeper sighed. "You have. Is it wrong of me to want you to marry? I would love for you to have a family of your own and, even more so, the security that you so dearly deserve."

"It is not wrong of you to want me to feel secure. However, I do not need a husband for that. I already have a family I am quite fond of—and that includes you."

Mrs. Acorn smiled again, and she nodded. "Just so. You are

more than capable of managing things on your own. Furthermore, you like it that way, and there is nothing at all wrong with that. Shall I fetch you a tea tray?"

"Is Grandmama coming here, or should I join her in the parlor?" Tilda didn't really want to abandon the correspondence, but she also didn't want to leave her grandmother to take tea alone after having done so the past two days.

"She said she would come here as her eyes have had enough needlework for today."

"Did you tell her about Vaughn behaving as our butler?" Tilda asked.

"I did not. I thought you would want to speak with him."

"I will, thank you." The man needed his rest, for a week at least, as the doctor had ordered. After that, they would determine his retirement.

Tilda realized she did not know if there was a settlement for him. Sir Henry ought to have provided him with one, but given the dismal state of his financial affairs, she rather assumed he had not. She would need to speak with Millicent to see if she could pay him a retirement settlement from the proceeds of the sale of the house and furniture. Even if she could, that may take time. Tilda suspected Vaughn would be with them for a while.

While she waited for her grandmother to arrive, Tilda returned her attention to the letter she'd been reading. It was from a far-flung cousin in Yorkshire.

"The day has turned dark with impending rain," Grandmama announced as she entered the sitting room. "I can't see well enough to continue, so we shall take tea here. How goes your work?"

"Well enough." She gave her grandmother an apologetic smile. "I'm sorry I've been so busy of late. We've had little time for our word games."

Grandmama sat in her favorite chair near the hearth. "It's

quite forgivable, my dear. You are helping poor Millicent in her time of need. Though, I can't say I understand Belinda's behavior. Her father—never mind her mother—would be most unhappy with her lack of engagement. Especially after what happened with Vaughn." Grandmama pursed her lips and shook her head.

"I'm not certain Millicent even told her about Vaughn," Tilda said.

"Such a shame. The girls were so close when they were younger. I saw there were photographs in that crate over there." Grandmama nodded toward a crate next to the desk. "I don't suppose there's one of the two sisters? It was done about ten years ago at their mother's behest. I imagine Millicent probably took it with her, however."

Tilda wouldn't have wagered on it. Millicent was quite put out by her sister's abandonment after their father's death.

Turning in the chair, Tilda bent at the waist to look through the crate just as Mrs. Acorn entered with the tea tray. She set about pouring out while Tilda searched for the photograph her grandmother had mentioned. There weren't very many—less than ten. She'd seen them sitting on the table in Sir Henry's parlor—someone had turned them back up after the funeral— as she'd walked by it and could recall each of them, including the one her grandmother had referenced.

"Here it is," Tilda said, removing it from the crate.

"You must see if Millicent wants it," Grandmama said. "She won't stay upset with her sister forever. We can keep it for her here until she would like to have it. Why don't you put it on the shelf over there where I can see it?" Grandmama accepted her teacup from Mrs. Acorn.

Tilda stood and set the photograph of Millicent and Belinda on the shelf beside a photograph of herself from a few years ago. Grandmama had insisted on having it done as well as one of herself, since they had none of Tilda's grandfather or father.

"Perhaps you should put all the photographs out," Grandmama said. "It's a shame for them to be piled in a crate."

While Tilda didn't agree, she also didn't care enough to debate the issue. "Mrs. Acorn, just leave my tea on the tray. I'll get to it."

The housekeeper nodded and left. Tilda removed the photographs from the crate one by one and set them about the room wherever she could find space. When the box was empty, she reviewed the photographs in her head, mentally cataloging what should have been there.

"There's a photograph missing." Tilda walked around and checked again.

"You're certain?" Grandmama asked before taking a sip of tea. She set her cup down on the saucer and picked up the biscuit Mrs. Acorn had set on the edge.

"Absolutely." The missing photograph was the one of four gentlemen with only two of the men identifiable—Sir Henry and someone Tilda didn't know. Or wouldn't recognize now, for the photograph had to be more than twenty years old. The only reason she knew who Sir Henry was in the image was because he'd pointed it out to her at some point. She tried to recall who the other men were but could not.

Hands on her hips, Tilda looked at her grandmother. "It was that very old photograph of Sir Henry with three other gentlemen."

Grandmama nodded. "I know the one." She waved her biscuit. "It's probably still at his house."

That was the simplest—and best—explanation. Tilda hadn't packed that crate. Ravenhurst had done so just before he'd left. If she couldn't find it at Sir Henry's, she would ask the earl if he'd seen it. She feared the thief may have taken something after all. He could have grabbed it on his way out after striking Vaughn. Or, perhaps, the photograph had been in his possession all along, and Vaughn hadn't noticed. The villain could have tucked it into his clothing.

But why would he steal an old, almost impossible-to-discern photograph?

Perhaps it was to do with the men in the photograph. Tilda had no idea who they were, besides Sir Henry. If the photograph was indeed missing, she would need to determine their identities. This investigation grew by the moment.

Still, it was possible the photograph was just left at Sir Henry's. As her grandmother had said, that was the best explanation. Tilda had enough to investigate and didn't need to add more to the pile.

"I need to make a trip over there before dinner anyway," Tilda said. "I've one more crate to fetch. I'll look for the photograph when I go."

Grandmama leaned forward, her brow creased. "You can't go by yourself. Not with the threat of that thief skulking about."

The footmen were no longer watching over the house since no one was in residence. Tilda would bring her father's pistol, though she wouldn't tell her grandmother that. While the weapon would make Tilda feel safer, because she knew precisely how to use it, Grandmama would be horrified. She'd accepted that Tilda conducted investigations, but she would not approve of her carrying a pistol.

"I won't be there long, Grandmama. I promise." Tilda went to the tea tray and plucked up her cup, taking a long sip of warm brew.

Grandmama looked up at her with a pleading expression. "I won't be able to persuade you not to go, will I?"

"No. Please don't worry. In fact, I think Ravenhurst's footmen are still there," Tilda fibbed.

"That makes me feel better. What a welcome support the

earl has turned out to be." Grandmama sat back in her chair with a deep sigh. "Still, do be careful, dear."

"Always." Tilda took a last sip of tea and set her cup down. Then she nipped a biscuit and strode from the room to fetch her hat and gloves—and the pistol.

Tilda would have walked to Huntley Street, for it was only about a mile, but the drizzle was fast turning to a steady rain. Instead, she hailed a hack on Wellbeck Street to convey her to Sir Henry's.

As she walked up to the door, she was glad they'd taken all the funerary markers down—just in case that had been the reason for the attempted theft. Tilda was also glad to be rid of the black. In just a few more days, she would be finished with her fortnight of mourning wear and could return to her regular wardrobe.

Removing her key, she moved to unlock the door. However, before she could fit it into the lock, she noted the door wasn't latched. A shock of fear washed over her, sparking her pulse to race.

She took a deep breath and told herself to remain calm. Then she removed the pistol from her reticule. Steadying herself, she pushed the door gently open and stepped softly inside. She did not close the door behind her in case she needed to flee.

Cocking the pistol, she held it up and moved slowly into the sitting room, positioning her back to the front of the house and keeping an eye on the corridor that led to the rear of the house in case whomever was here—*if* someone was here—was in the parlor or upstairs.

Heart racing, Tilda held her breath as she stepped into the sitting room. Then everything happened at once.

Someone came at her, ramming his body into hers and knocking her to the floor. She tried to pull her arm around to fire the pistol at him but wasn't fast enough. Nevertheless, she gripped the weapon tightly, as if her life depended on it—and it did.

The man covered her, his body pinning her to the floor. "Wait. *No.*"

Tilda recognized that masculine voice. The weight that had momentarily held her down now lifted.

She whipped her arm into position and pointed the pistol at the brigand, thinking she had to be wrong about his voice.

But she was not. Crouching over her was the man she least expected to break into Sir Henry's house and accost her—Lord Ravenhurst.

CHAPTER 11

"What the bloody hell are you doing here?" Miss Wren exclaimed, her green eyes sparking.

For a moment, Hadrian couldn't quite process with his mind what he was seeing: Miss Wren in a heap on the floor with a pistol directed squarely between his eyes. Mentally shaking himself, he managed to finally find words. "Good Lord, I am so sorry! Let me help you up. Though, perhaps you could put the pistol away, so you don't accidentally shoot me."

"If I shoot you, it won't be accidental." Her reply could have frozen the Thames.

She lowered the pistol and released the hammer before tucking it into the pocket of her dreadful black gown. Hadrian, his hands bare, grasped her hands and pulled her up to stand. He thought of what might have happened if her hands had been bare too. Would he have seen something? He hoped not, for that would feel like prying. And yet, he couldn't deny wanting to know more about her, including how her hands felt in his.

Immediately releasing him, she brushed her gloved hands

over her skirts, her features drawn into a deep frown. "I'm still waiting for you to explain what you're doing here and why you leapt upon me."

"I heard the door open and thought you were the thief returning."

"As you can see, I am not." She continued to glower at him, but her expression smoothed. "And why are you even here? The door was unlatched, and I also thought the thief had returned. And that he'd knocked me to the floor." The frown returned.

"Please except my sincerest apologies, Miss Wren. I came here to ensure that the thief *hadn't* returned."

She narrowed her eyes at him. "How did you get inside?"

He glanced away rather sheepishly. "I confess I own a device that will release a locking mechanism."

Now her eyes rounded, and her nostrils flared. "Why would you have one of those?"

He shrugged. "My valet gave it to me."

"Seems like there ought to be more to that story, but I shan't inquire after it just now." She gave him a high-browed stare. "You still owe me a story about a mistake that spared you being married. Perhaps someday you'll share your secrets. For now, I am troubled that you would take it upon yourself to break into my cousin's house."

"I meant no harm," Hadrian vowed. "I truly was trying to make sure the house remained secure." Though that hadn't been the primary purpose of his visit. He decided it was best to divert the conversation. "Why are you here with a pistol? Where did you even get that?"

"It is my father's, if you must know. My grandmother was concerned for my safety when I informed her that I was coming here."

"She takes no issue with you going about brandishing a pistol?" Hadrian would be surprised if that were the case.

Miss Wren gave him a haughty stare. "She is not aware I have it with me, and I would not have been *brandishing* it if I hadn't thought someone had broken in—and rightly so, I might add." She glanced around the room. "Did you find that all is, in fact, well?"

"I haven't been here long."

Her gaze fixed to the left of him, and she drew in a sharp breath. "It *is* here."

Hadrian saw that she was looking at the photograph on the table. He'd brought it with him and set it down just moments before she'd arrived. Bringing it here was the primary reason for his visit. Well, not just *bringing* it here.

She moved toward the table. "I discovered this photograph was missing from that crate you packed up the other day. Grandmama felt certain it was probably still here, but I didn't think you would have missed it."

He had not. He'd removed his gloves that day when he'd been helping, and the moment he'd touched that photograph, a horrible vision had flashed through his mind. He'd seen the body of a dead young woman, her pale neck covered in bruises, her dark-brown eyes open and unseeing. He'd seen it long enough to recall those details but hadn't recognized the woman. His efforts to recall the vision for the next short while had resulted in nothing more than a seething headache. So, he'd tucked the photograph into his coat and taken it with him when he'd left.

"I must have," he lied.

She studied him a moment, and he wondered if she could sense he was fibbing. "I thought the villain must have stolen it, which begged the question why." She turned her attention to the photograph. "I wondered if it bore any significance."

It most certainly did, not that she would know that. Blast, but he needed to find a way to share his curse with her. "Do you know who the people are in the photograph? I imagine the one on the right is Sir Henry, though he looks much younger."

"Yes, but I don't know who the others are specifically, just that they are friends of his." She picked it up, and Hadrian tensed. Was he worried she would get the same vision? Of course she wouldn't. She hadn't been cursed with an infernal, inexplicable ability.

"It's a shame the two on the left are too blurry to identify. And I don't know the fourth man who is next to Sir Henry."

"They must not have been standing still enough. If they were moving even a little, they wouldn't appear correctly." Hadrian had brought the photograph back here in the hope of seeing the vision again. After taking it home, he'd tried repeatedly to summon it once more, but he'd been entirely unsuccessful. By returning the photograph to this place where it had resided for so long, he'd hoped he would see the dead woman again. Or something related to her. Anything that might help him determine what the hell he was seeing.

His head still ached. He massaged his temple briefly. He had to try again. At least once. "Do you mind if I take a closer look?" he asked.

"Not at all. I do wonder why he kept such a poor photograph, but I suppose a great many from that time were somewhat blurred." She handed him the photograph, and as soon as Hadrian gripped the frame, the image of the dead woman rose in his mind. He gasped and dropped the photograph. It clattered to the floor as he clasped his head, a brutal pain striking him.

"My goodness, Lord Ravenhurst! Are you all right?" Miss Wren moved closer—not that he could see her, for he'd closed his eyes. He could, however, feel her presence. And it was a welcome comfort.

"I'll be fine in a moment," he rasped, blinking his eyes open.

"I've seen you rub your forehead before. Do you suffer headaches from your attack?"

Hadrian managed to focus on her, to see the concern in her eyes. "Yes." It wasn't a lie exactly. He hadn't endured headaches like these—or the visions and sensations that accompanied them—before he was attacked.

"Come and sit down." She took his arm and guided him to the nearest seat—a chair. "What does your physician say?"

The pain in his head was lessening. Hadrian exhaled as he settled himself on the cushion. "That I could have headaches for months. I suffered a serious concussion." That was also all true. But he certainly hadn't discussed his visions with his doctor. The man would have committed him directly to Bedlam. Which was perhaps where he belonged. He wanted to tell Miss Wren, but he could *not*.

A dull throb remained, but Hadrian felt recovered from the vision. No, not from the vision but from the accompanying pain. The vision would haunt him for some time. He'd seen the young woman in more detail just then. Her lips were purple, like the bruises at her throat. Her hair was brown with strands that had come loose against her cheeks. A white cap perched atop her head, but it was askew. She wore a blue patterned gown several decades out of fashion with low shoulders and puffed sleeves. A cameo was pinned to the neckline.

He felt a surge of sadness for her. Who was she? What had happened to her? And what did she have to do with Sir Henry?

Hadrian had to think the two people were connected. Why else would he see that vision of her in Sir Henry's house whilst touching an item that belonged to him? More than anything, Hadrian wanted to move about the house and learn what else he might see from touching various objects and furniture.

Miss Wren moved to pick up the photograph and put it back on the table. She was unaffected, not that he expected her to experience what he had. But damn, this was frustrating. And lonely. He couldn't tell anyone for fear he was going mad. To say it out loud was to make that fear manifest, he realized.

Miss Wren stood to the side watching him, her expression tense and full of worry.

"I'm feeling much better now," he said, hoping to ease her tension.

"I'm glad to hear it." She seemed to relax slightly. "You should go home and rest, but I did not see your coach outside."

"My coachman will return shortly." Hadrian hadn't wanted his coach to be parked outside for the neighbors to see and report back to Miss Wren or Mrs. Forsythe. "Perhaps we should look around the house to make sure everything is as it should be." That way he could try to learn more—if his unreliable curse would cooperate. When he'd helped with moving and packing things, he hadn't sensed anything beyond domestic visions with their accompanying routine emotions—until he'd touched the photograph. Now was perhaps his last chance to try to see something helpful. "We could also ensure that the rooms are indeed empty of everything save the furniture."

"That is probably for the best," she said with a nod.

Hadrian stood. "I'll go upstairs."

"Thank you. I need to fetch a crate from the study. That was the other reason I came, besides searching for the missing photograph." She started toward the door, then stopped, turning back to face him. "Please take it easy. If your head hurts too much, you should really go home."

"I can't until my coach returns," he said with a smile. "I'm fine, truly. I promise I will be careful. I've been dealing with this for weeks. I'll make sure the front door is locked before I go upstairs."

She nodded once, then Hadrian left the parlor.

Upstairs, Hadrian looked for Sir Henry's bedchamber.

Finding it at the back of the first floor, he surveyed the room. There was a bed, an armoire, a chest of drawers, a small table beside the bed, and a cozy chair near the fireplace, but it looked devoid of life. There were no personal items. Even the bed had been stripped of everything but the mattress.

Hadrian first went to the chair by the dark, cold hearth. It looked as though it had seen many years of providing Sir Henry comfort. Hadrian contemplated sitting in it, but he feared what a connection of that nature, involving his entire body, would bring. Although, for that to work, he would need to remove his clothing, and he certainly wouldn't want to chance Miss Wren finding him like that.

He ran his bare fingers along the back of the chair. There was nothing at first, then he felt a general sense of relaxation and warmth. These sensations were followed by something darker and sharper—worry or fear. Or both.

Moving slowly about the room, he touched the various pieces of furniture and kept experiencing the same sensations. The worry and fear began to overtake the other. When he reached the bed, he touched the headboard and felt a wave of comfort that was quickly disrupted by a rush of disappointment and anger, then sharp, stringent fear.

A vision came. However, it wasn't the dead woman. It was a gaming table. There were faces but he couldn't seem them clearly. A card before him flipped over, as if turned by his own hand. It signified loss. The disappointment and fear intensified. Then there were a series of visions, flickering before him in rapid succession. All of them horrible losses.

Had Sir Henry been a gambler? Was that the reason for the poor state of his finances?

Hadrian's head was now pounding once more. He removed his hand and put it to his forehead, closing his eyes as he sought to massage the pain away.

Taking slower breaths—for his heart had been racing—

Hadrian worked to ease himself. When he felt a little better, he turned toward the door and froze. He was not alone.

Miss Wren stood leaning against the frame, her head cocked to the side. "I think it's time you explain to me whatever it is you've been hiding."

CHAPTER 12

*T*ilda had watched as Ravenhurst put his hand on the bed. She'd almost spoken then, but she'd seen him flinch. Lines of pain streaked across his forehead and around his mouth. It was precisely how he'd reacted to the photograph downstairs and to Dr. Selwin the other day.

He straightened, letting his hands fall to his sides. "It's just my head aching. You were right. I should go home. I'll wait in the sitting room until my coachman arrives."

"Balderdash." She pushed away from the door frame and walked into the room. "You touched that bed and had some sort of reaction. The same thing happened when you took the photograph from me downstairs. And when you shook Dr. Selwin's hand the other day."

He blanched.

Tilda went on. "Since we met, I've had the sense you were withholding something. Your explanations for how you knew things never quite added up to the correct sum, beginning with why you arrived here the day after Sir Henry died."

Exhaling, he leaned back, almost perching on the edge of

the mattress. "If I tell you the truth of the matter, you will think me mad. Hell, *I* think I'm mad."

"You have always struck me as a thoroughly even-tempered and intelligent gentleman. Nothing about you suggests so much as a hint of lunacy." She frowned at him. "Do not try to avoid telling me the truth, else our association will end right here, right now. I can't work with something who won't be honest with me. Furthermore, how can I do my best for this investigation if I don't know all the facts?"

He held up his hand, his expression weary. "All right. I haven't told a soul about this, but I will tell you. You will think I'm barking mad." His gaze sharpened. "Don't say I didn't warn you. And please do not have me committed to an asylum."

There was a desperate note to his plea that belied any sarcasm. He was actually concerned that she may doubt his sanity. Tilda moved closer to him so that they stood just a couple of feet apart. "I won't do that. I can see this is of grave concern to you. Tell me what is happening to cause pain in your head, because *that* I believe."

"It started after I was concussed."

"When you were attacked?"

He nodded then winced faintly and put his hand to his temple briefly. "The headaches come along with other unwelcome occurrences. I...see things. Or feel...sensations."

"What do you mean?"

"As I was recuperating, I realized I still had the ring I'd stripped from my assailant's finger as he attacked me. When I handled it, I would see things, almost as if they were memories, but they weren't mine. None of what I saw, which were just fleeing images really, made sense." He put his hands in front of him, almost as though he were trying to touch something she couldn't see. "The more I tried to understand what I was seeing in my mind, rather, the more I tried to conjure these things for longer periods of time so I *could* understand them, the more my head would ache. Amidst all the nonsense, I was able to recognize the monument to the Great Fire."

She had to think that would be confusing and frightening. No wonder he hadn't wanted to tell anyone. "If you knew these weren't your memories, what did you think you were seeing?"

"The only thing I could reason—and reason seems a far stretch as I truly feel as though I may be losing my mind—is that I was seeing the assailant's thoughts and memories." He still sounded as if he couldn't quite believe it. "Whatever I was seeing, was coming from the ring, which he had worn."

"So, the ring is some sort of connection between you and him?" She couldn't keep from sounding both astonished and skeptical. It was all absolutely fantastical, and yet she believed him completely. It wasn't just that his fear and worry were palpable. She trusted him. She'd continued to trust him even when she'd been certain he was hiding something. Now that she knew why, it all made sense to her. And she gave a great deal of credit to sense.

"Something like that."

"Do you have the ring with you?"

"Always." He pulled it from his pocket and held it out to her in his palm. "Do you want to see if you feel anything?"

She was afraid to touch it, which was silly. "Do you see anything now?"

He shook his head. "But I am trying not to. While I often put my mind to seeing whatever an object or person can show me, I also instruct my mind *not* to do those things."

"And does it work?"

"It seems more effective than trying to see things," he said with a sardonic smile. "I'm grateful for that much, at least." He tucked the ring back in his pocket.

"What did you do after you saw the monument?" Tilda found herself torn between wanting to talk to him about the ability itself and the desperate need to know where these visions had led him.

"I decided my best hope of finding anything was to go to the place I recognized—the monument. I had also seen a sign with a bell. I was lucky to happen upon the Bell, an alehouse, almost immediately."

"That is most fortunate. Do you think these visions are trying to tell you something?"

"No, because if they were, they would do so clearly and immediately instead of making me work so hard," he said with exasperation. "My apologies, I find this curse most burdensome. Where was I with my tale? The Bell. I found the alehouse and went inside. I had the ring with me, of course, but it wasn't until I touched a table that I saw something that I recognized. Rather, someone."

Tilda could hardly believe what she was hearing. The man had visions. That gave him headaches. And they'd led him to... someone. She suddenly knew. "It was Sir Henry."

"I have always known you are quite clever," he noted with a smile that flattered her more than it should have, especially just now when she ought to be seriously considering whether he actually was mad. Except that ring and those visions had led him to Sir Henry, and she was more convinced than ever that Sir Henry's death had not been caused by a heart attack.

"That led you here the day we met."

"Yes, it did. Now, you can see why I have not been completely honest with you. This...curse makes no sense." He scrubbed his hand over his eyes. "I quite detest it actually."

"But it's been helpful." She thought through what he'd said. The ring had been worn by his assailant and that had led him to the Bell, which had in turn led him to Sir Henry. "I see now why you believe Sir Henry is somehow connected to your attacker."

"Yes," he said with enthusiasm, his eyes brightening. "The

visions showed me Sir Henry. My attacker knew Sir Henry. Of that, I am convinced."

He removed his hat and set it atop the mattress. Then he ran his hand through his dark hair. She'd never seen him do anything so...informal before. She felt they were moving into a new stage of their association. Friendship didn't quite describe it, at least to Tilda. But then her experience with friendship was limited. She only knew that she felt closer to him and wanted to help him.

"I want to understand this...power," she said slowly. "Touching the ring gave you visions, but so did the table?"

He nodded. "I can see things and feel sensations when I touch objects and people with my bare hands."

"People too?" Tilda recalled his reaction to Dr. Selwin. "You saw something when you shook Dr. Selwin's hand."

"I only felt sensations in that instance, but yes. Shaking his hand activated the curse."

She noticed the way he referred to this ability and could see just how much it taxed him. "This affects you greatly. I am amazed you've kept this burden to yourself for so long."

He pushed away from the mattress to stand straight. "I didn't see I had any choice. To tell someone would be to admit I am careening down a path of madness." There was a bit of levity to his tone, but she knew he had a real fear that his sanity was in question, at least to him.

"You are not mad," Tilda said. "At least, you don't appear to be. But I can see how this...ability would be terrifying."

"It is that," he said with a faint smile.

"Tell me about the sensations you felt when you shook Dr. Selwin's hand," she urged, eager to learn everything she could of what he knew.

Brows pulling together, Ravenhurst seemed to be concentrating. "I felt his agitation and fear, as well as his deception."

"That had to be unnerving." To feel fear and agitation was

unsettling enough, but to feel those things and not know why would make one question their sanity. Tilda understood why he would call this a curse. "I was sure the doctor was hiding something, so I'm not surprised to hear you felt a sense of deception."

Ravenhurst looked at her in open admiration. "You seem to be good at discerning that, and without the aid of an abominable curse."

"Perhaps." She found it fascinating that he could sense people's emotions by touching them. Would he be able to do that if he touched her? She realized they had never touched bare skin to bare skin. "Goodness, how are you not bombarded with visions and sensations constantly?" A curse indeed.

"It isn't consistent. And I don't see visions or feel anything touching objects at my home or when my valet touches me as he trims my hair or helps me dress. I suppose that's because I handle those things regularly or that they are mine, meaning anything I would see or feel would be my own memories and emotions, and I already have those inside me. And with Sharp, my valet, I don't know if I feel any sensations. I haven't paid attention, and perhaps whatever I would feel would not stand apart from what I am currently feeling." He blew out a breath. "I honestly don't understand how it works or where it came from, but none of this happened before I hit my head on the pavement several weeks ago."

Tilda uncrossed her arms. "What a burden this must be," she said softly. "I am sorry, though it has been helpful. I don't blame you for not telling me about it."

"I couldn't even imagine where to begin," he said with a chuckle. "Speaking of inconsistency, the photograph downstairs is a prime example. When I picked it up the other day, I saw a very clear image, but then I couldn't see it again until today." He hesitated, his features darkening. Whatever he had seen, it wasn't good. "I saw a young woman, her neck bruised and her eyes open—unseeing. She was most certainly dead."

Tilda gasped. "How horrifying."

"It was. Nevertheless, I strove to see it again in the hope that I might recognize her. But when I wasn't able to conjure the image again, I took the photograph with me when I left. I brought it back today." He gave her a sheepish look. "I hope you'll forgive me."

"Well, that solves one mystery," she said lightly. "I do understand—why you couldn't tell me and why you wanted to borrow the photograph."

"I thought if I returned it to where I'd first seen the dead woman, I might be able to conjure the image again."

"And you did, earlier when you took the photograph from me." She'd seen him go pale and grab his head, but she'd never imagined the true cause of his reaction.

"Yes. I saw her more clearly than the first time. I made out a few additional details such as her hair and eye color—light brown and brown respectively. I still didn't recognize her." His expression was pensive. "And I would say she looked to be from a different time. Her gown was of a style my mother wore when she was younger. I've a painting of her from the 1830s. The neckline and sleeves matched that of the gown the poor woman was wearing in my vision."

"Do you think you're seeing a woman who died decades ago?"

"That is my suspicion, but who can say?" He cut his hand through the air. "Who can say whether anything I see is accurate? You say it's helpful, but only enough to be extremely aggravating because it's never the whole story. I also came back today so that I could walk about the house and touch things to see what else I might learn." He rubbed his head again, his brow deeply furrowed.

She didn't need an odd ability to see his agitation or feel his frustration. "What about the headaches?" she asked softly. "Are you in pain now?"

"Somewhat, yes." He dropped his hand to his side. "Once they start with a vision or sensation, the pain will linger—even though it lessens—for hours. The more I demand of the ability, the more intense the pain. Sometimes I have to give up, at least for a while."

That sounded horrible. It was any wonder he even tried to have the visions. "You must take care of yourself. Perhaps you shouldn't be trying to see anything."

"I've thought about that, but it's deuced difficult when you see something like a dead woman, which raises so many questions." He met her gaze with a dark look. "It's also unsettling enough that you can't *not* think of it or want to know everything about it."

"I can understand that. I haven't seen her in my mind, and I'm quite eager to learn her identity. I'm sure you feel even more pressed for answers."

"That's exactly it. Why am I even seeing her? Why did I see Sir Henry?"

"It's as if something or someone is trying to communicate with you, to lead you to answers," Tilda said.

"Yes, but I can't imagine who or what. Rather than try to resolve that, I am focused on these urgent questions—who is that woman and what is her connection to that photograph?"

"I would guess she is somehow tied to the men in the photograph. Pity we can't ask Sir Henry."

"Yes, though perhaps that is why he is dead," Ravenhurst said, provoking a shiver to move up Tilda's spine.

"Perhaps," Tilda agreed. "I think we must treat the investigations into your attack, Crawford's murder, and Sir Henry's death as one."

His features relaxed with relief. "Thank you. I know they are all connected. We just have to determine how."

Tilda's mind was spinning. "You're hoping that by touching other things here in Sir Henry's house, you may find some answers?"

He glanced around the room. "That is my hope, though here in his bedchamber, I'm not seeing anything to do with the dead woman." He returned his focus to her. "Was Sir Henry a gambler?"

"I recall he liked cards, but I can't say what his wagering habits were. I could ask my grandmother. She would know far more than I do."

"I have the sense he lost a great deal of money on several occasions. I see different gaming tables and I feel loss, disappointment, even despair. If he'd lost large sums, that could explain the state of his finances."

Tilda blew out a frustrated breath. "Well, that does not support the theory of embezzlement by Mr. Hardacre."

"Perhaps, but I still think we should call on Mr. Hardacre."

"Of course we will," Tilda said. "A good investigator follows every path to gather as much information as possible, if only to rule things out."

He smiled at her. "And you are nothing if not a good investigator."

"Thank you." Tilda's mind was still whirring too fast to indulge in his flattery. "I suppose it's also possible that Sir Henry could have gambling losses *and* Hardacre could have been stealing from him. Wait! Why didn't we find any IOUs as we emptied the house? Especially in Sir Henry's study."

Ravenhurst shrugged. "It may be that Sir Henry never used them. Perhaps he covered his losses as soon as they happened. It would explain his lack of funds. It may also explain what happened to your grandmother's investment. Perhaps Sir Henry was in deep enough that he had to steal from her."

Tilda sucked in a breath. She hadn't considered that Sir Henry could have done something so despicable. It was too shocking. "I can't believe he would do that." Tilda would hate for her grandmother to find out he'd done that. Or for Millicent, who was already suffering enough with the state of things. Though, matters could be worse for her if there were IOUs for her to deal with. "I will speak to my grandmother and to Millicent. They will know whether Sir Henry was a gambler, but it seems as though he was."

"Do we trust my visions completely then?" Ravenhurst asked. "I confess, I am not always entirely confident. I can't even explain why they happen."

"They haven't steered you wrong yet, have they?"

"I don't think so. I only wish this…ability was more reliable or that I understood it better." Again, he sounded understandably frustrated. "I do wonder if it will disappear entirely when I am fully recovered. The doctor said it could be several months before my headaches eased."

"We should go downstairs," Tilda said, thinking he needed to rest, at least for a short while. "Perhaps there is some tea in the kitchen, though I believe we gave what was left to the cook and the maid."

"I'd rather go through the rest of the house and see what I may learn."

Tilda frowned at him. "I don't think that's wise. Your head is already aching. You can come back another day. I'll meet you so you don't have to break into the house," she added wryly.

He smiled. "I do appreciate your concern, but my head is feeling better. I should like to attempt at least one more room. The study probably, since that is likely where Sir Henry spent the most time aside from his bedchamber."

"That or the parlor. But start with the study. That way, I can search it one more time. Perhaps there's an IOU stuck at the back of a drawer in his desk." She turned and walked from the bedchamber.

She heard the earl following behind her as they made their

way downstairs. "What do you suppose Sir Henry has to do with a woman who perchance died decades ago and with the man who attacked you?"

"I can't begin to guess," Ravenhurst replied. "The other question burning in my mind is why someone stabbed me, Crawford, and Sir Henry. I think we can agree that Sir Henry did not die of a heart attack."

Tilda paused at the bottom of the stairs and turned to look up at him. She hadn't wanted to make the conclusion just yet, but that was what she believed. "Yes, we can agree. I suppose that means we can also agree that he was likely murdered."

Ravenhurst stood a few stairs above her. "I think so."

She cocked her head. "Do you suppose there's a chance Crawford is one of the men in the photograph?"

"He would have been too young. If that photograph is from the 1830s—using the era of the clothing the woman in my vision was wearing—Patrick Crawford would have been a young man. I suppose he could be one of the blurred figures on the left." He inclined his head. "It is an interesting theory."

Turning, Tilda continued toward the study. "I hope we're able to review Inspector Padgett's reports. We need to find your assailant. He is what connects you to Sir Henry."

"I am frustrated by whatever is happening at Scotland Yard," Ravenhurst said, his tone hard. "Padgett didn't conduct a thorough investigation and the confidentiality of the reports is highly suspect. I wonder if he is not tainted in some way, especially since you said corruption is rampant in the police."

"You may be right, but as I keep saying when it comes to the police, we need to tread carefully." Tilda wanted to believe they were all as honest and well-meaning as her father. No, it wasn't that she wanted to believe they were. She wanted them to *be* that way. It occurred to her that she ought not to bribe anyone anymore, not if she wanted to be true to her father's legacy.

"I understand," Ravenhurst replied. "But that doesn't make

me less irritated." He flashed her a smile that make her belly tickle. "We could start our search for my assailant at the Bell. It's on Fish Street Hill."

"Excellent." Tilda felt a surge of excitement. She was glad to have no more secrets between her and the earl. "Between your gift and my investigative skills, we will find him."

"It is not a gift but a curse," Ravenhurst said with considerable bitterness. "If given the choice, I would rather we solve this case using *our* investigative skills."

She did not miss his use of the word *our* and was surprised to find she didn't mind having him as a partner, or at least an assistant. "Are you just going to start touching everything now?"

"I suppose so." His mouth tipped into a lop-sided smile. "Do you see how this makes me look entirely mad?"

Suppressing a giggle, Tilda began searching the study. In the end, she found nothing and Ravenhurst's explorations were completely unfruitful. Tilda thought that may be for the best since his head was still paining him.

Ravenhurst's coachman had returned, and the earl insisted on driving Tilda home. They secured the house with plans to return, perhaps the next day.

"We have a great many things to do, it seems," Ravenhurst remarked as the coach moved along Huntley Street.

"We do indeed," Tilda agreed. "We still need to call on Mr. Hardacre. However, our first priority must be locating your assailant. When shall we visit the Bell?"

"I wondered if you might want to go this evening," he suggested. "I imagine the alehouse is busy on a Saturday night. It may even be that the assailant is there."

"You would recognize him?" she asked.

"Perhaps. I saw his eyes clearly, but he wore a covering over the rest of his face."

"So you must get very close to everyone and look them in

the eye," Tilda said with a laugh. "This could be rather diverting."

He smiled. "I shall endeavor to amuse you. You've a most charming laugh."

Tilda appreciated the compliment. She didn't think anyone had ever commented on her laugh. "All right, we will go this evening. What shall I tell my grandmother?"

"That I am taking you to a play?" he suggested.

"No, I must tell her I've gone to play cards with friends." A play would encourage her grandmother to think there may be more between Tilda and Ravenhurst when he was merely her client. And, apparently, her friend. "You will need to pick me up on Bulstrode Street."

"Eight o'clock?"

Tilda nodded. How exciting her life had suddenly become.

CHAPTER 13

*H*adrian's coach was parked and waiting on Bulstrode Street well before eight that evening. He wasn't going to risk Miss Wren being out alone. As it was, he'd considered walking to meet her, but he'd settled for parking near the corner, and Leach, his coachman, had assured him that he could see Miss Wren the moment she departed her house and walked toward them.

She arrived at the coach at a minute past. Hadrian heard Leach greeting her, then the door opened, and she climbed inside. She took the forward-facing seat, which Hadrian had left for her.

"Good evening, my lord." Her gaze assessed him briefly as she arranged her dark gray cloak about her ebony skirts. She wore the same small black hat she'd worn to the funeral, with the addition of a rather stunted feather atop her red-gold hair, which was fashioned into a simple style.

"Good evening, Miss Wren. Ready for our adventure in the east?" he asked as the coach began to move.

She smiled, her features alight with enthusiasm. "I'm quite

looking forward to it, actually. I rarely do anything this exciting."

"What about going to plays?" he asked, referencing his earlier suggestion for what she might tell her grandmother was her destination this evening.

"On a very rare occasion. I've been to the theatre just two or three times."

He could imagine it was not within her budget to do so. He wondered at her unmarried state and had to assume it was by choice. She was attractive, intelligent, and could clearly run a household. "I'd be delighted to escort you sometime—along with your grandmother. If we went alone, people may think we are courting." He smiled.

Miss Wren's gaze snapped to his. There wasn't a hint of amusement in her expression. "But we are not courting."

"No," he agreed, regretting the jest. He hadn't meant to make her uncomfortable. "I confess I am surprised you aren't wed." And that comment was somehow better? This was a moment in which Hadrian's curiosity had the better of him.

"I'm satisfied as a spinster," she replied. "My grandmother hopes I might fall in love and marry as she did, but I've no interest in such things." A mild shudder passed over her, giving evidence to not only a lack of interest but perhaps an active distaste.

"You never considered marriage? Not ever?" He wasn't sure he'd ever met a woman who hadn't.

"Do you find that odd?" She sounded surprised. "My parents weren't particularly happy together. I suppose that didn't encourage the matrimonial state in my view."

Hadrian nodded. "Mine did not enjoy wedded bliss either."

"You still haven't told me about the mistake you avoided," she said expectantly.

"True." He inclined his head. Though he rarely spoke of that time, he didn't mind telling Miss Wren about it. "I was betrothed several years ago. I caught Beryl, my fiancée, in a... compromising position with another man. We decided it was best to end our betrothal. She married the other man—Chambers—instead, and I am grateful I was not trapped in what would surely have been an unhappy union."

Hadrian had believed he loved her. They hadn't shared a grand, romantic, all-encompassing passion, but he'd held great affection for her and believed they would get on well together. How wrong he'd been. "I've since decided I am content as a bachelor, so I do understand your satisfaction with spinsterhood."

"Well, if we don't make the perfect situation for friendship between a man and a woman, I don't know what would."

"You make an excellent point. We *are* friends then?" He hoped so.

"Yes, as well as professional associates." Her gaze moved over his clothing. "You're dressed very simply this evening. Are those even your garments?"

Hadrian glanced down. "They are not, actually. I didn't want to look like an earl. My valet quickly assembled something from his own wardrobe. He's a trifle thicker than I am through the middle, so he nipped the pants in at the waist, and the waistcoat has pins at the back."

She appeared impressed. "How enterprising of him."

"I should blend in better with the patrons of the Bell in this costume."

"I daresay I already blend in with this horrid gown." She looked down at her dress and made a face. "No one would mistake me for a lady from the west end. Not until I speak, anyway."

"Should we alter the way we speak?" he asked.

Miss Wren shrugged. "I can approximate a Cockney accent, though that's a little farther east than where we're going." She slipped into it just then, and he was impressed by her yet again.

"I don't think I can do that." He didn't even try. "Perhaps I'll let you do most of the talking."

She arched a brow at him. "Do you think you can? I've noticed you sometimes can't contain yourself."

He chuckled. "That is a fair assessment. My curiosity often controls my mouth. I will endeavor to be more cautious." Sobering, he wanted to make sure they were both cautious about everything, not just their speech. "We are hoping to find my assailant—a man who has killed, if our theory is correct. We must be on our guard. Did you bring your pistol?"

"I did." She clutched her reticule, which sat on her lap, more tightly. "And yes, we must be vigilant. If we find him at the Bell, it may be easier to question him as it's a public place. However, if we can at least obtain his direction, it may behoove us to verify where he lives then return with Inspector Lowther."

"Or Inspector Teague," Hadrian said. "He has become invested in these investigations. Due to my incessant questioning, I'm sure." He chuckled again.

"Either would be fine," Miss Wren said. "I did like Teague's manner when he came to Sir Henry's house the other day after Vaughn was attacked." She glanced toward his pocket. "I plan to use the ring to identify your attacker. Perhaps someone at the Bell has seen him wear it."

"Brilliant," Hadrian said.

They arrived at Fish Street Hill a short while later. Hadrian departed the coach and helped her down. The coachman would await them, but Hadrian had no idea how long they'd be.

Hadrian escorted Miss Wren toward the river and into the Bell, which was bustling with patrons. He immediately looked toward the table where he'd seen the vision of Sir Henry and pointed it out to Miss Wren. They could not sit there, however, as it was occupied.

Instead, they moved toward the bar where a grizzle-faced man in his fifties was serving ale. Hadrian caught the man's attention and asked for two pints.

The barkeep fetched the ale and set the glasses in front of Hadrian and Miss Wren. Hadrian paid the man more than the ale cost and looked toward Miss Wren.

"We're lookin' for a particular bloke," she said in her impressive Cockney accent. "Got somethin' what belongs to 'im."

Hadrian removed the ring from his pocket and showed it to the barkeep. "Tall fellow with a long face and wide-set dark eyes." That was about all Hadrian could say to describe his assailant.

The barkeep studied the ring in Hadrian's palm. "I dunno the man, but there's a chap who comes in sometimes to see Moll, one of the barmaids. She's mentioned him complainin' about havin' lost a ring. Ye could ask her about it."

"Where's Moll then?" Miss Wren asked before glancing about the common room.

"The red-haired one in the green dress over there." The barkeep gestured toward one of the tables where a curvaceous young woman laughed as she stood next to a table of rowdy men.

Hadrian froze. He'd seen that face before. The first day he'd touched the ring and seen visions, she was one of the people he'd seen.

"Thank ye," Miss Wren said to the barkeep with an appreciative smile. Indeed, there was an air of flirtatiousness about it, something he'd never seen from her before. What was she doing?

They turned from the bar, and Miss Wren took his arm. He steered them away from Moll and the table of men. "I know her," Hadrian whispered urgently. "Not her, but her face."

Miss Wren locked her eyes with his. "In a vision?"

Hadrian nodded. "The first day I had them, I saw her, but I didn't know who she was."

"Then we can surmise she definitely knows the man who was wearing that ring." Mis Wren's eyes gleamed with anticipation.

"My assailant," Hadrian said grimly, his pulse hammering.

"Just so." Miss Wren sipped her ale and wrinkled her nose.

Hadrian sampled his and decided it was worse than when he last visited. "Why did you smile at the barkeep like that? Were you flirting with him?"

"I'm playing a role, and that includes charming the barkeep. It is a useful skill in conducting investigations."

"You are rather good at it. Not just being charming." Though she was particularly good at that, and he found himself wishing it was directed at him. Was he jealous? Perhaps a little. "The role-playing in general. You were excellent at Dr. Selwin's and tonight, you are nothing short of marvelous with that accent."

She blushed. "I have been conducting investigations for about four years now. I am glad to hear that I have some measure of skill."

"You do indeed. I am most fortunate to have made your acquaintance."

Moll left the table of men and moved behind the bar where she spoke with the barkeep for a moment. Then she came directly over to them. "I'm Moll. I 'ear you wanted to speak with me?" She most definitely had a Cockney accent.

Miss Wren smiled at the barmaid. "Evenin', Moll. My friend 'as a ring what may belong to someone you know."

"Lemme see," Moll said, pivoting slightly to look at Hadrian.

He held the ring out on his gloved palm once more. Moll picked it up and squinted at the gold. "That an M?"

"Yes," Hadrian said.

Moll nodded and dropped the ring back onto Hadrian's

glove. "Looks like the one Fitch used to wear but he lost it awhile back—some time after Epiphany, I think."

Hadrian exchanged a look with Miss Wren. That timing aligned with when he was attacked, which was a couple of weeks after Epiphany.

"Ye know Fitch well then?" Miss Wren asked.

"Aye," the barmaid replied. "We spend some time together now and again."

"Do you know where 'e lives?" Miss Wren flashed a coin at the woman. "We'd like to return the ring."

Moll took the coin and tucked it into the pocket of her patched gown. "'E lodges over the cheesemonger up on East Cheap. Just past Pudding Lane. On the first floor overlookin' the street. 'E may not be there, as 'e's out most nights, but ye can try."

Miss Wren cocked her head and squinted one eye at Moll. "Is 'e a friendly sort, or will 'e not take too kindly to us showin' up at 'is door?"

"Depends on 'ow much 'e's 'ad to drink," Moll said with a faint curl of her lip. "Jes tell 'im straightaway ye 'ave 'is ring, and 'e'll be thrilled. Losing it made 'im right angry, said it was a special gift."

"Do ye know who from?" Miss Wren asked.

Moll shook her head. "'E wouldn't say. Fitch was private-like about his work. Doesn't like to talk about it. Doesn't like to talk much at all," she added with a glint in her eye and a heated smile.

"Do you know what kind of work he does?" Hadrian desperately wanted to know the answer to this question. Was it possible someone had hired him to attack Hadrian, or perhaps more accurately, to kill Crawford?

"Why does it matter?" Moll asked almost crossly. "Ye're askin' a load of questions."

"Jes curious is all," Miss Wren said with a wave of her hand.

"My cousin likes to talk." She sent Hadrian a quelling glance. He nodded almost imperceptibly in response.

Miss Wren gave Moll a wide smile. "Thank ye, Moll. We appreciate yer 'elp."

Tucking her hand around Hadrian's arm, Miss Wren pulled him toward the door. He opened it for her as she stepped outside and followed her into the brisk night. A stiff breeze whipped around them, and Miss Wren pulled her cloak more tightly around her.

"My apologies," Hadrian said. "I was only trying to learn as much as we could."

"I know you were," Miss Wren replied without a trace of Cockney. "But it was clear to me that she doesn't know the specifics of Fitch's work."

"I thought so too, but I wanted to make every effort."

Miss Wren pivoted away from the river, and they started up Fish Street Hill toward East Cheap. "Do we think Fitch is the man we're looking for?" she asked.

"He must be, particularly since I recognized Moll from a vision."

She sent Hadrian a fiery look. "I am most eager to question him."

Hadrian paused and touched her elbow, drawing her to stop. He turned toward her. "But should we? Perhaps we should return with Teague now that we know where Fitch lives."

"We could, but you heard what Moll said. Fitch may not even be home, in which case we could search his lodgings." Her eyes glittered with excitement, and it was most infectious.

"That would be most helpful." Still, he wanted to be very cautious. "We must be prepared for violence."

She lifted her reticule slightly. "I will have my pistol at the ready when we knock on his door. Perhaps I should do the talking again. I'll do as Moll suggested and inform him from outside the door that I have his ring. I'll also say that Moll sent me."

Hadrian wondered why he hadn't thought to bring his own pistol. "As soon as he opens the door, he's likely to recognize me." Hadrian frowned.

She was quiet a moment, her features pensive. "We should have thought of that. I don't think you can come with me."

"What?" Hadrian's heartbeat was already fast with anticipation but now it jumped into a near panic. "Absolutely not. You can't face a killer on your own."

"You can stand just out of sight," she said far too reasonably. How did she not appear even slightly agitated? "Let us assess the situation. If we can't do this safely, we'll leave and return with Teague."

"I'm thinking we should do that straightaway," he said, though with less heart than he ought to have. The truth was that he wanted to confront his attacker, and he was very close to doing that.

Her brow creased, and the way her lips pressed together, he could tell she was thinking. "What we are most hoping to learn is *why* Fitch attacked you, killed Crawford, and how he knows Sir Henry. Given where he lives and what we learned of him from Moll, I think it's logical to deduce that he did not act without direction."

"No, I don't think he did. Why go all the way to Westminster to stab people?"

"Except we must consider that his motive was indeed theft since he stole items from Crawford. Perhaps he didn't steal from you because you'd surprised him by fighting back."

"But why stab me without even asking for my valuables?" Hadrian argued. "And why kill Crawford?"

She shrugged. "Perhaps he's bloodthirsty?" Exhaling, she shook her head. "That was somewhat in jest. All right, we believe he was carrying out a directive from someone else. *That* someone is our true villain."

Hadrian experienced a thrilling jolt. "*Yes.*" His mind worked quickly. "What if I offer to compensate him for telling us who directed him to stab me?"

Miss Wren started walking toward East Cheap once more. "Whilst I'm sure Fitch would be eager to take your money, we can't trust what he will say. He may misdirect us. We must assess the situation when we arrive."

"You make an excellent point." Hadrian was gladder than ever to be in her company.

They passed several people, some with their heads down as they went about their business. One trio was loud and jolly as they staggered past.

They turned onto East Cheap, and Hadrian noted Pudding Lane was just up ahead. As they neared the intersection, he saw the sign for the cheesemonger's shop. It was the second storefront after Pudding Lane.

"Where do you suppose the entrance is to the lodgings above the shop?" Hadrian asked as they approached the cheesemonger.

"I shall hope it's just to the side of the store entrance. Otherwise, it may be in an alley behind the building."

They were fortunate because it was indeed to the right of the cheese shop entrance. Hadrian opened the door, and the hinges creaked. A stairwell rose before them. It was dark, save the light from the street lamp filtering in through the open door.

"I am making a mental notation to carry a candle and matches for our future endeavors," Miss Wren said.

"A wise plan. For now, let us leave the door open for the meager light we can glean from the lamp outside. Can you see well enough to go up?"

"I believe so." She put her hand against the wall as she climbed the stairs and moved slowly. "My eyes are adjusting."

He followed just behind her, ready to catch her should she misstep. But she made it to the landing without incident.

There were two doors on the landing. The one on the left clearly led to the lodging that faced the street. And it was ajar.

Hadrian grabbed Tilda's arm. "The door," he whispered.

She nodded. "I see," she replied, her voice barely audible. She removed the pistol from her reticule.

There was a noise in the lodging that sounded like a piece of furniture moving. A muffled curse followed. Then the door opened wider, and a young man rushed out.

Upon seeing them, his eyes rounded. "I didn't do anythin'! He were like that when I got here!" He pushed past them, nearly stumbling down the stairs in his haste.

"Wait!" Hadrian called, the young man's words settling into Hadrian's brain: *he were like that when I got here.*

Like what? A chill ran down Hadrian's spine.

He exchanged a charged look with Miss Wren. "Tread carefully," she whispered, lifting her pistol.

The other door opened to reveal a petite woman with a mess of dark hair pinned atop her head. "Wot's the racket?"

"You may want to go back inside," Miss Wren said with barely a glance toward the woman. Miss Wren's focus was entirely on the open door of Fitch's lodging.

Hadrian stayed close to Miss Wren as she crossed the threshold into Fitch's room, for it was a single room.

"Oh no." Miss Wren gestured to a small table near the window that overlooked the street below.

"Bloody hell." Hadrian left her side and strode to the table where a body was seated in a chair and hunched over onto the table. He quickly removed his gloves and stuffed them into his pocket.

Grimacing, he grasped the back of the corpse's collar and

lifted his head, heaving him back against the chair. Hadrian shuddered as recognition gripped him. The man's lips were slightly apart, his eyes open and unseeing. "That's the man who attacked me."

"You're certain?"

Hadrian hated the shaft of terror that ripped through him as he recalled the moment of the blade slicing into his side. "Yes. I won't ever forget his eyes."

CHAPTER 14

Tilda's gaze moved down Fitch's neck. "I'd say the cause of death is obvious."

"Garrote," Ravenhurst said grimly.

"Death?" This was followed by a high-pitched shriek from behind them.

They both turned. The neighbor stood just inside the threshold, her hand pressed her to her mouth. That was all Tilda could make out from this distance in the dark. They needed illumination.

"He's dead?" the neighbor asked, lowering her hand.

"Yes. Would you fetch a constable, please?" Ravenhurst asked. There was a tremor in his voice that Tilda had never heard before.

The neighbor dashed out, and Tilda realized they would need to take advantage of whatever time they had before the police arrived. She tucked her pistol back into her reticule.

"We haven't much time," she said, looking about for a candle or lantern. The room didn't have much, and it had been pillaged. The drawers of the dresser were pulled out. One was even on the floor. The mattress sat askew on the bed frame.

Hurrying to the small hearth, she found a candlestick and a few matches. She lit the wick and carried it to where Ravenhurst stood over the dead man.

"Grisly," she breathed as a shiver rippled through her. She set the candlestick on the table. "The police will be here soon. We should search the room before they do. More importantly, you need to employ your gift, your *curse*, to see what you can learn. Touch everything. Starting with him, I suppose."

The earl put his hand to Fitch's head, starting at the top then moving his fingertips down behind his ear to his neck. Ravenhurst took a deep breath and slid his fingers forward until he touched the wound. She noted that his eyes were still open.

"You don't need to close your eyes to see visions?" she asked.

"No," he replied, his voice husky. "In fact, closing my eyes seems to prevent them from happening."

Tilda watched him closely and realized she was holding her breath. She let it out and tried to calm herself. This was her first time discovering a dead body. It was both exhilarating and terrifying. How she wished she could talk to her father about it. The old but familiar pain of loss swept through her.

"I can't see or feel anything," Ravenhurst said. "Perhaps this curse doesn't work when I touch a dead person."

"That's a shame." Tilda turned to survey the ransacked room. "I daresay someone has already searched this room."

Ravenhurst moved away from the body. "It does look that way. I wonder if they took anything."

"I don't suppose we would know. Let's see what we can find. I'll search, you touch."

Ravenhurst nodded. Besides the pulled apart dresser and the tumbled bed, there was a cabinet and a threadbare chair that was lying on its side near the hearth. He went to the cabinet.

Tilda strode to the dresser. The top drawer was only slightly open. She pulled it farther out and searched the contents. It contained just clothing which had been shoved to one side. The second drawer had more of the same plus a few linens, all in a tangle. There was also a small pouch that clanked as if there were coins inside.

She emptied the contents into her palm. "I found a small amount of money. If the murderer was a thief, he ignored a few pounds." She tipped the coins back into the pouch and replaced it in the drawer.

The third drawer was empty on the floor, and the bottom drawer was sideways and also empty.

"Nothing of interest here, save the money," she said, turning from the dresser. "It's odd the killer would leave money unless that wasn't what he was after." She moved toward the bed.

"I'd like to find the knife Fitch used to stab me," Ravenhurst said from the cabinet. "There are utensils here, a few bowls, a platter, a jug of ale, and some cups. No knives, not even one he might use to eat with."

"Can you help me lift this mattress?"

Ravenhurst joined her. "I'll lift, you look."

She bent at the waist and surveyed the ropes strung across the bed. "Nothing. And I don't see anything beneath the bed either."

"I wish we could find the knife," Ravenhurst said with a frown. "It would be excellent evidence."

"We wouldn't be able to prove it was the knife he used, but if he had one, it would support your identification of him." She met his eyes, which looked somewhat frenzied. "Your confidence that he attacked you is very solid evidence."

Ravenhurst's gaze moved to the dresser. "Where's the money you found?"

Tilda fetched the pouch, and he followed. She handed it to him quickly, afraid they were nearly out of time.

Reaching inside he pulled out a coin. His forehead creased, and a grimace passed over his features.

"You see something," she whispered.

"There's a man." The earl's eyes seem to focus on something, but it was just the dark corner. "He's well dressed, but I can only see his back."

Tilda was holding her breath again. Exhaling, she waited patiently for him to say more. At length, he set the coin on the top of the dresser.

"That's all I get," he said as he reached into the pouch once more. He withdrew another coin. Nothing seemed to happen.

"The police will be here at any moment." Tilda strained to listen for footfalls on the stairs.

Scowling, Ravenhurst deposited the coin on the dresser next to the first one and took out a third coin.

The earl's eyes rounded, and his nostrils flared. Then he gasped. His jaw tightened, and he pressed his free hand to his temple.

Tilda wanted to ask what he was seeing but she didn't want to disrupt him. She also wanted to ease his pain for she could see this was hurting him.

"Careful, Raven." She realized she hadn't finished his name but that was because he'd gasped again.

"I can't," he said, breathless. "Take it."

Plucking the coin from his palm, Tilda smoothed her other hand along his forehead and temple. "Easy now," she murmured, gently cupping the side of his head. "Do you need to sit?'

"One moment." He breathed heavily and closed his eyes. His head pressed against her hand as if he were seeking the comfort she was offering.

Then he wobbled, and Tilda moved her hand to clutch his elbow. "Steady," she said softly.

"I saw Sir Henry," Ravenhurst said darkly. He opened his eyes and fixed on her.

Before he could say more, Tilda heard someone on the stairs. "They're coming." She tucked the coin into her reticule then hastened to return the coins from the top of the dresser to the pouch, which she took from Ravenhurst. She wanted the police to find everything as it was.

Minus that one coin, which she and Ravenhurst may need again at some point.

Tilda barely dropped the pouch into the drawer before the constable appeared at the doorway.

The man stepped into the room, his hand gripping a club like Tilda's father. "I'm Police Constable Barker." He was close to thirty with dark facial hair along his jawbone. His nose was short and blunt, his eyes round and apprehensive. "I've been told there's a murder."

The neighbor stood at the doorway but didn't come in.

"It appears that way," Tilda replied. "I am an investigator. My client, Lord Ravenhurst, and I came to speak with Mr. Fitch. However, he has been the victim of a garrote."

Barker moved closer, his gaze wary. "An investigator, you say? Never heard of a lady investigator." He looked toward Ravenhurst. "Evening, my lord. Is what she says true?"

"It is," the earl said with a clipped tone. "Miss Wren is investigating a matter that the Metropolitan Police's A Division closed prematurely. I was stabbed by this man." He pointed at Fitch's body.

The constable's eyes rounded. "Bloody hell. Pardon me, my lord. You're sure it was him?"

Ravenhurst's gaze was haughty. He'd never looked more like an earl. "Completely."

Nodding, the constable looked about the room. "Was the place like this when you arrived?"

"Yes," Tilda replied. "The door was ajar."

"There was someone else 'ere," the neighbor called out.

Barker turned his head toward her. "You saw someone else here?"

"No, but I 'eard 'im. Least, I don't think it was one of these two."

Redirecting his attention to Tilda and Ravenhurst, Barker asked, "Was there someone else?"

"There was," Tilda said with a nod. She described how they found the door ajar and then described the young man who'd rushed out of Fitch's room.

Barker stopped her part way so he could take notes. He stuffed his club into his belt then took a notebook and pencil from his coat. He asked Tilda to start over then scribbled in the notebook.

"There will be an inquest," Barker said. "You'll both be called to testify, I'm sure." Probably not tomorrow as it's Sunday. I would say Monday is most likely."

"Certainly," Tilda said. "We'll be on our way if you don't need anything else. If so, you know how to find us." She and Ravenhurst had provided their full names as well as their direction. She hadn't been surprised to learn the earl lived on Curzon Street in the heart of Mayfair. His house was likely old and large and very elegant.

They didn't speak until they were outside on East Cheap. There, they passed two more constables who hurried into Fitch's building. Ravenhurst massaged his head as they walked toward Fish Street Hill.

"Are you all right?" Tilda asked. She recalled the catch in his voice earlier, and he'd seemed just...off since they'd found Fitch. "I know it can be jarring to find a dead body."

He looked over at her. "You know this from experience?"

"Er, no. But my father found many in his days working for the police, and he never really became accustomed to it."

"It's more than that," Ravenhurst said, his tone ragged.

"Seeing Fitch again, even dead…it took me back to the night he stabbed me. It all happened so fast. I didn't have a chance to feel afraid. Tonight, I felt a terror I've never experienced." He stopped and she did too. His eyes met hers, and they were dark with emotion. "Though he was dead, I realized this was the man who'd nearly killed me. He irrevocably changed my life, and not just because what he did to me triggered this horrible curse."

She could see he was shaking. Overwhelmed by concern and a slight fear of her own, Tilda touched his arm. "You are here, and you are safe." It seemed simple to say that, but it also seemed right.

He blinked. "I know. I just didn't grasp how much the attack affected me."

"It's completely understandable." Tilda curled her hand around his arm, clasping him tightly as she guided him to continue walking, slowly, to the corner where they turned onto Fish Hill Street.

"It's bloody infuriating," he growled. Tilda could feel the rage emanating from him. "I think I also realized that since Fitch was already dead, I wouldn't find the answers I seek, that I *need*. Nor would I have justice."

Tilda was upset by that too. "I'm sorry, Ravenhurst. You deserve that."

"And I'll still have it." His gaze found hers once more as they walked. "We will find the true villain—whoever hired Fitch to stab me and kill Crawford."

"As well as however Sir Henry is connected to this." Tilda was more committed than ever to discovering the truth.

"Sir Henry is the key, I think." Ravenhurst's voice changed. The anger gave way to a bright enthusiasm. "I didn't finish telling you about what I saw."

"You don't have to now," Tilda said, though she was desperate to hear. She didn't want to overtax him.

"I must." He glanced at her once more. "You need to know what I know."

Tilda smiled. She had told him something like that. "Yes."

"I definitely saw Sir Henry when I touched that coin. He was lying on the floor looking up, his eyes wide, his lips moving."

"Could you hear him?" Tilda didn't know if he heard anything when he saw these visions.

"No, I don't hear sound. God, I think that would be even more terrifying." He exhaled. "Sir Henry looked pale." Ravenhurst moved his left hand to his right side. "His hand was pressed to his side like this. That's about where I was stabbed."

Now it was Tilda's turn to gasp. She lifted her hand to her mouth. Though they'd suspected this, to hear this was how Sir Henry had died was still shocking. That was *if* they trusted the earl's visions.

"The carpet beneath him was distinctive," Ravenhurst continued. "It was a muted brown with dark red flowers with gold centers. I'd know it if I saw it."

"That's good," Tilda said. "But we need real evidence. Your visions, however helpful, don't help us prove anything." Her mind worked as she ruminated what their next move should be. "Now that we know Fitch also stabbed Sir Henry, we need to visit the place he was killed."

"We need to find out where that is."

"I will call on Millicent tomorrow and ask. In fact, Vaughn may even know," Tilda realized. "I will ask him when I get home."

They arrived at the location where Ravenhurst's coachman had left them—and the coach was already there. The coachman said he was growing concerned when they hadn't returned.

"All is well," Ravenhurst said with a smile that didn't quite reach his eyes. He helped Tilda into the coach, and she took the rear-facing seat.

"You are always supposed to sit facing forward," the earl said as he climbed inside.

"Not tonight," she said with a shake of her head.

"I don't mind facing backward," he mumbled.

Tilda swallowed a smile. Once they were moving, she asked, "Can we conclude that Fitch killed Crawford? We know he stabbed you and killed Sir Henry."

"I think we can," Ravenhurst replied with confidence. "I am all but certain I was stabbed by mistake." His blue eyes were animated, glittering in the light from the lamp hanging on the side of the coach, his jaw set with determination. "I believe Fitch was looking for Crawford the night he stabbed me."

"You said Crawford walked the same street you were on that night on his way to a weekly card game and that you and he share the same coloring and build. You think Fitch mistook you for Crawford."

"Yes, and when he saw my face, he realized his mistake and fled. Perhaps he meant to steal from me as he did from Crawford."

"To try and make it look as though he were a footpad." She felt a wave of compassion for the man opposite her, a man she'd come to like and respect. "You were simply in the wrong place at the wrong time."

"Unfortunately," he said with deep irony. "Then, the very next Tuesday, Fitch located his quarry and completed the job he was likely assigned. We just need to determine who hired him and why."

Tilda kept trying to fit the loss of her grandmother's investment into this puzzle, but she wasn't sure where it fit. "I still don't understand how the potential embezzlement of my grandmother's funds figures into what happened to Sir Henry."

"We still need to interview Hardacre," Ravenhurst said. "We should do that Monday."

"Yes. I don't wish to put it off any longer. Will you come to see Millicent with me tomorrow? Then we can go directly to where Sir Henry was killed."

He muttered something that she thought may have been a curse. "I can't join you to call on Mrs. Forsythe. My mother comes for tea every other Sunday. It used to be monthly, but after my attack, she came weekly. I finally persuaded her that fortnightly would be sufficient."

"That's nice that she cares about you." Tilda wasn't sure her mother would be bothered to come visit her from Birmingham, even if Tilda had been stabbed. "I'll call on Millicent and fetch you when I'm finished."

"I'll look forward to it." His lips lifted in a half-smile, and it filled Tilda with a surprising warmth. She'd been quite worried about him.

"Please take good care this evening and tomorrow," she said. "And if you aren't up to going to the club tomorrow night, we can go on Monday." Though it would be torturous to wait.

Tilda supposed she could go without him, but after tonight's excitement, she realized she liked having someone with her. Not just anyone, but Ravenhurst. He valued her as an investigator, and he made her feel protected. No one had done that since her father had died.

Ravenhurst met her gaze. "I do appreciate your concern, but nothing will keep me from pursuing our investigation tomorrow."

"Good. I confess I didn't really want to go alone."

Now the earl smiled fully, and Tilda's belly fluttered again. "That pleases me greatly."

~

The following afternoon, Tilda caught a hack to Millicent's house near Bedford Square. She was a little tired as she'd tossed and turned, her mind awash with details of the investigation for some time before finding sleep. In truth, she'd also been thinking about Ravenhurst. She hoped he was able to sleep well. His revelations regarding the attack and the emotions he was feeling after finding Fitch were most affecting and remained with her.

She'd completed her initial invoice for her investigative services and expenses for the earl, but she hadn't brought it with her. It just hadn't seemed right to demand payment in the midst of his...turmoil. But she would soon, as the added income would be most welcome now that Vaughn had joined their household, at least temporarily.

Departing the hack, Tilda went to the door and was shortly admitted by Millicent's butler, a robust, younger man with pink cheeks and high brows. He took Tilda upstairs to the drawing room and said Mrs. Forsythe would be with her directly.

Tilda had sent a note earlier, so Millicent was expecting her. A moment later, a maid entered with a tea tray. She set it on a table near the settee.

Millicent entered, her black skirts gliding about her ankles. Tilda was nearly giddy with relief that today was the last day she needed to don mourning clothes. Tomorrow would mark a fortnight since Sir Henry's death, and Tilda could return to her normal wardrobe, thank goodness.

"It's good to see you, Tilda," Millicent said as she pressed a kiss to Tilda's cheek.

Tilda reciprocated, and they sat down whilst the maid poured out the tea. As the maid departed, Millicent put teacakes on two plates and handed one to Tilda.

"Do tell me how Vaughn is faring." Millicent said.

"Much better. We are having trouble keeping him abed, in fact. He can't seem to stop butlering."

Millicent laughed softly. "That is the Vaughn I know. I'm glad to hear it. I received a note from Cook yesterday, and she is all settled in her new position. Dora also sent a note. She's been offered a position in a noble household. She's over the moon."

"I'm delighted for her and not at all surprised," Tilda said with a smile. "She was incredibly helpful in emptying your father's house."

"I can't thank you enough for doing that. My husband met with a solicitor, not Whitley, on Friday, and the house will be sold, we hope, with due haste."

"I do hope there will be enough money to provide Vaughn with his retirement settlement," Tilda said.

Millicent looked down at her lap. "I don't think there will be. Belinda is demanding her share of whatever we have left over, and I doubt she will care to contribute to Vaughn's retirement. Unfortunately, I don't think I'll be able to convince my husband to do so either," she said quietly. "He is very angry about my father's mismanagement."

Tilda wanted to point out to both Millicent's husband and Belinda that Sir Henry's mismanagement was not Vaughn's fault, and he shouldn't be made to suffer. "Well, someone is going to need to take care of Vaughn."

"I am hoping you will yet find some of Papa's money or your grandmother's investment," Millicent said brightly, with perhaps a touch of naivete. "Have you learned anything more?"

"I have not. I haven't had a spare moment to continue my inquiries, but I will keep you apprised."

"My apologies," Millicent said after swallowing a bite of teacake. "You have been terribly busy, and that is my fault. I shall not pester you about the financial matters. I know you will do your best. You've such a keen mind."

"I will do my very best," Tilda vowed, thinking of Vaughn and that she would make sure he was cared for, even if she didn't know how at the moment. Though she still planned to speak with Hardacre, she doubted she'd be able to recover her grandmother's investment. "Millicent, I am concerned that your father may have lost the money on his own. Are you aware he liked to gamble and that he may have lost great sums?"

Millicent blanched. She'd picked up her tea, and the cup rattled in her saucer. "You didn't find more IOUs, did you?"

Tilda blinked. "I didn't find any. *Are* there IOUs?"

Setting the cup down without drinking from it, Millicent put her hands in her lap and worried her fingers. "I found several in the bottom drawer of Papa's desk. I thought we could pretend we didn't know they existed."

Apprehension gripped Tilda's chest. She dearly hoped Millicent hadn't destroyed them. "Do you still have them?"

Millicent nodded, and Tilda exhaled with relief. "I can fetch them now." She met Tilda's gaze. "Please don't be angry with me for keeping them from you. I was hoping they would just go away. It's not as if there's any money to pay them."

"I doubt they will go away," Tilda said softly. "But perhaps I can help you deal with them."

"Thank you. What would I do without you?" Millicent sniffed as she rose.

Tilda sipped her tea and ate her cake whilst Millicent was gone. The discovery of IOUs was not surprising, given the visions Ravenhurst had seen in Sir Henry's bedchamber.

Millicent returned and rejoined Tilda on the settee. "I'm sorry I didn't tell you about these. I should have done." She handed a small stack of papers to Tilda, her features etched with sorrow and concern. "I didn't realize my father was in such a terrible situation. It seems he was keeping a great deal from everyone—his financial situation and his health. Was there anything else we didn't know?"

Tilda decided now was not the right time to tell Millicent that her father had been murdered. "You have much to deal with right now, not the least of which is your grief." Tilda gave her an encouraging smile.

"You know what that feels like," Millicent said quietly as she picked up her teacup.

"I do indeed," Tilda replied. She put her attention to the IOUs lest she get caught up in the past. She had no time for that at present.

There were six IOUs for varying amounts. The smallest was sixty pounds to someone called Theodore Morehouse. There was another for one hundred and two pounds to Farringer's. Tilda looked over at Millicent. "Do you know what Farringer's is?"

Millicent paled slightly. She set her teacup down and smoothed her hands over her lap. "That is where my father died. It's a gaming club near Covent Garden."

Tilda's pulse quickened. She'd planned to ask about that after she reviewed the IOUs, but now she didn't have to. The date on the IOU from the club was from December. So, he was likely a regular customer. She reached over and patted Millicent's hand before continuing her review of the IOUs.

The rest were to gentlemen, but it was the last one that made Tilda swallow a gasp. It was for five hundred pounds to —Martin Crawford. He had to be related to Patrick Crawford. It was too much of a coincidence. She could hardly wait to show it to Ravenhurst.

"May I keep these?" Tilda asked. "I'm going to ask for Ravenhurst's advice on how to deal with them."

"Please do," Millicent said with another sniff. "I haven't the faintest idea what to do, and I'm afraid these people will seek repayment from my husband. I haven't even showed them to him. One of the reasons he is so upset about the lack of money is because my father apparently told him there would be an inheritance."

"I see. Did Sir Henry convey anything specific?"

Millicent shook her head. "No, and that is the source of some of my husband's frustration."

Tilda folded the IOUs and slipped them into her reticule. The final information she sought from Millicent would be most delicate, but it was important that Tilda ask.

"Millicent, I am sorry to ask you what I'm about to, but I'm afraid I must. I know it's a troubling subject. Could you describe for me the wound you saw on your father when you prepared him for the funeral?"

Now Millicent looked almost gray. Her lips quivered. "I don't like thinking of it. Not just the wound, but the entire ordeal. He was so pale and there was an odd smell about him." She put her hand to her nose and took a moment. Turning her head, she looked Tilda in the eye. "Why do you want to know about this?"

Tilda now didn't think she could avoid telling her the truth. She tried to speak as gently as possible. "Ravenhurst and I suspect your father may have been murdered. I don't want to say too much about that until we have more evidence, but this IOU to Farringer's will certainly help us." Tilda wasn't sure how yet, but she suspected it, and the Crawford IOU, were important pieces of evidence. At the very least, it connected Sir Henry to both entities, though he was already tied to Farringer's since he'd died there.

Millicent began to cry, and Tilda put her hand on the woman's shoulder. "I'm so sorry. I didn't mean to cause you upset," Tilda said. "I would not have asked if it wasn't vitally important."

Nodding, Millicent pulled a handkerchief from her pocket and dabbed at her eyes. "I know. You've been nothing but kind and helpful. I am so grateful." She wiped her nose and took a deep breath. "To be honest, I didn't look at the wound too closely. It had been stitched, and the thread was still there. The area around it was discolored."

"And where was it exactly?" Tilda asked, removing her hand from Millicent and placing it in her lap.

Millicent put her palm to her right side. "Here, where his ribs terminated."

"Thank you, Millicent. If you think of anything else, will you let me know?"

She met Tilda's gaze once more. "I will. I promise I'm not keeping anything else from you. And you'll tell me when you know more about what happened? Especially with the money?"

"Of course." Tilda would make sure that she and Ravenhurst called on Hardacre tomorrow. She needed to put more focus on the potential embezzlement—and see how, or if, it was tied to Sir Henry's murder.

CHAPTER 15

*H*adrian kept glancing at the clock, not that tea with his mother concluded at a specific time. More, he was wondering if Miss Wren was currently with her cousin and whether the visit would be fruitful. He was also not entirely sure when Miss Wren would arrive, but she'd sent a note earlier saying it would likely be close to five. He would make sure his mother was gone by then, for he'd no wish to introduce his mother to his private investigator. His mother would be scandalized that he'd hired a woman.

"You seem distracted today," Hadrian's mother, the dowager countess, noted from across the small, round table in the library. She possessed his same blue eyes, but the shape of her face was completely different. Her nose was short and slightly upturned, her chin round and small. She smiled easily, and where his father had been serious and intellectual, she was cheerful and typically in search of amusement. She enjoyed shopping, visiting museums, and frequenting the theatre. She also had a large group of friends with whom she took tea, dined, and played cards.

"My apologies," Hadrian said before taking another sip of tea. His cup was now empty, and he didn't plan to refill it.

"Is there something occupying your mind?" she prodded, her light-brown brows raised.

He replied with something that was somewhat true. "I returned to Westminster last week, and I've a great many things to catch up on." Which he'd been mostly ignoring in favor of his investigation with Miss Wren.

"That is understandable. I imagine your colleagues are glad to have you back."

"Indeed, though I am shocked that someone was attacked the week after me, and I didn't know about it." Hadrian probably ought not have mentioned that to his mother. He didn't wish to upset her, and she'd been most distressed after his attack.

Her brow creased, and she didn't meet his eyes. "I didn't think it would be helpful to your recovery to hear about that."

"You knew of it?" he asked.

She nodded. "Mrs. Crawford—Mrs. Martin Crawford, his mother—is a friend. Not a close one, but we circulate in the same groups. It was a terrible shock. As was your attack."

"Are you aware they both happened in the same place?"

"I'd heard Crawford's was in the vicinity of where you were attacked. Was it exactly the same? How peculiar."

"Indeed."

Hadrian's butler, Collier, entered. Tall with a rather forbidding brow, he possessed an air of solemnity that belied his penchant for ribald jests. "My lord, Miss Wren has arrived."

Damn. Hadrian hadn't expected her this early, else he would have instructed Collier not to announce her in that manner. The last thing he needed was his mother's interrogation regarding Miss Wren. Furthermore, his mother would now demand to meet her, and Hadrian hadn't warned Miss Wren that might happen.

The dowager fixed her blue eyes on Hadrian. "Who is Miss Wren?" She blinked expectantly.

"An associate," Hadrian responded. "She is helping me with an investigation. I can't say more than that, I'm afraid."

"*She* is an investigator? That is unusual."

Hadrian bristled at the emphasis she'd put on Miss Wren's sex. "Her father was with Scotland Yard, and her grandfather was a well-respected magistrate. I would say it is in her blood."

"Wren?" his mother asked. "That does sound familiar."

Hadrian rose. "Collier, please inform Miss Wren that I will be with her directly. The dowager and I are just finishing tea." He met the butler's gaze. "I require my hat and gloves as well as my overcoat."

"Yes, sir." Collier departed.

His mother stood from her chair. "I can see you are wanting me to leave, and I suppose we were finished with our tea. You'll at least permit me to meet Miss Wren?"

There was no avoiding that now. "Of course."

"And you are obviously leaving with her," his mother continued. "Where are you going?"

"I'm afraid I can't discuss it, Mother. I do hope you understand."

Her eyes narrowed as a worried expression commanded her features. "Is this to do with your attack? I know how eager you were to learn why it happened."

"I promise I'll explain in due time." He hoped he would be able to, meaning he and Miss Wren would have solved this complicated case.

Hadrian escorted his mother from the library through the family parlor and into the staircase hall. He looked to the right toward the entrance hall and saw Miss Wren.

The moment his mother stepped into the entrance hall ahead of him, Hadrian said, "Good evening, Miss Wren. Allow me to present my mother, the dowager Countess of Raven-hurst. Mother, this is Miss Matilda Wren."

His mother moved closer to Miss Wren and smiled. "I'm delighted to make your acquaintance, Miss Wren, though surprised. My son hasn't mentioned you or your association." She sent Hadrian a mildly accusatory glance.

Hadrian quashed the urge to roll his eyes. His mother was a gatherer and purveyor of information, which was to say, she was a gossip. There were reasons he didn't tell her things and what was more, she knew it.

Miss Wren dipped into a curtsey. As she rose, she gathered her dark gray cloak more closely in an apparent attempt to cover her gown. "It's my pleasure to meet you, my lady. I did not mean to arrive at an inopportune time." She sent a worried look toward Hadrian, and he gave her what he hoped was a slight but reassuring nod.

"Your timing is perfect," Hadrian said. "My mother was just leaving." He turned to the dowager and bussed her cheek. "Always a pleasure, Mother."

Collier appeared with her hat and gloves. She took the hat and set it atop her head then received the gloves. "Thank you, Collier." Looking to Hadrian, she said, "Perhaps next time, you can invite Miss Wren to tea so that we can become acquainted."

"I doubt she will be available, Mother," Hadrian replied. "Miss Wren is a busy woman."

His mother smiled at Miss Wren as she pulled on her gloves. "She can consider it and perhaps rearrange her sched-ule, if necessary."

Miss Wren merely returned her smile. But there was a nervous glint in her eyes.

Collier held the door, and Hadrian's mother departed. The butler then handed Hadrian his hat.

"I'm sorry if my mother made you uncomfortable," Hadrian said to Miss Wren as he donned his hat. "I hadn't meant for the two of you to meet. She is incurably and overwhelmingly inquisitive."

She regarded him with a faint smile, her eyes dancing with amusement. "That is where your curiosity comes from then."

Hadrian laughed. "Apparently."

"I should not have arrived so early," she said. "But I was rather eager to see you."

Her words filled him with a surprising heat. "It's quite all right. I trust you've news to share."

"I do, indeed." Her eyes glowed with ill-concealed excitement, and now Hadrian was overcome with anticipation. "First, tell me how you are."

"There is little a good night of sleep can't repair," he said, pleased that she would ask.

He took his gloves from Collier and quickly pulled them on then allowed the butler to help him with his coat. "Thank you, Collier. We'll be taking a hack." Leach had the night off.

Collier inclined his head and sent a brief smile toward Miss Wren. He then opened the door, and Hadrian escorted Miss Wren outside.

"I really am sorry I arrived so early," Miss Wren said with a shake of her head. "I wasn't thinking."

"Your impatience indicates you may have learned something helpful."

"Quite. First, we are on our way to Farringer's. It's a gaming club near Covent Garden."

"I've heard of it. Some of my colleagues go there." He hailed a hack and paid the driver to take them to Farringer's.

Once they were situated in the vehicle, they traveled toward Piccadilly via Half Moon Street.

Hadrian turned his head to the left to look at Miss Wren. "How was your visit with Mrs. Forsythe? Clearly, you obtained the name of the location of Sir Henry's death."

"It was very informative. As it happened, I didn't even have to ask about the location. I started by asking whether Sir Henry was a gambler, and she confessed that she'd found several IOUs."

"Several?" Hadrian stared at Miss Wren.

"Six in total, but the number is not the shocking part. Two of the debtors are most surprising. The first is Farringer's, which is how I learned that was where he died."

"And the second?" Hadrian held his breath.

"Martin Crawford. I assume he is a relation to Patrick Crawford?"

Hadrian had to snap his jaw closed. "His father." He sat back and let this information sink into his brain for a moment. "This links Sir Henry to the other murder victim. I think we can conclude Patrick Crawford was killed by Fitch, if we hadn't already."

"I agree," Miss Wren said as they traveled along Piccadilly. It was not quite five, but it was Sunday so while the traffic was brisk, it was not thick. They would arrive in Covent Garden relatively quickly, he should think.

She went on. "Lastly, I asked Millicent about her father's wound. She said the stitching was still present, and the flesh was discolored around it. The wound was located here, at the base of his ribs." Miss Wren pressed her hand to her right side.

"Precisely where I was stabbed." Hadrian's side twitched in recollection. "It seems Fitch had better aim with Crawford and Sir Henry."

"Didn't you grab him when he attacked you?" Miss Wren asked. "Perhaps your actions saved your life."

"It's possible. It's also possible that once he saw I wasn't his quarry, he fled before finishing the job." Hadrian was still thinking of the IOUs. "How much did Sir Henry owe Crawford?"

"Far more than he owed anyone else—five hundred pounds."

Hadrian gaped at her. "Good heavens, that's a sum."

"There was no date, so there's no telling how old it is. The others had dates, however. The one from Farringer's is from December, for one hundred and two pounds."

Hadrian was focused on the larger IOU at the moment. "Martin Crawford died last year—not long after the new year, I think. To loan Sir Henry such a large amount seems to indicate they knew each other well, don't you think?"

"I would assume so. You don't loan money to people you don't know, particularly a sum like that."

"I think we should call on Mrs. Patrick Crawford and perhaps Mrs. Martin Crawford as well," Hadrian said. "My mother and the elder Mrs. Crawford are social acquaintances. Can you believe my mother knew of Patrick Crawford's death and didn't tell me about it? She didn't want to upset me during my recovery."

Miss Wren hesitated before responding, "That was thoughtful of her, perhaps?"

"Would you not be annoyed if your parent had kept such information from you?" he asked drily.

"Touché. Although, my father would not have kept such a thing from me. He would understand my need to know," she said confidently.

"And your mother?"

"Since we only exchange letters monthly, I daresay she wouldn't tell me anything in a timely fashion for no other reason than she was otherwise engaged." Miss Wren lifted a shoulder. "We have never been very close, and I can't say that it bothers me. One does not miss what they never had."

Hadrian wasn't sure he believed that. There were many times he'd longed for a deeper connection with his father. But perhaps it was easier for Miss Wren to think of her mother in such terms. "I'm sorry to hear that. My mother can be an imposition sometimes, but we care for one another."

"When will you call on Mrs. Crawford?" Miss Wren asked, changing the subject, which was for the best—both because it had been verging on maudlin and because he was quite eager to focus on their investigation, which seemed to be picking up speed like a boulder rolling downhill.

"Perhaps tomorrow after we call on Mr. Hardacre?"

The hack stopped in front of Farringer's, and Hadrian stepped out of the vehicle. He helped Miss Wren down and nodded toward the driver.

Turning with Miss Wren, he surveyed the entrance. It was an unassuming establishment with wide windows on each side of the wooden door emblazoned with a gold H.

A footman in livery opened it for them as they approached. For all its styling as a "club," Farringer's appeared to be just a fancy gaming hell.

They stepped into what was likely supposed to be an elegant main room with chandeliers and mahogany tables and chairs. However, there was a worn quality to everything, as if it had looked quite splendid five or more years ago and was in need of refurbishment.

As it was early, there was hardly anyone about—just a few patrons and a liveried employee standing in the corner.

"Should we sit down?" Miss Wren murmured.

"I suppose we could. Then we could ask to speak with the proprietor."

"We should speak with as many people as possible."

"Agreed." Hadrian escorted her farther into the room. A man in a black coat and gold waistcoat entered from a doorway at the back.

"Good evening," the man said, with a polite smile. He was of average height with a sharp chin and narrow forehead. "Have you come for supper?"

"Yes." Hadrian decided that was as good a reason to be here as any, rather than immediately asking what he knew about a murder that had occurred here nearly a fortnight ago and had been covered up.

"And perhaps some cards or dice after," Miss Wren said with the hint of a mischievous smile.

Hadrian chuckled. "As the lady wishes."

The man led them to the doorway he'd just come through. They entered a dining room that looked slightly more polished than the main room. But the carpet! Hadrian recognized it immediately.

Miss Wren snapped her gaze to his. She must be wondering if it was the same as he'd seen in his vision. It certainly fit the description he'd given her.

He gave her a slight nod. "I do like this carpet," Hadrian said to the man taking them to a table.

"You'll also find it in our gaming rooms," the man said.

Sir Henry may not have been killed in this room then. Hadrian supposed it made more sense if he'd died in one of the gaming rooms since he'd been a gambler.

"Before we sit to eat, would you mind if we took a look at them?" Miss Wren asked. "The gaming rooms, I mean. I'm very curious. This is my first time in an establishment such as this." She blinked demurely, her demeanor one of suppressed excitement. She really was excellent at assuming a role.

"Of course," the man replied.

"Thank you," Hadrian said as they moved toward a different doorway than that which they'd entered. "Are you the proprietor?"

"The manager. My name is Dunwell. I work for Mr. Farringer."

They stepped into one of the gaming rooms. This one was clearly for dice and offered six different tables of play. Only one was occupied with players at the moment.

"Oh, splendid," Miss Wren said with glee. She glanced at the carpet, which matched that of the dining room.

"If you prefer cards, we've two rooms on the opposite side."

"I'd love to see them, if you don't mind." Miss Wren gripped Hadrian's left arm more tightly. Once Dunwell led them back into the main room, she leaned close and whispered, "Shouldn't you remove your gloves and touch something?"

Hell, of course he should. Hadrian took off his right glove and kept it in his left hand. As they moved through the main groom, he grazed his fingertips against a chairback. He felt exuberance and anticipation. He saw nothing.

By the time they reached the first card room, he'd touched several pieces of furniture but hadn't gleaned anything of import. Stepping into the card room, however, he had the sense he'd been there before. That was an altogether new sensation. There was no one present at the moment, which suited Hadrian.

It was a small room with four tables, set up for a tournament perhaps. He pulled Miss Wren toward one of the tables and put his palm atop the green baize covering the mahogany. Instantly, he felt an overwhelming number of sensations and saw a haze of figures. It was all too much, and pain streaked through his head. He pulled his hand away. This method of investigation was simply not going to work here.

"We came here because it was recommended to us by a friend," Hadrian said. "Sir Henry Meacham? Regrettably, he died here nearly a fortnight ago."

Dunwell had seemed reserved, but now his features seemed to shutter. "Oh yes, the man who collapsed."

"Was it in here?" Miss Wren asked.

"I can't recall. It was a sad situation. I'd rather not discuss it, if you don't mind."

"Terribly sorry," Hadrian said, frustrated to be shut down so quickly. "He was a good man. We are naturally curious as to how he met his end. His family members are most distraught."

"I can imagine." Dunwell's gaze flicked to Miss Wren's black costume but said nothing. Did he wonder if she was part of Sir Henry's family? Hadrian realized it would seem odd for a woman in mourning wear to be out to supper, let alone gambling.

Dunwell moved toward another door. "The other gaming room is through here."

"I do think I'm ready to eat, actually," Miss Wren said.

"Back to the dining room then," Hadrian turned with her toward the main room. Dunwell hastened to precede them and led them to the dining room once more, where he seated them at a table near the center of the room.

"Your waiter will be with you shortly." Dunwell disappeared into the main room.

"Well, that was disappointing," Miss Wren said.

"We couldn't have expected to walk in and learn that Sir Henry had been stabbed to death," Hadrian reasoned. "A false story was created and given to Scotland Yard. I have to think these employees must have been part of the lie."

"That is a great many people to keep quiet," Miss Wren noted as she glanced about the room. "Even if they contained the situation to that room, there had to have been witnesses."

"Except Fitch would have stabbed Sir Henry where there was likely no one to see him. What if the entire event was planned and concealed?"

Miss Wren's eyes rounded. "You mean Sir Henry was lured here to his death?"

"I'm merely discussing possibilities." Hadrian saw their waiter coming toward them, a young man in his middle-twenties with long sideburns.

"Evening," he said with a nod.

"Good evening," Hadrian said. "We'll have a bottle of claret."

"Right away, sir." The waiter took himself off.

"He does not know you are an earl," Miss Wren said quietly. There was a gleam of mischief in her eyes.

"Does that amuse you?"

"Perhaps a little. Does it bother you to not be addressed appropriately?"

"Not in the least. Now, I sent him to fetch wine so that he will have something to do whilst we ply him with questions." He gave her a pointed look. "I think you must play the bereaved relative, particularly since you are dressed that way."

"Oh, goodness, I shouldn't be dining out in mourning wear." She grimaced.

"I thought the same, but upon reflection, I hardly think it matters in a place such as this." He gave her a wry look.

The waiter returned and set about opening the wine.

Miss Wren looked up at the waiter, her expression sad. "I hope you won't think this odd, but we've come here tonight so that I may feel closer to my dear departed cousin. He died here recently."

The waiter dropped the wine opener onto the table. "I see." His voice seemed to have climbed.

"I don't suppose you were here that night?" Her gaze turned imploring. "I should love to speak with someone who saw him before he collapsed."

Hadrian gave her credit for using the story that had been concocted. He touched her arm. "There, there," he murmured in support.

She sent him a grateful glance before returning her attention to the waiter. "His name was Sir Henry Meacham. He was a genial fellow with more charm than a person had a right to possess. You would certainly recall meeting him. Please tell me you did. It would be such a comfort to me."

The waiter managed to pull the cork from the bottle, despite the slight tremor in his hands. It seemed evident to Hadrian that he was nervous. "I did see him that night, and he was most amenable. I'd met him before, of course."

"Of course," Miss Wren said smoothly. "I know he liked to

come here. He always had wonderful things to say about the hospitality and the dining service."

Again, Hadrian was impressed with her skills of flattery. The young waiter blushed faintly.

"I don't suppose you could tell me how he was before he collapsed?" Miss Wren asked. "It's only that we'd like to know he didn't suffer. His daughters would take particular comfort in that."

The waiter paled as he poured the wine into the glasses. His hand shook even more, and the neck of the bottle clacked against the rim of the second glass.

"It's all right," Hadrian said in a low tone. "We know Sir Henry's death may not have happened as was told."

Sucking in a breath, the young man snapped his gaze to Hadrian. "I'm not to speak of it. You'll put me in a great deal of trouble."

"We don't wish to do that," Miss Wren said softly.

"Talk to the doorman," the waiter whispered. "Gregson might be able to tell you more. But I cannot." He set the bottle on the table and rushed off before they could discuss ordering dinner. Not that Hadrian was interested in that, and he doubted Miss Wren was either.

"Shall we go and speak with the doorman?" he asked.

Miss Wren was already rising. "Directly."

Hadrian reached into his purse for money and set enough for the wine and a bit extra on the table. Then he stood and escorted her from the dining room. They moved quickly to the exit.

As soon as Hadrian opened the door, the doorman standing outside took over, holding it open as Miss Wren passed outside. Hadrian joined her, then they turned to face the doorman.

Hadrian hadn't noticed when they'd arrived that the man was a burly fellow with wide shoulders and legs like tree trunks. Even his hands were large. He looked more like a guard than a doorman, but perhaps he was both. An establishment such as Farringer's likely had need of someone who could enforce the peace when necessary.

"Good evening," Hadrian said affably. He decided not to waste any time or bother with prevarication. Reaching into his purse once more, he withdrew two pounds and handed them to the doorman. "I'm Lord Ravenhurst. There is more of that if you can answer my questions."

The man's eyes widened slightly, but he tucked the bills into his coat without comment. "Evening, my lord."

Hadrian spoke just above a whisper. "Gregson?" At the doorman's nod, Hadrian continued, "We understand you may have some information about the death that occurred here nearly a fortnight ago. Sir Henry Meacham died and was said to have had a heart attack. We know he did not. We know he was stabbed."

The doorman's nostrils flared, and his neck reddened. "I'm not allowed to discuss that. What I will tell you is that if you ask more questions, you'll draw attention that you don't want." He briefly met Hadrian's gaze. "You don't want to become entangled with any of this."

"We know who committed the act," Hadrian continued. "A man called Fitch. Do you know him?"

The doorman blanched, the red in his neck fading until he was quite pale. He said nothing, but Hadrian had his answer. "Are you aware that Fitch is dead?" he asked next.

The doorman wiped his forehead. "Please, you must go," he croaked. Then he glanced over his shoulder at the door.

Miss Wren edged closer to him, her voice a sharp whisper. "Are you afraid for your life if you are seen speaking with us?"

The doorman nodded. "Especially now you've told me about Fitch. *Please*, leave me be."

The door opened suddenly, and the doorman grabbed

Hadrian's elbow. His upper lip curled back in a threatening sneer. "I told you to go." He turned his head toward the manager who stood in the doorway. "This gent doesn't know when to stop asking questions that can't be answered."

"I see." The manager gave Hadrian a cold stare. "I must ask you to leave and not return. We have tried to put the unpleasantness of the death behind us, and it is not good for you to be here dredging it up. It was most upsetting for the employees, you must understand."

Hadrian pulled his arm from the doorman's grip. "I do. My apologies." He took Miss Wren's arm and guided her away from the doorway. He did not speak until they rounded the corner away from Covent Garden.

"If that didn't reek of concealment, I don't know what would," Miss Wren said.

Hadrian looked for a hack. "I do hope we didn't get the waiter or doorman into trouble."

"I do too. That could be quite dangerous for them, considering what happened to Sir Henry." She paused and cast her eyes down. "I want so badly to find out what happened to him. He deserves that. As does Millicent."

"So do you," Hadrian said, gently touching her arm.

She lifted her gaze to his and nodded. "Thank you." Taking a deep breath, she straightened her shoulders. "Given that we have already found a dead body and we are now worried about the safety of others embroiled in this series of crimes, perhaps it is time we share what we've learned with Scotland Yard."

"You may be right, though I worry their involvement will frighten some of the people we hope to convince to speak to us. Regardless, we must prioritize the visit to Hardacre. You've put it off long enough in favor of everything else." Hadrian waved down a hack and paid the driver to convey them to the Wren household first and then to his house on Curzon Street.

As they traveled to Marylebone, Miss Wren thanked him

for his concern about calling on Hardacre. "After speaking with Millicent today, I would very much like to resolve the matter of my grandmother's investment and Sir Henry's lack of funds."

"That is more than understandable."

They then reviewed what they'd learned at the club, and Hadrian described what he'd seen and felt in the card room when he'd tried to use his ability. "I only wish this frustrating curse had been more helpful," he said somewhat bitterly. What good was the damned thing if he couldn't control it? At least he didn't have a lingering headache.

"I imagine it's difficult to use that ability when we are somewhere that there are or have been a great many people. How would you detect or see anything amidst a sea of sensations and visions?"

"I shall have to learn to use it better, I suppose. Though, I was rather hoping it would fade in time, as I continue to heal from my fall when I was attacked."

"It may yet do that, and then you won't be able to use it more efficiently. Or at all." She gave him an encouraging smile. "Though, without it, we would not have met."

She was right about that. "And there would be no investigation," Hadrian said. "I would be stewing in my certainty that a common footpad wouldn't stab me with no one to listen to my rantings."

Miss Wren laughed as the hack stopped in front of her house, and Hadrian climbed down to help her out. As soon as he did, a figure moved toward them. Hadrian tensed.

The man stepped into the light of the streetlamp. "Good evening, Lord Ravenhurst, Miss Wren."

"Good evening, Inspector Teague," Hadrian said. "I'm surprised to find you lingering about Miss Wren's house."

"I went to yours first, but your butler informed me you were out." Teague looked to Miss Wren. "Your grandmother told me you were out as well."

Hadrian felt Miss Wren stiffen. She would be concerned about her grandmother having to speak with an inspector who was looking for her granddaughter.

Teague glanced between them, his gaze moving back and forth. "I think it's time you told me precisely what it is you are up to with regard to Sir Henry Meacham."

CHAPTER 16

"May we go inside?" Inspector Teague asked.

Tilda frowned at him. "I suppose, though I wish you hadn't called on me at home. My grandmother doesn't need to be troubled by Scotland Yard." Though her grandmother was aware of Tilda's investigation, she did not know things were escalating.

Ravenhurst told the driver of the hack to go then returned to Tilda's side. "Shall we go in?" He gave her a slight nod, as if he understood her concern.

Tilda led them to the door and into the entrance hall. Mrs. Acorn came rushing in. "Oh, Tilda. And Inspector Teague." Her lips pressed together, and her gaze was flat. She also seemed bothered by Teague's presence. Her expression eased into a smile when she addressed the earl. "Good evening, Lord Ravenhurst."

Ravenhurst returned her smile. "Good evening, Mrs. Acorn."

Tilda removed her hat and gloves and handed them to the housekeeper then hung her cloak on its peg. "We'll be in the sitting room for a few minutes." She turned to Ravenhurst. "Will you take Teague in? I'll be along directly."

"Of course." The earl gestured for the inspector to precede him into the sitting room.

Turning to Mrs. Acorn, Tilda whispered, "Was Grandmama upset by the inspector's call?"

"She was...concerned," Mrs. Acorn replied.

"Please tell her I will explain everything as soon as they leave. And ask her to remain in the parlor—I assume that's where she is?" At Mrs. Acorn's nod, Tilda continued, "I shan't be long."

"There is something else." Mrs. Acorn withdrew a sealed piece of parchment from the pocket of her apron. "A constable from the City of London brought this by earlier. I didn't tell your grandmother."

Pursing her lips, Tilda broke the seal and scanned the paper. It was a summons to the inquest for Mr. Paul Fitch at the Bell on Fish Street Hill tomorrow morning at ten o'clock. Tilda was to be interviewed as a witness. Presumably, the same summons had been delivered to Ravenhurst.

"Thank you, Mrs. Acorn." Tilda tucked the summons into her pocket.

Mrs. Acorn glanced toward the sitting room. "The inspector was most eager to see you. I do think he was hoping your grandmother would invite him to stay and wait for you."

"He's a decent sort. He may have information that will help my investigation." Pivoting on her heel, Tilda strode into the sitting room. The gentlemen were still standing, though both had removed and now held their hats.

Tilda didn't sit either. She wanted Teague to leave quickly so she could soothe her grandmother and assure her all was well. "Inspector, please get right to the point of your call."

"As you wish." Teague cleared his throat. "I understand the two of you found a man dead last night. A man called Fitch and whom you, Lord Ravenhurst, identified as the man who attacked you in January." He pinned the earl with a dark stare.

"Yes, to all of that," Ravenhurst replied evenly.

"How did you find him?" Teague prodded.

Ravenhurst looked toward Tilda. It was difficult to tell what he might be thinking. "We are not going to discuss our investigative methods with you at this juncture. Especially since this matter is being investigated by the City of London Police, which is separate from the Metropolitan Police."

Teague frowned. "That may be, but since you identified Fitch as the man who attacked you, it is also a matter for A Division. I would like to help." He looked to Ravenhurst. "You're certain Fitch was the man who attacked you?"

"Absolutely."

"Have you any idea who would kill him?"

Ravenhurst glanced at Tilda. His gaze seemed to silently ask whether he should answer. She decided to do it for him. "Not as of yet," she said, drawing Teague's focus. "However, we are working on it. We do, however, believe Fitch killed Sir Henry."

Teague's expression sharpened, and his brows pitched into a V. "Do you have evidence that Sir Henry was murdered? There will need to be an inquest."

"How do you do that without a body?" Ravenhurst asked. "Or do you plan to exhume him? That might be necessary since there is some dispute over his cause of death. We are certain he had a wound, and we will soon confirm that he did not suffer from a heart ailment."

"There are no plans to exhume Sir Henry's body," Teague said. "But that could change if I presented new evidence."

"Does this mean you believe that Sir Henry was murdered?" Tilda asked the inspector.

"It does not." Teague looked to Ravenhurst. "But I am troubled by Padgett's refusal to share information about your and Crawford's attacks. I have had no luck speaking with him or even seeing the confidential reports for myself. Since I have exhausted my efforts, perhaps you'd like to speak with the superintendent. He'll be in tomorrow, if you'd like me to set an interview for you in the afternoon."

"That would be helpful," Tilda said, wondering at the inspector's motive. "Why have you taken such a strong interest?" She recalled Ravenhurst telling her that Teague's curiosity was piqued.

The inspector gave her a determined look. "I want to make sure we have not closed cases prematurely. Accurately solving crimes is top of my priorities."

"So, you're helping us because you want to," Tilda asked with great skepticism. "And you are not assigned to do so, nor should you be, at least not whilst you are working."

"That's correct. This is my personal time."

Tilda folded her arms across her chest. "What do you expect us to pay you?"

Teague looked aghast, his eyes rounding briefly. "Nothing." He wrinkled his nose in distaste. "I don't approve of that, though there's not much I can do about it."

"Commendable of you," Ravenhurst said. "We do not require help at this time, but that may soon change. When it does, we'll inform you with alacrity."

Teague put his hat back on his head. "I hope you will. Justice must be served."

Tilda thrilled at the inspector's ethical commitment. "I completely agree. You say you've exhausted your efforts with Padgett and the confidential reports. Is there anything else you can do to obtain information about Ravenhurst's attack and Crawford's murder?"

"There were constables involved in both cases, though I'm not sure who they are. I will find out and question them," he said firmly. "Since you mentioned bribery, you should know that Padgett is not above taking money for...*assistance*."

"That makes sense," Ravenhurst said with distaste. "Why else would my and Crawford's cases be closed so quickly and without thorough investigation?"

"Men like Padgett infuriate me," Teague said. "But there is nothing I can do. The superintendent is aware of these corrupt practices but believes they do not impair the work we do. I disagree."

"Perhaps he'll change his mind if we can show him that Padgett has prevented justice from being done."

"Particularly for an earl," Teague remarked with a curled lip. "Superintendent Newsome cares very much how members of the House of Lords regard the Metropolitan Police."

"Because Scotland Yard relies on us for support," Ravenhurst said. "I may have to use that to my advantage, though I've wondered if that's any better than bribery."

"If your influence will effect change, I'm in favor of it," Teague said before making his way to the entrance hall. "I'll arrange for your interview with Newsome and send word of the time. Good evening, and Miss Wren, please apologize to your grandmother for my imposition."

Once the inspector was gone, Ravenhurst turned to Tilda. "I'm so sorry this came to your doorstep," Ravenhurst said with great care.

"Teague is not the only police official who came here today." She pulled the summons from her pocket and handed it to Ravenhurst to read. "I assume one will have been delivered to your house as well."

"I suppose we'll be busy most of tomorrow." He returned the summons to her, and she slipped it back into her pocket.

"We must postpone our call on Mr. Hardacre yet again," Tilda noted with considerable disappointment.

Ravenhurst gave her a sympathetic look. "Perhaps the inquest will go quickly. It won't take the jury long to declare Fitch's death a murder."

"They won't have a guilty party, however. I can't think there is any way the killer will be present."

"I tend to agree," Ravenhurst said grimly. "It will be an interesting event, to be certain. I'll pick you up shortly after nine. You go and speak with your grandmother now. I'm sorry for any upset she may have suffered."

"Thank you for coming in to speak with Teague," Tilda said.

"Of course. I'll see you in the morning." Ravenhurst left, and Tilda bolted the door.

Turning, she shook her shoulders out and prepared herself for the conversation with her grandmother. Tilda walked into the parlor, and her grandmother immediately looked toward her.

"Come and sit, my dear," Grandmama said with a smile.

Tilda took the chair near her grandmother's. "I'm sorry you were disturbed by Inspector Teague."

"I'm sure you'll tell me what he wished to speak with you about. I know you were just talking with him—and Lord Ravenhurst—in the sitting room." Grandmama looked at her expectantly.

"You know that Lord Ravenhurst hired me to investigate his attack. The investigation has...expanded. We now know that the man who stabbed Lord Ravenhurst killed others." Tilda took her grandmother's hand. "Including Sir Henry. He did not die of a heart ailment."

Grandmama lifted her free hand to her mouth, but it did not stifle her gasp. "This is absolutely dreadful. Does Millicent know?"

"I spoke with her about it today. Ravenhurst and I still have much investigative work to do."

"Is the earl assisting you in this?"

"He is," Tilda replied. "He's most invested in finding out why he was attacked—and understandably so."

"I'm just so shocked to hear about Sir Henry. First, my

investment goes missing, and now we learn he was murdered." She blinked at Tilda. "Are those things related?"

Tilda didn't want to discuss the possible embezzlement after revealing Sir Henry's murder. "Were you aware that Sir Henry had a penchant for gaming?"

"Oh, yes. He and your grandfather never said no to whist." A nostalgic smile lit Grandmama's face. "They loved playing in tournaments."

"And did they wager? Sir Henry died with several IOUs."

Grandmama's features creased. "Sir Henry did occasionally wager more than he ought, but your grandfather kept him in check. I hadn't thought about the fact that without him, Sir Henry may not have had anyone giving him wise counsel." The color drained from Grandmama's face. "You think he gambled away my investment?"

"It's possible," she said softly, squeezing her grandmother's hand. "But we don't know for sure yet."

Anger lit her grandmother's eyes. "It was foolish of me to allow him to manage my money."

"You didn't really have a choice. He was our only male relative." Tilda loathed how women had such little control over their lives. "However, now we must ensure the management falls to me. With whatever funds we have."

Grandmama nodded. "You will do splendidly. And you will solve Sir Henry's murder. I'm exceedingly glad you are on the case. Your father would be so proud of you."

Tilda swallowed. She did not trust herself to speak just then.

After a moment, she said, "Tomorrow, Lord Ravenhurst and I must attend an inquest and provide testimony. The man who stabbed him and Sir Henry has been killed, and Lord Ravenhurst and I found the body." Tilda had no choice but to tell her the truth, as the details of the inquest may very well be printed in the newspaper, which her grandmother would see.

Grandmama's eyes rounded and she put her hand to her chest. "You didn't witness his death, did you?"

"No, and I promise you we were very careful."

"You really are an investigator," her grandmother said with a measure of awe.

Mrs. Acorn came in. "Dinner is ready."

Tilda's grandmother pushed herself up and looked at Tilda. "I had Mrs. Acorn hold it while you were speaking with the gentlemen." She walked into the staircase hall, but before Tilda could follow her, Mrs. Acorn handed her another envelope.

"This was delivered shortly after you left this afternoon," the housekeeper said. "I didn't want to bother you with it when the earl and inspector were here, nor did I want to give it to you with the more official-looking document."

"Thank you, Mrs. Acorn. I'll be in to dinner directly." Tilda didn't recognize the hand that had scrawled her name on the envelope. Opening it, she removed the letter—and a pound note.

The brief message was from Inspector Lowther. He said he couldn't accept her money as he was not able to help her. He concluded by writing:

You must leave the matter of Ravenhurst's attack alone. Even your father would have turned his focus elsewhere. Please take very good care.

Tilda frowned at the letter. If Lowther had been here in person, she would have argued with him. Her father would not have walked away from this investigation. There were too many unanswered questions. Too many things that did not make sense.

And why was Lowther warning her off? Her stomach suddenly felt hollow. He wasn't corrupt too, was he? Well, beyond accepting bribes.

That *was* corruption.

Tilda had to accept that she didn't know who she could

trust at Scotland Yard, not without her father's guidance. Teague seemed honorable, but could she really know for certain?

She didn't have time to investigate the members of A Division, not when she was already consumed by her other investigation.

One thing did seem certain. If an inspector was telling her to stop her investigation, she was likely on the right path to discovering the truth. Tilda replaced the letter and the pound note into the envelope and tucked it into her pocket.

She would find Sir Henry's killer and she would see him brought to justice. Just as her father would have done.

CHAPTER 17

*H*adrian had arrived home last night to the same summons that Miss Wren had received. Then, this morning, a note from Inspector Teague had been delivered. He'd set an appointment for them to meet with Superintendent Newsome at Whitehall at four that afternoon. Hadrian hoped the inquest would be finished by then.

His coach arrived at Miss Wren's. A few moments later, he knocked on the door and was greeted by Vaughn.

Hadrian stared at the man. "I didn't expect to see you, Vaughn. I trust this means you are feeling much better?"

The elderly butler seemed slightly more stooped than before his attack, but his color was improved. He smiled faintly at Hadrian. "Good morning, my lord." He held the door for Hadrian as he stepped into the entrance hall. "I am doing well, thank you. I find being bedridden abhorrent."

Was he now acting as butler for the household? Hadrian would have been surprised to learn that Miss Wren and her grandmother could take on another retainer. "I do hope you are taking good care. It is always wise to follow a physician's direction."

Vaughn closed the door and shuffled to a chair. "I have my chair here. And if I become too tired, I can repair to the parlor." He gestured toward the room off the entrance hall where they'd spoken with Teague yesterday evening.

Hadrian wondered what Mrs. Wren would think of their probably-not-butler draped across the settee. He didn't know her well, but suspected she would not be nearly as horrified as his mother if such a thing happened.

Miss Wren's grandmother came into the entrance hall then, as if conjured by Hadrian's thoughts of her. She was dressed in black and moved spryly for a woman of her age. Or perhaps Hadrian was only noting that because Vaughn had moved so moribundly.

"Good morning, Lord Ravenhurst," Mrs. Wren greeted him as Vaughn sat in his chair. "Let us await my granddaughter in the parlor." She looked toward Vaughn. "You'll inform Tilda where we are? Not that she won't have figured it out."

Vaughn inclined his head. "Yes, ma'am."

Mrs. Wren preceded him into the parlor and took a chair near the window that looked out to the street. She waited until Hadrian sat opposite her in another chair before she spoke. "It seems we have a butler. At least temporarily. Mrs. Acorn found him stationed in the entrance hall early this morning. He declared the household in need of his services and himself in need of being out of bed." She shrugged.

"You are very kind to allow him to recuperate here."

"Where else would he go? I'm not sure where he *will* go when he's recovered, in fact." Mrs. Wren inhaled through her nose. "Tilda is working that out."

Hadrian realized Miss Wren worked on a great many things. "She is very capable. At least, that is my observation."

"It's an astute one," Mrs. Wren said with a nod. "You will find few young women with her intellect and efficiency. But I suspect you already know that since you've been working together on this investigation. Last night she explained how Sir Henry was murdered." A shudder passed over her small frame. "I still can't quite believe it. His sudden death was shocking enough. I want to thank you for joining with Tilda in this investigation. I feel better knowing she is not doing this alone. You do me a kindness by supporting her."

"She does me a kindness by agreeing to work together," he said with a smile.

Mrs. Wren chuckled. "You are a smart man."

Miss Wren entered the sitting room, and Hadrian had to blink to make sure he was seeing the same person. It was remarkable what the absence of black did for one's appearance. He'd not seen her in anything but mourning clothes since that first time they'd met.

Today, she wore a blue walking dress trimmed in navy blue, and a jaunty hat pitched forward atop her red-gold hair. He hadn't forgotten that she was pretty, but he perhaps hadn't realized she was truly beautiful.

"There you are Tilda," Mrs. Wren said. "We were marveling at your investigative abilities."

A very faint pink stained the upper arch of Miss Wren's cheeks. "I'm sure that isn't necessary," she murmured. She looked to Hadrian. "I'm ready to depart."

Mrs. Wren rose from her chair, and Hadrian jumped up to offer assistance if she needed it. But she waved him away with a smile. "I'm not quite old enough to require help—usually—but I do appreciate the sentiment. I wish you both a productive day." She sent her granddaughter a pointed stare. "I shall antici-pate your report later."

"Of course," Miss Wren said before turning and walking into the entrance hall. "Don't get up, Vaughn. Lord Ravenhurst can open the door for me."

"But it is my calling, miss," Vaughn said, sounding slightly put out.

Hadrian hastened to open the door. "I'm sure you can open it for her when she returns." He smiled at the butler then escorted Miss Wren to his coach.

When they were settled inside—her on the forward-facing seat and him on the rear-facing—Hadrian said, "You've a butler now, apparently."

"So it would seem," she said with the hint of a smile. "It's temporary, of course, but I do need to determine his retirement. Millicent informed me that there will likely not be enough money from the sale of the house to provide him a settlement."

"That is unfortunate. What will you do?"

"I'll manage somehow. We can't turn him out."

No, she wouldn't do that. Hadrian resolved to find a way to help her, though he doubted she would accept assistance. "If you provide me with an invoice for your services so far, I would pay you immediately."

She reached into her reticule and withdrew an envelope, which she handed to him. "Here you are."

He smiled. "I'll send payment over as soon as I am home."

"That is kind of you." She straightened, smoothing her hands over her lap. "Are you ready for the inquest today? My father told me about countless inquests he'd attended. I found his retelling of them fascinating. Such a spectacle with the body laid out on a table, the jury behaving with self-importance, the crowd of people outside eager for information. Not to mention the journalists recording the story." She cocked her head. "Are you concerned about your name appearing in the newspaper? The presence of an earl, as a witness no less, at the inquest will likely draw much attention."

"I hadn't considered that," he said.

"We must also consider that Fitch's killer will now be aware that you—and I—are conducting an investigation."

"Who do you think his killer is?" Hadrian realized they

hadn't discussed that beyond the idea that Fitch's murderer could be at the heart of everything. "Do you think he killed Fitch to ensure he didn't implicate him?"

"That seems the likeliest reason for Fitch to have been murdered. It's too coincidental for a man we know killed or attacked three separate people to have been randomly garroted in his home." She pursed her lips. "I do hope this doesn't take all day."

"I hope not either, as we have an interview with the super-intendent this afternoon at four. Teague sent a note this morning."

"I confess I'm not at all certain what to ask him," she said with a worried expression. "If we come straight out and accuse his police of corruption, I suspect the interview will end."

"You are probably right."

"One thing I would love to ask but I am not sure I dare is why one of his inspectors would tell me to stop investigating your attack."

Hadrian gaped at her. "Who did that and when?"

"Lowther sent me a note yesterday, along with my pound note, urging me to cease the investigation. He went so far as to suggest my father would do so, which is utter nonsense." She clucked her tongue in disgust. "My father would never walk away from an investigation."

"This is most concerning." Hadrian wondered if Teague was the only inspector at A Division who was interested in justice. "Why do you think Lowther would do that?"

She shrugged. "I can't say, but it gives me encouragement that we are on the right path. Lowther may be trying to keep information hidden, as Padgett is likely doing with making those reports confidential. It's all part of an effort to conceal the truth." Frowning, she added, "I have decided not to engage in bribing anyone any longer."

"How will you obtain information without playing along with their game?"

"I'm not sure yet, but I can't support the concealment of information which leads to the suppression of justice."

"I do admire that," Hadrian said with a smile. Sobering, he added, "I wonder if someone, Padgett perhaps, asked Lowther to tell you to back away from the investigation."

"That would make the most sense," she said.

"What of your edict that we tread carefully with Scotland Yard?" Hadrian asked. "This note from Lowther concerns me."

"Let us ask Teague about it since he's so keen to help."

"Excellent idea." Hadrian would feel better if Teague was aware of Lowther's actions. Perhaps he could even explain them.

The coach stopped a few minutes later, and Hadrian helped Miss Wren onto the pavement. Hadrian had told his coachman he wasn't sure how long this would take. He was going to park the coach just around the corner and wait for them.

People were already gathered outside the Bell. Hadrian escorted Miss Wren through the crowd toward the door.

"Lord Ravenhurst, why are you here?" someone, presumably a journalist, asked.

Hadrian ignored them and opened the door for Miss Wren to precede him into the tavern. Fitch's body lay atop two tables pushed together, and a sheet covered his form.

"There's Constable Barker from the other night," Miss Wren whispered, looking toward the uniformed man speaking to an older gentleman who Hadrian suspected was the coroner. With gray hair and sharp eyes, the coroner possessed an air of authority despite his small stature.

A group of well-dressed men stood to one side. Hadrian assumed they were the jury.

Another constable came toward them. "Good morning. You are Lord Ravenhurst?"

"Yes, and Miss Wren." Hadrian pivoted toward her.

"The witnesses are sitting just over here." He led them to a grouping of chairs. Fitch's neighbor was already present, as was Moll, the barmaid, and the barkeep of the tavern. Most surprisingly, the man they'd seen leaving Fitch's lodging was also there.

Miss Wren took a chair, and Hadrian sat beside her, which put him next to the young man they'd encountered. He looked frightfully nervous. In his early twenties, perhaps younger than Miss Wren, he had a thin face and wide-set eyes. He fidgeted with his hands and chewed his lip.

The coroner began the inquest then, starting with selecting twelve jurors. There looked to be close to twenty gentlemen who'd responded to the summons. One who wasn't chosen left, and the rest remained to watch the proceedings.

Next, the coroner announced the name of the victim and described the circumstances surrounding his death. The jurors then moved to examine the body. They encircled the table, and the sheet was removed. The view of Fitch was mostly obscured by the men around the table.

This continued for some time as the coroner indicated the wound that had caused his death. There could be no doubt that the jury would find the cause of death to be murder.

Fitch was covered once more, and the jurors moved to an area with twelve chairs where they sat to listen to the witnesses give their depositions. The coroner started with Hadrian.

Standing, he went to sit near the jury in a chair designated for the witness. A clerk sat at a table and recorded what Hadrian said. He detailed how they'd found Fitch, and that Hadrian had fetched the constable.

"How did you come to be at Mr. Fitch's lodging?" the coroner asked, his eyes assessing as he addressed Hadrian.

"I have a ring that belonged to him." Hadrian suspected he would lose the ring as evidence, which he was loathe to do, however he couldn't not mention it. The barmaid, Moll, would most certainly bring it up in her testimony.

"And how did you come to possess it?"

"The deceased stabbed me on the twenty-first of January," Hadrian replied. There were a few gasps. He glanced at the jury to see they were watching him intently. Several were frowning. "In my attempt to defend myself, I grabbed his hand and somehow removed the ring. I then hit my head on the pavement when I fell and didn't realize I had the ring until several days later."

"You did not give this ring to the Metropolitan Police?"

"No, as I said, I didn't know I had it. And the case was closed rather quickly," he added.

The coroner nodded. "How did you find Mr. Fitch?"

This was where things became difficult. "He said something that night about the Bell, so I came here to find him." It was an utter fabrication, but what else could Hadrian say? "I spoke with the barmaid there." He gestured toward Moll whose expression was stoic. She'd been crying earlier if her reddened nose was any indication. "She directed us to Fitch's lodgings."

"'Us'?" the corner asked. He glanced toward Miss Wren. "You are referring to yourself and Miss Matilda Wren?"

"Yes. She is my private investigator. I hired her to help me find Fitch." This garnered a few snickers, irritating Hadrian. He wished he could tell who they'd come from. He'd set them straight.

"Miss Molly Hennings gave you Fitch's address, and you went there directly on Saturday evening?" the corner pressed.

"Yes."

"Upon arriving, did you encounter a man leaving Fitch's lodging?"

"We did," Hadrian confirmed. "He said, 'he were like that when I got here,' presumably in reference to Fitch and the fact that he was dead."

"Could you identify this man if you saw him again?" the coroner asked.

"Definitely." Hadrian glanced toward the young man beside him. He'd gone quite pale.

"Do you see him here?" the coroner prodded.

"I do. He is sitting to my left."

"Please note that Lord Ravenhurst is referring to Mr. John Prince."

The coroner moved on to ask Hadrian about their exchange with the neighbor and what exactly they found in Fitch's room. Hadrian described how the room had been ransacked and Fitch's body—its position and the wound they'd discovered.

"Thank you, Lord Ravenhurst," the coroner said. "We appreciate your time today and ask that you remain in case I need to ask you any further questions."

"I am happy to assist in the carriage of justice." Hadrian moved from the witness chair back to his own. No sooner was he seated than the coroner called for Miss Wren to testify. Hadrian gave her an encouraging nod.

Miss Wren sat in the designated witness chair. Hands folded demurely in her lap, she appeared serene and collected in her blue walking dress with its fabric buttons up the front from her waist to the collar at her neck. Her costume may have been slightly out of fashion, but she looked smart. Her gaze was clear and sharp as she awaited the coroner's questions.

"You are Lord Ravenhurst's private investigator?" the coroner asked.

"Yes," she said evenly but with a warm lilt to her tone that revealed her pride in being addressed in such a manner.

"When did you begin working with him?"

"After the death of my grandfather's cousin, Sir Henry Meacham," she replied.

The coroner's dark brows rose. "There is another death?"

"Yes, and another that occurred the week after Lord Ravenhurst was attacked," she said. "Mr. Patrick Crawford was stabbed in the same location along Whitehall as Ravenhurst. Unfortunately, Mr. Crawford did not survive his injury."

Hadrian wanted to applaud her for bringing that up.

"In your investigative opinion, do those deaths have aught to do with the death of Mr. Fitch?" the coroner asked.

"I believe the death of Mr. Crawford was committed by the person who stabbed Lord Ravenhurst, and that was Mr. Fitch. The coincidence of the two crimes so close together in the same place and in the same manner is too striking to ignore. Furthermore, Lord Ravenhurst noted that he surprised his assailant. That could have been due to his defensive maneuvers, but it could also be because the attacker was expecting someone else. Mr. Crawford attended a card game every Tuesday at the White Stag on Whitehall. Lord Ravenhurst was attacked on his way from Westminster to Whitehall on a Tuesday. Furthermore, Ravenhurst and Crawford share the same build and coloring. It's entirely possible the earl was targeted by mistake, particularly when you consider that Crawford was attacked the very next Tuesday in the same location. Crawford was likely the person Fitch had meant to stab in the first place."

"That is an interesting theory, Miss Wren," the coroner said slowly. It was hard for Hadrian to determine if the coroner meant that seriously or sardonically. "However, you do not have evidence to support it," the coroner clarified.

"For now." She sounded slightly terse, not that Hadrian could blame her.

The coroner went on to ask her about visiting the Bell and speaking with the barmaid then continuing to Fitch's lodgings. She corroborated everything Hadrian had said and was soon dismissed.

When she returned to sit beside him, Fitch's neighbor, Lilian Tolman, was called to give her deposition. She was shaky and clearly nervous, her gaze mostly focused on the floor and her voice was low.

The coroner asked her how she knew Fitch, how long they'd been neighbors, and the last time she'd seen him before his death.

She said it had been at least a day, perhaps two, that they kept different hours.

"Do you know what Mr. Fitch did for work?" the coroner asked.

"'E worked for a fancy club near Covent Garden, 'ad a special uniform with gold buttons and everything." She sounded a trifle envious.

Miss Wren touched Hadrian's arm. She was clearly thinking what Hadrian was, that Fitch was perhaps an employee at Farringer's. Hopefully the coroner would confirm that.

"Son of a bitch," Moll whispered from behind them. Hadrian glanced back at her to see she was scowling faintly. He thought back to their conversation with her, and she hadn't said what Fitch did for work. Perhaps she hadn't known and was irritated that his neighbor did?

The coroner next asked Lilian if she'd noticed any visitors going to his lodging over recent days or even weeks. She nodded in response. "The man next to the earl there. 'E's visited a couple times in the last fortnight or so."

Hadrian looked toward the young man, Prince, once more. He'd gone from white to gray.

The coroner went on to ask Miss Tolman a few more questions about fetching the constable then dismissed her. Next, he called the barmaid to testify.

Moll said she'd had an intimate relationship with Fitch for several months. She admitted she loved him but didn't think he returned the sentiment. She told the coroner about Hadrian and Miss Wren coming into the Bell looking for Fitch because they had his ring.

When she was finished, the coroner called the barkeep as well as a few people who lived nearby and knew Fitch or had occasion to see him regularly. Notably, there was no one from Farringer's present, which Hadrian found odd—if that was indeed his employer. A neighbor who lived across East Cheap from Fitch gave testimony that he'd seen John Prince going into the door that led up to Fitch's lodging sometime on Saturday but couldn't say when.

Next to Hadrian, Prince had tensed. Then he was called to testify next.

"How do you know Mr. Fitch?" the coroner asked.

Prince wiped the back of his hand over his mouth. "I don't know 'im, not really."

"But you were seen visiting him on multiple occasions and visiting his lodgings the night he was found dead," the coroner said. "Why would you visit a man you didn't know?"

"I asked 'im about 'is job," Prince said, fidgeting with a button on his coat. "'E 'ad a fancy costume for it, and it looked like it paid really well."

The door opened then, and an inspector came into the alehouse. He went directly to the coroner and spoke to him in a low tone. Hadrian could not make out what they were saying. The inspector handed something wrapped in cloth to the coroner.

After pulling the cloth back to see the contents, the coroner nodded. Then he set it on the table next to Fitch's body.

The coroner shot a look toward Hadrian. No, not Hadrian. Toward Prince beside him. "Mr. Prince, you may return to your seat for now."

Shit. What was happening?

The inspector who'd come in sat in the corner, and the coroner asked Constable Barker to testify. Barker ran through the events of the evening, including finding the money in Fitch's drawer.

"Did you find the weapon used to kill Mr. Fitch?" the coroner asked.

"No, we did not."

The coroner thanked him and said he was finished. As Barker returned to his seat, the coroner asked the inspector who'd just arrived to offer testimony.

Square-jawed and nearly bald when he removed his hat, the inspector had small, dark eyes. His name was Chisholm and he'd been employed by the City of London Police for nineteen years. He'd been assigned to oversee Fitch's case and apologized for his tardiness today.

"I understand you have a good reason for being late," the coroner said. "Would you please share it with everyone?"

"Certainly," Chisholm replied crisply. "We were searching the lodging of John Prince. We found a length of wire with blood on it. Something used to garotte someone. It was tucked beneath Prince's bed."

"I didn't put it there!" Prince called out, his eyes bulging and his face turning red. "I don't 'ave nothin' like that!"

"Mr. Prince, please remain quiet," the corner demanded crossly. "I will question you again after the inspector, and you will have an opportunity to refute what has been said."

For whatever reason, Hadrian believed the young man. His declarations today and the night they'd found Fitch simply rang true to him.

Removing his glove, Hadrian reached over and touched Prince's hand. "It will be all right," he murmured.

Nothing was happening. Hadrian kept his hand on Prince's, willing a vision or even the slightest sensation. There! Prince was afraid. And he was desperate to be believed. Hadrian did not detect deception. He removed his hand and pulled his glove back on.

Hadrian was confident this young man had nothing to do with Fitch's death. But why was someone trying to make it look like he was the killer? And why had he been in Fitch's room?

Miss Wren leaned toward Hadrian and whispered, "I think Fitch's murderer is trying to ensure someone else takes the blame."

So, he plants the garotte wire under Prince's bed...but that didn't account for the witnesses who'd testified that Prince had visited Fitch or the fact that they had seen Prince coming out of Fitch's lodging when Fitch was dead inside the room. "What motive does Prince have for killing Fitch?" Hadrian asked quietly.

"That should be the glaring hole in this farce," she replied with an edge to her tone.

The coroner addressed the inspector once more. "Have you any notion as to why Mr. Prince would want to kill Mr. Fitch? It's already been established that the murderer left money in Mr. Fitch's lodging, so he can't have been robbing the man."

The inspector cleared his throat. "It seems to have been a simple disagreement about Miss Hennings."

Hadrian looked over to see Prince's reaction. He looked down, his face flushed.

"Please explain," the coroner said.

Inspector Chisholm took a deep breath. He did not so much as glance toward either Prince or the barmaid. "Prince has tried to gain Miss Hennings' favor on multiple occasions. I'm sure she'll tell you this is true, if you care to ask her. Though, we will ensure her testimony is entered at trial."

"Trial?" Prince whispered. He slumped in his chair.

The coroner dismissed the inspector and asked the barmaid to return to the witness chair. She confirmed that Prince had flirted with her and made romantic overtures, but she'd said she wasn't interested because she was with someone else.

Then it was Prince's turn to give further testimony. He was sweating profusely, and he looked as if he wanted to take flight, not that Hadrian could blame him. His entire demeanor made him appear nervous and guilty, which was a shame since Hadrian knew he was innocent.

The coroner asked Prince if he was acquainted with Miss Hennings. Prince admitted he did know her and that he had been hoping to draw her notice. The coroner asked if he'd done more than just hope.

"I asked 'er to 'ave an ale with me once or twice," Prince replied, his lip quivering.

"You live by yourself, Mr. Prince?" the coroner asked.

"Yes," the young man said shakily.

The coroner pinned him with a dark stare. "How do you manage that? What is it you do for employment?"

Prince turned white again. "I work at the docks."

"That pays enough for you to live on your own?"

"My lodging is very small." Prince looked utterly defeated.

"Thank you, Mr. Prince. You may return to your seat." The coroner was quiet a moment then drew a long breath. "The jury will now confer and determine the findings of the inquest."

"Can I leave?" Prince asked Hadrian, his eyes desperate.

"You should not," Hadrian advised.

"I didn't kill 'im," Prince swore, looking toward the body on the table.

Inspector Chisholm approached them. His gaze was fixed on Prince. "I don't know how the inquest will turn out, Mr. Prince, but you will need to come with me when it concludes."

"Are you going to arrest me?" Prince asked.

"It's possible," the inspector said. He looked at Hadrian. "Would you mind moving so I can sit next to Mr. Prince?"

Hadrian stood, and Miss Wren joined him. "I saw that you took off your glove and touched him. What happened?" Miss Wren asked quietly.

"I felt that he was telling the truth. He's petrified."

Miss Wren looked at him intently. "We have to find the real killer."

Hadrian moved to Prince's other side and leaned down. "Go with the inspector. All will turn out well. Miss Wren and I will find the man who killed Fitch."

Prince looked up at him in complete dejection. "I don't want to 'ang."

"You will not," Hadrian vowed. They needed to move quickly to save this young man further turmoil. This would not be easy for him.

In the end, the jurors found that Fitch had been murdered by garotte, and the coroner indicated there was at least one suspect, Mr. John Prince, who was then taken into custody by the City of London Police. The young man's sobs could be heard on the street as the conclusion was read by the coroner— or so the newspapers reported.

"We can't let Prince hang for a crime he didn't commit." Hadrian said.

Miss Wren met his gaze with determination. "We will not."

CHAPTER 18

fter making their way through the throng of people outside the Bell, Tilda hurried alongside Ravenhurst toward his coach. The journalists outside had asked the earl question after question, but he'd ignored them all. A few followed Ravenhurst and Tilda to the coach and were still trying to ask questions as Leach ushered them into the vehicle. When the coach pulled away, Tilda relaxed against the seat.

"Persistent, aren't they?" she asked wryly.

"Quite." Ravenhurst checked his pocket watch. "We've plenty of time to call on Mr. Hardacre. I instructed the coachman to take us to Walton Street."

Tilda was glad they could finally do so. "Thank you."

It took them some time to reach Walton Street near Brompton Crescent in the far west end. On the way, they discussed the inquest. Hardacre's home was a smart, new terrace with wrought iron across a narrow first floor balcony.

"He retired very well," Tilda noted as they stood on the pavement after exiting the coach. "Embezzlement would allow for that, I imagine."

"Quite." Ravenhurst escorted her to the door where a butler answered promptly.

The earl gave the butler his card and asked to see Mr. Hardacre. Tilda couldn't deny that Ravenhurst's privilege was rather helpful to their investigation.

"I will see if Mr. Hardacre is receiving." The butler invited them into the entrance hall and closed the door then walked upstairs.

"Do you suppose there is a Mrs. Hardacre?" Tilda murmured.

Ravenhurst shrugged. "I hadn't considered it."

A few minutes later, the butler returned. "If you will just follow me."

He led them up the stairs to the drawing room. Two tall windows opened onto the narrow balcony that overlooked the street below. The room itself was elegantly appointed in gold and ivory. Tilda assumed a woman had decorated it.

"The Earl of Ravenhurst, eh?" a voice creaked from the doorway.

They turned as Mr. Hardacre ambled in. He leaned on a cane and moved slowly. Of average height, he was slightly stooped, though not as much as Vaughn. Hardacre was almost completely bald, yet he had the thickest, whitest brows Tilda had ever seen.

"Good afternoon, Mr. Hardacre," Ravenhurst said. "We're sorry to disturb you, however, we've come on a matter of urgent importance."

"Sit down then," Hardacre said as he lowered himself into a chair. He set his cane against the arm and settled back with a huff. "Do I know you? Terrible thing to ask, but my memory's not what it once was, I'm afraid."

Tilda and Ravenhurst settled themselves on a settee. "I'm sorry to hear that," Tilda said. "No, you don't know us. You were solicitor to my grandfather's cousin, Sir Henry Meacham."

Hardacre's impressive brows climbed. "Oh yes, Sir Henry. Jolly chap. I'd received notice of his death, but I regret I was unable to attend the funeral. I don't go out too much these days. I did send a card. I *think* I sent a card." His wide brow furrowed, and he shook his head.

"That was kind of you," Tilda said. "I'll get right to the reason for our call."

"What was your name?" Hardacre asked, interrupting her before she could continue. "Did I forget that already?"

"Actually no. I am Miss Matilda Wren."

Hardacre's brow creased once more. "Wren? Sounds familiar. But everyone knows Christopher Wren." He chuckled.

Christopher Wren was, in fact, Tilda's ancestor, but she did not mention that fact. "Perhaps you recall my father, Thomas Wren? He died eleven years ago and at that time, the funds that he'd been managing for his mother—my grandmother—came under the control of Sir Henry as her closest living male relative. However, it seems that money has disappeared."

Hardacre blinked at her. "Disappeared?"

"Mr. Whitley, who took over as Sir Henry's solicitor when you retired, says there is no record of my grandmother's investments. I am hoping you will recall what happened to her money." Tilda held her breath.

Ravenhurst scooted forward on the settee and fixed Hardacre with a serious stare. "It is of vital importance we learn the truth, Mr. Hardacre, whatever it may be."

"Who are you again?" Hardacre asked. "Sir Henry's nephew?"

"No, I'm Ravenhurst."

"Ah." Hardacre nodded and tapped his finger to his temple. "I can remember a dinner that occurred twenty years ago, and yet something you tell me right now will likely be forgotten in a matter of minutes."

"You remember Sir Henry then?" Tilda prodded. Hardacre had referred to him as delightful.

"I do. Always cheerful with a wicked sense of humor. Horrible with his finances though." Hardacre shook his head and looked down for a moment.

"Horrible how?" Tilda asked. When the man didn't respond for a long moment, Tilda said, "Mr. Hardacre, we were discussing some investments Sir Henry would have made on behalf of his cousin's widow, Mrs. Alexander Wren. That would have been some eleven years ago. Would you recall that?"

"Not entirely, but the name is familiar. Like Christopher Wren," he added with a smile.

Tilda sent a frustrated look toward Ravenhurst who, thankfully, appeared more patient. She was worried this would be a fruitless errand. But they'd had to try.

"Do you know what happened to those investments?" Ravenhurst asked. "Whitley, your successor, has no record of them."

"He wouldn't." Hardacre said this with a surprising certainty. "Can't imagine Sir Henry would have held onto anything for eleven years. He spent money as fast as he got it. Terrible gambling habit. I distinctly recall him completely bleeding through his wife's inheritance in just a few years. Never missed a whist tournament."

"That's true," Tilda said softly. "You're certain?" She had to ask for confirmation.

"Absolutely. As I said, I can remember things from long ago quite well. Sir Henry was a singular fellow. He always felt so badly when he lost large sums—he was particularly upset after he went through the last of his wife's money. But then he'd come up with a way to make the money back, though it was always a gamble, and rarely successful." Hardacre's forehead creased, and his brows nearly met over his eyes, resembling a long, white caterpillar. "Now that I think about it, I believe he did borrow from a fund to pay a debt. That might have been your grandmother's money."

Tilda sagged against the back of the settee. "I gather he didn't repay the loan?"

"Can't imagine he did. Always short of funds, that one. Indeed, I recall he once considered blackmailing someone." Hardacre waggled his brows. "Absolutely salacious!"

Tilda straightened and sent a shocked look toward Ravenhurst who returned the same.

The earl directed his attention back to Hardacre. "Do you know who he meant to blackmail?"

"Someone with plenty of money. In the end, he didn't do it." Hardacre shrugged. "Said he was too afraid he'd be found out."

"You're certain he likely spent my grandmother's funds?" Tilda had known it was possible, but having a definitive answer meant there was no hope.

"Sir Henry spent every shilling he could get his hands on." Hardacre blinked at her. "Who was your grandmother?"

Ravenhurst cleared his throat. "Mr. Hardacre, we know you also took money that didn't belong to you. Did you embezzle Mrs. Barbara Wren's investment funds eleven years ago or at any time since?"

Hardacre appeared affronted. "Embezzle? I did no such thing. I charged a fair fee for my services."

Tilda wondered if Hardacre perhaps didn't recall embezzling money or even realized he'd done so. It was possible that in his mind, he'd done nothing wrong. But she didn't believe he'd stolen Grandmama's money, not when he seemed to recall Sir Henry and his spendthrift behavior very well. And since Tilda now knew he'd been an inveterate gambler and risk-taker, she had no trouble believing he'd pilfered her grandmother's funds, particularly since he'd always avoided discussing financial matters with Tilda.

"Thank you, Mr. Hardacre." Tilda rose. "We appreciate your time today."

"Glad I could help." His expression was blank as he regarded her, and she could tell he'd forgotten who she was.

"Good day, Mr. Hardacre," Ravenhurst said before escorting Tilda out of the drawing room and then down the stairs.

The butler showed them out, and Ravenhurst handed her into the coach. Tilda heard him direct the coachman to Scotland Yard in Whitehall. But her mind was reeling with what they'd just learned.

Ravenhurst sat opposite her, and the coach began moving. "That was a worthwhile errand, albeit a disappointing one. I'm sorry."

"I'm so angry." Indeed, Tilda's hands were shaking. "That money should have ensured my grandmother's comfort in these later years."

"It is an awful situation," he said quietly. "I wish there was something I could say or do."

There was nothing to be done. The money was gone and had been for some time. No wonder Sir Henry had never wanted to speak with her about increasing their stipend. "I'm surprised he didn't steal the first investment too, but then Grandmama would have had nothing to live on."

"At least he showed a modicum of restraint." Ravenhurst spoke gently. She knew he was trying to soothe her, but there was no way to soften this blow.

"I will also need to tell Millicent." Tilda's stomach churned. "She held out hope I would find some money."

"I am doubly sorry that you have to be the bearer of more bad news. Perhaps you don't tell her about the potential blackmail."

"No, I'll leave that part out. Though that was an interesting tidbit."

"Agreed," Ravenhurst said.

They were quiet a few minutes as they traveled east toward Whitehall. Tilda's blood began to cool, her anger giving way to sadness and dread. She did not look forward to the conversations with her grandmother and Millicent.

Diverting her attention from her financial problems, Tilda said, "What is our goal in meeting with Superintendent Newsome?"

Ravenhurst squared his shoulders against the seat. "My primary objective is to ask for the supposedly confidential reports of my attack and Crawford's death. I think you mut also tell him about the note from Inspector Lowther."

"I fear you are right, though I dislike causing any trouble. I suppose it's fair to say that Lowther started the trouble by sending that note."

"Yes, that exactly." Ravenhurst's eyes narrowed. "I am torn between wanting to complete this investigation ourselves and informing Scotland Yard of what we have learned, which indicates they should not have closed my case or Crawford's, and that they must investigate Sir Henry's death."

"We could do both," Tilda suggested. "Teague is ready and eager to help at any moment. We must first present proof that Sir Henry was murdered, or that he at least died suspiciously, and the matter deserves an inquest. That requires a body, however." Tilda could not afford to exhume Sir Henry, and she doubted Millicent would be able to pay for it—or that her husband would even allow the expense.

"I would pay for it," Ravenhurst said, his gaze gentle.

She hadn't said a word, and yet he had easily discerned the obstacle. "You couldn't."

"Why not? I want to discover who was behind Sir Henry's death as much as you do. Perhaps more. Because that person is responsible for my attack and these horrid visions. You are my private investigator, and this is merely another expense." He wasn't wrong about that.

Setting aside the matter of exhumation for now, she said, "You could argue that person—because of your visions—inadvertently triggered an investigation that may very well bring them to justice."

Ravenhurst grinned. "That's rather poetic."

As they neared Whitehall, she said, "I do hope Superintendent Newsome is open to hearing what we have to say about your case and Crawford's, as well as Sir Henry's death. This is another time when I daresay your rank will be of considerable assistance." Tilda wasn't sure she could have secured an appointment with the superintendent.

"Your connections to Scotland Yard should also prove useful," Ravenhurst said. "I would hope that Newsome would be eager to listen to the daughter of one of his best sergeants."

"That's kind of you to say," Tilda said quietly. "But my father died more than a decade ago. I am not sure his legacy carries much weight."

"It should, particularly since he died in service." Ravenhurst sounded most authoritative on that point.

"We are going to suggest that one of his inspectors may have corrupted investigations outright. We must be prepared for the superintendent to take umbrage."

"Alas, it must be done," Ravenhurst said firmly. "Padgett has worked to bury these investigations, and I would know why. Teague said he was corrupt, and I trust him to tell us the truth."

"The question is who would have bribed him to tamper with your investigation and that of Crawford's murder?"

The earl's eyes gleamed with zeal. "That, my dear Miss Wren, is what I would like to know."

～

a short while later, they were seated in the superintendent's office awaiting his arrival. It was a quarter hour past their appointed meeting time when Newsome finally entered. In his early fifties, he was a tall man with thin sideburns and thick gray hair. His eyes were wide set and a rather unnerving shade of pale blue. He looked as if he could see through you. Hadrian imagined those eyes were quite useful in interrogations.

"Afternoon, Ravenhurst, Miss Wren. I'm sorry to have kept you waiting." He joined them at a table where a clerk had set a tea service shortly after Hadrian and Miss Wren had arrived. "Ah, tea will not come amiss. I see you have already poured out for yourselves, excellent."

The superintendent poured his cup and took a satisfying sip, indicative by the sigh he let out as he returned the cup to its saucer. "Inspector Teague tells me you have questions about the investigation into that nasty attack you suffered in January. I am terribly sorry that happened, my lord. It does look as though you've recovered well."

"I have, thank you. As I understand it, no one has been caught and charged with the crime, yet the case has been closed."

Newsome rested his elbows on the arms of his chair and steepled his fingers together. "Yes, that is, unfortunately, what happens sometimes."

"Except Lord Ravenhurst *did* find the man who stabbed him," Miss Wren said evenly. "We found him dead in his lodgings two nights ago. He'd been garroted."

Unsteepling his hands, Newsome let them drop toward his lap. "I am aware of that. In fact, I just came from a meeting about the inquest earlier today. You were there, I believe? I understand that man's killer has been arrested by the City of London Police." He looked to Hadrian. "Since the man you identified as your attacker is dead, I would say the case is most definitely closed."

Though the interview had barely started, Hadrian's patience was thinning already. "I suppose that is true, however the investigation into the death of Mr. Patrick Crawford, MP, should be reopened. I believe he was killed by the same man who stabbed me."

"Well, then that case would be solved too then, wouldn't it?" Newsome said pleasantly.

Hadrian exchanged a frustrated glance with Miss Wren. She leaned slightly toward Newsome. "At the very least, the reports regarding both investigations should be amended to indicate the identity of the culprit."

"How do you know they haven't been?" Newsome asked, his brows climbing.

"Because the reports are confidential, and we haven't been able to see them," Miss Wren replied flatly.

"I find it perplexing that they are classified as confidential," Hadrian said. "If these attacks were indeed due to a common footpad, it makes no sense that they would be secreted away."

The superintendent frowned. "You raise a good argument, and I'm afraid I don't have an answer for you."

"Perhaps you could look into the matter so that you *could* have an answer," Hadrian suggested with a bland smile.

Miss Wren moved her hand slightly so that she brushed Hadrian's leg. He looked at her, and she sent him a warning glance. Hadrian realized he may have overstepped. Even for an earl.

"We have another matter we think requires Scotland Yard's investigation. My grandfather's cousin, Sir Henry Meacham, died a fortnight ago. He was reported to have collapsed at a club called Farringer's near Covent Garden. However, we believe the true cause of his death has been misrepresented,

and that he was stabbed in the same manner as Lord Ravenhurst and Mr. Crawford."

Surprise flashed over Newsome's features. "Do you think he
was killed by the same man? The one who was killed and for
whom there was an inquest today?"

"We do," Miss Wren said.

Newsome picked up his tea for another sip. "I realize your
father was a respected sergeant with the Metropolitan Police
and that your grandfather was a highly regarded magistrate, but
you are hardly qualified to make such deductions, Miss Wren."

The condescension from the superintendent made Hadrian's blood boil. He could only imagine how it made Miss Wren
feel. He looked over at her and observed a tic in her jaw.

"I would argue that my lineage makes me uniquely qualified," she informed him cooly. "Ravenhurst and I are still
working out the connections, but Mr. Fitch seems to have been
an employee at the gaming club where Sir Henry died. From
there, someone took his body to his physician, Dr. Selwin, who
determined he'd died of a heart attack—without conducting an
autopsy. However, when Sir Henry's daughter prepared him
for the funeral, she noticed a stitched wound on his right side.
This is inconsistent with the cause of death listed on his death
certificate. I will also note that a death certificate would not
have been necessary, and its existence raises more questions."

Hadrian wanted to stand and applaud.

Newsome was not as impressed—he shrugged. "Just
because Sir Henry had a wound doesn't mean his death was
caused by it. And whilst a death certificate may not have been
necessary, it seems a wise course of action in this situation.
Please do accept my condolences, Miss Wren."

Miss Wren pursed her lips. "We have reason to believe Sir
Henry may not have been suffering from a heart ailment at all,
which would mean the death certificate contains false informa-

tion. The wound to his side seems the likelier cause of death." She pinned the superintendent with a direct stare—Hadrian was in awe of her confidence. "We are prepared to have his body exhumed."

Surprise widened Newsome's eyes. "His next of kin supports that?"

"Yes," Miss Wren said as she gripped her reticule. The action was a tell that she was not being completely honest, not that Hadrian was going to dispute anything she said.

Before Newsome could pursue that line of questioning, Hadrian said, "You should know that we have spoken to employees at Farringer's. It is clear to us that his death was not ordinary. Indeed, I am surprised there wasn't an inquest."

Newsome tapped his fingers on the desk briefly. "You say the cause of his death was inaccurately documented as a heart ailment. Are you saying the physician was wrong?"

"Wrong, or he lied," Miss Wren said without looking away from the superintendent.

"That is a weighty accusation." Newsome took another sip of tea. Setting the cup down, he returned his attention to Miss Wren, but his gaze had gone cool. "Miss Wren, I highly doubt your father would approve of you doing the work of our good inspectors. I suggest—highly—that you leave the investigating to them." He shot a look toward Hadrian. "I would give you the same counsel, Ravenhurst."

It occurred to Hadrian that Lowther's note could have been written as a direct result of the superintendent himself learning of Miss Wren's investigation and wanting her to stop. Perhaps it was best if they didn't mention it. He would not, though Miss Wren might—and he couldn't prevent her.

Hadrian saw that Miss Wren's neck was flushing red above her blue gown. He could not remain silent and sent the superintendent an icy stare. "Perhaps if we'd felt the police had done their job more thoroughly, we would not be compelled to investigate these matters ourselves."

"Perhaps you didn't know my father very well, Superintendent Newsome," Miss Wren added quietly but firmly. "If you did, you would know that he would be my staunchest supporter. Everything I know about investigations and solving crimes I learned from him."

Again, Hadrian wanted to cheer. He noted that Newsome's jaw had tightened, and there were lines around his mouth. He appeared to be growing annoyed or losing patience. Or both.

Hadrian forced a small, brief smile. "I'm confident Scotland Yard would prefer to learn the truth and ensure justice is served."

"Except—by your assertion—your attacker and Crawford's and Sir Henry's murderer is already dead," Newsome replied flatly. "Justice has already been dealt."

"Fitch was not acting on his own," Miss Wren said. "What reason would a man such as him have for stalking gentlemen so far from where he lives and in such a manner that would potentially increase his risk?"

Impatience flashed in Newsome's gaze and his features darkened. "I fail to see why this is pertinent. Mr. Fitch is dead. The crimes you claim he committed are therefore solved. Furthermore, everything you have presented today is circumstantial, and while I sympathize with your plight, Ravenhurst, I simply don't have the resources to pander to an earl who wishes to play investigator."

Hadrian stood, and Miss Wren joined him. "While that may be, I should, at the very least, be allowed to review the report of Inspector Padgett's investigation. If you are not able to provide it to me, I shall ask the Home Secretary for his assistance."

"You needn't bother him," Newsome said gruffly, his jaw moving with agitation. "I will obtain the reports and deliver them to you personally. I trust you will keep them confidential, since that is what they have been classified." He glanced toward Miss Wren as if trying to communicate that she wasn't allowed to read them.

"I should like to know why Padgett classified them in that manner," Hadrian said. "You can inform me when you deliver the reports." He looked to Miss Wren with a subtle nod toward the door.

"Thank you for your time, Superintendent Newsome," Miss Wren said tightly.

Newsome rose. "I am glad to help." He smiled, but the expression did not extend to his eyes—those seemed to say he was not at all pleased to have to assist them. "Ravenhurst, if there is some conspiracy or plot to murder Crawford, Sir Henry, and you, why are you still alive? At least, why hasn't someone tried again to kill you?"

"I don't believe I was the intended victim," Hadrian replied. "Crawford was. He was known to visit a pub on Tuesday evenings for a card game with other MPs. I was mistaken for him. Fitch was quite surprised when I turned on him, and we made eye contact. That detail ought to be in the *confidential* report as I relayed it to Inspector Padgett when he interviewed me."

Newsome's nostrils had flared slightly as Hadrian had spoken, seeming to indicate he was not unmoved by Hadrian's argument. Perhaps he would truly consider looking into these cases.

Hadrian escorted Miss Wren from the man's office. They followed a corridor into the main reception area.

"I did not expect Newsome to be so dismissive," Miss Wren said as they made their way outside to Hadrian's coach.

"I can only hope we've opened his eyes to certain facts he may not have been aware of. I didn't like that he tried to deter you. It sounded rather like the note you received from Lowther."

"I agree, which is why I didn't bring it up. It's possible Newsome advised Lowther to tell me to mind my own business." She scoffed.

Hadrian handed her into the coach. "I think we've made it clear we aren't going to do that."

"And you've threatened to go above him and speak to the Home Secretary," she said. "Will you really do that?"

Hadrian settled opposite her as the coach moved forward. "I may. It depends on what happens with the confidential reports, such as when I receive them and what Newsome has to say about Padgett's behavior." He met her gaze. "And I will most definitely share them with you."

Miss Wren chuckled. "The superintendent seemed to imply you should not. Because I am not properly trained, you see." She rolled her eyes, and he was glad she was able to find some humor in Newsome's obnoxious behavior.

"I am very sorry he said those things to you," Hadrian said. "You behaved wonderfully. I was quite in awe of your confidence and capability in dealing with him. He should wish he had more investigators like you."

Faint spots of pink stained her cheeks, and she glanced toward the window. "That is kind of you to say." A moment later, she gave Hadrian a dubious look. "Why do I think the reports will not appear?"

"I hope that does not happen." Hadrian really would speak to the Home Secretary in that case. "Tomorrow, we have our appointment with Selwin. I am keen to interrogate him about what really happened the night Sir Henry died."

"I am too. I think he must have been persuaded to falsify a death certificate. By whomever is pulling the strings."

"But we are no closer to discovering why," Hadrian said, feeling frustrated. He would think they were doing a poor job, but they were finding more answers than the police.

She returned her gaze to his. "Perhaps Sir Henry's IOUs are the place to look for motivation."

"Someone killed him because he couldn't pay?" Hadrian shook his head. "That would be illogical, for then you wouldn't ever get paid."

"Does that mean Millicent can ignore the IOUs she found?" Miss Wren asked, sounding hopeful.

"Probably, though she should perhaps contact each of the holders and simply state that she is unable to repay because her father died bankrupt."

Miss Wren nodded. "I'm sure her husband can help her with that." Her brow creased. "But why would the IOUs have caused someone to kill Crawford?"

"There is that link between the IOU to Martin Crawford, but why was his son murdered?" Hadrian shook his head. "There is a connection between Patrick Crawford and Sir Henry. I think we should call on his widow tomorrow after our appointment with Selwin."

"Do you think she'll see us?" Miss Wren asked. "Though it's been almost two months since her husband's death, she may not be receiving."

Hadrian pressed his back against the squab. "We have to try. I am hoping your presence will smooth things."

"Why?" Miss Wren sounded surprised. "I don't know her."

He shrugged. "Because you're a woman?"

She laughed. "That is hardly a reason to think I will help matters, but I suppose it can't hurt."

"Perhaps you should don black again," Hadrian suggested.

Miss Wren grimaced. "As much as I detest that idea, that is very smart."

"Why do you detest it?"

"The thought of wearing that mourning gown even one more day..." She shuddered in clear revulsion. "Still, I will do it."

"I appreciate your sacrifice," he said with a faint smirk that made her smile in return. He was glad for that, for he knew this had been a trying day for her. And she had yet to speak with her grandmother about what they'd learned from Hardacre. Her day was not going to improve.

"Ravenhurst?" she said, as they neared Marylebone.

"Yes?"

"We haven't spoken much of the vision you had with the photograph at Sir Henry's house—not since we found Fitch."

"No, we haven't." Hadrian's thoughts of the dead woman had been pushed aside by the vision he'd seen of Sir Henry dying. "My mind has been too focused on what I saw from Fitch's coin. And on finding Fitch dead." Hadrian's sleep last night had been interrupted by a dream of Fitch coming after him again, this time with a garotte.

Miss Wren nodded. "Understandably so. But Sir Henry is somehow linked to this dead woman. We have to consider that she is a part of all this."

"Do we?" Hadrian wasn't sure. "Her appearance seemed to indicate she likely lived decades ago. I can't see how she would be involved with Sir Henry's death at all."

"I can't disagree with that assessment, however, I find it troubling that Sir Henry had something to do with a dead woman, even if it was some time ago. I just wish there was someone we could ask." She tapped her finger on the seat next to her leg. "Please don't suggest Millicent. While she may have been alive at that time, I can't imagine she'd know anything about a dead woman."

Hadrian agreed it was unlikely Sir Henry's daughter would know anything. "You could ask her about who his friends were at that time. Perhaps we could speak with them."

"I suppose I could do that." A faint grimace passed over Miss Wren's features. "I need to tell her about there being abso-lutely no money."

"You'll also need to mention the possible exhumation," he said gently. "I'd be happy to accompany you."

"I will consider your kind offer." She took a deep breath. "That is not a conversation I look forward to having."

The coach arrived at her house, and Hadrian saw her to the door. Vaughn admitted her with a very butler-esque nod.

Back in his coach, Hadrian became consumed with thoughts of the dead young woman. Who was she? What did she have to do with Sir Henry?

He thought about her the whole way home but was no closer to concluding how she might be involved with their current mystery. Hadrian feared the mystery of her identity and her—what looked to be—violent death had died with Sir Henry.

CHAPTER 19

*D*onning the dreaded black gown after only one glorious day of freedom from it nearly drove Tilda to tears. Or would have if she was one for crying, which she was not.

She hadn't even come close last night when she'd informed her grandmother of Sir Henry's utter perfidy. Unfortunately, Grandmama *had* shed some tears, some in sadness but mostly in anger.

Tilda had vowed to her they would be all right, that she would find a way to ensure they were comfortable. Ravenhurst's payment for her investigative services certainly helped, but the investigation would not last forever. And now Vaughn was a member of the household—or she'd have to provide him with a retirement settlement. Tilda had decided not to tell her grandmother last night that they now had a permanent butler—that news could wait for when she was not so upset.

As she walked into the entrance hall to await Ravenhurst's arrival for their appointment with Dr. Selwin, Vaughn rose from his chair.

"No need to get up, Vaughn," she said. "I'm only waiting for Lord Ravenhurst to arrive."

"It's quite all right, miss. I needed to get up anyway. The parlor requires dusting."

"Mrs. Acorn will take care of that," Tilda said, waving him back down. "You should be resting as much as possible."

"Bah, I can dust, and Mrs. Acorn has a great many tasks already. Honestly, your household requires a butler. It's good that I am here." Tilda found him very dear and couldn't deny she didn't mind having him here. She just had to find a way to continue to support the addition.

Ravenhurst knocked on the door, and Vaughn shuffled to open it. "Good afternoon, my lord."

"Afternoon, Vaughn." Ravenhurst stepped inside. He carried a beautiful bouquet of bleeding hearts, camellias, and carnations.

"You brought flowers?" Tilda was slightly taken aback.

"I know how hard it was for you to don the mourning gown today." He gave her an apologetic smile full of warmth and understanding. Tilda's insides fluttered like a bird taking flight. "And yesterday was difficult. I hope these will cheer you."

Tilda took the bouquet, smiling. "They're beautiful. Thank you." She didn't tell him that the only person who'd ever given her flowers had been her father. Every year on her birthday, he gave her a posy, which was no small feat in November.

And now, she had to blink back stupid tears. Turning away from the earl, she handed the flowers to Vaughn. "Would you put these in a vase for me, please?"

"Of course, miss. They are as lovely as you." He smiled before moving slowly from the entrance hall.

Tilda faced the earl once more. "That was very thoughtful of you."

He smiled at her, his blue eyes crinkling at the edges. There was a youthful quality to certain smiles he offered—the ones that appeared the most genuine. They seemed to originate from a place of warmth and joy. "You deserved something nice," he said. "You may want to grab your cloak. It started raining as I arrived."

Tilda fetched her cloak from the peg and drew it around her with the earl's assistance. He then held the door open for her, and they moved outside. She hurried to the coach as it was raining quite steadily.

When they were settled inside and on their way, the earl fixed his gaze on her. "I hope you won't mind my asking, but how did things go with your grandmother last night?"

"She was distressed to hear that Sir Henry had used her money to settle his gambling debts. Then she was sad. Then she became rather angry. In the end, she had a second glass of sherry."

Ravenhurst's brows arched. "That is not the norm, I take it?"

Tilda shook her head. "Rarely. Only to celebrate or if she is upset, the latter of which is almost never. At least not to the extent that requires a second glass of sherry. She didn't even have one after we learned Sir Henry had died. Or after I told her he'd been murdered."

"Well, I am sorry for that. Hopefully, she slept well anyway."

"She says she did. Thank you for inquiring after her." Tilda did not mention her worries about the household or Vaughn in particular. She preferred not to think about those concerns just now. She would rather focus on their upcoming interview with the doctor.

As it was a short journey to Harley Street, they were nearly there.

"I do hope Dr. Selwin is accommodating today," Tilda mused, though she knew it was incredibly unlikely. "However, I suspect he will try to keep our meeting short."

"I'm curious to see what he will present to us as evidence of diagnosing and treating Sir Henry's heart ailment."

The coach stopped outside his office, which was also his residence on the upper floors. The rain had let up a bit, but a persistent drizzle leaked from the clouds.

The earl departed and ushered Tilda inside. The clerk was wearing half-moon glasses today and peered at them over the top as they entered.

"Good afternoon," Ravenhurst said jovially. "I'm sure you remember us from last week. We're here for our appointment with Dr. Selwin."

The clerk removed her glasses and pursed her lips. "You do not have an appointment with him. You are meeting with me so that I may give you the dates of Sir Henry Meacham's visits with Dr. Selwin." She handed Tilda a paper with dates along with short descriptions. "Those are from the past year. I trust that will be sufficient."

"No, it will not," Ravenhurst replied brusquely. "How do we know these weren't fabricated? We want to see the diaries for these dates."

"I'm afraid I can't share those with you," the clerk said coldly. "Then you would see other patients' information."

"We promise we won't be looking at anything but Sir Henry's appointments," Tilda said in growing frustration. Which was silly. It wasn't as if she'd expected anything different. Except she had. She'd thought that Dr. Selwin would be here at least.

"I must insist we speak with Dr. Selwin," Ravenhurst demanded.

The clerk clasped her hands atop the desk and gave him a cool, patient stare. "He is not here."

Tilda folded the paper with the dates and tucked it into her reticule. "We'll return when he is."

Turning on her heel, she stalked to the door. Ravenhurst got there just before her and escorted her outside. He closed

the door behind them with perhaps a tad more force than was
necessary.

"I was expecting difficulty but not outright rudeness,"
Ravenhurst said.

Tilda looked toward the building. "She's probably lying
about him being gone. I'll wager he's in his office."

Ravenhurst's eyes glittered in the murky afternoon light.
"There is one way to find out." He turned abruptly and stalked
back into the office. He bypassed the clerk entirely and went
straight into the sitting room where they'd met Selwin last
week. Then he went into the doctor's private office.

Dr. Selwin bolted up from behind his desk, turning the
shade of a beet. "You can't just come in here!"

"We have an appointment," Tilda said politely as Ravenhurst
closed the door.

"We require a bit of your time," Ravenhurst gave the doctor
a serene smile, but Tilda could see the angry pulse in his neck.
"Please sit."

Selwin dropped into his chair, his color fading, and his
shoulders drooping. His hands were also shaking.

"We have questions for you regarding the night Sir Henry
died," Tilda said, moving closer to the desk.

"I can't speak to you," Selwin said quietly, his voice a dark
rasp laden with fear.

Ravenhurst dragged a chair from around the desk to sit
close to the doctor. "You can and you must. It is clear to us that
you have lied about Sir Henry's death. He was stabbed at
Farringer's then brought here, wasn't he?"

Tilda was surprised by the earl's aggressive approach, but
she didn't mind it. Indeed, there was something...invigorating
about watching him take control and assume a position of
authority.

Still ghastly pale, Selwin lifted his gaze to Ravenhurst, but
only for a moment before dropping it back to his lap. "Yes. He

was already dead when he arrived. His clothing was soaked with blood, and I could see it must have come from a wound to his right side."

"Who brought him?" Ravenhurst asked.

Tilda was mesmerized by Ravenhurst's manner. He stared fixedly at Dr. Selwin and spoke in a calm but demanding tone. He looked and sounded like a father disciplining a child. There was a sense of dominance about him but also of kindness.

"They worked at the club," Dr. Selwin replied shakily. "A couple of blokes carried him in and a third man, he was the one in charge, told me I needed to clean Sir Henry up and write a death certificate saying he'd died of natural decay."

"This man simply instructed you, and you complied?"

"He threatened me with a pistol, and one of the blokes waved his bloody knife around whilst the other returned to the coach. I assumed the knife was used to kill Sir Henry, and I feared I would be next." The doctor's voice trailed off to nothing.

"Did you invent Sir Henry's heart ailment for the death certificate?" Ravenhurst asked.

Dr. Selwin nodded.

Tilda's lip curled. "Which is why you couldn't just show us your diary or tell us last week when it was that you diagnosed Sir Henry. Why even bother with a death certificate? The cause of death would be recorded in the burial registry."

The doctor bent his head toward his lap. "The man in charge said it would ease things with the police."

Ravenhurst frowned at the doctor. "Why would the police be involved?"

"The goal was that they wouldn't." Dr. Selwin worried his hands, flicking his fingers then flexing his palms. "After I cleaned Sir Henry up, I took his body to his house where I delivered it to his butler and informed him what happened. I gave him the death certificate to provide to Sir Henry's next of kin."

Tilda stared at him, aghast. "Sir Henry was a patient of yours. I believe you took care of his wife when she became ill and died. Even if you were threatened, how could you treat him in this way?"

When Selwin lifted his head to look at her, she saw tears in his eyes. "He did not give me a choice. The man in charge made it clear he was not asking me but telling me what to do." He sent her a fearful look, and Tilda almost felt bad for intimidating him. "He also paid me a good sum."

Ravenhurst made a sound of disgust in his throat. "You've had ample opportunity since then, when you were not actively being threatened, to report the incident to the police," Ravenhurst said, still sounding calm while Tilda wanted to shake Selwin until his teeth rattled. "Or did you prefer to accept the money and remain complicit?"

Selwin's chin wobbled. He sniffed then wiped his hands over his eyes. "I am not proud."

"What are the names of these men who brought Sir Henry here?" Ravenhurst demanded.

"I don't know. They didn't say, and I didn't ask. The two men who carried him were in livery, as if they were footmen. The man in charge wore evening clothes—a black coat and white waistcoat."

Tilda looked at Ravenhurst the moment he looked at her. Their silent communication was that they both knew who this was—the manager of Farringer's, Dunwell, who they'd met. And Tilda would bet Fitch was one of the men in livery. Likely the one waving a knife around. She had to admit that was likely terrifying for the doctor. Still, Ravenhurst was right, Selwin could have reported the incident anytime in the past fortnight.

Ravenhurst turned his attention back to the doctor. "How much did they pay you?"

Selwin adjusted his gaze down once more and spoke quietly. "Thirty pounds."

That much! Tilda wanted to demand he give it to her as recompense. Instead, she glowered at him. "You must come with us to Scotland Yard now and repeat to the inspector what you told us."

Selwin shook his head violently. "Absolutely not. It's risky enough that I spoke to you. Those men are dangerous. They were very threatening when they were here. The one with the knife in particular. He was quite menacing. And he threatened to go upstairs and harm my wife." Selwin broke down completely then into great sobs.

"I understand you were frightened," Ravenhurst said soothingly. "But now is the time to make things right."

Selwin pivoted in his chair and opened a drawer in his desk. He dug into the back and withdrew a folded piece of parchment. "I received this day before yesterday, along with another ten pounds." He shoved the paper at Ravenhurst.

The earl glanced up at Tilda before he unfolded the paper. He read it aloud:

Remember that you must remain quiet. People who talk lose their tongues.

And more.

So do their family members.

Another sob leapt from Selwin's mouth. He clapped his hand over his lips and slid down in his chair. He looked utterly defeated.

Ravenhurst looked up at Tilda with a frown. She pursed her lips. What were they to do?

"I am leaving London for a while," Selwin croaked. "We're going to visit my wife's sister and her husband in Oxford." He pulled a handkerchief from his pocket and blew his nose.

"You can't leave until you give testimony," Ravenhurst said darkly, his eyes narrowing slightly. "I will ensure a constable is put on guard here so that you will be safe. I will arrange that immediately."

Selwin shook his head vigorously. "I will be gone within the hour. We've already packed, and the coach is being readied as we speak. You can't make me stay!" Selwin jumped up.

Ravenhurst slowly got to his feet. "No, we can't. But know that if you leave, you may also be charged with a crime. Indeed, I will do everything I can to ensure that happens."

Selwin turned gray. "Please. I never asked for any of this."

Tilda put her hand on her hip and glared at the doctor. "Sir Henry didn't ask to be murdered and have that concealed. Have you any care for right and wrong? For justice?"

"I do." Selwin's shoulders curled in, and his voice was small. "I will help you. Just let me take my wife to her sister's, then I will return tomorrow."

"If you don't, I'll make sure you're found and brought back," Ravenhurst said. He looked at Tilda, and his eyes were darker than she'd ever seen them.

"What about that note?" Selwin asked, his gaze moving to the paper in the earl's hand.

"I'll be keeping it." Ravenhurst moved toward the door and opened it, holding it for Tilda.

She pinned the doctor with a furious stare. "You should be ashamed. I pray your wife doesn't learn how poorly you've behaved. I doubt she would forgive you. I certainly won't."

Spinning on her heel, Tilda stalked through the doorway. She continued quickly to the outer office where she didn't spare even a glance for the clerk. Ravenhurst wasn't fast enough to open the exterior door.

Outside, she muttered a curse under her breath. "How can we just let him leave London?" she asked.

"Do you recommend I tie him up until Inspector Teague can arrive?" Ravenhurst guided her to the coach.

The rain had stopped but there was a cold wind. It felt

refreshing against Tilda's heated face. "We should call on Teague." She hoped he was at Scotland Yard, for they really did require his help. Whomever was behind everything was a very dangerous person.

"I'd prefer to call on Mrs. Crawford first." He glanced at her gown. "You've gone to the trouble of wearing that garment you detest, so it seems we should ensure it wasn't for naught."

Tilda did not want to wear it again any time soon. "Yes, let's go visit Mrs. Crawford. Then we can inform Teague about Selwin's crimes. Do you think he'll be arrested?"

Ravenhurst lifted a shoulder and helped her into the coach as Leach held the door. "It's possible. I certainly won't advocate for leniency."

Tilda thought of poor Sir Henry, stabbed and carted off; the truth of his death concealed. Now they needed to determine why.

CHAPTER 20

*W*hen the coach turned onto Grenville Street near Clarendon Square, the rain started to fall in buckets. It suited Hadrian's dark mood. He'd wanted to throttle Selwin upon learning what he'd done to be complicit in concealing Sir Henry's death. And for what? Money?

And keeping his family safe, Selwin had said. Hadrian understood fear, but if the villains had been reported to Scotland Yard at any point during the past fortnight, they would likely already be in custody awaiting trial. Indeed, Fitch would probably still be alive.

He looked over at Miss Wren. She'd barely said anything since they'd left Selwin's. For her, this was even worse because Sir Henry was family. He could imagine how angry she must feel.

The coach stopped in front of the Crawfords' address. A mourning wreath still adorned the door, and he could see black hangings through the windows.

Hadrian wished they didn't have to bother Crawford's widow, but it was critical to move their investigation forward.

They had to establish the link between Patrick Crawford and Sir Henry. "Ready?" he asked Miss Wren.

She blinked a few times and pushed away from the back of the seat. "Yes. Let's make the most of this black dress, shall we?" A small smile passed over her lips, and Hadrian was grateful for the moment of levity.

He stepped from the coach and helped her down then escorted her to the door. "I hope this isn't too upsetting for Mrs. Crawford. I'm not sure what to do if she refuses to see us."

"I know. I've tried not to think about that," Miss Wren said, sending him a worried glance.

Taking a deep breath and sending up a prayer, he knocked on the door. A moment later, it opened to reveal the butler, an older, stern-faced man with dark, bird-like eyes that moved over Hadrian and Miss Wren with speed and intensity.

Hadrian presented the man with his card. "Good afternoon. We would like to see Mrs. Crawford, if she is receiving. I was a colleague of her late husband. I was also attacked in the same manner as he was, only I am here to tell the tale." He felt it was important to mention the latter as it may increase their chances of being received.

"I see," the butler said. "Come in while I ask if she is available to see you. She is not currently receiving callers outside of family."

"We understand," Miss Wren said softly with a gentle nod.

The butler looked over her again, his gaze lingering on her mourning costume. "If you'll just wait here." He departed the entrance hall for the staircase hall which was visible through an arched doorway.

Hadrian removed his gloves and noted Miss Wren watching him. "Just in case," he whispered.

The tension grew palpable as they waited. What would they do if Mrs. Crawford refused to see them? They'd continue to Scotland Yard. Hadrian wanted to return to Farringer's, but as they'd been banned from visiting, that was not an option. Hadrian was keen to confirm Fitch as an employee.

The butler appeared in the staircase hall and came back into the entrance hall. "Mrs. Crawford will see you. I'll take you up to the drawing room."

They followed the butler into the staircase hall and up to the drawing room. Candles flickered, but the space was dim and held a melancholic air as the curtains were drawn and black crepe covered multiple mirrors. Mrs. Crawford was not present, but she would presumably be along directly.

Miss Wren moved farther into the room toward a central seating area. Suddenly, a cat jumped up from the settee over the back onto a table situated behind it. Several photographs were turned down, and the feline knocked one off as it leapt from the table to the floor and dashed from the room, cutting a wide berth around Miss Wren and Hadrian.

Miss Wren lifted her hand to her chest. "That surprised me."

"Apparently we surprised the cat." Hadrian moved to pick up the photograph. He couldn't help looking at it and froze. It was identical to the one of the four men at Sir Henry's. And it provoked the same flash of the dead woman in Hadrian's mind. But the vision was different. He viewed the woman from a different angle. And he could see the lower half of a man's legs on the other side of her body.

Hadrian sucked in a breath, and the vision flitted away like a butterfly. He blinked at the photograph in his hand. It wasn't exactly the same as Sir Henry's. The figures on the left weren't quite as blurry. Indeed, the second from the left was almost identifiable, as if he'd been convinced to hold still for this version of the photograph.

"What is it?" Miss Wren asked, moving to his side. She gasped. "Oh!"

"What are you doing?"

Hadrian and Miss Wren turned toward the doorway at the sound of the shaky, feminine voice.

"That is supposed to be turned down," Mrs. Crawford said. She was about Hadrian's age, beautiful but terribly thin. She was also pale with dark circles beneath her eyes, perhaps indicating she didn't sleep well.

"It was," Hadrian replied. "I'm afraid we spooked the cat, and it knocked the photograph to the floor. I was merely picking it up."

"I see," Mrs. Crawford said, walking slowly toward them. She wore a high-necked ebony gown. It was far more fashionable than Miss Wren's, but it was terrible that Mrs. Crawford should have to wear it. She was a young woman and ought to be laughing and wearing vibrant colors.

Miss Wren gave her a warm smile. "This is Lord Ravenhurst, and I am Miss Matilda Wren. My grandfather's cousin is in this photograph." Miss Wren took it from Hadrian and showed it to Mrs. Crawford. "Here." Pointing to the man on the far right, Miss Wren went on, "This is Sir Henry Meacham. He died a fortnight ago. That is why I am also wearing black."

"I'm sorry for your loss," Mrs. Crawford said. "My father-in-law is the man next to Sir Henry."

"Is he?" Miss Wren studied the photograph. "I didn't know that. They must have been friends."

"I think they must have been, though that image was taken some thirty years ago, I believe. The date is on the back."

Hadrian took the photograph from Miss Wren. "May I?" He was asking Mrs. Crawford if he could remove the plate from the frame. "I'd like to see the date. Sir Henry's didn't have that." Actually, it might have. They'd never thought to look.

"You can take it out of the frame, if you like," Mrs. Crawford said.

Anticipation curled through Hadrian as he removed the plate from the frame. He read the year etched on the back.

"1839," he said, thinking the clothing that the woman in his visions wore fit that time period. Except she wasn't in the photograph, just the visions that accompanied it. How he wanted to find out who she was!

Hadrian put the plate back into the frame. "I don't suppose you know who the other men are?"

Miss Wren gave Mrs. Crawford a faint smile. "Sir Henry's daughter doesn't know, and she is wondering if they were good friends of her father's."

"I don't know, I'm sorry," Mrs. Crawford said.

Loath to set the photograph down in case he might glimpse the vision once more, Hadrian held it for a moment longer. He fixed on the image, on Sir Henry and then on Martin Crawford beside him.

The vision burst into Hadrian's mind once more, along with a searing pain. He saw the woman, but she was nearly upside down due to the vantage point. Was he seeing her from Crawford's perspective versus Sir Henry's? He tried to see more of the man whose legs were visible. Up, up to the man's middle...higher. There.

It was Sir Henry, but thirty years ago.

The pain in Hadrian's head intensified. He felt Miss Wren touch his arm. She took the photograph and set it face down on the table with the others. He blinked and saw the concern in her gaze.

"Thank you for seeing us, Mrs. Crawford," Miss Wren said softly. "I can imagine how difficult this time has been for you. I am so very sorry for the loss of your husband."

"He was such a good man." Mrs. Crawford's voice broke on the last word. Her nose twitched as she pulled a handkerchief from her pocket. "Can't manage without a steady supply of these," she said with a fleeting smile. She pressed the handkerchief to her nose.

"Yes," Hadrian said, sounding gruff. He cleared his throat

gently. "He is much missed in the Commons."

"So many of his colleagues have sent notes and flowers. Their concern is much appreciated." Mrs. Crawford focused on Hadrian. "My butler told me you were also attacked. I didn't know anyone else had been."

"Yes, the prior Tuesday and in the same location, in fact."

Mrs. Crawford's blue eyes rounded. "What a striking coincidence."

"Exactly my thoughts," Hadrian replied. "I didn't even learn your husband had been attacked until recently. I find it very troubling. So much so that I visited Scotland Yard to determine what they had done to investigate the two crimes."

"They didn't do much, in my opinion," Mrs. Crawford said with clear acrimony. "They closed Patrick's case quickly after concluding a footpad had killed him. Then the inspector told me they would likely never find the perpetrator. Of course they wouldn't as they didn't even look."

"Was this Inspector Padgett?" Hadrian asked. "I understand he was assigned to both cases."

Mrs. Crawford wrinkled her nose in distaste. "Yes. I didn't care for him."

"Neither did I," Hadrian said in solidarity. "I have been trying to review the reports, but he classified them as confidential, so I haven't been able to see them." Perhaps Superintendent Newsome was even now trying to deliver them to Hadrian. He hoped so but would not hold his breath.

"Can I ask why you are here?" Mrs. Crawford asked. "It almost seems as if the two of you are investigating these cases since Scotland Yard is not."

Miss Wren smiled. "That *is* what we are doing. As you can imagine, Lord Ravenhurst has a particular interest and hired me to conduct an investigation."

"He hired you?" Mrs. Crawford asked with surprise.

"Miss Wren is incredibly qualified in such matters," Hadrian said. "She is close to proving the man who attacked me and killed your husband also killed her grandfather's cousin."

Mrs. Crawford put her hand to her mouth. She blinked, but a tear escaped each eye. Lifting the handkerchief, she quickly swabbed her cheeks. "You know who killed Patrick?" She looked from Miss Wren to Hadrian.

"We think it's most likely he was killed by the man who attacked Lord Ravenhurst," Miss Wren replied. "The earl has positively identified him. However, he is, unfortunately, dead."

The woman wobbled, and Miss Wren rushed to her side, sliding her arm around Mrs. Crawford's waist. "I've got you," Miss Wren murmured.

"I'm sorry," Mrs. Crawford said softly. "This is shocking to hear."

"Come and sit." Miss Wren guided her to the settee, and they sat down together.

Hadrian took a chair opposite them. "I'm sorry this is so upsetting. Please know that we are only trying to discover the truth. What we are missing is the link between your husband and Sir Henry." Although, it seemed the connection may actually be between Sir Henry and her father-in-law, the man in the photograph, particularly since Martin Crawford had loaned Sir Henry money.

"All I can say is that my father-in-law was friends with Sir Henry. I'd forgotten we even had that photograph, but it was one of many things Patrick's mother gave him when his father died last year." Mrs. Crawford fell silent a moment, then her eyes rounded briefly. "Wait, I do remember who one of the other gentlemen is. He came to my father-in-law's funeral. His name is Erasmus Blount."

Hadrian felt a rush of excitement. Hopefully Blount was still alive and well. "I don't suppose you could give us Mr. Blount's direction?" He held his breath and glanced toward

Miss Wren whose attention was entirely focused on Mrs. Crawford.

"He lives in Brighton. He's infirm. I think it was difficult for him to come to London last year. He sent a card after Patrick died saying he wasn't able to make the trip for the funeral." Mrs. Crawford shook her head. "I don't know why I didn't recall all that sooner." She looked at Miss Wren. "I suppose grief takes up too much space in my head sometimes."

Miss Wren patted the woman's hand. "We're just grateful you recalled something that could help us."

"How does this help?" Mrs. Crawford asked.

"We will speak with Mr. Blount," Hadrian said. "Hopefully, he will be able to tell us more about how your father-in-law and Sir Henry are connected."

Miss Wren tipped her head toward Mrs. Crawford. "Would you know anything about an IOU Sir Henry had with your father-in-law?"

Mrs. Crawford shook her head. "No. You could ask my mother-in-law, but I do not recommend it. She is completely devastated by Patrick's death. She has removed to the country. Not even her grandchildren could bring her joy." Mrs. Crawford sniffed.

"That's a shame," Miss Wren said consolingly.

Mrs. Crawford looked toward her. "Was Sir Henry also stabbed?"

"He was, and someone tried to make it appear as though he'd died of natural decay," Miss Wren replied. "I would surmise that your husband's death was made to appear a random attack by a footpad who'd gone too far."

"But a footpad stabbing his victims didn't make sense to me," Hadrian said. "Which is why I hired Miss Wren to look into the matter."

Mrs. Crawford's brow pleated with confusion. "But you

said you identified the culprit and that he's already dead. Is the matter not resolved?"

Miss Wren shook her head. "No. We don't believe the man who killed your husband and Sir Henry had a motive to do so. It's much more likely that he was paid to...do what he did."

"How cold." Mrs. Crawford looked down at her lap and sniffed.

"We won't bother you any longer." Miss Wren touched Mrs. Crawford's hand briefly before standing. "Thank you again for permitting us to see you. I will keep you in my thoughts."

"And my children please," Mrs. Crawford said before dabbing at her eyes with her handkerchief. "They're so young. I worry they won't remember him at all. Forgive me." She squeezed her eyes shut and hurried from the room.

"Poor dear," Miss Wren said.

"I feel very badly for her loss and more committed than ever to finding out what happened." Hadrian stood and went to the photograph. Without hesitation he picked it up as he cleared his mind, opening it to whatever he might see.

A bolt of pain shot behind his eyes. The dead woman, Sir Henry...to the right, another man but only his midsection was visible. And his hand. He was wearing a ring on his little finger.

"*Ravenhurst.*" Miss Wren jolted him from the vision.

"I liked Raven better, actually," he said without thinking. His head throbbed. That must be why his hand was pressed against his forehead. He'd been completely engrossed in what he'd been seeing. And what he'd seen...Excitement shot through him, obliterating the pain for a moment.

"You saw something touching that photograph," Miss Wren said in a low voice. "It happened when you picked it up from the floor too. I saw your reaction."

He still held the photograph, but for now, he was just feeling a mash of emotions: fear, horror, guilt. "I saw the same dead woman," he said. "But from a different perspective. From

Crawford's, I would imagine. I could see Sir Henry standing on the other side of the woman's body. There was a third man. I saw part of him—his hand." Hadrian blinked and fixed on Miss Wren. "He was wearing a ring on his little finger. A ring bearing the letter M."

She gasped, her eyes growing wide. "The ring you have?"

Hadrian removed it from his pocket, glad he hadn't had to surrender it—yet. He did not see or feel anything touching it, and he realized he hadn't since they'd found Fitch. Looking at the ring, he was confident it was the same one he'd seen in his mind. "Yes. Whomever originally owned this ring was with Sir Henry and Crawford and the dead woman. Probably thirty years ago." He looked down at the photo. "I believe that when I touch this, I am seeing the memories of the person it belonged to. Looking at the photo triggers these images."

"So, today you are seeing Martin Crawford's memories. And with Sir Henry's photograph, you saw his. Both men share the horrible memory of this dead woman," Miss Wren said darkly. "Why don't you see the memories of the man wearing the ring? You *have* the ring."

Hadrian handed her the photograph and pulled the ring from his pocket. Slipping it onto his finger, he took a deep breath. His head still ached horribly. Nevertheless, he took the photograph back. There was nothing for a long moment, then a flash of color—the dead woman's blue patterned dress. The pin on her bodice.

The woman wasn't dead. She smiled prettily, her eyes narrowed with desire. She said something, but Hadrian couldn't hear her. He thought it might be, "Kiss me." Then her eyes closed, and her mouth opened, as if she were moaning.

Hadrian's view was from above her. Hands encircled her neck. She didn't flinch. She arched her head back, seeming to welcome this abuse. The hands squeezed. Her eyes flew open, and she began to struggle. Her hands closed around the man's wrists. Her face paled. She opened her mouth, her eyes wide with panic. Then she went limp.

The photograph fell from his grip. He blinked. It took him a moment to focus on Miss Wren. She held the photograph. Her face was a mask of worry. "What did you see?" she whispered.

"The man who wore this ring killed her. He choked her." Hadrian tried to make sense of it all. "She didn't mind at first—they were...intimate." They'd been having sex. Hadrian was sure of that now. The man had begun to choke her, and she'd seemed to enjoy it. Until he'd gone too far.

Miss Wren's jaw dropped. "How ghastly. Are you all right?"

"I am very glad this curse doesn't belong to you." His head felt like it had been split open with an axe. He removed the ring and slipped it back into his pocket. Then he massaged his forehead. "We should go."

"We need to visit Erasmus Blount with due haste," she said quietly.

Hadrian nodded then wished he hadn't, for his head was still throbbing. "Tomorrow. I'll purchase our tickets to Brighton. We'll leave early."

CHAPTER 21

After leaving the Crawford residence that afternoon, Hadrian had conveyed Miss Wren to Mrs. Forsythe's, where Miss Wren planned to discuss the potential exhumation as well as query her about the friendship between her father, Martin Crawford, and Erasmus Blount. It was Miss Wren's hope that she would be able to learn the identity of the fourth man in the photograph. They both felt certain he was the killer —of the poor young woman, of Patrick Crawford, and of Sir Henry. And Fitch.

They'd decided that whilst Miss Wren did that, Hadrian would call on Inspector Teague to inform him of what they'd learned regarding Selwin. Teague had wanted to speak with Selwin directly, of course, and, when he'd learned the doctor had left town, he'd been angry. He was at least glad to know where Selwin had gone so the police could retrieve him if he didn't return as promised.

They'd also discussed Hadrian's and Miss Wren's meeting with Superintendent Newsome as well as the inquest. Hadrian had also mentioned Newsome's condescending attitude toward Miss Wren as well as the note she'd received from Lowther.

Teague hadn't been surprised as the police generally didn't like people meddling in their investigations, even if cases had been closed or the investigating party had the appropriate skills, which Teague had agreed Miss Wren possessed.

Hadrian had been pleased to hear it and looked forward to informing Miss Wren that she had at least one supporter at Scotland Yard. Hadrian was still waiting for the "confidential" reports on his attack and Crawford's murder. At this point, he doubted he'd ever be allowed to read them.

It was past nine that evening as Hadrian sat at his desk in his study, writing out a timeline of events, beginning with the photograph taken in 1839. His head still ached, but a glass of whisky had soothed the rougher edges of the pain.

Hadrian's butler, Collier, stepped through the open doorway of the study. "I'm sorry to disturb you, my lord, but a man arrived at the servant's entrance asking to speak with you. He says his name is Gregson and that he has information you want."

Shooting out of his chair, Hadrian nearly dashed downstairs. However, they ought to speak in confidence rather than in the scullery. "Show him up, please."

Collier hesitated. "I shouldn't ask, but is he involved in your investigation?"

Hadrian hadn't shared the specifics of his investigation, but he'd told Collier, as well as his valet, Sharp, that he was hunting the man who'd attacked him and that the search had expanded to include a variety of crimes.

"He is," Hadrian said. "I'm quite surprised he is here."

"I'll bring him up." Collier turned and left.

Hadrian paced whilst he waited, questions swirling in his mind. He'd hoped for the chance to speak with the doorman or the waiter but wasn't sure how or when that would happen. This was incredibly convenient and timely given what they'd learned from Selwin earlier.

He wished Miss Wren were here. Hadrian would do his best to recall every detail of the interview as well as make sure he didn't miss asking something critical.

"My lord, Mr. Gregson is here," Collier said from the doorway.

Gregson, his hat crushed between his meaty hands, walked slowly into the study. He looked around the room, his gaze wary. Then his focus settled on Hadrian.

"Welcome, Mr. Gregson." Hadrian glanced toward the butler. "Thank you, Collier."

The butler departed, closing the door behind him with a definitive click.

Hadrian regarded the doorman—he was not wearing the Farringer's livery but a cheaply made brown costume. Anticipation thrummed through Hadrian along with a bead of apprehension.

"I appreciate you agreeing to meet with me, my lord." Gregson sounded as uncertain as he looked.

"I'm quite pleased to see you, actually." Hadrian gestured toward the small seating area near the hearth radiating heat from the burning coals. "Please have a seat."

Gregson went to one of the chairs and seemed to hesitate. Ultimately, he perched on the edge as if he hadn't really wanted to sit.

"Do make yourself comfortable," Hadrian said.

The man had been fearful when they'd met, and now he'd come here in spite of that. Hadrian didn't want him to be nervous—or afraid. Still, Hadrian would be on guard in case Gregson was here for nefarious purposes, though he very much doubted it. The man did not exhibit the demeanor of someone intent on malice. "May I pour you a glass of wine, or perhaps you prefer whisky?" Hadrian offered.

Gregson blinked. "Er, no, thank you, my lord."

Hadrian took the chair that faced Gregson's. Sitting, he gave the man an encouraging smile. "It is very brave of you to come here. I know it can't have been easy."

"Do you know why I'm here?" Gregson asked in seeming surprise.

"I can surmise the reason. It was evident to me that you were afraid to say much at Farringer's the other night."

Gregson nodded. "That's right. Then Dunwell came outside." He grimaced and twisted the hat in his hands. "He was vexed about you and your lady friend asking so many questions."

"Did you tell him what we discussed?" Hadrian asked, worried for the doorman since he knew that Dunwell was involved in the concealment of Sir Henry's murder—at least. What else had the man done?

Shaking his head, Gregson wiped one hand over his brow. "Just that you were asking about Sir Henry, and I refused to talk to you and was trying to make you leave."

"That was smart." Hadrian wanted to get to the purpose of the doorman's visit. "Why did you come here tonight?"

"You said Fitch died. I heard he was garroted." Gregson's shoulder's twitched, and he lost a shade of color.

"He was," Hadrian confirmed. "Did you work with Fitch at Farringer's?"

Gregson nodded. "He was a doorman too. Been there longer than me. I only started last fall."

Hadrian's pulse thrummed. "I have learned more information since I saw you the other night. I know that Sir Henry's body was transported from Farringer's to his physician's office on Harley Street. Were you and Fitch the ones who moved him?"

Gregson pressed his hand over his mouth. He stared at the burning coals for a moment before dropping his hand to his lap. He looked at Hadrian with sorrow and regret in his eyes. "Yes. I was working at the door that night, and Fitch was inside. Sometimes we'd have gentlemen who couldn't hold their liquor or some who get angry and irrational when they lose. The inside man would toss them out."

"I see. Do you know what happened inside? Sir Henry was stabbed, but it would be helpful to know who stuck him." Hadrian prayed the man could say it was Fitch.

"I don't know what happened for certain," Gregson replied. It was disappointing to hear, but he likely knew *something* helpful. "Dunwell bade me help them move the body out the back before anyone could see. It seemed no one witnessed what happened in the card room. It was just Dunwell and Fitch. And the dead man."

Gregson took a breath before continuing. "I could see the man—Sir Henry—had been stabbed. There was a great deal of blood, and it originated in one area on his right side. I would have thought it was a pistol shot, but I didn't hear that." He swallowed. "And Fitch always had a knife handy—in the top of his boot."

Why hadn't Hadrian thought to search Fitch when they'd found his body? Though, if there had been a knife on his person, it would have come up in the inquest. Perhaps whomever had killed him had also known it was in his boot and had taken it.

"Do you think Fitch killed Sir Henry?" Hadrian asked.

"If I was a betting man, I would put money on it, but I'm not. Sometimes Dunwell pays Fitch extra for jobs on the side." Gregson hesitated before adding, "I did wonder if Fitch killed people for money."

"What made you think that?"

Gregson lifted a shoulder. "He was sharpening his knife one night several weeks ago. I thought I saw dried blood on the blade, but I wasn't certain. Even so, Fitch was a scary bloke. He was good for a laugh, but I wouldn't have wanted to prick his temper. Just after the new year, he beat one of the waiters at

Farringer's until his eyes were swollen shut—because the waiter made a jest about Fitch wearing a new gold ring. The waiter asked who Fitch had stolen it from. Fitch didn't like that, said it had been given to him fairly as payment. Then he'd beat the waiter."

Hadrian's heart had begun to race faster when Gregson said Fitch had beaten someone—this was likely one of the first visions Hadrian had seen—and then picked up speed at the mention of the ring. "Did this ring have an M engraved on it?"

Gregson blinked. "That's right. How'd you know?"

Exhaling, Hadrian pulled the ring from his pocket and held it out on his palm. "Because I took it from Fitch's hand the night that he stabbed me in January. Have you any idea who gave it to him for payment?"

"I don't. He never said, and after he thrashed the waiter, no one dared ask him anything. No one spoke to him unless he talked to them first."

"He sounds charming," Hadrian said drily. He wanted to get back to what happened the night Sir Henry died. "After you moved the body, you and Fitch took it to Harley Street. Did Dunwell accompany you?"

"Yes. He came with us to make sure certain things were done. I don't know what because I was made to wait in the coach. Dunwell said the physician had to write out a death certificate before we could take the body to its home."

Hadrian studied the man for a moment. "Surely you must realize there is danger in working at Farringer's after what you've been asked to do?"

"I do. I've found a new position and gave my notice today. Dunwell wasn't pleased. He told me I shouldn't leave and that I definitely shouldn't talk."

"Did he threaten you?"

"Not outright, but I confess I'm afraid, especially since Fitch was killed. But then I read that they arrested the man who murdered him."

Hadrian frowned. "I'm sorry to tell you that I don't believe that man killed Fitch."

Gregson's features turned ashen. "So, the killer is still about?"

"Yes, but I am close to finding him. You will need to give testimony regarding Sir Henry's death to Scotland Yard."

"Will I be in trouble?" Gregson asked, fear lurking in his gaze.

"No. You will explain that you were acting as instructed by your employer, and from what you told me, you weren't aware that you were involved in a crime." Hadrian glanced at the clock. "It is rather late to be going to Scotland Yard, and I have prearranged plans in the morning. I could pick you up later tomorrow afternoon and take you to Whitehall. Where do you lodge?"

"I don't think I want to go there if Fitch's killer is still lurking," Gregson said, his voice trembling. "Fitch was killed at his lodging."

"You can stay here," Hadrian said. "You'll lodge in the mews with my coachman."

Gregson's shoulders sagged with relief. "Thank you, my lord."

"Come, I'll take you to the mews." Hadrian stood. He was brimming with excitement over what he'd learned and couldn't wait to share it with Miss Wren in the morning.

~

*R*avenhurst was punctual as usual despite the early hour. Tilda had watched his coach arrive and rushed to the door. Vaughn was downstairs polishing something that didn't need polishing.

"Good morning," Ravenhurst said, his expression livelier than normal. Indeed, his gaze was positively brimming with excitement.

"You look as if you've something to share," Tilda said as she stepped outside.

"I do, indeed. Let us settle ourselves in the coach." He escorted her to the vehicle where Leach was holding the door for them.

Tilda barely waited for him to be seated before demanding to know what he'd learned. "I assume your visit to see Teague revealed something new?"

"Actually no, it wasn't Teague. Gregson, the doorman from Farringer's, came to my house last night. He was ready—eager even—to tell me what he'd been keeping from us the other night."

Tilda sat forward on the seat, desperate to hear. "I'm sorry I missed this interview."

"I am too," Ravenhurst said with a light chuckle. "Indeed, I wished you were there with me. It wasn't the same hearing this information without you. I thought I might come over and tell you, but it was around ten o'clock or so."

"That's too bad. I do not retire early, but I suppose that is rather late to call. Still, in future if you have vital or even thrilling information to impart, I won't mind you coming at that hour. You won't disturb me."

"I'll keep that in mind."

Tilda wanted to get back to what happened. "Gregson just showed up at your house?"

"At the servant's entrance. He resigned his post at Farringer's. He was smart enough to realize he needed to find new, safer employment."

"I'm glad. Did he confirm that Fitch worked there?" Tilda held her breath even though she was all but certain.

"Yes. He was another doorman. He was also paid by

Dunwell to complete other jobs outside the club. Gregson wasn't entirely sure what those were but suspected Fitch may have killed someone." Ravenhurst arched his brows. "Fitch had a knife with dried blood on the blade some weeks back."

Tilda was both unsurprised to hear this and shocked by it just the same. "Perhaps from when he killed Crawford. Or stabbed you."

"Precisely. Fitch does not sound as though he was a pleasant individual. Gregson related a rather unsavory tale of Fitch beating one of the waiters just after the new year when the waiter insinuated Fitch had stolen something. I saw this in one of my very first visions, but I had no idea what it meant." Ravenhurst paused, and Tilda was sure he was about to reveal something important. "Fitch grew violent when the waiter joked that he had to have stolen a gold ring that he was wearing."

Tilda sucked in a breath. *"With an M engraved on it."*

Ravenhurst nodded somewhat triumphantly. "I showed it to Gregson, and he said it was the same, that Fitch received it as payment."

"From the man who strangled that poor woman thirty odd years ago. I don't suppose Gregson knows who that man is?" Just as she'd been sure that Gregson would confirm Fitch's employment at Farringer's, she was certain he didn't know the killer's identity.

"That would be too easy for us, wouldn't it?" Ravenhurst said with a sardonic smile. "Gregson did convey Sir Henry's body to Dr. Selwin's—along with Fitch and Dunwell. The manager made Gregson stay in the coach while Selwin stitched up Sir Henry and falsified the death certificate."

Tilda's heart pounded. "Did Gregson confirm that Fitch murdered Sir Henry?"

Ravenhurst blew out a frustrated breath. "Unfortunately, no, because he was stationed outside at the door when it happened, but Fitch was inside, and Gregson thinks it's likely he killed Sir Henry. Sir Henry appeared to have been stabbed, and Gregson noted that Fitch always had a knife in his boot."

"How convenient for a killer," Tilda murmured.

They arrived at the London Bridge station, and the coachman opened the door. Ravenhurst climbed down then helped Tilda from the coach.

Moving quickly, they found their platform and Ravenhurst guided her to their carriage, holding the door as she stepped inside. There was a cushioned bench covered in dark-red velvet on either side of the compartment. They sat down opposite one another.

Tilda couldn't help thinking that if Ravenhurst hadn't been employing her, she would have been sitting in the uncovered carriage in the rear, for that was all she could afford. And it likely would have been a stretch at that.

"Did you take Gregson to Scotland Yard?" Tilda asked, resuming their conversation from the coach.

"Not yet. As I said, it was rather late, and we were leaving early this morning. I am going to take him later this afternoon, and you are, of course, welcome to join us."

"I wouldn't miss it."

She thought of Fitch being murdered and worried Gregson may face a similar fate even if his involvement hadn't been as great. "Do you suppose Gregson is safe?"

"He certainly didn't think so. Once I told him I thought the man arrested for Fitch's murder was innocent, he was afraid to return to his lodgings. He spent the night in my mews with Leach. He was enjoying a breakfast in the servants' hall when I left this morning and will spend the day working in the mews until I return—he insisted."

"I'm glad you did that," Tilda said, thinking the earl was a singular gentleman. She hadn't met anyone like him. In many ways, he reminded her of her father. He was kind and thoughtful. And just.

"How was your visit with Mrs. Forsythe yesterday?" Ravenhurst asked, demonstrating his thoughtfulness.

"I was worried Millicent would be upset about the possibility of exhuming her father's body, but she was not. On the contrary, she is eager to have answers about his death, and if an autopsy will help, she is in favor of that." Tilda paused before adding, "She was also eager that someone else cover the expense. I do thank you for offering that."

"Just another expense of the investigation," Ravenhurst said. "I'm relieved she did not take issue with it."

"When I asked about her father's friendships with Crawford and Blount, Millicent could only say that Blount had sent a condolence card after Sir Henry's death." Tilda grabbed the carved wooden arm of her bench as the train lurched forward. "She recalled her father having a group of friends who gathered periodically for card parties and annually for a hunting party in the fall, but as it didn't affect her in any way, she'd paid no attention. She couldn't say whether Blount was part of that group or not. How was your meeting with Teague?"

"He was most interested to learn about Selwin, though he was not pleased that I let him leave town. I kindly reminded him that I am not a constable and that the police had closed the case without proper investigation."

Tilda smirked. "How did he take that?"

"He understood. I have the sense he is frustrated with how these investigations were handled. He really does seem to want to find the truth."

"Because he is apparently uncorrupted, unlike Inspector Padgett." Tilda narrowed her eyes. "I should like to know what Padgett's specific role is in everything. Was it just closing the cases and making the files confidential, thereby ensuring no one investigated and learned the truth?"

"I look forward to discovering that too. We are making good, and faster, progress," Ravenhurst said intently. "It feels as though we are getting close to discovering what we need to crack this open."

"Do you think if Blount can identify the fourth man in the photograph, we'll learn the identity of the person behind everything?"

"Yes, but I'm trying not to get ahead of myself," he said with a laugh.

"I did bring Sir Henry's photograph to show to Blount." She'd tucked it into her reticule.

Admiration flashed in Ravenhurst's eyes. "That was smart. I suppose I assumed he had one too, since he was also in the photograph."

"He might, but I didn't want to take the chance he didn't or that he wouldn't know what photograph we were asking about. That was thirty years ago. It's possible he doesn't have it anymore, if he ever had one, and may not even remember it."

They spent the rest of the journey discussing the case. Ravenhurst removed a piece of parchment from his coat. "I've written out a timeline of events as we know them as well as a list of players in this ever-expanding scheme." He handed her the paper.

Tilda smiled. "I've done the same." She pulled her version from her reticule and gave it to him.

Ravenhurst laughed. "It is good that we are partners." They fell silent as they reviewed the other's notes.

"We have a puppeteer who is pulling all the strings," Tilda began.

"The man who originally owned the M ring and who killed that young woman in 1839," Ravenhurst continued.

"That man is also responsible for Sir Henry's death as well as that of Patrick Crawford." Her gaze locked with Ravenhurst's. "And the attack on you."

"Which was meant for Crawford. Just think, if Fitch had never made that error, the puppeteer might have succeeded in his machinations."

"Aside from not knowing who he is, we've still no idea why he did all this."

Ravenhurst cocked his head and looked out the window at the passing countryside. "We know he killed someone thirty years ago and two men were with him and the body. Both those men—well, the son of one—are dead. Killing them ensures his secret is safe."

"But why would he kill them now? To keep them from revealing his crime? Why not do that thirty years ago?"

"Something had to have triggered this series of events," Ravenhurst said. "I hope Blount will be able to identify the fourth man in the photograph and that he can tell us about the dead woman."

Tilda snapped her gaze to him in surprise. "You think we should ask him about her?"

He gave her a dark look. "I think we must."

Silence reigned for some time as they both lost themselves in thought. Tilda watched the passing countryside but was too preoccupied to enjoy it. Which was too bad since she'd rarely left London.

When the train at last approached the station, Tilda felt a rush of anticipation. Soon they would have answers.

CHAPTER 22

Upon arriving at the train station in Brighton, Hadrian hired a hack to convey them to Erasmus Blount's house near Queen's Park. He escorted Miss Wren to the door.

"I'm nervous," she whispered as they stood at the top of the steps. "What if Blount isn't even home?"

"He will be." *He had to be,* Hadrian thought.

He knocked, and a stout housekeeper answered the door. Handing her his card, Hadrian smiled. "Good afternoon, we've come from London to see Mr. Blount." He hoped mentioning how far they'd traveled would help their cause.

The housekeeper eyed them skeptically. "I see. Are you acquainted with Mr. Blount? Do you know he is infirm?"

"We are not acquainted," Miss Wren replied gently. "Forgive our intrusion, but Mr. Blount was a friend of my cousin's. He died recently, and I'm hoping Mr. Blount can provide some information that would comfort our family during this time."

"I'm sorry for your loss," the housekeeper said as she opened the door wider. "Please come in, and I'll inform Mr.

Blount you're here. I'm sure he'll want to provide solace, if he can. I'll be back directly."

The housekeeper left the small entrance hall for the staircase hall. They waited anxiously for her return a few minutes later, at which time she led them up to the small drawing room overlooking the street below.

Mr. Blount, presumably, sat in a chair near the hearth, his feet propped on a footstool. Beside him stood a table piled with books and newspapers. He was fully dressed, but his clothing was a bit rumpled, as if he'd been sitting in the chair all morning. Glasses perched on his nose as he fixed his gaze upon Hadrian and Miss Wren.

"Lord Ravenhurst?" Blount asked in a graveled tone.

Hadrian inclined his head. "Yes, and this is my private investigator, Miss Wren."

Blount's eyes focused on her. "My housekeeper says your cousin died recently and that I can provide you with some information. Who was your cousin?"

Hadrian noticed he did not invite them to sit. However, he moved closer to the man's chair, and Miss Wren accompanied him.

"Sir Henry Meacham," Miss Wren replied.

Blount began to cough. He pressed a handkerchief to his mouth as his face reddened with his exertion. When he'd recovered, he reached for a glass of water on the table beside his chair and took a sip.

"We are terribly sorry to disturb you," Miss Wren said. "We would not have done so if it was not of critical importance."

"I was aware Sir Henry died," Blount said with another light cough.

"Yes, his daughter told me you'd sent a condolence card. Thank you."

"I don't think I can help you at all." Blount did not meet

their gazes. Instead, he looked into the fire. "I haven't seen Sir Henry in a great many years. And we did not correspond."

"We don't wish to take up too much of your time, Mr. Blount," Miss Wren said. "I'll get straight to the reason we came. I have a photograph that belonged to Sir Henry, and we are unable to identify the fourth person in it. Since you are in the photograph, we hoped you could tell us who he is." She removed the photograph from her reticule and showed it to Blount.

The man began to cough again and had to gasp for breath when he finished. "I can't help you."

Hadrian could see the man was struggling, but they were desperate for his help. "Mr. Blount, please. This is you with Sir Henry and Martin Crawford. Please, will you tell us the identity of the fourth man?"

Blount coughed once then took another drink of water. He reached for the photograph and brought it in front of his face. "He's blurry."

"So are you," Hadrian said. "But Mrs. Patrick Crawford recalled that you are the second man from the left. Is that not you?" For a brief moment, Hadrian feared Mrs. Crawford had been mistaken.

"It is me." Blount sounded defeated. He muttered something that sounded like, "Lord, forgive me," then exhaled. He pointed to the man on the right. "That's Henry and that's Crawford." His finger moved to the man next to Sir Henry. "This is me." He pointed to the second man from the left. His hand shook as his finger gravitated to the left, to the blurriest of the figures. "And this is Ardleigh."

"The Viscount Ardleigh?" Hadrian said in surprise.

Blount nodded then thrust the photograph back at Miss Wren. "I loathe that photograph."

"It isn't very good, is it?" Miss Wren said with a trace of levity. "Did you not have your own? This belonged to Sir

Henry, and Mrs. Crawford has the one that belonged to her father-in-law."

"I had one once, but I burned it. Ardleigh had one too. No one is blurry in his. He kept the best one because he paid for them to be taken."

"That was in 1839," Hadrian noted. "Where were you?"

"At Ardleigh's estate in Essex. Ardleigh hosted hunting parties every fall. That was the last one we attended." Blount coughed again then frowned. "You must leave."

"We will in a moment, I promise," Miss Wren said softly. "This is so very important, and I deeply appreciate your help." She looked over at Hadrian, and he knew this was the only chance he'd get to ask what they most needed to know after learning Ardleigh's identity.

Though Hadrian knew that Ardleigh had likely killed the woman he saw in his visions, he purposely posed a vague question. "Mr. Blount, what does a dead young woman have to do with this photograph?"

The older man's coughing resumed, much worse than before. He turned scarlet and struggled to breathe. A middle-aged woman rushed into the room and frowned at them. She wore a starched white apron and a cap. Hadrian presumed she was a nurse.

She waved an herbed sachet before Blount. "There now. Easy. Try to breathe."

Blount struggled but eventually caught his breath, and the coughing subsided. The nurse turned her head toward Hadrian and Miss Wren. "You need to leave Mr. Blount alone now."

Shaking his head, Blount took the glass of water that the nurse offered him. He took a drink then gasped a long breath. "Leave us, Nurse. They will depart shortly."

The nurse did not look pleased, but she bustled from the room.

Fixing Hadrian with a dark stare, Blount asked, "How do

you know about the woman?" His gaze moved to Miss Wren. "Did Henry tell you before he died?" His tone held an accusatory note.

Miss Wren shot a surprised look at Hadrian. "He did not. I can't tell you how we know, but we do."

Blount sniffed then looked down for a moment. "I suppose it is well past time the truth is told. Why don't you sit?" He waved at the settee nearby.

Hadrian and Miss Wren sat down together and exchanged anxious looks.

Removing his glasses, Blount set them atop one of the books on the table beside his chair. He massaged the bridge of his nose. At last, he said, "Ardleigh has always had an eye for young women. In our youth, he was, I suppose, very attractive, and the fairer sex typically sought his attention. Mostly, he would flirt, but later we learned that he took things much farther, most often with those in his employ." Blount met Hadrian's gaze, his features tired. "He gets rough with them sometimes. That's what he told us when we stumbled upon him standing over the woman at the hunting party. She was *not* in his employ but the daughter of a neighbor. They'd met for a tryst near where her father's property met Ardleigh's. That happened the day before the photograph was taken."

"He killed the young woman?" Hadrian already knew the answer of course.

"He said it was an accident, that she was enjoying his attentions. Ardleigh had his hands around her neck while they were —" Blount sent a sharp look toward Miss Wren. "Perhaps you shouldn't be hearing this."

"It's fine, Mr. Blount," she said. "My father was a sergeant for the Metropolitan Police, and I am a private investigator."

"Do go on, Mr. Blount," Hadrian said.

Blount sipped his water before continuing. "Ardleigh found

pleasure in causing distress to his bed partners. In this instance, he went too far. He said he accidentally killed her."

Miss Wren's face lost a bit of color, but she said nothing. Hadrian felt an urge to reach over and take her hand. He did not. Later, he would provide comfort—if she wanted it.

"Ardleigh was most distraught. He was sobbing. We all believed him. Well, all of us but perhaps Sir Henry. Turns out Ardleigh had done this before. Four years earlier, he'd had another 'accident' with a maid at his house in London. Sir Henry had helped him clean that up too."

"Is that what you all did with this young woman he killed at the hunting party?" Hadrian asked. "You 'cleaned it up'?"

Blount's chin quivered, and his hands were shaking again. "We helped him bury her. Her family was devastated that she'd disappeared. I hate that those poor people have no idea what happened to her." Another coughing fit claimed him. Tears streamed down his cheeks. Hadrian couldn't know if they were from coughing or deep regret.

When Blount was recovered, Miss Wren held up the photograph. "You all posed for this the next day as if nothing happened?"

"We didn't want to. Crawford wanted to leave first thing, but Ardleigh had already arranged and paid for the photograph. He insisted we all stay, that we'd been friends too long." Blount coughed a bit and drank more water. "The four of us were never together again after that. Crawford kept his distance from all of us. I think Sir Henry and Ardleigh remained friendly. I left London a few years later. I hated running into Ardleigh and the memories it stirred." Blount wiped his hand over his nose as he looked down at his lap. "I hate myself still."

Hadrian and Miss Wren exchanged a sorrowful look. What could they say to Blount that would ease his heartache? Was it even their place to do so?

"It's good that you're telling the story now," Miss Wren said with a small, heartening smile. "We will do everything we can to bring Ardleigh to justice."

"I can't imagine how difficult it has been for you to hold these secrets and to share them now," Hadrian said. "I hope it will be easier to repeat what you've told us to an inspector from Scotland Yard."

Blount shook his head. "I can't possibly travel to London."

"Of course not, nor will anyone expect you to," Miss Wren assured him. "The inspector can come here and take your statement."

"Will it even matter?" Blount asked, sounding defeated. "The crime happened so long ago, and it didn't even take place in London."

"While that is true, it seems that crime is connected to the deaths of Patrick Crawford and Sir Henry. A man was paid to kill them. He wore a gold ring with the letter M engraved on it that was given to him as payment."

"That ring belonged to Ardleigh." Blount coughed. "The M is for his surname, Mattingly. Before he became the viscount, everyone called him Matty. Though, I'm surprised he would give that ring away. His father gave it to him."

"Perhaps he was willing to trade anything to keep his secrets buried," Hadrian said.

"That I believe with every fiber of my being. Whenever I saw him before I left London, he would ask if I'd kept 'our' secret." Blount sneered. "Ardleigh made a point of ensuring we all had a stake in what happened and in keeping it quiet. If he paid someone to kill Sir Henry, he must have thought Sir Henry had exposed him or was going to."

Miss Wren let out an audible breath. Hadrian looked over at her to see she'd closed her eyes for a moment. When she opened them, he saw a bright vigor. She angled herself toward him on the settee. "Whitley said that Sir Henry believed he was going to come into a sum of money. What if he blackmailed Ardleigh? Hardacre said he'd considered blackmail before."

"You are brilliant," Hadrian said with a quick smile. "But why was Crawford killed?"

Blount spoke. "I can't say why Martin's son was killed, but of the three of us who were with Ardleigh that day, Martin would have been the one to reveal what happened. He was so horrified and even tried to walk away whilst we were digging the poor girl's grave."

"Why didn't he?" Miss Wren asked.

"Ardleigh convinced him not to, said he was already part of what happened." Blount frowned, deep creases forming around his mouth. "Martin wasn't entirely persuaded at first, and that was when Ardleigh became frightening. He didn't threaten violence specifically, but there was a cold malice in his behavior that left me with no doubt that, accident or not, Ardleigh would not balk at taking a life."

"How awful," Miss Wren murmured. "Is there any chance Ardleigh may have thought Martin Crawford shared the secret with his son? Perhaps Ardleigh was afraid Patrick Crawford would expose him."

"It's baffling. I suppose I should be glad he didn't kill me too." Blount succumbed to another coughing fit, and Hadrian decided they ought to go.

Hadrian nudged Miss Wren. She looked at him and nodded. They stood.

When Blount had regained himself, Hadrian said, "We can't thank you enough for speaking with us."

"Yes," Miss Wren agreed. "We are sorry we had to trouble you, but I'm sure you understand how important this is."

Blount looked up at them, his eyes watery. "I should tell you one more thing. The young lady wore a brooch on her gown, a cameo carved from coral. It fell to the ground when Ardleigh and Crawford carried her to where we dug the hole for her body. Henry picked it up and pocketed it. Ardleigh and Craw-ford didn't notice, but I saw. I don't think Henry knew that I did. I have never said a word about it—until now."

Miss Wren stared at Blount, aghast. "Sir Henry had a piece of evidence?"

"He did then. Perhaps he used it to blackmail Ardleigh." Blount took a sip of water. "I hope you can stop him. It's time. I don't want to think about how many other women he's hurt—or worse."

Hadrian didn't want to think of that either. He'd been eager to solve this case as quickly as possible for John Prince's sake. However, now a speedy resolution was vital. They needed to stop Ardleigh before more people were hurt or killed. "With your help, we are several steps closer to putting an end to Ardleigh's reign of terror."

"I hope so." Blount leaned his head back against his chair and closed his eyes. "Thank you. I'm sorry." Another tear slipped down his cheek, and this time there could be no question that it came from sadness and regret.

~

*T*ilda was brimming with thoughts and reactions to their meeting with Blount, but she and Ravenhurst had agreed to wait until they were situated in their compartment on the train. They'd had a quick repast of tea and cakes at the station but had kept their conversation to a minimum. Now that they were alone in the carriage, Tilda spoke.

"I think it's clear Sir Henry was blackmailing Ardleigh. Hardacre said he'd considered it in the past. Whitley said he was anticipating a sum of money. And Blount said he had evidence with which to execute the blackmail."

Ravenhurst listened intently, nodding at each thing she said. "I saw that brooch in my vision."

Tilda blinked at him. "You did?"

"Yes. I just didn't identify it as an object of importance."

"It's crucial. And I believe I know where it is." Tilda recalled the pretty coral cameo she'd found in Sir Henry's study last week. "It's in Millicent's possession."

"You're going to need to ask her for it," Ravenhurst said.

"I know. Yet again, I have to deliver upsetting news. She found that brooch whilst cleaning out her father's house and thought it was a nice reward for all the hard work she was doing after her father's death. I hate to take it from her."

"I understand." Ravenhurst looked out the window as the train pulled away from the station. "Just think what that poor young woman's family will do when they see it after thirty years. At last, they'll know what happened to their daughter."

Tilda put her hand to her mouth as a wave of sorrow swept over her. She hadn't allowed herself to think too deeply about the murdered young woman. Now that she knew the truth about who she was and what had happened to her, it was impossible not to imagine what she'd suffered and what her family had endured. "Ardleigh is a monster." A new wave of emotion surged within her—fury. She met Ravenhurst's gaze with determination. "We have to make sure he pays for his crimes."

"We will," he vowed, his expression hard.

Sir Henry was also to blame. He could have saved that family decades of heartache instead of keeping Ardleigh's secret. Tilda could scarcely believe the jovial man who'd been so well liked could be capable of such cold-heartedness.

After several moments of silence, Ravenhurst asked, "Do we have the evidence we need to ensure Ardleigh is found guilty?"

"Of which crime?" Tilda asked. "We can tie him to Fitch—who you can identify stabbed you—with Gregson's testimony about Ardleigh's ring being given to Fitch for payment. And

Gregson's testimony will put Fitch at Farringer's the night of Sir Henry's death."

"Selwin's testimony will prove Sir Henry was stabbed and that was his cause of death," Ravenhurst said.

"We need both of them to speak with Scotland Yard as soon as possible."

Ravenhurst nodded. "I'll make sure Gregson does that later this afternoon. Hopefully, Selwin will have returned—if not today then tomorrow. I will call at his residence and office."

"*We* will call," she corrected with a smile.

"Of course," Ravenhurst said with a nod. "Mrs. Forsythe can testify that she found the young woman's brooch at her father's house, and Blount will provide testimony that the brooch belonged to the dead woman, which her family will confirm."

"There is quite a bit of work to do to gather everything together. It's a pity your visions cannot be used as evidence. They have been incredibly helpful." Tilda gave the earl a wry smile.

Ravenhurst shuddered. "Can you imagine what that would mean for me? I'd be committed to an asylum, never to see the light of day again."

"I won't ever let that happen to you," she said quietly. "You are *not* mad. No one will ever hear of your curse from me."

"I know."

Their eyes met, and the shared secret bonded them. Though, Tilda already felt a special connection to him after all they'd experienced together. A strange heat bloomed inside her.

She looked away from him and sought to break the some- what awkward tension. "How I envy the inspectors who will be assigned these investigative tasks."

"It's a shame you can't be an inspector," Ravenhurst said. "Scotland Yard would be lucky to have you. You'd run circles around most of them holding that position."

Tilda laughed. "It's too bad you don't decide such things." Again, she felt the peculiar warmth that had come from their shared moment earlier. His flattery was affecting her too much, she reasoned.

Another moment passed before Ravenhurst asked, "What about Dunwell? It seems he could identify Ardleigh as the man pulling the strings."

"That assumes the viscount coordinated directly with him," Tilda reasoned. "Now that we know Ardleigh's identity, we should ask Gregson if he was ever at Farringer's."

"Excellent idea. We'll ask him as soon as we return to London."

"Good." She smiled as she smoothed her hands over her skirts and settled in for the long train ride. "Perhaps we should stop at Scotland Yard first and fetch Teague. That may feel safer to Gregson, and he is a key witness in this investigation."

"That's an excellent idea," Ravenhurst replied. "After, we can take Teague to call on Dunwell at Farringer's. I'd like to think the manager will be more inclined to talk to a police inspector."

"There's also Selwin, and I need to obtain the brooch from Millicent." She blinked a few times. "We've quite a busy afternoon and evening ahead of us."

"Teague can take care of Selwin since he needs to record his testimony," Ravenhurst said. "You and I can call on Mrs. Forsythe."

Except all their plans were completely upended as soon as they arrived at Scotland Yard and sought Inspector Teague. He met them in his office, and immediately Tilda realized something was wrong.

"We've news to share," Tilda began. "However, you look as though you have something of import to say as well."

Teague frowned at them. "Farringer's caught fire over night. Three people are dead, including the manager."

"Dunwell?" Ravenhurst asked, his eyes wide with shock.

Teague nodded. "The other two have not yet been identified. Dunwell escaped the building but died a short while after.
He was able to inform the constable that he'd been hit on the
head and lost consciousness."

"The fire was not an accident then," Tilda said, not that
she'd thought anything different.

"It does not appear that way. Thankfully, it was contained
before it spread, but the loss of life is unfortunate. F Division is
investigating."

Ravenhurst gave the inspector a grim stare. "We can
surmise who was responsible."

Teague's brows rose in surprise. "Who?"

"The man who would gain from Dunwell's death."

"What would he gain?" Teague asked.

"Peace of mind," Tilda replied. "Dunwell knew too much. As
did Fitch." She looked over at Ravenhurst. "We really need to
make sure Gregson is safe."

"We do." Ravenhurst stood, and Tilda joined him. "Teague,
come to my house with us. I've a witness there—he was a
doorman at Farringer's until yesterday. He will tell you a great
deal about the night Sir Henry Meacham was killed. We're
going to have his body exhumed and examined with a full
autopsy so there can be no doubt as to the true cause of his
death."

Teague shook his head as if he too had sustained a blow. He
rose from his chair and grabbed his hat. "You still haven't told
me who gains from Dunwell's death."

Tilda and Ravenhurst had started toward the door, but they
both looked back at the inspector over their shoulders. "The
Viscount Ardleigh," Ravenhurst said. "We'll provide you with
the details in the coach on the way to my house."

"Bloody hell." Teague followed them from the office.

Ravenhurst paused before they left the building. "I still

haven't received the confidential reports that Superintendent Newsome said he would deliver personally."

Teague pressed his lips into a thin line. "Newsome told me this morning that they've gone missing. He's furious."

"I hope he's directed his anger at Padgett," Ravenhurst said wryly.

Tilda stifled a smile. She sobered quickly as she thought of the fire and three people dying. There would be no interrogating Dunwell now.

They settled into Ravenhurst's coach, and for the first time Tilda shared a seat with the earl. They sat side by side facing forward whilst Teague was facing backward. It was no different than the times they had sat together on a settee, but the space in the coach was close, and for some reason Tilda was keenly aware of the earl's heat and...masculinity. Her reaction to the earl today was most perplexing. She attributed it to the excitement of all they'd learned.

In the coach, they told the inspector about their meeting with Erasmus Blount. Teague listened, sometimes slack-jawed, to every detail then sat mute for several moments.

Finally, he looked to Ravenhurst. "You have this ring with the M that belonged to Ardleigh?"

Ravenhurst withdrew it from his pocket. "I do."

Teague frowned. "You should have given that to Padgett when he interviewed you following your attack. He may not have closed the case so quickly."

"Somehow, I doubt that," Ravenhurst said with a sardonic edge. "However, I would have if I'd known I had it. My valet found it in my pocket and set it aside. By the time I realized it was in my possession, the case had already been closed."

Of course, Ravenhurst could not reveal the truth of why he'd kept it. She also wondered if it pained him to relinquish it, this object that had first transmitted the curse he'd gained.

Taking the ring, Teague looked at it closely before tucking it into his own pocket. "Perhaps I'll be able to persuade Superintendent Newsome to allow me to reopen your case."

"And that of Sir Henry and Patrick Crawford," Tilda said firmly. "Fitch may have been the attacker and the murderer, but he was not the man who is ultimately responsible. His widow and their young children deserve justice for what happened to her husband."

"I will do my best to ensure she receives it," Teague vowed. "I would like to accompany you to Sir Henry's daughter's house to retrieve the brooch that belonged to that young woman who lived next to Ardleigh's estate."

"All right," Tilda said. "Though, you must let me talk to Millicent. She is fond of that brooch, and she's had a great deal of disappointing news of late."

"Of course," Teague replied. His brow creased and his mouth drew into a frown. "With Dunwell dead and this doorman unable to directly identify Ardleigh as the man who hired Fitch—though the ring will help prove he was—it would be ideal if we could lure Ardleigh into a confession."

"About which crime?" Ravenhurst asked, echoing what Tilda had asked him earlier.

"All of them, preferably," Teague said with a humorless chuckle.

Tilda's mind worked out a plan. She doubted either of the gentlemen in the coach would care for it, but she believed it was their best chance—and it would work.

"Since Ardleigh has a penchant for disposing of people who know too much about his crimes, why not draw him out with a person who knows his crimes?" she asked.

Ravenhurst nodded slowly then his lips spread into a slow, rather wonderful smile. "Brilliant. Ardleigh will surely want to kill Gregson."

"I actually thought I would do it," Tilda said. "I could wear the brooch, as that would likely provoke him into doing something foolish. We lay a trap, he comes after me, and we snare him."

"Absolutely not," Teague said, shaking his head. "You can't endanger yourself in that way."

"I won't be in any danger," Tilda argued. "You will both be there—hiding—and I'll be perfectly safe."

"I might actually be persuaded to endorse this plan," Ravenhurst said cautiously. "However, I would much prefer to use Gregson as the bait. All we need do is send him home to his lodgings. If Ardleigh wants to eliminate him, he'll try, and we'll be waiting."

Tilda folded her arms over her middle. "That is too vague. We're just going to hide for who knows how long? I was thinking I would encounter Ardleigh," she looked at Ravenhurst. "You could arrange for that to happen. I would be wearing the brooch, and we'd discuss meeting at Sir Henry's funeral. I'd then mention that I will be at his house the next morning working on emptying it out. Ardleigh will be unable to resist the temptation of me being alone."

"That could work," Teague said, his eyes narrowed slightly. "But we really ought to use Gregson. I can station constables out of uniform about his lodgings. We'd catch Ardleigh without putting you in any danger."

"Except, how will you obtain his confession?" Tilda asked. When no one answered her question, she pushed for her victory. "That is what we need, and I will procure it. Furthermore, you will both be there to hear the viscount incriminate himself. You'll be hiding in or under furniture. And you can have constables out of uniform lurking out of sight outside the house."

"She makes a good argument," Ravenhurst said, sounding resigned. "I think we must adopt her plan."

"I fear you are right." Teague sent Tilda a shrewd look. "Has anyone ever told you that you should be an inspector?"

Tilda couldn't suppress her smug smile. "Very recently in fact."

CHAPTER 23

*H*adrian flicked a speck from his ivory waistcoat as his coach traveled to Miss Wren's house. He could scarcely believe it was just yesterday that they'd visited Blount in Brighton and learned that Ardleigh was the man they'd been seeking.

The viscount had always been friendly, charming even. Hadrian was sick about all the things the man had done. How did someone carry on normally with his life after committing such heinous acts? Hadrian couldn't understand it, nor did he want to.

Teague had interviewed Gregson who had been horrified to learn that Farringer's had caught fire. He'd then confirmed that Ardleigh had been to the club on several occasions, often with Sir Henry, including on the night of Sir Henry's death.

Gregson was doubly glad he'd left his position and none too eager to leave Hadrian's mews until Ardleigh was in custody. As an added measure of safety, Teague had arranged for a constable to watch over the mews.

Then they'd called on Mrs. Forsythe who was disappointed to have to relinquish the coral cameo, just as Miss Wren had said she would be. Miss Wren had gently explained that it belonged to someone else and needed to be returned. She did not think it was necessary to detail the horrors of Ardleigh's behavior and her own father's involvement in concealing it. She would find out soon enough, and Miss Wren would spare her until she could no longer do so.

Since Hadrian had already been invited to a reception hosted by the Duke and Duchess of Northumberland this evening, they'd decided it was the perfect event to encounter Ardleigh. As the attendees would be largely political players, Hadrian was certain Ardleigh would be present.

Miss Wren had balked at first but had then admitted that she didn't have anything appropriate to wear to such an event. Hadrian had offered to outfit her, but she'd resisted, saying that sort of expense was too far. So he'd reminded her that this was her plan. She'd agreed to charge him—responsibly—for the expense.

Hadrian had given her the money in advance to visit a dress shop and wherever else she needed to go to purchase what she needed. He'd given her strict instructions not to skimp, that she needed to fit in. If he were honest, he wanted her to have something beautiful and new since he was fairly certain she hadn't purchased garments in some time. He looked forward to seeing her.

The coach stopped in front of her grandmother's house on Marylebone Lane, and Leach opened the door of the coach. He was perhaps the only member of Hadrian's household who hadn't commented on how nice it was to see him attending an evening event again. Hadrian hadn't done so since January.

"Thank you for not mentioning the fact that I am going out for the evening," Hadrian said to the coachman.

Leach snorted. "I do know Sharp was delighted to press your fancy costume."

Indeed, Hadrian's valet had been positively giddy to prepare him for a night out.

Hadrian walked toward the front door, which Vaughn opened before Hadrian reached it. The butler welcomed him inside. "Good evening, my lord. Always a pleasure to see you."

"Thank you, Vaughn." Hadrian moved into the small entrance hall with its parquet flooring and thick green-and-gold carpet. "Likewise."

Hadrian wondered what Miss Wren was going to do about the butler given the lack of funds from Sir Henry. Perhaps there would be enough money to see him into retirement after the house was sold and the debts settled. Doubtful, but Hadrian would hope for the best. Whatever happened, he would make sure Vaughn was secure. The man deserved it, especially after he'd been assaulted.

Whilst the culprit of that particular crime remained unknown, Hadrian suspected it might have been Fitch doing one of his side jobs for Dunwell, but which had actually been for Ardleigh. Though, why would Fitch have gone to Sir Henry's? Hadrian hoped they would be able to answer all the remaining questions but realized that may not happen.

"Good evening, Lord Ravenhurst," Mrs. Wren said as she ambled into the entrance hall. "Tilda will be along in a moment. It's been some time since she prepared for an event like this."

"Did she have a Season?"

"No, she didn't want that." There was an almost wistful quality to Mrs. Wren's tone. "She came to live with me when she was seventeen. Though, her mother's new husband could have afforded to provide her with a Season. He and her mother reside in Birmingham, however, and either they decided they didn't wish to come to London for the Season, or Tilda convinced them she didn't want one. I suspect it was a combination of both."

But had Miss Wren really wanted one, deep down? If she hadn't thought it was available to her or that it would have been done begrudgingly, he could understand why she may have chosen to avoid it. He could also see her finding the entire effort to be nonsense given her outlook on marriage.

"I hope she will have a pleasant time this evening," Hadrian said.

"She told me you were going as part of your investigation but didn't say why." Mrs. Wren seemed to be fishing for information.

Hadrian could well understand why Miss Wren would not have explained the specifics to her grandmother. The woman didn't need to know that her granddaughter was luring a killer to meet her tomorrow. Hadrian had enough anxiety about it and wouldn't want Mrs. Wren to suffer the same.

He'd hopefully done a fair job of assessing and mitigating the risk of what they were about to do. They'd planned everything through, and Miss Wren would not be alone with Ardleigh at any moment. Still, the thought of her facing a man as despicable and capable of evil as Ardleigh was incredibly unsettling. Hadrian would do anything necessary to keep her safe.

Miss Wren came into the entrance hall then, beautifully garbed in an ivory silk gown with a black netting overdress. The dress did not cover her shoulders and the neckline had a V that was called the *en coeur* style. The coral cameo was pinned at the low point, easily drawing the eye.

Her hair appeared much the same as it did every day, but there was just a single ringlet hanging over her collarbone. Small pearls hung from her ears and ivory gloves encased her arms past her elbows. She looked elegant and lovely. Indeed, she took his breath away.

"You are stunning, Miss Wren," he said with a smile.

"Look how well you two match each other," Mrs. Wren noted.

Hadrian supposed they did since they were both wearing black and ivory. Perhaps he should have found a coral pin to stick in his lapel.

"That was not intentional," Miss Wren murmured. She met Hadrian's gaze. "Shall we go?"

He offered her his arm. "Yes."

Mrs. Acorn beamed as she placed an ivory shawl around Miss Wren's shoulders.

"Have a lovely time," Mrs. Wren said with a wide smile.

Vaughn held the door and whilst he wasn't grinning like the others, his eyes held a lively sparkle. It seemed everyone was delighted for Miss Wren to have an evening out.

Except, perhaps, Miss Wren. She didn't look especially pleased. No, she appeared anxious, but he could understand why since he felt the same.

They walked outside to his coach. The March evening was cool but dry, thankfully. Leach held the door and, as had become the norm, Miss Wren took the forward-facing seat.

When they were on their way, Hadrian noticed she hadn't relaxed at all. She looked pale in the light from the lamp streaming into the window from the exterior of the coach.

Rather than point out how she appeared, he said, "I confess I'm feeling anxious about this evening."

"I am as well, though perhaps not entirely for the same reasons you are." She sent him an almost shy look. "I've never been to an event such as this. I have never met a duke or duchess. I think you are perhaps only the second earl I have been acquainted with."

"You are most adept at conversation and know how to present yourself." Hadrian wanted to ease her worry. "You've nothing to be concerned about."

"Just the unknown," she said with a small smile.

He wanted to reassure her but realized it may not be possible. She would have to see for herself and soon would. "I'll be with you the entire time."

"I appreciate that. Just as I appreciate this gown and the many accoutrements that were required." She looked down at her costume. "I feel rather guilty about the expense for something I will only wear once."

"You don't know that," he said. "We may have occasion to work together again, and we may need to dress for evening."

"You anticipate hiring my investigative services in the future?"

"I may, who's to say? Or it may be that someone else engages your services and you decide you need my help." He was going to miss working with her, he realized.

"No one is going to engage me as a private investigator," she said with a harsh laugh. "Except for Mr. Forrest who occasionally employs me to assist with his divorce cases."

"Well, if you ever need assistance with them, I do hope you'll call on me. I am more than eager to help." This entire experience had been incredibly exhilarating and not just because he was uncovering the truth about his own attack. He enjoyed Miss Wren's company and watching her work. "Would you mind me recommending your services?" he asked.

She stared at him. "You would do that?"

"Without hesitation and with great vigor."

A bright, wonderful smile lit her face, and Hadrian didn't think he'd ever seen a more beautiful woman. His heart beat a little faster, and a heat moved through his body. Disconcerted, he turned his attention to plucking imaginary lint from his coat.

"How do you plan to introduce me?" she asked.

Everything had been moving at such a tremendous pace, they hadn't discussed that. "As we've done in the past, I was going to present you as a family friend."

"I'm sure that will provoke inquiries as to why we are together, particularly about me and my spinsterhood."

"No one will be foolish enough to ask anything, not tonight anyway. And if anyone has the gall to query me about you, I will set them straight." He gave her a firm look. "I will not tolerate any disparagement toward you."

Her mouth ticked up at the edges. "That's kind of you."

They arrived at Northumberland House near Trafalgar Square, a sweeping Jacobean structure that looked out of place now amongst the commercial surroundings. Leach opened the coach door, and Hadrian stepped down to assist Miss Wren.

She placed her gloved hand in his and looked up at the façade as she descended. "I've walked by this house a hundred times, probably. I never imagined I'd go inside."

Hadrian smiled at her as he tucked her arm through his. "Tonight, you shall."

The butler opened the door for them, and Hadrian felt Miss Wren tense. Her gaze moved about the splendid entrance hall. She squeezed his arm, and he instinctively put his other hand over hers.

They moved into the staircase hall, ascending the center steps, then turning to go up the right side to the first floor. The railing was ornate, but the ceiling was even more splendid. A large, extravagant chandelier hung over the center part of the staircase.

The sounds of conversation greeted them when they reached the first floor. They made their way toward the grand gallery, which was also a ballroom. Hadrian had been to Northumberland House on a few occasions, including once during his former fiancée's season. He'd danced with her at a ball here.

They entered the gallery where the duke immediately greeted him. With a large nose and jutting chin, the duke possessed an arresting countenance. He'd just inherited the title last year but had served in the House of Commons prior to that, so Hadrian knew him fairly well.

Hadrian introduced Miss Wren. She curtsied, and the duke gave her an approving nod. They continued on to meet Her Grace, the duchess. She was effusive in her welcome and laughingly asked if Miss Wren was related to Christopher Wren.

"I am, in fact," Miss Wren said. "He was my many times great-grandfather."

The duchess appeared quite impressed. "How extraordinary! Does His Grace know? He is quite enamored of Wren's work and enjoys a lively debate about whether Wren's plan for London should have been adopted after the Great Fire."

"I'm not sure he does," Hadrian replied. "We will be sure to discuss it with him later."

They moved along the gallery, and Miss Wren studied the paintings intently. "This is like being in a museum."

"I suppose so, yes. It reminds me somewhat of the Hall of Mirrors at Versailles." Which was now, in fact, a museum.

"I wouldn't know what that looks like."

"Similar to this, but...gaudier."

Miss Wren bit back a laugh. "I shall not aspire to visit then."

"You should, at least for the gardens," Hadrian said. "They are magnificent."

"We should look for Lord Ardleigh." Miss Wren turned from the wall of paintings and scanned the long room. "But there are so many people, and this is such a massive space. Truly, why does anyone need to live in such a place?"

"I agree it's excessive, but Northumberland House has been in their family since just after Queen Elizabeth died. I believe the Metropolitan Board of Works would like to demolish it as so many other great houses along the Strand have been, to make way for more commercial buildings."

"While I do think that is for the best, I'm sure it is distressing for their graces." She continued to look about the room then shifted her gaze to Hadrian's. "I've only met the viscount once and very briefly—at Sir Henry's funeral. You will have better luck finding him."

"True." He pulled her along the gallery. "Let us make a circuit until we find him. It may be that he has not yet arrived."

They spent the next hour meandering and chatting with a variety of people, all of them colleagues of Hadrian's—and their wives. A few of them looked askance at Miss Wren, and Hadrian hoped they weren't passing judgment as to her accompanying him. Though, Hadrian acknowledged their coming together was at least unusual.

But he didn't care. Their work here tonight was too important. It was worth the risk of social judgment.

At last, he spotted Ardleigh. "I see the viscount," Hadrian said. "He's about fifteen paces in front of us. He's speaking with Lord Dalwyn."

Miss Wren exhaled. "Finally."

"Are you ready?"

"More than." She started forward, and Hadrian kept apace.

A few moments later, they stopped next to the two gentlemen. They were dressed in their evening finery, and one or perhaps both of them carried a great deal of scent. Ardleigh made eye contact with Hadrian and smiled.

"Evening, Ardleigh, Dalwyn," Hadrian said. "Allow me to introduce a dear family friend, Miss Matilda Wren."

"That name seems familiar," Ardleigh said. His gray eyes assessed Miss Wren, moving over her in a fashion that made Hadrian want to knock him to the ground.

"We met at the funeral of my grandfather's cousin, Sir Henry Meacham," she said demurely, a smile teasing her lips. Was she being flirtatious? Perhaps she thought that would appeal to the viscount, and it probably bloody well would.

"Ah, yes, I recall now. Women always look so different out of their mourning weeds," Ardleigh said with a laugh.

"I'm sorry for your loss, Miss Wren," Dalwyn said with a kind nod.

"Thank you, Lord Dalwyn. It's been difficult for my grandmother, as she has of course known Sir Henry for some time. And his daughters are most bereaved, so I have been managing a great many things for them. He died quite suddenly."

Hadrian watched Ardleigh for any hint of a reaction. There was nothing, except perhaps that his features were unnaturally frozen. One might expect a look of sympathy at least.

"That is always unfortunate," Dalwyn replied with a furrowed brow—his expression was extremely sympathetic. "Though I suppose death is hard no matter how it arrives."

"Very true," Miss Wren said. "Compounding matters is the fact that it seems Sir Henry's death may not have been as we thought. We were told he died of a heart attack, but it now appears he was—" She cut herself off and glanced toward Hadrian with a distressed countenance. "I'd rather not say," she whispered.

Hadrian patted her shoulder. "It's all right," he murmured. He didn't want to add anything, for she was doing a stellar job needling Ardleigh. He hadn't yet reacted, but Hadrian saw a tic in his neck that belied his state of calm.

She lifted her hand toward the brooch, where her fingers fluttered gently before she lowered her arm once more. Ardleigh's gaze followed her movement and locked on the brooch. His lips moved, the lower one drawing in briefly. Hadrian looked to the man's hands to see if he did anything. The fingers of his right hand curled in slightly then straightened.

"That is a lovely brooch, Miss Wren," Dalwyn noted. Dalwyn! Not Ardleigh.

Miss Wren touched the coral briefly. "Thank you. It actually belonged to Sir Henry. Apparently, he found it some thirty years ago."

Ardleigh did the thing with his lip again. And his hand. His nostrils also flared. Was his flesh turning red above his collar?

"His daughter had forgotten about it, then we found it as we worked on emptying the house," Miss Wren continued. "Though, I've taken over managing all of that for her. She became too distraught to continue. Indeed, I'll be there again tomorrow morning to hopefully finish up. I'm just glad to be of help."

"How awful for her," Dalwyn said. "My wife was much the same when her father died. The grief strikes you in ways you can't expect."

"What made matters truly worse was someone breaking into the house and assaulting the butler, if you can imagine," Miss Wren said with quiet outrage. "Horrible people try to take advantage of grieving households."

Dalwyn's eyes rounded. "Ghastly!" He turned his head to Ardleigh. "What say you?"

"Ghastly, indeed." It was as if Ardleigh couldn't think of anything original to say. His eyes had flickered with worry when Miss Wren had mentioned the butler. Hadrian couldn't help wondering if the viscount had been responsible for that.

Hadrian suddenly recalled what Vaughn had said to Teague after he'd been attacked. He'd said he'd thought the brigand smelled like a woman.

Pivoting slightly toward the viscount, whom Hadrian was standing closest to, he inhaled deeply. The man's perfume filled Hadrian's nostrils. It smelled of flowers and neroli, and, yes, it was practically feminine. Hadrian knew in that moment that Ardleigh had broken into Sir Henry's, and he'd struck Vaughn. Had he been looking for the brooch?

Miss Wren again passed her hand near the brooch as she smoothed her fingers along the base of her neck. Was she taunting Ardleigh by gesturing to her neck since he'd strangled his neighbor's daughter?

The red above Ardleigh's collar spread farther up his neck. Hadrian concluded Miss Wren had more than completed her task.

Hadrian changed the topic to the business of Parliament, and after another ten minutes, they parted ways from the gentlemen.

When they reached the opposite end of the gallery, the tension in Miss Wren's grip on his arm finally dissipated. "Do you think he'll come to Sir Henry's tomorrow?"

"Without a doubt." Hadrian looked back down the gallery toward where they'd talked with the viscount. "I'd rather not say more here."

"Can we leave?" she asked.

His moved his gaze to hers. "Already? The supper will be served soon."

"I already ate dinner. Though, I do realize, your ilk are accustomed to late night dining. I can't imagine sleeping after that."

"My 'ilk' don't sleep afterward," Hadrian said with a laugh. "We're up for several more hours before falling into bed."

"Do you do that?" she asked. "For some reason, I can't quite see it. You seem far too responsible for such reck-lessness."

"It's true I do it less now than when I was younger, but I've had plenty of irresponsible nights." He suppressed a grin as he recalled some of his youthful exploits. "Now, it's sometimes necessary—the late nights, not the irresponsibility—if I'm engaged in business."

"What sort of business?"

He shrugged. "Discussions about bills in Parliament, happenings about the country that we should address, that sort of thing."

"You take your role in the Lords seriously. That is most admirable."

"I do, and thank you. Now, you can perhaps see the benefit in a late supper."

"No, thank you," she said primly. "Especially not tonight. I couldn't possibly eat after that encounter with Ardleigh. He quite turned my stomach. Besides, I've important business in the morning."

Hadrian sobered. "Yes, we do. Let us depart."

When they were situated in the coach, Miss Wren leaned forward. "Did you see the way Ardleigh tried to contain his reactions to the brooch and what I said about Sir Henry—and Vaughn being attacked?" She sounded almost giddy. "His neck even turned red."

"Yes, I noticed all that." He wasn't surprised she did too. "Did you note his perfume?"

Miss Wren's eyes rounded. "I did catch a vague scent, but you were closer to him than I was. Did he smell like a woman as Vaughn described?"

Hadrian nodded. "Neroli and tuberose, if I'm not mistaken."

"That is very specific." Miss Wren appeared impressed. "How did you recognize those scents?"

"My mother adores perfume and has had special recipes made at Floris. I am well acquainted with scents, and if I remember correctly, tuberose is often used to incite passion."

Miss Wren made a sound of disgust in her throat. "You don't suppose Ardleigh chose that fragrance to prey on young women?"

"Probably, as he is truly loathsome. And I am certain he broke into Sir Henry's house and hit Vaughn."

Her lip curled with disgust. "His villainy knows no bounds."

"It does not." Hadrian could not wait to see him pay for his crimes. "After I drop you off, I'll stop at Teague's and confirm our plans for tomorrow."

"He gave you his home address?" Miss Wren asked.

"He did. He's quite committed to catching Ardleigh in a confession and ensuring justice is done for everyone involved. And I am committed to ensuring you are safe."

"I will be fine. Both you and Teague will be nearby to swoop in at the appropriate moment." Clasping her hands in her lap, Miss Wren's face creased with sadness. "I can't keep from thinking of that poor young woman Ardleigh killed and how distraught her family will be when they learned what happened. I suppose it will just be good for them to know."

"That is the best we can do for them now," Hadrian said solemnly. "We can give them the truth."

"What time will you and Teague arrive at Sir Henry's?"

"Very early—just after dawn—and we'll go in through the servants' entrance. We don't want to risk Ardleigh arriving early and seeing us enter." They'd discussed where Hadrian and the inspector would conceal themselves. Miss Wren would be in the parlor where Hadrian would be inside an armoire that he and Teague would move from downstairs. Teague would be hidden in the voluminous draperies on the windows.

"I will arrive around nine," Miss Wren said. "With my pistol at the ready, should it be necessary."

Hadrian's anxiety from earlier returned with greater intensity. "I will hope it does not. Teague and I will be ready with pistols also. We won't let anything happen to you." Hadrian's insides clenched with apprehension at such a thought. He'd come to like Miss Wren a great deal. He was having difficulty thinking about not seeing her every day, but at least he would know that he could. If something happened to her, and he could not see her at all, ever...well, that was unconscionable.

"I shall ensure nothing happens to you either," she assured him.

Hadrian smiled at her. "With you watching out for me, I have nothing to fear."

CHAPTER 24

*T*ilda's father's pistol felt weightier than usual in her reticule as she stepped out of the hack in front of Sir Henry's, but perhaps that was due to the addition of the photograph, which she'd brought to taunt their prey if it became necessary. The house seemed ominous, and it didn't even have black in the windows or the yew wreath on the door any longer.

She felt a rush of sadness at how Sir Henry had met his end. He may have stolen her grandmother's money, concealed multiple murders, and attempted blackmail, but he hadn't deserved to be stabbed to death. Actually, her sadness wasn't so much for him as it was for Millicent and for her grandmother. It wasn't just his death that brought them grief, the knowledge of what he'd done would only compound that when they learned the truth.

Tilda dreaded that.

Unlocking the front door, she closed it behind her. Since Vaughn had been attacked—by Ardleigh, apparently—she'd been careful to bolt the door when she was here. Today, however, she would not, for that would foil their plan.

Anxious sweat dappled her neck and chest. She tried not to think of what Ardleigh was capable of. It wouldn't come to that today.

Glancing down, she lightly touched the coral brooch, which she'd worn again, pinning it to the bodice of her gray-green walking dress.

"You're wearing it again."

The low, almost seductive voice startled her. Tilda's heart hammered wildly. The viscount was already here.

He stood on the other side of the entrance hall, as if he'd walked in from the staircase hall where he'd likely been lurking. He wore a dark blue and gray suit and a black hat. Gray gloves covered his hands. His expression was serene, pleasant even.

Tilda had considered how she would play this scene with him. Was it better to behave as if she didn't know what he was talking about so he would perhaps reveal everything as he explained things to her? Or should she provoke him with what she knew to bait him into saying what he needed to incriminate himself?

Either would work, so she planned to see which way he led her. But first, she needed to get into the parlor where she would be closer to Ravenhurst and Teague, both for safety and so the inspector could hear Ardleigh's confession.

"Forgive me, Lord Ardleigh," she said, moving toward the parlor. "I am surprised to see you here."

"Where are you going?" he snapped, darting forward and grabbing her arm.

Tilda resisted the primal urge to cry out and dash away. She didn't want to spook him, nor did she want Ravenhurst or Teague to come running before she'd done what she needed to.

She gently pulled her arm from his grip. "I am merely moving into the parlor where it's more comfortable." She gave him a cool look that was quite at odds with the thundering of her heart before slowly continuing into the parlor.

"I am here because you all but invited me last night," Ardleigh said from behind her.

When Tilda reached the center of the room, she turned to face him. "I don't recall doing that." She cocked her head. "You've been here at least once since the funeral, haven't you?"

He blinked, but that was the only indication that she'd perhaps surprised him. "When would that have been?"

"When you were looking for this." She raised her hand to the brooch. "Sir Henry found this brooch when he helped you with that young woman—your neighbor's daughter, I believe."

The viscount lunged at her with a snarl. Tilda jumped back.

Instead of pursuing her, he took a deep breath. "All you need do is give me the brooch and forget whatever you think you know. Sir Henry was a fool to tell you anything."

"Sir Henry didn't reveal a thing to me." Tilda reached into her reticule. Her fingers brushed against the pistol, which gave her courage, and she pulled the photograph out. "I understand you have a better version of this photograph, one in which you are clearly visible."

Ardleigh did the same thing with his lower lip he'd done last night at Northumberland House.

Tilda pointed to the individuals in the photograph. "This is Sir Henry, and Martin Crawford, and Erasmus Blount, and lastly, you. It was taken in 1839, the day after Sir Henry found this brooch. He was blackmailing you with this, wasn't he?"

Exhaling, Ardleigh removed his hat and tossed it onto a chair. "I'd really hoped to keep this as pleasant as possible, but you keep provoking me." He fixed on her hair, and an unnatural light flickered in his gaze. "Pity you aren't a brunette."

Tilda's blood went cold. "Why, would you try to seduce me?" Reaching her arm out, she set the photograph on a small table.

"Seduction isn't always possible, though I do prefer it." He took a step toward her, and Tilda gripped her reticule. If he moved too close, she would remove the pistol and point it at him. And she'd alert Ravenhurst and Teague. They may not be able to see what was happening. She just hoped they—especially Teague—could hear.

Touching the brooch once more, Tilda said, "The young woman who owned this brooch had dark hair."

"You know a great deal. I suppose you also know her name was Susannah Baxter. What happened to her was an accident."

"Was it also an accident with the other woman in 1835?"

Ardleigh's eyes narrowed. "Sir Henry had to have told you about that. He was the only one who knew."

"I think it's best if you don't assume who knows what. A great many people know a great deal. We are aware of all your crimes."

"Does that include your grandfather?" His voice was taunting, but his eyes were flat.

Tilda began to shake. Though she'd never known him, she still felt love for the man she'd heard so much about from her father and grandmother. "No," she whispered.

Ardleigh took another step toward her, but Tilda was frozen, her gaze fixed on this monster. "I hated doing that, but he left me no choice. All he had to do was find a young footman guilty of strangling one of my maids, but he refused. So bloody righteous. And after Henry promised that his cousin would help me." Ardleigh tsked.

"What did you do?" Tilda's voice climbed.

"Put a burr under Wren's horse's saddle when we went for a ride one morning. Horse threw him. I'd hoped that would take care of it, but it did not. I had to hit him with a rock to finish the task."

How could he refer to her grandfather's murder as a 'task'? Tilda doubled over, her arms going around her waist. She felt as though she may toss up her breakfast. Ardleigh rushed toward her, catching her lest she fall. He held her gently, his voice soothing as he murmured, "There, there, sweet Matilda. I will comfort you."

With a loud cry, Tilda pushed at him. He grabbed her arm and threw her to the floor. Panic flooded her. "Raven!" she cried as Ardleigh loomed over her.

The sound of furniture scraping across the room filled the air. A body launched into the viscount, knocking him sideways, away from Tilda. Ravenhurst snaked his arms around Ardleigh as they both hit a table on their way to the floor.

Tilda scrambled to her feet and, hands shaking, pulled the pistol from her reticule. "Stop! I have a gun and will shoot you, Ardleigh."

"The bullet may hit Ravenhurst instead!" he taunted.

That was possible, as they were wrestling about. But then Ravenhurst slammed his fist into Ardleigh's gut, and the older man groaned. Rising above the viscount, Ravenhurst grabbed him by his lapels and pulled him up to the nearest chair, pushing him down onto the seat.

"You bloody bastard," Ravenhurst spat. "You're finished. As soon as the police arrive, you'll be arrested for your battery of crimes—the women in the 1830s, paying Fitch to kill Crawford and Sir Henry, killing Fitch yourself, starting the fire at Farringer's after hitting Dunwell over the head. And killing Alexander Wren." Ravenhurst didn't take his eyes from Ardleigh but said, "I'm so sorry, Tilda."

It was the first time he'd used her given name, and she was exceedingly glad. In that moment, she needed his care. It was a shocking realization as she prided herself on not needing that from anyone, not since she'd lost her father.

"You think you can prove all that?" Ardleigh sneered.

"Yes, we have evidence and a mountain of testimony from the likes of Selwin, Blount, and Gregson from Farringer's, not to mention what you admitted to Miss Wren today, all of which I heard."

"I didn't actually mean to start the fire," Ardleigh said without a hint of remorse. "I did hit Dunwell, and he grabbed at a lantern on his desk, knocking it over. It caught fire, and I decided that was a happy accident."

"You're not sane," Tilda said. "There is *nothing* happy about that."

The viscount's gaze was empty, his expression nearly blank. In that moment, Tilda was convinced he had a deficiency of some kind.

"Your list of crimes is extensive," Ravenhurst said, standing directly in front of Ardleigh. Tilda kept her pistol pointed at the viscount. "Unfortunately, they can only hang you once."

Suddenly, Ardleigh kicked out, connecting with Ravenhurst's shin. It was enough for Ravenhurst to falter, and Ardleigh leapt from the chair, shoving the earl to the side.

"Stop!" Tilda said, cocking the pistol.

But the viscount dashed toward the entrance hall. Thankfully, he was halted by the appearance of Teague and three constables.

Teague pointed his drawn pistol at Ardleigh. "Stop, or I will shoot you. Though, I would much prefer you undergo a trial so you can hang."

Ravenhurst had righted himself and moved to Tilda's side. "Ardleigh has confessed to a great number of things, including hitting Dunwell, starting the fire at Farringer's, and —shockingly—killing Miss Wren's grandfather, Alexander Wren."

"You've been busy," Teague said with cold disdain, his eyes glacial as they fixed on Ardleigh. "But now, you are finished. Take him into custody."

The constables moved toward the viscount who took several steps backward. He spun around, facing Tilda and

Ravenhurst, who'd recovered himself. Now, Ardleigh's eyes were wild as he looked frantically about, seeking escape.

"There is nowhere to go," Ravenhurst growled.

Ardleigh's gaze fixed on the brooch Tilda wore. "She didn't want to die," he whispered. "Susannah loved me. She was such a sweet, little bird. But what was I to do with her? I was already wed, and her demands were unrealistic. You see, I had no choice." He'd killed her on purpose.

"And what about the maid before her?" Tilda asked quietly. "Or the countless other women you have likely killed?"

"Not countless," he said, lifting his gaze to hers. "Only six. Though, I've had my eye on a new maid who came to us recently. Dora. She's a pretty thing with such a light in her brown eyes."

Dora? Tilda had to stop herself from shooting him right there. He had to be talking about Sir Henry's maid, Dora Chapman. "You're a vile monster," Tilda said.

He gave her a haughty stare. "I am your better, my dear." In an astonishing, single movement, he picked up a small table that stood nearby and swung it out toward Tilda. She bent low and twisted to avoid the strike, but the table legs caught her thigh as she heard the report of Teague's gun. At least, she assumed it was Teague's.

Ravenhurst caught her, hauling her up against him as the constables descended around the viscount who now lay sprawled on his stomach. A wet spot formed on his back as Tilda worked to catch her breath.

"Damn. I really didn't want to shoot him," Teague said. "Is he dead?"

One of the constables who was bent down next to Ardleigh shook his head. "Not yet. His breathing is rough."

"I hope you can hear me," Ravenhurst said. "You will rot in hell, and that is precisely where you belong."

Tilda felt a rush of emotion as she watched the viscount and heard him struggle to breathe. The hate she felt for the man was overcome by sadness over all the death he'd caused. There was a small bit of solace in that. With Ardleigh dying, there would be no trial. The truly horrible things he'd done could be largely kept quiet. Mostly, she just didn't want her grandmother to know that he'd killed her husband. It seemed unnecessary to reopen the wound of that loss and make it worse.

Teague moved into the parlor. "I'm sorry I wasn't able to be here earlier. I was called away." He frowned deeply. "But it looks as though you had things in hand."

"For the most part," Ravenhurst replied. His arm was still around Tilda, and she was quite content to settle against his side. "I do wish you could have heard the things he said."

"I heard plenty just then," Teague said. "Susannah is the neighbor he killed in 1839?"

Tilda nodded. "Susannah Baxter. You'll want to contact her family as soon as possible." She looked at Ravenhurst and smiled then stepped slightly away from him as she needed her hands to remove the brooch.

"Don't," Ardleigh rasped.

"You still here?" Teague grunted.

Tilda handed the inspector the brooch. "I'm sure her family will be glad to have this back."

"Yes, and they'll be able to confirm its provenance." Teague slipped the brooch into his pocket and removed the ring. Crouching down near the viscount, he said, "This your ring, Ardleigh?"

Shockingly, Ardleigh tried to reach for it. "That rat demanded it for killing Crawford, said a job like that required special payment."

"Were you angry when he stabbed me instead?" Ravenhurst asked.

"Furious. But he took out the right man a week later."

Ardleigh coughed. "Fitch wasn't the cleverest, but he was keen to work." He closed his eyes for a moment and wheezed.

"Why kill him then?" Teague asked.

"Wanted more money. Mentioned blackmail, which Henry had already tried. When I found out it was him that night at the club, I didn't hesitate to tell Fitch to get rid of him, which he did without blinking. Greedy bastards." Ardleigh's voice had weakened, and he coughed again.

Tilda wanted as many answers as they could get before the man expired. "If Sir Henry was blackmailing you, why kill Crawford?"

"Thought it was—" Ardleigh took a stuttering breath. "Crawford. His father told me a few years ago he'd shared what happened with his son. Couldn't live with the guilt. Crawford the Coward, I called him." Ardleigh attempted a smile, but it looked more like a grimace.

"What about Padgett?" Ravenhurst demanded. "Did you pay him to limit his investigations and then bury them?"

"Didn't cost much. I just...needed...it all...to go...away." The viscount's body convulsed briefly, and he went completely still, his gray eyes fixed on nothing. In death, he looked the same as he had in life—emotionless and empty.

Teague rose. "Seems as though your theories proved accurate. Every case will need to be reopened and corrected."

Ravenhurst sent Teague a dark look. "And Padgett must be excluded from that enterprise, since it sounds as though Ardleigh bribed him. His corruption cannot be ignored."

"Speaking of corruption, don't forget John Prince in the City of London," Tilda noted as she tucked her father's pistol back into her reticule. "We heard Ardleigh confess to killing Fitch, which means someone planted that false evidence."

Ravenhurst nodded at Tilda. "Since Ardleigh confessed to trying to corrupt a magistrate to hide his crimes and to bribing

Padgett, I think it's possible, if not likely, that he paid someone at the City of London Police to frame Prince."

Tilda glared at the corpse on Sir Henry's floor. "Or Ardleigh planted the murder weapon in Prince's lodging himself."

"I'll ensure that is all investigated," Teague said. "At least, I will do my best. I have no sway with the City of London Police, unfortunately."

"You're a good man," Ravenhurst said.

Teague slipped his pistol back into its holster and addressed the constables. "Let's carry him out." He looked to Ravenhurst and Tilda. "Take a bit to collect yourselves, then if you wouldn't mind coming to Scotland Yard to give your testimony, I'd appreciate it."

Ravenhurst nodded. "Of course."

"Inspector," Tilda said. "Could I ask that you try to keep the fact that Ardleigh murdered my grandfather out of the newspapers? My grandmother doesn't need to know the truth. It would do a great deal of harm and absolutely no good."

"I understand." Teague looked at her with sympathy. "I will do my best." He directed the constables to carry Ardleigh's body outside to the wagon. He glanced toward the floor. "At least there's no mess to tidy."

Tilda laughed, surprising herself. She pressed her hand to her mouth.

"Thank you, Inspector," Ravenhurst said, moving to show Teague out.

Putting her hands on her hips, Tilda exhaled, her mind running over the events of the morning. Ravenhurst returned. "I'm sorry that didn't go quite as planned."

"I was surprised to find Ardleigh was already here," she responded, feeling surprisingly shaky now everything had concluded, and the danger was past. But perhaps that was why she was feeling unsettled now—she hadn't allowed herself to before.

"I heard him come in probably an hour before you arrived. It was incredibly difficult to stay quiet, particularly when you came in the door, and I heard him address you." Ravenhurst's features tensed. "I was ready to spring to action, and I nearly did when he grabbed you."

"I'm glad you were in place and ready, just as I am glad you did not intervene immediately. In the end, it all worked out, I suppose. I can't say I'm sorry he's dead, especially after hearing what he did to my grandfather." Tears burned her eyes, but she blinked them away before they could fall.

"Neither can I." Ravenhurst came toward her, stopping just shy of touching her. "I am so sorry about your grandfather."

"It's strange because I never met him, but I feel as though I know him from everything my father and grandmother told me." Tilda had to blink again lest the tears return. She lowered her hands to her sides. "My father admired him greatly. Their relationship sounded very similar to the one I had with him— my father, I mean. To know they were both killed is distressing."

"Ardleigh isn't going to hurt anyone again, and for that we must be grateful." Ravenhurst picked up the table that Ardleigh had tried to use as a weapon and set it right. "Did he hurt you with that?"

"Not really. It was a glancing blow. Are you all right from tussling with him?"

"Fine. Punching him was rather gratifying, I must say." He smiled, and Tilda nodded, thinking it must have been.

Tilda picked up the photograph. It had fallen from the table when the viscount had swept it up. "I doubt Millicent will want this, and I certainly don't."

"Burn it, as Blount did," Ravenhurst suggested. "I certainly don't want to touch it ever again. I wonder if we ought to accompany Teague to Brighton to tell Blount what happened."

"I think we should," Tilda said, sliding the photograph back into her reticule with the intention of giving it to Teague as evidence. "I imagine Ardleigh's death will be a relief, as will the return of Susannah's brooch to her family. I can't think Teague will seek to charge Blount with anything."

"I agree," Ravenhurst said. "After Leach drops us off at Scotland Yard, I'll have him return to my house to convey to Gregson that Ardleigh is dead. He will be greatly relieved. Are you ready to go now?"

"I am." Tilda glanced about the parlor, thinking of all the time she'd spent here recently. "I'll be quite happy if I don't have to return to this house."

"If you do, I will eagerly accompany you. Indeed, I insist upon it." Ravenhurst offered her his arm and escorted her out.

CHAPTER 25

*A*fter several grueling hours at Scotland Yard providing testimony and answering questions, including from Superintendent Newsome, Hadrian and Miss Wren had gone to the City of London Police to ensure John Prince was released. As it happened, they'd arrived just as he was being set free. They'd been able to speak with him, and he'd been overjoyed and grateful for their help in proving he was innocent.

When they were settled back in the coach, Miss Wren said, "That is the part of investigation that is so rewarding—discovering the truth and ensuring innocent people don't pay for crimes they don't commit." Her features darkened. "I feel so badly for that poor footman who was convicted of the maid's death in 1835 after my grandfather refused to find him guilty."

After looking through records at Scotland Yard, they determined the young man had been transported to Australia. Teague said it was unlikely they'd be able to find him or restore him to England, but perhaps he'd already found his way back. "I thought about trying to locate him," Hadrian said.

Miss Wren looked at him with surprise. "That would be a

monumental task. And would perhaps require a journey to Australia. Do you have time for that?"

He was fairly certain she was jesting. "No, but I could hire someone who might be interested."

"You don't mean me?" Miss Wren asked with a light laugh. "I've no interest in traveling across the world, at least not right now. My grandmother needs me."

"I actually meant I could hire someone in Australia. I will look into it. I would even pay for the footman's passage back to England if he wished to return."

"Would you want to come back to the country that had seen you corruptly convicted of a murder you hadn't committed?" Miss Wren shuddered. "At least he wasn't hanged."

"A small mercy," Hadrian murmured.

Miss Wren stifled a yawn. "Pardon me. It has been a rather long day."

Hadrian had to press his hand over his mouth to cover his own responding yawn. "Indeed, it has." He'd risen much earlier than normal, and they'd been up late the previous night at Northumberland House. That seemed so long ago now. "We must start again early tomorrow to travel to Brighton."

They'd arranged to accompany Teague to visit Erasmus Blount. And this afternoon, Superintendent Newsome had traveled to Essex to speak with the Baxters about their daughter's death and to return her brooch. Teague would ask Blount for the location of Susannah's body so that could also be communicated to her family.

"I'm glad to make the trip," Miss Wren said. "And relieved there will be no charges against Blount. I daresay he isn't long for this world anyway."

"No charges for Selwin either, though he is not to produce death certificates or participate in any inquests." Hadrian wasn't certain how he felt about that. Selwin could have saved the lives of Fitch, Dunwell, and the others who'd died in the fire at Farringer's.

As the coach arrived at Miss Wren's, Hadrian's stomach grumbled. They'd barely eaten all day, just some terribly dry meat pies that had been delivered to them at Scotland Yard. He was inclined to ask Miss Wren to dine with him but imagined she was eager to get home. Perhaps another time.

Hadrian escorted her to her door. "I'll pick you up in the morning, then."

"Thank you. I can hardly believe we've completed the investigation." She smiled. "There were times I thought we'd never discover the truth."

"It was a very tangled web. Next time, I shall hope for something simpler."

She arched a brow. "You seem quite interested in there being a next time."

"I can't deny that I have enjoyed working with you, Miss Wren. I would most eagerly hire you again and recommend you. And I can only hope you might need to consult with me at some point."

"I confess, your special ability was most helpful with the investigation. I'm torn between appreciating its use and not wanting you to suffer the burden any longer."

"I'm becoming used to it. Somewhat," he added with a smile. "Touching people, such as shaking hands, is the most disconcerting part. I'd like to find a way to stop that. Except for when we need it." Laughing, he shook his head. "Apparently, I am also torn."

Miss Wren laughed with him, and it was lovely. He wouldn't mind touching her, and yet he wasn't sure how he felt about seeing her memories or feeling her emotions. That seemed incredibly intrusive.

Vaughn opened the door, interrupting their conversation.

"Miss Wren, it's good you are back. Mrs. Wren was growing concerned."

"It was a very busy day, Vaughn," Miss Wren replied as she stepped into the house. "I've much to report, including the identity of the man who hit you."

Hadrian wished he could stay and participate. But this was not his household.

"Indeed?" Vaughn's eyes narrowed. "I should like to have words with him."

"Unfortunately, he has already drawn his last breath, and that is for the best. He was a truly horrid person." She shook her head. "Not a person at all, really. Rather, a beast." Pivoting, she looked at Hadrian. "See you in the morning."

"Yes. Sleep well." The door closed, and Hadrian returned to his coach.

The sun was setting as they traveled to Mayfair. Hadrian realized he was frowning. He felt quite morose, actually. Whilst he knew he would see Miss Wren tomorrow, he didn't know when he would do so after that. Their investigation was finished. What reason would they have to spend time with one another?

He wanted her to have another case soon, not only because he could hope to become involved, but because he knew she needed the income. That reminded him that she owed him another invoice. She would likely give it to him tomorrow morning. Miss Wren was nothing if not efficient.

But that would be the end of his payments to her, and she still needed money to support her new butler and perhaps even afford a dress now and again. She would not accept additional funds from Hadrian, even if he tried to explain that she more than deserved it after all she'd done to solve this mystery.

An idea struck him. His lips curved up. It might just work. He would dispatch a note to the Whitley before he left for Brighton tomorrow morning.

He turned his mind back to investigating another case with her. Perhaps she'd have need of his unique gift.

When had he started thinking of it as anything other than a curse? Was it because it had pushed him to meet Miss Wren? He definitely considered that a boon.

He wondered how his ability would work in the future. Would it stop now that this case was solved? The things he'd felt and seen had seemed to direct him—and Miss Wren— where they needed to find the truth.

Regardless, he would be cautious in touching things—and people—going forward.

Surprisingly, he thought of touching Miss Wren, and not in an entirely platonic manner. He'd felt a fierce need to protect her that morning when Ardleigh had gone after her. Hadrian was certain he would have killed the man without hesitation if it had become necessary.

But it had been a moment of heightened emotion and sensation. It only made sense that Hadrian had wanted to keep his partner safe. He decided it didn't need to be more than that.

❦

The following Tuesday, Tilda sat in the parlor with her grandmother and Lord Ravenhurst. Sun streamed in through the window, which always made Grandmama happy. She was also delighted the earl had returned. She'd been sad about not seeing him as often as they had been.

Tilda had been disappointed by that too. Far more than she'd expected to be. She certainly liked and respected the earl, but she'd never imagined their association to continue after the investigation concluded.

Then, today he'd called socially, surprising her. Perhaps they would remain friends, which seemed an oddity given his station compared with hers. Not to mention their unmarried states. Could they really be permitted to be friends?

"Tilda, you must tell Lord Ravenhurst our good news." Grandmama smiled toward the earl.

Tilda directed her attention at Ravenhurst. "Mr. Whitley has finally sent the summary of Grandmama's investment account. In the course of searching for records for the second investment, he found a sum of money in an account in Grandmama's name."

"That's wonderful," Ravenhurst said with a broad smile.

"Yes, and now we can now afford to keep Vaughn on," Grandmama said.

Ravenhurst paused before sipping his tea. "As butler?"

"We did suggest he retire," Grandmama said. "However, he implored us to allow him to serve as butler. I must say, he presented an impressive argument as to why we needed him."

Tilda suppressed a laugh. There was nothing he'd mentioned that either wasn't already being done before he arrived or that needed doing as often as he suggested. What it did mean was less work for Mrs. Acorn.

The finances would still be a bit strained, but Tilda planned to invest a small portion of the money Whitley had found for added security. She just needed to determine how.

"Ravenhurst, I wonder if you might assist me in locating a competent and respected solicitor to invest some of this money we received. I do not wish to continue with Mr. Whitley. I think a fresh start is best."

"My solicitor can certainly help. I'll set up a meeting straightaway, if you like." He set his cup down. "I have a bit of news to share. Teague sent me a note this morning informing me that Padgett has retired, and unfortunately Blount passed away yesterday."

"He also sent me the news," Tilda said. "Though, I'm disappointed Padgett was allowed to retire and not prosecuted for his corruption."

"I also found that disappointing," Ravenhurst replied. "However, I can't say I'm surprised after what you've told me about the culture of bribery that exists."

Tilda had decided she would no longer pay for information. It might make her investigations more difficult, but she couldn't, in good conscience, support the practice any longer, even if it did help certain members of the police force support their families.

Grandmama nearly scowled. "Such a horrible practice. Tilda, your father and grandfather never would have approved of such behavior."

No, they would not. Tilda's heart clenched as she thought of how her grandfather had died for that very principle.

"I was sorry to hear about Blount, but it is not a shock," Ravenhurst said.

Tilda nodded in agreement. "Perhaps he realized he'd done what he could to make things right and was ready to depart. Although, nothing could be made truly right." When they'd traveled to Brighton, Teague had informed them that the Baxter family had taken the news about their daughter quite poorly. Tilda hoped they would be able to find peace.

Teague had also informed Tilda that Ardleigh's widow was leaving London. She'd been devastated to learn of her husband's crimes and said she would never show her face here again. So many lives lost and ruined by that horrible beast.

"Did Teague mention how it's too bad you can't work for the Metropolitan Police?" Ravenhurst asked.

Tilda laughed. "He did."

"Well, I am glad you cannot," Grandmama said as she took a biscuit from the tray.

"He also wrote that he looked forward to working with us

again, should we have the opportunity," Tilda said, looking at Ravenhurst.

"He wrote the same to me." Ravenhurst's gaze was warm. "I hope we have that chance. You know where to find me if you require my … skills."

She glanced at his bare hands, for he'd removed his gloves for tea. Did he see anything when he touched the teacup or the arm of his chair? Perhaps he felt a sense of something. "I do indeed," Tilda said, thinking his particular skill could perhaps be useful the next time Mr. Forrest hired her.

They finished tea a while later, and Grandmama retreated to the sitting room. Tilda walked the earl to the entrance hall, where he set his hat atop his head. Vaughn was somewhere else in the house.

Tilda looked at his bare hands again. "I wondered if you saw anything when you touched the chair or the teacup."

"I did not," Ravenhurst responded. "I haven't seen or felt anything since the investigation concluded. Perhaps I was only meant to solve this case, and now I'm back to normal."

She smiled. "I'm sure you are pleased about that. I know how troubling you found that curse. Furthermore, the accompanying headaches were terrible."

"You're not wrong about that. However, without that … gift, there would have been no case to solve, and I would not have met you." His gaze locked with hers, and she felt that same peculiar heat in her belly that had begun to haunt her in Ravenhurst's presence.

The way she thought about him since the other day, when he'd held her close after Ardleigh had attacked her with the chair, had shifted. She couldn't deny a sense of warmth and security when she was in his presence or, really, just when she was thinking about him.

"I keep meaning to ask you about the device you have to release locks," Tilda said, changing the subject lest her thoughts continue down a path she didn't particularly want to travel. "You said your valet gave it you and would explain why, but you never did."

Ravenhurst chuckled. "It was somewhat of a joke, actually. After my fiancée and I ended things, Sharp gave me the device as a sort of universal key. He said I could use it to unlock any woman's heart and be certain of her feelings."

Tilda laughed. "I can't decide if that's very sweet or incredibly silly."

"It's both," he replied with a grin. "Sharp is a very caring valet. I could not manage without him."

The idea of having a personal attendant was incredibly foreign to Tilda. She was reminded again of the huge divide between her and the earl, at least in their social standing.

"Thank you for coming to tea, Ravenhurst."

He hesitated then said, "You could call me Hadrian. Or Raven, if you prefer."

Both seemed almost unbearably informal, but when he'd called her Tilda the other day, she'd liked it immensely. Perhaps it was because she had so few people in her life who were close enough to her to use her given name. She liked that Ravenhurst —Hadrian—was part of that circle. Did that mean she would keep seeing him?

Tilda didn't have an answer for that, but she did respond to his suggestion. "I would be delighted to call you Hadrian if you agree to call me Tilda."

"It would be my privilege." He looked at her hand, as if he were going to take it. Then he quickly drew his gloves on and did so. "Until our next meeting."

How she wished his hands had remained bare. Was he hesitant to touch her because of what he might see or feel? That could be awkward. Still, she found herself hoping she might have cause to touch him.

Alas, that would not be today. Or in the coming days. Or anytime in the future that she could see.

He opened the door and walked toward his coach. Tilda watched him go before closing the door. She noted there was a letter on the table where Hadrian's hat and gloves had been.

Tilda plucked up the envelope and opened it, scanning the contents. It was from Mr. Forrest. He had a case for her!

A woman was seeking divorce and needed help proving her husband's infidelity and abuse. Tilda froze when she saw her name: Mrs. Beryl Chambers.

Hadrian's former fiancée.

Don't miss the next book in the Raven & Wren series, A WHISPER AT MIDNIGHT when Tilda agrees to help Hadrian's former fiancée secure a divorce from her husband. But when her husband is murdered, Tilda must find the killer and bring them to justice...even if the trail leads her to Hadrian.

Would you like to know when my next book is available and to hear about sales and deals? **Sign up for my Reader Club newsletter** which is the only place you can get exclusive bonus books and material.

Join me on social media!

Facebook: https://facebook.com/DarcyBurkeFans
Instagram at darcyburkeauthor
Threads at darcyburkeauthor
Pinterest at darcyburkewrite

And follow me on Bookbub to receive updates on pre-orders, new releases, and deals!

I hope you'll consider leaving a review at your favorite online vendor or networking site!

I appreciate my readers so much. Thank you for reading!

ALSO BY DARCY BURKE

Historical Mystery

Raven & Wren

A Whisper of Death

A Whisper at Midnight

A Whisper and a Curse

Historical Romance

Rogue Rules

If the Duke Dares

Because the Baron Broods

When the Viscount Seduces

As the Earl Likes

The Phoenix Club

Improper

Impassioned

Intolerable

Indecent

Impossible

Irresistible

Impeccable

Insatiable

The Matchmaking Chronicles

Yule Be My Duke

The Rigid Duke

The Bachelor Earl (also prequel to *The Untouchables*)

The Runaway Viscount

The Make-Believe Widow

Marrywell Brides
Beguiling the Duke

Romancing the Heiress

Matching the Marquess

The Untouchables
The Bachelor Earl (prequel)

The Forbidden Duke

The Duke of Daring

The Duke of Deception

The Duke of Desire

The Duke of Defiance

The Duke of Danger

The Duke of Ice

The Duke of Ruin

The Duke of Lies

The Duke of Seduction

The Duke of Kisses

The Duke of Distraction

The Untouchables: The Spitfire Society
Never Have I Ever with a Duke

A Duke is Never Enough

A Duke Will Never Do

Lord of Fortune

Captivating the Scoundrel

Contemporary Romance

Ribbon Ridge

Where the Heart Is (a prequel novella)

Only in My Dreams

Yours to Hold

When Love Happens

The Idea of You

When We Kiss

You're Still the One

Ribbon Ridge: So Hot

So Good

So Right

So Wrong

Prefer to read in German, French, or Italian? Check out my website for foreign language editions!

ABOUT THE AUTHOR

Darcy Burke is the USA Today Bestselling Author of historical romance and mystery and contemporary romance. Darcy wrote her first book at age 11, a happily ever after about a swan addicted to magic and the female swan who loved him, with exceedingly poor illustrations. Join her <u>Reader Club newsletter</u> for the latest updates from Darcy.

A native Oregonian, Darcy lives on the edge of wine country with her guitar-strumming husband, incredibly talented artist daughter, and imaginative, Japanese-speaking son who will almost certainly out-write her one day (that may be tomorrow). They're a crazy cat family with two Bengal cats, a small, fame-seeking torbie named after a fruit, an older rescue Maine Coon with attitude to spare, an adorable former stray who wandered onto their deck and into their hearts, and two bonded boys (a Russian Blue and a Turkish Van) who used to belong to (separate) neighbors but chose them instead. You can find Darcy in her comfy writing chair balancing her laptop and a cat or three, attempting yoga, folding laundry (which she loves), or wildlife spotting and playing games with her family. She loves traveling to the UK and visiting her cousins in Denmark. Visit Darcy online at <u>www.darcyburke.com</u> and follow her on social media.

facebook.com/DarcyBurkeFans

instagram.com/darcyburkeauthor

pinterest.com/darcyburkewrites

goodreads.com/darcyburke

bookbub.com/authors/darcy-burke

amazon.com/author/darcyburke

threads.net/@darcyburkeauthor

tiktok.com/@darcyburkeauthor

Printed in the USA
CPSIA information can be obtained
at www.ICGtesting.com
LVHW041549300724
786905LV00007B/161